Hyperion's Shield

Book One
Of
The Scales of Torma

NATHAN SCHIVLEY

For Ellie, Neil and Leah.
Never be afraid to try.

First came the tormen.

Like most children, the tormen fought.
When they proved incapable of governing themselves,
the Tormada were created.

The fights turned into wars.

But throughout the centuries, one thing has remained true.

The Scales of Torma have always been in balance.

CHAPTER ONE
Night Runners

Loras strained his ears against the quiet of the night, searching for any sound of the nearby Gartune. Beside him, his best friend Tinko struggled to contain his nervous breathing. Each gasp from the portly teenager betrayed their location. Loras glared down at Tinko and, in return, Tinko placed his hand over his mouth in an attempt to muffle his breathing. All was quiet.

A large merchant cart stood in front of the alley that Loras and Tinko had selected to hide in. The cart was overloaded with various dried meats, canned goods, bottled elixirs and other sundries—all ripe for the picking. Many years ago, a merchant would have never dared to leave their cart unattended overnight. But ever since the Gartune occupation, and the strict curfew which they imposed, merchants were sometimes faced with a tough decision at the end of the day. A late customer could result in the merchant not making it home before curfew. In which case the merchant had a choice to make; slowly push the cart home and try to avoid getting caught by a Gartune sentry, or leave the cart and sprint home before the curfew bell rang. As it was, abandoned carts were not uncommon in Reysa.

"We can't stay here all night," said Loras uneasily as he peeked through the spokes of the cart's front wheel. He could only see a little ways down the street. A small trickle of light filled the translucent tubes that ran along the buildings next to the road. Eighteen years ago, the street would have been ablaze with light emanating from the tubes. This was one of the few times where Loras was actually thankful for the energy restrictions. He and Tinko would have had a hard time hiding in a fully-lit street.

Tinko scooted up to join Loras. He warily poked his head out from behind the cart and looked slowly to the left and then to the right. The street remained empty.

"This is the last time I listen to you," whispered Tinko. "We should have been home an hour ago. You know what happens if we get caught out past our curfew."

Loras sometimes thought that Tinko allowed himself to be persuaded to break the rules only for the opportunity to say, "I told you so" when they got caught. But, they had never been caught, so Tinko was forced to settle for preemptive scoldings. Both boys knew one day Tinko would get to rub it in Loras' face in earnest, but neither of them wanted today to be that day.

"I think he's gone," said Loras. "We can make a run for it."

"Wait," said Tinko. He pointed down the street. A hint of violet reflected off the corner of a building a block away. The all-glass facade, typical of most buildings in Reysa, gave the boys just enough warning to duck back behind the cart.

Only one thing wore violet in Reysa.

It wasn't long before they heard the metallic tap of metal on stone as the Gartune appeared around the corner and headed towards their location. The giant sentry strode lazily towards the alley, tapping his metal staff on the sidewalk in time with every step. Tap... tap... tap.

Loras could hear Tinko's breath accelerating next to him. Even in the darkness of the alley, he could sense his friend's wide-eyed gaze and knew that he was covered in sweat. The time to make a run for it was quickly closing. Soon, they would be trapped.

The tapping was only about ten feet away when Loras made his decision. He rose from his crouch and was about to bolt out into the street when Tinko, using a surprising amount of strength, pulled Loras down next to him until they were face to face. Loras could see that Tinko was terrified. His eyes were the size of saucers and they seemed to plead with him. *Don't leave me*, they said.

Loras pressed himself up against the back of the cart and pulled Tinko down next to him. The boys pressed their knees up into their chins, becoming as small as possible. The Gartune was only a few steps away. Tap... tap... tap.

The tapping stopped in front of the cart.

Tinko gasped and Loras immediately put his hand over his friend's mouth. A drop of sweat dripped onto his hand. They listened.

There was a rustling in the cart. Bottles clinked as the towering Gartune shuffled through the selection of tonics. The boys held their breath and their wide, unblinking eyes locked onto each other. The sound of a cork popping echoed through the alley and the Gartune took a large swig then immediately spit the contents out in front of him. A spray of sour-smelling liquid shot over the boys and splattered on the ground next to their feet. They both pulled their legs in even tighter to their bodies. Above them, the Gartune angrily threw the bottle against the wall, shattering it to pieces. "Ech!" He exclaimed then continued to rummage through the cart until he found another bottle. Loras and Tinko braced themselves as the Gartune took another drink. "Hmmmm..." rumbled a deep voice. More bottles clinked together. Eventually, the Gartune finished making his selections. He let out a large belch, sniffed the air a couple of times, then turned and continued lazily down the sidewalk, tapping his staff along the way.

3

When the tapping was a good distance off, the boys exhaled.

"I thought that was it," whispered Tinko between breaths. "We were goners for sure."

"Oh stop being so dramatic," said Loras. "Come on, let's get out of here before he tells his friends about the free drinks."

Loras began to stand up but Tinko, once again, placed a firm hand on his shoulder. "Wait," he said pleadingly. "Just give me a moment to catch my—"

Loras shrugged off Tinko's hand and jumped out from behind the cart. "Let's go!" He said over his shoulder and then took off across the street. When he had reached the other side, he crouched behind a trash can and ventured to look in the direction where the Gartune had gone. There was no sign of the violet-caped sentry so he waved that the coast was clear. Tinko's round face poked out from behind the cart. Loras waved again, more urgently this time. "Come on!" He exclaimed as loudly as he dared. Tinko slowly stood up then took a couple of tentative steps around the cart. He bent his head outside of the alley and looked both ways like a pre-schooler learning to cross the street.

Loras' patience had ran out. "See you at home!" He shouted across the street without any attempt to lower his voice. *That'll get him moving,* he thought. He turned and ran through the adjacent side street. Behind him, he could hear the wheezing of his out-of-shape friend trying to keep up, but he didn't slow down. He couldn't. Loras was overcome with a rush of nervous energy. Obstacles like shrubs, trash cans and benches were no match for his youthful exuberance and he easily hurdled anything in his path. Whereas Tinko was slow, Loras was fast. Where Tinko was weak, Loras was strong. The two boys were polar opposites of each other in their physicality. It also didn't hurt that Loras had a large reserve of pent-up teenage angst to propel him through the night air.

Fortunately, only the furthest of Torma's three moons, Ramala, was full that night. Most of Reysa was shrouded in darkness. The "middle city" where Loras and Tinko now found themselves, consisted of tightly-spaced merchant buildings of medium height. These were nothing compared to the colossal, curving skyscrapers of the inner city. But like the structures at the center of Reysa, the middle city buildings were made almost entirely of glass. Their surfaces were purposely designed to reflect and enhance the sun's rays, making Reysa appear to glow during a cloudless day. But that was before.

Loras paid no attention to his friend, quickly lengthening the distance between them as they raced through side streets, cut through patios and jumped over the occasional hedge. Well, Loras jumped. Tinko strategically circumvented the obstacles which pushed him even further behind. It didn't take long before they had traversed the narrow streets of the middle city and entered the "outskirts" where most Reysene lived. Here, the streets widened and the buildings became smaller and more spread apart which meant there were less places to hide. The boys were much more out in the open here, but Loras was not concerned. His legs were a blur as he raced through the familiar streets. The cool night air dried the sweat from his face and refreshed him as he ran. He was invincible. Nothing could catch him. Not even a Gartune.

After about five minutes of full-on sprinting, Loras reached his home. The house was like most of the others in Reysa; small, simple and made of glass. The walls were opaque but the glass in the windows was transparent. Light tubes similar to the ones in the center of the city ran the perimeter of the roof. However, these tubes did not contain any glowing liquid. The light, little that there was, was reserved for the central parts of the city. Citizens were responsible for providing their own light in the outskirts. Most of the time that meant candles if the household could afford them. Candles were expensive.

Loras waited in his front yard for almost a minute before Tinko came panting up behind him. Completely winded, Tinko immediately collapsed to the ground in front of a row of hedges and put his head between his knees. "I thought you said you had taken up jogging, Tink," said Loras as he flopped down next to his friend. Too tired for a rebuttal, Tinko shot his friend a piercing look instead. Loras only smiled.

Suddenly, a person holding a candle appeared in the window of Loras' house and peered outside. Tinko ducked behind a bush. Loras frowned at his friend and shook his head disapprovingly.

"What?" said Tinko looking up. "What if *he's* in there?"

"He's not," said Loras as he frowned at the person silhouetted in the window. He rubbed the newly-arrived stubble on his chin, thinking about what his next move should be.

"How do you know?" Tinko lifted his head above the bush to take a look. The person in the window leaned forward and the candlelight illuminated the side of her face.

"See, it's just her," said Loras.

"Oh, thank the gods," said Tinko. "I've had enough excitement for one night." He got to his feet, brushed himself off and headed for the door. Loras did not follow him.

"The longer you wait out here, the worse it's going to be, ya know," said Tinko over his shoulder.

"I can't even see her face but I can tell she's frowning," grumbled Loras. The girl in the window spotted Tinko approaching the house then immediately looked towards the bushes. The candle illuminated more of her face as she turned. She had the same dark skin and light eyes as her brother. They both wore their blonde hair similarly; long and unfettered by braids or adornments, only hers was a bit longer. She cupped her hand over her eyes and peered out the window in Loras' direction. After a brief scan of the yard her eyes locked on to Loras and she scowled. Loras returned her glare.

"Fine, you stay out here in the cold and have your little stare off," said Tinko as he reached for the door. "I'm going in."

Loras thought for a moment then begrudgingly walked towards the house while maintaining an unblinking glare with his twin sister. When he was a few feet from the entrance, he tripped slightly on a rock, which caused him to blink and break eye contact. The hint of a grin cracked on the face of Loras'

sister before she left the window and went to meet the boys.
They had not set two steps inside the house before Regan let
them have it.

"I really thought this was going to be the night!" shouted
Regan as she stalked towards the front door. "This was going
to be the night when I got a knock on the door saying my
brother had been caught and put in jail!"

"Well that sounds familiar," said Loras brushing past his
sister while giving Tinko a sideways glance.

"But it wasn't—" stammered Tinko.

"Shut up!" interrupted Regan. "I'll get to you in a minute."

"No need to be rude to Tink," said Loras as he continued
towards the kitchen. "You know if it was up to him, we would
have been home hours ago."

"And why can't you ever listen to him? He's the only one
with half a brain between the two of you and yet you never
heed his advice," shouted Regan at her brother's back. "Why
do you always have to break the rules?"

"Because the rules are stupid!" shouted Loras. "It's only
eight o'clock!"

"Actually, it's eight thir—" Tinko interjected.

"Shut up, Tink!" shouted Loras and Regan simultaneously.
Tinko raised his hands in surrender and joined Loras in the
kitchen. He opened the refrigerator and began pulling food out
onto the counter.

"It doesn't matter if the rules are stupid," continued Regan.
"The consequences for breaking them are not. It's only because
of this one," she pointed towards Tinko, who was greedily
stacking slices of meat and cheese atop a large piece of bread,
"that you haven't been caught already."

"Ha!" shouted Loras. "You think *he's* the reason I haven't
been caught yet? If it were up to him, I'd have been caught ten
times already! He's just waiting for the day he can walk up to
my cell and say 'I told you so'."

"He's not entiwely wong..." said Tinko through a mouthful
of sandwich.

7

"You two don't get it, do you?" said Regan. "You think if you get caught you just go to some nice little jail for a few days? You think you can have *visitors*? When someone gets caught after curfew, they go away–for good! When have you ever heard of someone being released from jail, let alone getting visitors?"

Tinko stopped chewing his food. He and Loras exchanged glances.

"Ah, you don't know as much as you think you do," said Loras, waving his hand at his sister. He walked over and took a bite of Tinko's sandwich. Regan crossed her arms, and the furrow in her forehead deepened.

"I know more than you, meager achievement as that may be. And besides, did you ever stop to think about how your actions might affect other people? I've been pacing for the last thirty minutes, wondering where you were; wondering if some Gartune is dragging you by your feet off to gods-knows-where."

"Well nobody told you to worry about me!" shouted Loras, his temper rising. "You're not my mother, so stop acting like it!"

"*Somebody* has to act like it!" shouted Regan.

"Somebody has to act like what?" said a dirt-covered man as he walked in through the kitchen door. A tired woman in similar condition followed behind him. Each of them hung a grimy hard hat on a hook by the door then wiped their hands on a towel that may have once been yellow but had long since turned a dark shade of brown.

"Your son still thinks that the rules don't apply to him," said Regan, her voice still raised. The man and woman both gave Loras the same, tired look. It was a mixture of frustration and a hint of empathy, as if deep down they understood his need to break the rules, although they would never tell him that.

Underneath the layer of dirt that had come to serve as a second skin, Loras and Regan's parents were as hard as stone. Their features were all straight edges and sharp angles. Even their hair was cut short and straight, a stark departure from the long wavy locks that they had donned before they adopted the twins. Several Reysene had cut their hair similarly over the years, although a few still maintained the traditional look, as if the length of their hair signified their defiance of the Gartolians. Loras once asked his parents why they had cut theirs, and his mom responded with a half-smile that she liked being able to see her husband's ears. Loras suspected that it truthfully had something to do with the difficulty of washing dirt out of so much hair.

There was only one thing about the twins' parents that wasn't rigid—their eyes. They had tired eyes. Not from work but from worry; the kind of exhaustion that only a parent can know. Both parents pointed those eyes at Loras, waiting to see what elaborate excuse he would have this time, but it was Tinko that spoke up first.

"It wasn't our fault," explained Tinko. "We had to hide from a—" Loras shot his friend a fierce glance that quickly silenced him.

"Hide from a what?" Asked Loras' mom. Her tired face suddenly turning anxious.

"It was nothing..." said Loras in a voice barely above a whisper.

"Did a *Gartune* see you?" exclaimed Regan.

"It was nothing!" shouted Loras.

Loras' father strode toward his son and placed a hand on the young man's shoulder. He brought his face within an inch of Loras' and stared him directly in the eyes. Loras could smell the dirt on his face. Dirt and sweat; that was his father. If he were to die tomorrow, it wouldn't be the lessons he had taught his son, lively dinner conversations or the memories of playing in the yard (if those memories had even existed) that Loras would remember. It would be his smell.

"Loras," his father squeezed his shoulder as he said his son's name, "you are no longer a child. We cannot tell you what to do. Not that we ever could." He straightened up and let his hand slide off of his son's shoulder. Then he let out a sigh and looked at his wife. She gave him a small nod as if to say, *continue.*

"Perhaps we have done you an injustice by not properly instilling the fear of the Gartune in you."

Loras frowned at his feet. "What's there to be afraid of..." he grumbled to himself.

"A lot!" interjected his mother. "More than you can imagine!" Loras' father raised his hand to calm his wife.

"You have never been caught by a Gartune, so you don't understand," he continued. "And now it's too late. If they had caught you as a boy, then they would have taught you a lesson—one that you would have never forgotten—but then they would have let you go afterwards. But that leniency expires when you get to a certain age. If they catch you now..."

"Save your breath," sighed Regan. "He won't listen."

"He thinks he's inwincible," added Tinko, through another mouthful of sandwich.

"He thinks he's a Reytana," said Regan, locking eyes with her brother. She gave him a strange look. There was fear and frustration there, but also a hint of something else. Loras thought it might have been pride, but that didn't align with anything that his sister had been preaching to him all these years. Still...

Tinko choked on his sandwich and coughed up a large piece of bread into his hand. He looked around sheepishly, trying to decide where to put the half-eaten glob. Everyone watched him, waiting to see what he would do. Cut off from both the sink and the trash can, he eventually bowed his head in defeat and placed the glob in his pants pocket. Regan curled her lip in disgust. Loras snorted.

Loras' father turned back to his son. He looked him over slowly, as if trying to decide what to say next. "Loras, the Reytana are gone. And they're not coming back. If you get caught by a Gartune, there will be nobody to save you. There would be nothing your mother or I could do. Do you understand?" Loras looked down at his feet and nodded.

"Look at me, Loras," said his father as he took a step toward his son. "Tell me that you understand."

"I understand," said Loras.

"Then I think it's time you all went to your rooms," said Loras' mom. "I'm sure professor Lucan has provided you with enough homework to occupy the rest of your evening. Tinko, you will of course be sleeping here again tonight?" Her voice trailed up as if it were a question that they didn't already know the answer to.

"I already made the couch up for him," said Regan. The heat in her voice had cooled. "Come on, Tink. I'll grab your pillows out of the closet." Tinko quickly walked over to join Regan. As he passed the sink, he slid his hand into his pocket and nonchalantly flung his linty sandwich glob into the drain. "Gross," said Regan.

Loras didn't speak to anyone for the rest of the night. He locked himself in his room and lay on his bed with his arms crossed behind his head. He gazed out through his window into the night sky. Ramala's faint glow outlined the rooftops of the adjacent homes. The night air was quiet, but Loras thought he could hear a faint, metallic tapping far off down the street. "Stop imagining things," he said to himself aloud, as if speaking the words made them more powerful. He closed his eyes and tried to think of something else. His mind wandered back to the conversation in the kitchen

Not that it was much of a conversation, he thought. *More like a scolding.*

He expected it from Regan, but it was rare that his parents contributed to the chiding. That wasn't really fair though. The reason that his parents hardly ever scolded him was because they were rarely around to do so. Perhaps if they had been home more, they would have had more opportunities to scold him, and this particular admonishment wouldn't have felt so strange. No matter. Regan had filled that void admirably for many years. But something about the look in his father's eyes that evening began to take over Loras' thoughts. It was not like his father to show that much emotion. So why now? He toiled with that question for several hours before eventually drifting off to sleep.

The views of education vary greatly between the Reysene and the Gartolians. Traditionally, the youths of Reysa are raised to be free thinkers. Their instructors encourage them to ask questions and test the boundaries of the known world. On the contrary, Gartolian children are taught that their lessons constitute an irrefutable catalogue of truths that are to be accepted and, more importantly, followed without question. These differing philosophies, imparted at such an early age, contribute to the starkly different worldviews that the Reysene and Gartolians develop as they grow into adults.

- Chapter Seven of *The Crescent Wars*, by Nicholas Baston

CHAPTER TWO
The Lost Reytana

Loras could feel the power of the sun coursing through his body as he stormed across the Battle Plains toward the Gartolian invaders. The Reysene army ran at his heels, led by five hundred of his own Reytana soldiers, their eyes burning like yellow flames. Across from him, the violet capes of the Gartune waved behind them as they charged forward with their staffs raised high.

The gap between the two charging armies narrowed. Now it was two hundred meters. Now one hundred. Fifty. With military precision, the Gartune stomped their eürocs in unison and an array of fault lines went shooting through the ground towards the Reytana. Right before the ground split in front of him, Loras leapt into the air, his light sword flashing in the sun...

"Loras, wake up!"

Loras immediately jumped up from the desk that had been serving as his pillow. His classmates stifled a familiar laugh as Loras' daydreaming had become an almost daily occurrence lately. He brushed his long golden hair out of his eyes as the last wisps of his dream dissolved into the back of his mind. *To be continued*, thought Loras.

Now that he was awake, Loras had to deal with another relentless foe—his professor. He and professor Lucan had been having their own battles for several years. The professor was tough on everyone, but when it came to Loras, and in particular his daydreaming habit, the professor could be ruthless.

When he dreamt that he was a Reytana, Loras had unique powers. In addition to the extreme height and strength that all Tormada shared, The Reytana could channel the power of the sun. These solar-fueled abilities were in direct opposition to the powers of the other race of Tormada—the Gartune, whose powers were derived from the ground.

Unfortunately, here in the classroom, Loras had no special abilities. He could not form objects from light and he could not cause the ground to shake. He was just a normal torman, and Professor Lucan had a special knack of reminding Loras just how un-special he was. It was not that Loras was dumb. He just lacked... motivation. Loras knew that Lucan's own *special* form of motivation was coming unless he could somehow prove that he had been listening.

Professor Lucan stood at the front of the classroom waiting for a response from his daydreaming pupil. Loras frantically looked around the room, searching for assistance. Lucan's classroom, like most of the classrooms in the school, was in dire need of updating. The glass-covered walls were cracked in several places. Little pieces of folded paper propped up the legs of the desks so that they were all even. Most of the textbooks were old, their spines broken and their pages ripped. If not for the meticulous mending of the professor, most of them would have been unusable. Lucan salvaged what he could, for there were no funds to replace the old tomes. Reysene education was not a top priority for the current government.

Loras continued to look around the room, in search of aid. He knew better than to look in Regan's direction but he could still feel her disapproving glare boring into the back of his skull.

Half of the students grinned mischievously at him when they met his gaze, the others—the younger ones—looked away nervously. Since there were less teachers now, different grades had been combined into a single class which meant that the ages of the students varied by a few years. Loras was one of the oldest in the class. Due to the combining of the grades, the room should have been overcrowded with students. But it wasn't. With the majority of the Reysene adults assigned to work on "the project," many school-aged children had to fill the jobs that had been vacated by their parents. And they weren't the good jobs. Most of the manual labor, the sanitation and the service jobs in Reysa were now performed by teenagers.

Of course, the Reysene children had a choice. They could choose to go to school instead of work if they wished. They could also choose to eat or not. The decisions were one in the same. So most chose to work. It was the Gartolians' way of oppressing the youth, without actually forcing them to miss school.

The Reysene would not let their youth go entirely uneducated, so they insisted that some of the children attend class. They claimed that the selection was random, but everyone knew that only the children who appeared to possess the most potential were "chosen" for education. Those fortunate few were allowed to bring one companion. It could be a young sibling, a friend... a twin brother.

Loras gave up. Nobody was going to help him out of his jam. In fact, most of the students wanted to see what kind of retribution awaited their classmate. There was nothing left for Loras to do but blurt something out and hope that it somehow related to whatever Lucan had been teaching.

"Yes, uh... eight, sir," stammered Loras.

"Eight what?" asked professor Lucan with an eyebrow raised.

"The answer is eight," replied Loras.

"And what was the question, exactly?"

The class giggled again. They had seen this routine many times. It was always entertaining to watch Loras squirm and try to guess what he had missed.

Professor Lucan stood at the chalkboard with his arms crossed, waiting on Loras' answer. He was one of the oldest professors at the school, and both his appearance and disposition reflected his seniority. Though he was short for a torman, he held himself in a way that made him seem taller. His shoulder-length hair had long since faded from golden-blonde to white and he had a matching beard—a rarity among the Reysene—but it fit him and his profession well.

Loras looked like he was about to answer the professor when Regan hissed at him from across the aisle. "Just be quiet," she said.

Loras scowled at his sister then slunk back down in his seat. *Back to being my mother again,* he thought.

Tinko leaned over the desk behind Loras and whispered something under his breath. Loras turned his head slightly to try to hear what he was saying. Tinko whispered again, louder this time, but it was still unintelligible. Loras gave his friend an irritated look and then returned to face the professor.

"It seems that my lesson has bored our Loras to sleep once again," continued Lucan. Loras turned red as he stared hard into his desk. The grain of the wood began to swirl as water filled the teen's eyes. He quickly wiped his face, hoping that nobody had seen his eyes shimmer.

"Since Reysene history, the history of *your own people,* is apparently not riveting enough for you, let's try something new today. Tell me, Loras, what *will* hold your attention long enough to keep you out of your afternoon coma?"

This has to be a trick, thought Loras. *He's just looking for another way to punish me for sleeping in his class again. Nothing I pick will be correct.*

Out of the corner of his eye, Loras could see his sister shaking her head at him. He chose to remain silent.

"Nothing?" asked professor Lucan. "There's nothing rattling around in that brain of yours that demands answers?"

Actually, there was one thing that Loras would love to discuss, but he knew it was forbidden. *Although...* his professor had opened the door. If there was any time when Loras might be allowed to mention this topic, maybe this was it. Still, it was probably best to play it safe. He was already on Lucan's bad side today.

Lucan slowly walked over to Loras until he was standing directly over him. He bent over and laid his chalk-covered hands on the teen's desk. The smell of book leather and glue filled Loras' nose as Lucan leaned closer. Loras continued to avoid his professor's gaze. His hands began to sweat as he gripped the edge of his desk as tightly as he could. The wood in his desk began to swirl again but he continued to hold his tongue.

"I can see your wheels spinning, Loras," whispered professor Lucan as he hovered over his student. "There's something up there gnawing at you. Spit it out! Maybe there's someone else in this room who shares your thirst for knowledge."

He knows what I want to say. He's goading me. It's as if he wants me to get myself in trouble, thought Loras. Professor Lucan had always been rough on Loras, but this was a new kind of torture. *Maybe I should just do what he says and spit it out. Everyone else in this classroom wants to know as well.* Loras looked up from his desk and peered around at his classmates. Everyone was staring at him, waiting to see what he would do next. He peered over at his sister. Loras asked her with his eyes, *should I do it?* Regan answered him with another subtle but stern shake of her head. *She's right,* thought Loras. *She's always right. This must be a trap.* He remained silent.

A few moments of tense silence hung in the air while the professor waited to see if Loras would give breath to the question that had inched its way to the tip of his tongue. Finally, Loras looked up at Lucan. He searched the professor's face for any clue as to what his next move should be. But Lucan's face showed nothing; only a raised eyebrow. Loras gave up.

"I think we should talk about whatever you want to talk about, professor," said Loras as he folded his arms onto his desk and slouched back in defeat.

"Very well..." said Lucan. Loras thought he saw a brief flicker of disappointment in the professor's face as he walked back to the front of the classroom.

"Why don't we change gears and talk about that number *eight* which Loras was so kind as to provide us with? Who can tell me the significance about the number eight?"

"There are eight moons in our solar system," shouted one student.

"Very good," answered Lucan, "what else?"

"My curfew is eight o'clock," grumbled a boy.

"Everyone has the same curfew as you," sneered a girl in the back.

"Stop whining."

Tinko's hand shot up in the air.

"There have been eight Great Wars."

"Very good, Tinko," exclaimed Lucan. "Let's talk more about those, shall we?"

As professor Lucan turned his back, Loras kicked his leg behind him and hit Tinko's foot. The pink-faced boy let out a little grunt. Tinko was the teacher's pet. He always had all the right answers and it irritated Loras to no end.

"What was that for?" whispered Tinko. "I was trying to help you!"

"Next time try harder!" said Loras.

Professor Lucan continued with his lecture. "There have been eight Great Wars between the cities of Reysa and Gartol," Lucan announced as he pulled down a map over the chalkboard. The map showed the northern half of the planet Torma, or The Crescent, as it was referred to. The Crescent represented the civilized portion of the planet, or at least all that was known to be civilized. No torman had ever ventured beyond the confines of The Crescent, or if they had, they hadn't returned to tell their tale. One did not have to study the map long to see why this was the case.

The eastern half of the map was covered by the great Delucean Sea. Its vastness had never been fully charted; partly because it was so large, and partly because tormen, in general, were wary of the water and only traversed it when it was absolutely necessary. Even the Tormada, with their enhanced strength and powers, avoided the water.

To the west was Dellwood Forest, a great expanse of green which was outlined on its western edge by a concave line of mountains that stretched from the top of the map to the bottom. It was easy to see where the name "The Crescent" had come from.

It was difficult to tell from the two-dimensional map, but the Crescent Mountains were no mere range of rocky cliffs. Their peaks extended above the clouds so that, on most days, one could not see their tops. Some people actually believed that where the mountains stopped, the sky started, and that was the reason they could not be crossed.

Between the sea and the forest was a large, desert-like expanse with the words "Battle Plains" scribbled over it. A thin, black line ran through the center of the area. At the southern terminus of the line, built into the base of a great canyon, was the city of Gartol. At the northern end of the line, atop a large, flat cliff overlooking the Delucean Sea, sat the city of Reysa.

"There have been hundreds of battles and thousands of skirmishes between the two great races," continued professor Lucan as he circled the two cities on the map, "but only eight conflicts have been so great that their outcomes radically changed the course of history.

"The Eighth Great War ended almost eighteen years ago. Prior to that, Reysa and Gartol had been at relative peace for almost a hundred years—one of the longest armistices in history. It was a time of cooperation and advancement. Gartolian and Reysene engineers were collaborating on enhancements to the light rail." Lucan pointed to the black line on the map that connected Reysa and Gartol. "There was even talk of a summit between our King Atholos and King Hadrian of Gartol. But, of course, we know now that the summit was nothing more than a trap. "

Lucan paused for a moment. His eyes became tired as he glanced longingly out one of the windows, as if he was searching for a time that had long past. Outside the window, the streets of Reysa were empty except for a handful of Reysene who walked briskly with bowed heads along the sidewalks. Before the occupation, the streets would have been bustling with people talking and doing business. Vendors would have lined the sidewalks, hawking their wares while carefree children ran back and forth playing tag. But not anymore. The lifeless scene that Lucan saw outside jolted him back to reality.

"None of us saw it coming," Lucan continued with a dark tone. "King Hadrian's overtures of goodwill were meant to lull us into complacency, and more importantly, to buy him time. Time to complete the weapon he knew would cripple our city and its defenses.

"The war was relatively short," continued Lucan, "only lasting about a week. Though they fought valiantly, King Atholos and our Reytana defenders were no match for King Hadrian and the Gartune once they unleashed the shield."

Lucan paused and again gazed out the window of his classroom. His eyes were now as dark as his tone.

"And the instrument of our defeat is now a part of our daily lives."

He turned back to face the class. They looked bored.

"I sometimes wonder what it is like for all of you to have been born into such a situation; to have known nothing else. Reysa was a wonderful city and oh, to have seen her light up at night..."

The corners of Lucan's eyes began to glisten. Slowly, defiance shimmered through the pools in his eyes. Lucan lowered his head slightly and his voice became as hard as stone. His next words were almost a whisper. "There will come a day when you will see her again as she was," said Lucan as he continued to stare out the window, his gaze fixed on something distant and unseen. "They're out there... waiting for the right time... and when they return, we wi—" Lucan stopped himself abruptly as if awoken from a trance. He looked out across the class. The students' faces were fixed on their professor, waiting to see what he would say next. But the defiance had left Lucan's eyes. The speech was over just as quickly as it had started.

The class was taken aback by the sudden show of emotion from their normally even-keeled professor. A few chuckled under their breath. Regan shook her head disapprovingly. Tinko raised his hand but then thought better of it and lowered it awkwardly. Loras didn't know what to think, but he was definitely awake now.

Reliving the memories of the war had caused a momentary lapse in Lucan's judgment. He quickly stepped out into the hall to see if anyone had heard him. There was no one there. Steadying himself, Lucan took a deep breath and collected his emotions before stepping back into the classroom.

It was not often that the old professor lost his cool, but the few times that he did were usually a result of this subject matter. None of the other instructors dared talk about the war. For safety's sake, they tried to avoid discussing the Gartolians, especially the Gartune, as much as possible. But Lucan sometimes let his history lessons, particularly those about the wars, veer off into talk of Gartolians. The students loved it because, like anything that was taboo, it was exciting to discuss.

Though tales of the battle were usually told in dark corners and in hushed tones, the students had been hearing about the Eighth Great War throughout their lives. As with most stories of the sort, the tales were ripe with exaggeration and often contradicted each other. It was hard to tell what was true and what was legend, especially since most people who actually fought in the war were now gone.

Naturally, the students had lots of questions and few people to answer them. They suspected that professor Lucan had the answers. Up until this point, he had chosen not to reveal many.

Lucan had told the story of the Eighth War a few times before. He usually recounted it the same way —without getting into any specifics and only telling the students what they already knew, or rather what the "approved Gartolian history" would allow them to know. And he always stopped at the same point because if he told the story any longer, he would approach the forbidden subject—the same subject that Loras had almost broached just a few minutes earlier.

Loras studied his professor carefully. *Maybe he really did want me to bring it up.*

Loras was about to press his luck when Tinko's hand shot up in the air. Apparently, his best friend had also been thinking that perhaps today was the day for answers.

"But, Professor," said Tinko without being called on, "the Reytana should have returned eighteen years ago!"

Lucan turned his back to the students and began to slowly erase that day's lesson from the chalkboard. He gave a slow sigh as he did so, but he did not rebuke Tinko for his question. Tinko took his professor's silence as a sign to continue.

"They say that hundreds of Reytana died in the war," continued Tinko, "but when Reytana die, they are reborn shortly after. There should have been newborn Reytana in our pool of life, but they never came!"

"The deserters probably stole them," whispered a boy in the back of the room.

"Or killed them, more likely," quipped another.

The students became excited at this rare opportunity to voice their opinions on the forbidden subject and soon everyone was shouting their theories on the missing Reytana.

"Enough!" shouted Lucan. He had let this go too far already.

But it was too late. The cork was off the bottle.

The whereabouts of the missing Reytana was a very sensitive subject. tormen didn't know a lot about how Tormada were created or *re-created* as the case may be, but they knew that after either a Reytana or Gartune was killed, they were quickly replaced with a newborn. During the Eighth Great War, more Reytana than Gartune perished, but the Reytana who fell were never replaced.

However, there *were* hundreds of Reytana that survived the war. This was known. What was not known was the current whereabouts of the former guardians of Reysa, and more importantly, why they had not come back to liberate the city they had been sworn to defend.

Lucan walked to the windows and slowly drew the shades, peering outside before he did so. Then he walked to the classroom door and pulled it shut. The students whispered excitedly to each other. Was this the day that Lucan would finally tell them what happened?

"It was the seventh day of the war," Lucan began in a hushed voice. The students leaned forward in their seats. "The shield had taken its toll. King Atholos knew that our chances for victory were gone. Rather than sit behind our walls and wait for the inevitable while Reysa suffered under siege, Atholos decided to lead one final charge against the enemy. But when our king went bravely to meet Hadrian in battle, he went alone. The remaining Reytana were nowhere to be found. Some say that they had been ordered to flank the Gartolians from the forest, but that they were betrayed and the Gartune were waiting for them when they arrived and killed them all. Others say that they attempted to launch a surprise attack from the sea, but that Lyse was angry that day and drowned them. All we know is that when Atholos launched his attack, his fellow Reytana were nowhere to be found. And though he fought valiantly, King Atholos could not overcome the entire Gartolian army by himself. With Reysa undefended, King Atholos' death marked the end of the Eighth Great War, and the beginning of the Gartolian occupation. Mention of the Reytana who had deserted their posts was henceforth forbidden. For, if indeed they fled, then they had committed the greatest sin that a Tormada could commit—the sin of cowardice. They had abandoned their city and the people that they were sworn to protect. We refer to them now as 'The Lost Reytana.'"

Lucan paused for a few moments to collect his thoughts and then continued.

"After the war ended, we waited for the arrival of our newborn Reytana—the ones meant to replace those that fell in battle. History has shown us that it usually takes a couple of weeks after a Reytana dies before a replacement is delivered from the river into our pool of life. That's how long it takes for a Tormada's aura to reach The Scales, and then be delivered back into the river. Weeks passed, and nothing came. So we waited. A month came and went and still no Reytana infants. So we waited longer. Two months passed, and the result was the same. Eventually, we came to realize that our dead Reytana were not returning. These Reytana, we refer to as 'The Fallen.'"

Professor Lucan sat down in the chair behind his desk and looked out over his class. It was plain to see that the students had many questions to ask but they dare not interrupt him while he was telling his tale. Even Tinko was exercising restraint, although he had to sit on his hand in order to keep it from shooting into the air.

"But, Professor," ventured a brave student from the back of the classroom, "what if The Scales are broken? Maybe that's why the Fallen Reytana didn't return?"

Lucan simply shook his head. "One thing I can tell you for certain; The Scales of Torma are always in balance. They cannot be broken."

Lucan was exhausted. He looked as though he had aged about ten years in the past ten minutes. The weight of his story hung in the silent room for a few minutes until the professor decided that the lesson should be over for the day and so, to the delight of the students, they were let out of class early.

Loras, Regan and Tinko grabbed their things and began their walk home. It was the middle of the day and the sun was shining brightly. The city's glass buildings glistened just like they had in the days before the war. Reysa's architecture was like nowhere else in the world. Almost every structure was made of reflective surfaces. Most walls consisted of giant glass windows inside of shiny, metallic frames and there were very few straight lines or corners. Almost everything was slightly curved. Buildings varied in height and shape. There were no two alike. Because of the shape and variance of the structures, sunlight was reflected throughout the city in a beautiful array of color and luminescence.

When the sun shone, there were very few dark alleys or corners in the city. Shady spots were few and far between. And the Reysene, who absolutely bathed in the warmth of the sun were perfectly fine with that. In days past, the people spent the majority of their time outdoors. Today, they only went outdoors when necessary.

The reason was obvious. People avoided going outside because instead of the massive, golden-haired Reytana patrolling the streets, it was the malevolent Tormada of Gartol that were now in control.

An occupation of no less than one hundred Gartune patrolled the city of Reysa at all times. They spent their days walking the streets, intimidating the Reysene in every way that they could. The main instrument of their intimidation was their eüroc; a daunting staff made out of a mysterious ore that was a combination of stone and metal. Some thought that the staffs had magical powers. A simple stomp of the eüroc could cause a minor earthquake or cause a mound of rock to raise up out of the ground. And as if they weren't frightening enough in their natural state, the eürocs could *transform* at the push of a button. They were the perfect intersection of Gartolian engineering and violence. Those Reysene that had actually seen a Gartune use the weapon would not step within fifty feet of a soldier if they could help it.

The Gartune's pale skin, fierce violet eyes and violent disposition were in direct contrast to the appearance and demeanor of the previous regime of Tormada. The ornately carved eürocs that they all carried were symbols of fear and pain. Often times, the staffs were brandished for no other reason than to watch a passing torman jump out of the way.

The Reysene had never been afraid to walk the streets with the Reytana. Often times, a Tormada and a torman would be seen walking together while having a friendly discussion. It was quite a sight to see a full-grown Reytana, nearly two feet taller than any torman, bending down so as to speak at the same level as his or her shorter companion. The Reytana had been more than happy to help the smaller Reysene carry a burdensome load or to otherwise lend a hand in any way that they could. In contrast, the Gartune would rather stand and laugh at the tormen' struggles. The only time a Gartune would address a torman was to give them an order or to scold them.

It was because of this that Loras, Regan and Tinko chose to use the alleyways for their walk home. Rarely did a Gartune travel on the smaller streets because the paths were too small for a Tormada to comfortably traverse. This allowed the three teenagers to travel unmolested and discuss things that they wouldn't dare if they thought they might run into a Gartune.

Naturally, their thoughts were still on the "Fallen" and the "Lost" Reytana.

"I bet that the Gartune just keep killing the babies," said Tinko. "That's why none of us are allowed down at the pool of life. I'll bet they have a few soldiers stationed there and they just sit and wait until the Reytana babies show up and then kill them on the spot. It's like an endless cycle—baby dies, their aura goes back to The Scales and then they're reborn, only to meet a Gartune's dagger a few weeks later. They've probably been doing it continuously since the war."

"That's barbaric," said Regan. "A Tormada would never kill another Tormada newborn, even if it was of a different race."

"Oh, because the Gartune have such a strong sense of morality?" replied Loras.

"No, because the Tormada have a code," answered Regan. "It's about honor, not morality. The Gartune may be cold and cruel, but they would never—"

"Why am I not surprised that you would defend the Gartune?" interrupted Loras before his sister could finish her thought. He gave her a knowing look.

"Subtlety is not your strong suit, brother," said Regan coolly. "If you have something to say to me, say it."

Loras looked at Tinko who was becoming noticeably uncomfortable. This was a conversation that the siblings had delved into in the past, and Tinko obviously wanted no part of it.

"I'm not going to speak of your actions in front of Tink, but just know that I saw you two last week... and you should be ashamed!"

"Like I had any choice!" Regan exclaimed defiantly. "What would you have me do?"

"Not flirt with him, for starters!" answered Loras. "And look at your hair. You never used to braid it until he started coming around. Why is that?"

Regan's cheeks flushed. She turned her back to her brother in an attempt to hide her red face, but both boys had seen it clearly enough.

"Ok now, come on," interjected Tinko. Normally, he stayed out of it when the siblings fought but it looked like he was going to have to play peacemaker again. It was one of his least favorite characters, but one that he had been forced to play frequently as of late.

"Why do you think the professor chose today to talk about the Reytana?" Tinko blurted out in an obvious attempt to change the subject.

Silence. Tinko took that as a sign to continue.

"What if the Fallen Reytana are alive somewhere? Maybe the Lost Reytana captured them and they've all been hiding out and waiting until The Fallen receive their light, and then they're going to return and take back the city!"

Tinko grabbed a tree branch and began thrashing it around wildly as if he were brandishing a sword and the nearby trees were Gartune.

"Take THAT, you Gartune scum!" Tinko cried as he landed a rather clumsy thrust on the side of a tree.

Tinko's flailing had the desired effect and the twins let go of their quarrel and turned their attention to their friend thrashing around in the alley. Regan's scowl turned to a smile and she covered her mouth to mask her laughter. Loras decided to join in the battle and grabbed his own tree branch off of the ground.

"In the name of King Atholos!" he shouted as he struck a mighty blow to an innocent tree that now found itself under attack. Loras then twisted in the air and came around to the other side of the tree where he landed three precisely-placed strikes in blinding fashion.

"Wow," said Regan mockingly, "my brother the Reytana."

"Maybe I am, and I just don't know it yet!" exclaimed Loras as he continued his onslaught.

"Ummm, not to burst your bubble," said Tinko, "but you turned eighteen three weeks ago. I think you'd know if you were a Tormada."

"Maybe I'm just a late bloomer!" said Loras as he jumped off of a tree stump and attempted to hover in the air, only to come crashing down awkwardly.

"Well, Professor Lucan always did say that you were a bit slow..." said Tinko.

"Boys..." Regan sighed as she watched them turn their attentions from the trees to each other. Loras was the far greater athlete and enjoyed repaying the slower, fatter Tinko for his earlier brown-nosing in class.

"If the Reytana do return," Loras said as he landed a stinging blow on Tinko's arm, "I will join up with them! I will lead them straight to the capitol building, and the first person that I shall send to The Scales will be—"

Regan shot Loras a piercing look.

"No, not him," sneered Loras. He pushed Tinko all the way up against a wall with his flurry of tree branch parlays.

"Who then?" asked Tinko as he struggled to regain his breath.

"Dario!"

And with this declaration, Loras landed a mighty blow that cut Tinko's tree branch sword clear in half. He stood victorious with his hands raised in the air as Tinko doubled-over from exhaustion. Regan rolled her eyes.

Just then, a thunderous clanking sound of unfolding metal rose from around the city. Loras, Regan and Tinko looked up to see four enormous metal arms unfolding above them. The arms stopped unfolding a thousand feet above the city, each one about five hundred feet from the next and evenly spaced. As soon as they had finished unfolding, a curved steel plate emerged snakelike from the tips of each arm. The steel plates moved clockwise in a circular pattern until they met the adjoining arm and created an enormous circle. Three feet below the tips of the iron arms, four more steel plates emerged in the same fashion and continued until they had created another circle directly inside the first. The smaller circle fastened seamlessly into a groove in the interior of the outside circle. On and on this went in rapid succession until the steel circle had filled itself in. It was now a massive, steel saucer held up by the four iron arms.

"Is it four o'clock already?" asked Tinko as he looked up at the mechanical marvel covering the city.

"Time to get home," said Regan.

The three teens walked slower as their small alleyway was now covered by the giant saucer's shadow. The city of Reysa lay in darkness. The shield had blocked out the sun, just like it did for the first time nearly eighteen years ago.

To say that The Crescent represents the civilized portion of the planet Torma may seem like a loose application of the term when you consider that the area has only known limited times of peace in between centuries of chaos and war. But throughout the years, there has been one constant that has kept the region from devolving into complete anarchy – The Scales have maintained the balance of power between the Reytana and the Gartune.

- Chapter One of *The Crescent Wars,* by Nicholas Baston

CHAPTER THREE
The Fallen

The city of Reysa sat atop a soaring cliff that served as the northern terminus of The Crescent Mountains. Its eastern edge was a thousand foot drop directly into the Delucean Sea. Many centuries ago, the constructors of the city, under instruction from their god, Rey, had chosen this location because it received more direct sunlight than any other spot on the entire planet Torma. This was essential because the city, like its Reytana guardians, drew its power from the sun.

The capitol building of Reysa towered like a beacon at the highest point of the city. The multi-level glass structure soared several stories high and was slightly curved for the length of a semi-circle. Inside the curve was the most striking piece of its stunning architecture—an immense open-air courtyard. In the center of the courtyard lay the most important object in the entire city. The lotus.

The lotus was a large glass orb that spanned nearly twenty feet in diameter with a large, circular opening at the top.

Sprouting from its base were several petal-shaped solar panels that collected the sun's rays and converted them to energy. The energy was then collected within the glass orb and dispersed to the city via a network of translucent tubes. These tubes stretched out from the orb like vines across the courtyard.

Everyone in Reysa referred to the energy orb as "the lotus" because when it was full, the glowing orb with its solar panels and tube vines resembled a giant, radiating lotus blossom. However, it had not been full for nearly eighteen years. Currently, only a small pool of solar energy sat at the bottom of the orb; enough to power the basic needs of the city for just a single day.

It used to be that on a normal day in Reysa, enough solar energy was collected by mid-day to power the city for the next twenty-four hours. The remainder of that day's solar rays were converted into a reserve that was collected in the lotus. But ever since the solar shield was deployed, the lotus had not seen a solar ray after four o'clock in the afternoon. Thus had the Gartolians regulated and controlled the city's power supply since the end of the Eighth Great War.

Dario leaned against the window of the meeting chamber and stared down into the shadowed courtyard. A small amount of luminescent liquid swirled gently at the bottom of the lotus. The motion of the liquid created watery reflections of light that cascaded over the dark petals. Dario found it equally sad and calming at the same time.

Behind him, sitting around a long, glass table sat several pristinely-dressed Gartune. The Tormada of Gartol were meticulous by nature, but these statesmen took it to the next level. Each one considered their position as a politician to be a great honor, and they all yearned to advance as far as they could in this foreign government because they knew they would never have the chance to do so in their home city. In Gartol, King Hadrian was the government. His voice was the law. But here in Reysa, things were done differently and for an ambitious Gartune, it was a rare opportunity for advancement and, more importantly, for power. As such, none of the Gartune politicians missed an opportunity to one-up each other. One way they did this was in the way they dressed. Another was in the way they spoke up at these meetings. Dario found it all so petty and exhausting. And it was about to begin.

Each Gartune looked at Dario expectantly. The meeting could not begin until he sat down. It was a silly formality, but one that they adhered to. Keeping up the appearance of normalcy lent credibility to this farce of a government and allowed the Gartune to convince themselves that they were conducting business the same way that the Reytana had done so before the war. At first, the charade angered Dario greatly, but now it was merely a single annoyance heaped in with the mountain of aggravations that was his life.

Dario sunk into his seat at the head of the table and looked around with tired eyes as the Gartune settled in around the table. He slowly rubbed his forehead which held more wrinkles than a 'Mada of his age should have contained. His head didn't hurt, it was more of a habitual motion than anything else; a way to communicate his mood without actually having to speak. And his mood was always the same.

These weekly meetings were exhausting and Dario had long since begun to dread them. The room was filled with cheats, manipulators, liars and bullies. Had he met them on the battlefield, his light sword would have thirsted for the blood of these Gartune. But as it was, all he could do now was listen to their bile and obey their commands.

"You are looking old, my friend," said Rankin, captain of the Gartune regiment and second-highest ranking Gartune in Reysa. His squinty eyes were a darker shade of purple than his fellow Gartune, making them almost black. That trait would have given him a menacing appearance if it wasn't cancelled out by his patchy facial hair—a defect that he tried to cover up by growing his goatee longer than normal. Gartune were very particular about their beards. Every other 'Mada at the table had a neat, clean, low-cut goatee that accentuated their square faces. But not Rankin. His beard betrayed him and it was seen by his peers as a sign of weakness; an imperfection that implied greater character faults within.

"Even now, I can see that your light is fading," continued Rankin. "I think it may be time that you stepped down and let a younger 'Mada fulfill your duties."

"I still have enough light for this room," replied Dario as he continued to rub his temple. Though his title as governor of Reysa may have been as empty as the lotus' energy orb, it was still his and he would not let the city's highest political office fall to a Gartune.

"It does not take any great amount of strength to be your puppet, only a flexible spine," Dario continued. "As long as I can hold a pen, I can hold this office."

"That's the spirit!" A young Gartune—the only one who had chosen not to take a seat when Dario did—sauntered over to the head of the table and picked up Dario's hand for closer examination. "I'd say these old fingers have at least two or three years of penmanship left in them! Perhaps you should take this time to learn how to write, Rankin."

Rankin scowled at the younger Gartune but said nothing. He dare not give voice to his thoughts. But it was no secret that Rankin, having formerly served as the chief Gartune in Reysa prior to Xander's arrival, hated him and yearned to regain his lost position. Xander was the youngest 'Mada in the room by far and did not have the experience or ambition required to fulfill his duties. But he had one thing that the other Gartune did not—a father that was the king. It wasn't even a week after Xander received his metal that he had supplanted Rankin as chief Gartune in Reysa. But for the past five years, Xander had shown no interest in the job. He was simply there because his father had ordered it. Meanwhile, Rankin's embarrassment for being demoted turned into a smoldering hatred for the prince. And the worse part was, Xander knew it and he didn't care.

"So what great mandate would the king have me sign into law today?" asked Dario as he leaned forward at the head of the long table full of pretend statesmen. One of the Gartune slid over a document to Dario as he explained its contents.

"His majesty, King Hadrian thinks it would be wise to move the city's curfew from eight o'clock to six o'clock."

"Six o'clock?!" cried Dario. "Does your tyranny have no end? Is it not enough that you have blocked our sun? We barely have enough energy to cook our food and light our houses."

"You are lucky that we give you that much!" exclaimed one of the Gartune. "It would take but the flick of a switch and we could shroud your city in darkness for the entire day!"

"The sentries have reported several instances of mischievous behavior during the six o'clock hour," continued Rankin. "King Hadrian trusts that you will agree with his suggestion... for the safety of the city."

"For the safety of the city!" cracked Xander. Other than Dario, only Xander realized the ridiculousness of this process, and he enjoyed sneaking in the occasional undermining comment. The other Gartune at the table squirmed in their seats. A few snuck the prince a sideways glance, but they said nothing.

"For the safety of the city," sighed Dario as he signed into law the document that lay before him. He had no choice. The only reason that the Gartune, and more specifically King Hadrian, allowed Dario to retain his position as governor of Reysa was because he did everything that he was ordered to do, and because they figured that the Reysene would sooner listen to one of their own. Well, sort of their own. For Dario was the only Reytana left in Reysa.

"We would like you to make the announcement this evening," requested Rankin, although it wasn't a request. "The law shall go into effect immediately."

"Is there anything in particular that you would like him to wear, whilst he delivers the good news?" interjected Xander with a wry smile. He walked behind the governor and clapped his hands on his shoulders. "Perhaps some big floppy shoes and a red nose?"

This time, each Gartune at the table shot their prince a piercing glare, but as always, they said nothing. Dario's face was a mixture of anger and exhaustion. Years ago, it would have shown only anger.

Xander leaned over the old Reytana and whispered in his ear. "If you prefer, I can make you a vest with a bulls-eye on it. So that the citizens have something to aim for."

"Forget the vest. Put it on my forehead," replied Dario. Xander laughed and clapped the old Tormada on his shoulders.

At least you've kept your sense of humor, old boy. These meetings wouldn't be any fun if you had lost it," said Xander.

"On to new business," declared Rankin, turning away from Xander. "My spies have sent back reports of a Reytana being spotted in Dellwood Forest."

"I too have heard a similar report," interjected an eager Gartune from the end of the table.

"As have I!" added another and then another until the table was full of Gartune confirming the reports as if they were the first to have to discovered them.

"What say you, Dario?" asked Rankin. "Have you heard any news as to the current whereabouts of your brethren?"

"As always, I have heard nothing," answered Dario defiantly, "nor do I care where they may be hiding. Those cowards are of no interest to me or my city. "

"He lies!" shouted a Gartune. "He knows where they are and he won't tell us!"

"Why would he?" said Xander. "We ask him the same question each week and he gives us the same answer. If he knows their whereabouts, then he has decided not to reveal it to us. No amount of threats will change that. In fact, I think if you asked him to choose between revealing the hiding place of the deserters or being thrown into the Delucean Sea then old Dario here would probably come dressed in his swim suit to our next meeting."

Dario let slip a quick smile. Though he would never admit it, out of all the people in the room, he disliked Xander the least.

"Regardless," continued Rankin. "We should send a search party into the forest to investigate this further. Three hundred Reytana cannot remain undetected forever. "

"Agreed," said the rest of the Gartune in unison.

"Is there any other business for the governor before he announces the new curfew?" asked Rankin. Nobody replied. "Good," said Rankin. He turned to Dario. "I have prepared your remarks. They are on your desk. I suggest memorizing them rather than reading off the paper. It will look more natural that way."

"You mean it will look like I thought of it myself," replied Dario.

"Exactly," smiled Rankin.

With that, the meeting was adjourned until the following week. As the Gartune began to file out of the room, Dario put his hand on Xander's shoulder and motioned for him to wait behind.

"Interested in that vest afterall?" asked Xander after the last Gartune had exited.

"I wear a bulls-eye every day I walk outside. I don't need a vest," answered Dario.

"Then what is it that you need? I have somewhere to be."

Dario's tone became pleading, a voice that he would never show in front of the others.

"Please, it has been almost two years since I have checked on them. Five minutes is all I request."

Xander's puckish demeanor was replaced by a rarely-seen air of seriousness. Dario's request was a dangerous one and he could see that his pleading made Xander uncomfortable.

"They're fine. They haven't changed yet," replied Xander.

"Please," Dario asked again, but this time he added defiantly, "it is my right!"

Xander leaned in close to the governor and inspected his face while he thought. Dario stared straight back into his eyes as the two stood in silence for several seconds.

"Look around you," said Xander. "You have no rights anymore. I thought you had accepted that."

"I still have this one," answered Dario. He was no longer pleading. "I wouldn't expect a torman to understand, but you are a Tormada for gods sakes! There is a code! Your father would understand."

Xander's eyes narrowed. "Perhaps. Although, if your plan is to depend on the understanding of my father, I fear you will be sorely disappointed. Don't forget who put them there in the first place."

The Gartune prince stood and thought for a moment while he rubbed his neatly-cropped goatee. Finally, he spoke.

"Come. Do not speak."

Without another word, the two left the meeting chamber and turned the opposite direction that the others had gone. Dario followed directly behind the Gartune prince. The two Tormada walked through several corridors and down several steps until they had traveled far below the capitol building and into the very heart of the cliff itself.

Eventually, they came to a long, dark corridor that was unlike any of the others that they had passed through. This hall had not been in existence for very long. The floor, walls and ceiling were made of chiseled rock. Small torches were placed every thirty feet along the hall in order to illuminate the path. The corridor was only wide enough for one Tormada at a time and Xander set a brisk pace. His eüroc tapped in perfect time with his footsteps as they went deeper underground. Dario found that his breath was starting to come quicker and beads of sweat began to form on his forehead the further along they went. It seemed as if the walls and ceiling were closing in on him. Dario knew to expect this reaction from his body, and so he said nothing and pressed on in silence. Meanwhile, the Gartune in front of him strode along easily, his staff tap, tap, tapping lazily on the ground.

Dario and Xander walked along the corridor until they came to an iron door that was built into the side of the rock wall. The door was guarded by two Gartune sentries who leaned half-asleep on their eürocs. They clamored to attention when they saw the Gartune prince approach.

"Stand aside," commanded Xander.

"I'm sorry sir, but your father told us that we were not to admit anyone without his clearance," stammered one of the guards. "Do you have an authorization?"

Xander gave his eüroc a quick stomp on the ground. Two precise shockwaves flew along the ground directly at the Gartune sentries. The sentries' knees buckled instantly when the tremors hit the spot where they were standing and they stumbled to the ground, dropping their staffs as they fell. It took nearly half a minute for the guards to regain their composure, at which time the first guard removed a large keychain from his pocket and unlocked the door.

Xander gave the guards a disapproving look as he and Dario walked through the doorway. After they had entered the chamber, Xander's face changed back to its normal, irreverent self.

"That was almost worth the trip down here," he said with a malevolent grin.

The chamber that Dario and Xander entered was a vast, dimly lit cavern. The cave was long and narrow with a high ceiling from which small, candlelit chandeliers hung. Bits of molten wax dripped off of them, making small "ping" sounds as they hit the stone floor. There was only one entrance or exit to the room, and they had just walked through it. The cavern air was musty and filled with the stench of rotten food and excrement.

Each side of the chamber contained a long row of cells, each one roughly ten feet by ten feet in area. The walls and ceiling of each cell consisted of three-inch-thick iron bars and the floors were solid granite with a hole dug out in the middle.

Every cell had but one occupant – a teenage boy or girl. Skinny, shivering and covered with grime, some of the youths were huddled in the corners of their cells. Others were standing with their hands gripped onto the bars of their cage.

As Dario and Xander slowly walked down the row of cells, the prisoners watched their every step. Silent rage filled Dario as his eyes met those of the imprisoned teens. He fought to compose himself. In order to occupy his mind, he focused on inspecting each boy and girl for cuts and bruises—any signs of injury. Other than those characteristics that are symptomatic of malnutrition and lack of exercise, Dario found no signs of mistreatment.

Dario stopped in front of one of the cells. In the back corner sat a slender boy, his knees pulled up to his chin. His golden hair was covered in grime and stretched all the way down to the floor. Two curious eyes peeked through a small space between his hair and the top of his knees. Dario met the boy's gaze and the two looked at each other for a few, long moments.

"Can they talk?" asked Dario.

"Why don't you ask it," replied Xander, refusing to look at the prisoner.

Dario started to address the boy but his tongue caught in his throat. He didn't know what to say to the creature huddled behind the bars. The boy simply stared at the old Reytana, his gaze wide and curious. A small cough from down the row broke the silence and provided an excuse for Dario to continue his examination of the cells.

When they had reached the end of the row, Dario turned to Xander.

"They will receive their light soon. They cannot live like this once they have matured into full grown Tormada."

"We know," answered Xander.

"So what are you going to do? I can't believe that you have kept them alive this long only to kill them and recapture them as babes?"

"There is a plan and it is none of your concern," replied Xander cooly. His tone suggested that he was done with this line of questioning. Dario wanted to press the issue further, but he decided not to. He was fortunate enough that Xander had allowed him to visit the prisoners.

"Have you seen enough?" asked Xander.

"Yes, I have seen enough," answered Dario in a voice no more than a whisper.

The two Tormada turned and walked back down the row of cells toward the door from which they had come. This time, Dario could not bare to look into the cells. He tried to console his guilt by reminding himself that they were all alive and unharmed. But the ambiguous answer that Xander had given him caused his heart to fill with dread. What exactly did the Gartune have planned for the Fallen Reytana?

"I do not need to tell you to keep silent about where we have just been," said Xander as they exited the chamber.

"No, you don't," answered Dario.

"Good. I would not have taken you to the cells had I not been confident in your ability to keep a secret." Xander scanned the old Reytana's face for any reaction to his comment but found none. "Well, I am already late for my appointment so I will leave you here. I gather you can find your way back before you pass out?"

"I'll be fine," replied Dario. "It's just been awhile since I've been underground."

Xander placed his hand on Dario's shoulder. "You may want to work on acclimating yourself, old boy." Dario could not help but hear the ominous hint in his voice.

With that, Xander turned and left the governor alone in the corridor. Dario attempted to take his mind off of Xander's comment and the wave of claustrophobia that was trying to swallow him. He shifted his thoughts to how he was going to deliver the news about the city's new curfew. It would not be taken well. He supposed that was good. Anger was good. It meant that the Reysene had not given up; that they still cared.

Dario knew that his citizens detested him. After all, he was the face of the government that had been oppressing them for eighteen years. The Reysene needed someone to direct their anger towards and that was the burden that Dario had willingly accepted. *Better that they hate me than someone like Xander or Rankin*, he thought. Dario could handle the derisive whispers and the hateful stares. Rankin, on the other hand, would kill you for looking at him sideways. *It is better that the bile is directed towards me*, thought Dario. *But it does take its toll.*

Dario entered his stateroom and walked to the wall of windows that faced the courtyard. Leaning up against it, he returned his gaze to the nearly-empty lotus. The tiny pool of light at the bottom represented an evening's worth of power and that was all. Once the light was gone, the city would be powerless. Dario could relate. Soon, he too would be empty.

After a few moments, Dario watched as Xander crossed the courtyard and passed through one of the several glass arches that led to the city. Dario had a good idea of where he was headed, and it terrified him.

It is rumored that the god Rey, herself, instructed the first Reysene on how to build the city of Reysa. Though their technological capabilities prevented them from constructing some of her more elaborate building designs, they had the framework of the city laid out for hundreds of years. When the Reytana eventually arrived, their strength and powers allowed the Reysene to complete their glass city in the sky, thus fulfilling Rey's grand vision.

- Chapter Four of *The Crescent Wars,* by Nicholas Baston

CHAPTER FOUR
Twilight

Though the city had been shrouded in darkness for the past four hours, Xander could tell that the sun was just now setting. In Reysa, the only difference between dusk and four o'clock in the afternoon was that a faint purple hue reflected off some of the buildings on the east side of the city as the sun dipped over the horizon. He couldn't help but admire the view as he casually strode through the center of the city.

The most ingenious function of the Gartolian sun shield was that it actually moved throughout the day to follow the path of the sun. The shield's four arms were attached to giant military tanks on the ground that moved in accordance with the sun's position so that the shield was always angled directly between the sun and the city, thus ensuring that no rays snuck through to the energy orb. As soon as the last bit of sun had dipped over the horizon, the shield began to disassemble itself.

Starting from the inside out, the steel discs retracted back into their respective arms, which then folded down neatly into the four tanks on the ground. Xander watched the entire process as it unfolded above him. *Impressive as always,* he thought. The hulking marvel of Gartolian engineering was a stark contradiction to the subtle, flowing grace of Reysa's skyline, but it was beautiful in its own way.

There were no streetlights, lamps or torches in Reysa. Instead, translucent tubes outlined the edge of nearly every structure. These tubes ran along the tops of the city's walls and wrapped around the circumference of each building. At night, when the sun went down, these tubes filled with solar energy and illuminated Reysa. Before the Gartolian occupation, the city absolutely glowed at night. But now, the tubes only contained a faint trickle of light—just enough for Xander to see his way through the darkness.

The Gartune prince strode down the streets of Reysa, twirling his eüroc lazily at his side. As he passed the glass buildings that lined the street, he allowed himself a couple of quick glances at his reflection in the windows. He liked what he saw. Most people did. He had the striking dark features of a Gartolian, but without all of the *hardness.* His light skin was a shade darker than most of his kin, a result of being stationed so close to the sun these past five years. His eyes were a deep shade of violet. A near ever-present grin also added to his appeal, even though the smile usually held more mischief than mirth.

As he traversed the densely populated central city, Xander took note of the Reysene as he walked past them. It wasn't quite eight o'clock yet so the citizens still had every right to be outside of their houses, *until tomorrow anyway.* However, when they saw the prince of Gartol, they immediately changed direction or moved to the other side of the street, all the while keeping their eyes fixed on his eüroc. Xander had never wielded his staff against a Reysene, nor did he have any desire to. A eüroc was an instrument of war; to use it on a defenseless torman would be a defilement. At least that's the way that Xander viewed it. He knew that some of his fellow Gartune did not have the same reservations, and that is why no Reysene would come within twenty feet of him.

Xander strode lazily through the main plaza at the center of the city. In years past, this had been a bustling marketplace full of vendors hawking their wares and street performers dancing and singing for loose change. It was also a meeting place where Reysene would come and enjoy a drink at one of the many cafes and restaurants that lined the open square. But not anymore. Now, the plaza was nearly empty.

A few vendors still attempted to make a living selling junk or trinkets that they likely stole from a forest city like Arsdale or Woodhaven. Most of these merchants were not Reysene, but waifs – tormen who lived in the woods. Xander recognized one of the vendors; a crippled man who walked with a cane and had the look (and smell) of a woodsman all over him. Unlike most tormen who approached a Gartune, this man did not cross to the other side of the street. Instead, the man kept on walking his original path which took him right next to the Gartune prince. Shockingly, when the woodsman came abreast of Xander, he did not tilt his head to the ground, but rather he looked up and gave the Gartune a friendly nod and then limped away.

The balls on that guy, thought Xander. A thought struck him: *first, Dario dares to ask me for a favor, and now this guy thinks he's my best friend. Perhaps my good nature is being mistaken for weakness.*

Xander considered this for a while but then decided that Dario probably wanted to die anyway, which explained his actions, and the woodsman was probably just crazy (as were most people who spent their entire lives eating grass and sleeping in trees). There was no doubt that tormen were still terrified of him, especially the Reysene. Xander smiled. During his five years as commander of the Gartune occupation, Xander had only found one Reysene that was unafraid of him, and it was her home that he now approached.

Loras and Tinko had resumed their tree branch battle in the front yard of the twins' home. When they glimpsed the approaching Gartune, they immediately threw down their branches. Fighting, whether real or play, was forbidden amongst any of the citizens of Reysa.

"It's lucky that I came by," said Xander to Loras, "otherwise I think the fat one may have bested you."

Loras gave Xander a scathing look, but he dare not say a word. Xander liked to torment Loras because he knew how much Loras hated his visits. Though he was only five years Loras' senior, Xander treated the Reysene as if he was much younger. Every chance he could, Xander made a point to antagonize the hot-headed teen. But each time, Loras simply stood and stared right back at the prince. If a look could kill, Xander would have already died a thousand deaths.

"Where might I find your sister this evening, Loras?" asked Xander. Still glaring, Loras nodded toward the kitchen and then he and Tinko skulked down the street.

"Curfew's coming soon, boys," said Xander over his shoulder. "Better get inside while you still can…"

Xander walked into the house as if it were his own, for he had been there many times. But even on his first visit to Loras and Regan's home, he did not knock or wait for an answer. He simply walked in unannounced. Knocking was a courtesy that was reserved for equals and Xander did not have any of those in Reysa.

Xander found Regan in the kitchen cleaning up the dishes from dinner. She had cooked for her brother and Tinko as she did most nights. Her parents would not be home for another couple of hours. They, like most Reysene adults, had been "selected" to work on the secret project under the city. For most of the twins' lives, their parents had spent dawn to dusk working on this project. They only saw their children briefly at night, and even then, they were too tired to spend much time with them. Holidays were skipped. Birthdays were five minute affairs before bedtime. There was only a cake if Regan decided to bake one. The other parents in the neighborhood—those that had avoided being chosen for the secret project—helped out as much as they could, but Loras and Regan essentially raised themselves. Their parents were simply two people who slept in the same house as them.

"Don't you have someone else that can do that?" asked Xander as he entered the kitchen.

"Unfortunately, the servants took the day off," responded Regan. She did not lift her eyes from the dishes. If any other Reysene had addressed the prince of Gartol in such a manner, they would have been beaten. But Xander was amused by Regan's quiet defiance. It was one of the reasons why he enjoyed coming to see her.

Xander had first met Regan two years ago. She was hurrying home with a bag full of groceries when she turned a corner and accidentally bumped into the prince. Xander had been talking to a couple of Gartune soldiers when the Reysene girl had collided with his backside. Her groceries went flying everywhere. Immediately, she apologized to the prince for running into him. The soldiers berated her for her carelessness, but Xander said nothing. He simply watched the girl as she went about collecting her groceries off the ground.

There was something different about this girl; something that separated her from other Reysene of her age. She had the same long, golden hair, lithe frame and dark, tan skin that was common amongst her race. Undoubtedly, she was beautiful. But there was something in the way that she went about collecting her things that struck Xander. Eventually, he realized what it was. She was not scared.

Any other Reysene would have been quivering with fear as they frantically searched for their groceries. Some may have just left the food on the ground and run away. But not Regan. She calmly picked up each and every item and returned it to her bag, all while being heckled by two armed Tormada three times her size.

Finally, Regan had returned all of her groceries back to her bag; all except one can of soup that she could not find. The soldiers laughed to themselves as they watched Regan searching everywhere for the remaining can. Then Regan saw why they were laughing. The can was under the massive boot of one of the soldiers.

The soldiers looked down at her with evil smiles as they waited to see what she would do. Regan looked down at the can for a few moments and then did something totally unexpected. She reached underneath the soldier's boot and quickly yanked the can out from under it, sending the Gartune reeling backwards to the point where he lost his balance and would have fallen had his companion not caught him.

The Gartune soldier was furious. As soon as he had regained his balance he rushed at the Reysene girl, his eüroc held above his head, ready to strike. Just as he was about to land a crushing blow, Xander stepped in front of the girl and caught the staff in his hand.

"You would kill this girl for a can of soup?" exclaimed Xander.

"I would kill her for her disgrace!" replied the soldier.

"You disgraced *yourself*," answered Xander in disgust. "A little torman girl almost upended you. Had I not intervened just now, she probably would have finished the job!"

The soldier's scowl shifted from Xander to Regan and then back to Xander before he finally lowered his staff. Angry as he was, he dare not challenge the prince. Seeing as how there was nothing left to be said, the soldiers turned and walked away fuming, leaving Xander alone with the Regan.

"I don't know what to say," whispered Regan. "Thank you for saving my life."

"I hate to see a can of soup go to waste," answered Xander. He smiled and put his hand on the girl's shoulder. He expected to find her shivering but she was steady as a rock. She didn't even flinch when he touched her. Xander then offered to walk Regan back to her house, and she accepted with a silent nod. The two walked side by side on the street, inspiring more than a few shocked looks from nearby Reysene. Xander cracked a few jokes to see if he could get the girl to laugh, but all he managed were a few polite smiles. When they arrived at her home, Regan thanked Xander once again for his assistance.

"Perhaps it was fate that put that can of soup under Bonner's foot," said Xander. "Otherwise, you might not have had the pleasure of meeting me." Xander grinned at the girl and she smiled politely back at him. "I think I'm going to have to step up my game if I'm going to get a laugh out of you," said Xander.

"I'm afraid I'm not much of a laugher," replied Regan.

"Challenge accepted!" exclaimed Xander impishly. And ever since that day, Xander had made it a point to stop by a few times a week to try to crack a smile from the Reysene girl.

Xander sat on the kitchen counter and sorted through a bowl of fruit as Regan finished with her dishes.

"I think I set a new record on the way over here today," said Xander as he tossed a ripe andal pear up in the air. "I counted twenty-seven Reysene that crossed to the other side of the street when they saw me coming."

"Perhaps they thought that you would trip them," said Regan as she put away the last dish.

"You know me better than that," said Xander. "I do not deny that there are some of my kin who participate in that sport, but I have never harmed one of you and yet you still act as if I might strike you down at any moment. Do I have some unknown reputation as a torman abuser?"

"You are the son of King Hadrian. You command the only Tormada in the city. That is more than enough reason for a Reysene to walk on the opposite side of the street from you."

"Ah, but answer me this," said Xander as he took a bite of the pear, "We treat the tormen in Gartol the same as we treat you, but they do not flee from us," said Xander.

"And what exactly is the fate of a slave who flees from his master?" asked Regan.

"The tormen in Gartol are not slaves." Xander's tone began to lose some of its light-heartedness. "They are subjects. They work and do what they are told because that is the way the gods intended—for the Tormada to rule and for the tormen to obey. It has always been that way."

"It has always been that way *in Gartol*," answered Regan.

"But not in high-and-mighty Reysa, where the Reytana carry the groceries and wash the feet of the Reysene, is that it?" asked Xander. "How would you know anyway? The only Reytana that you have ever known is Dario. Does he not instruct and you obey?"

"Is it *he* that instructs?" questioned Regan. She was walking a thin line now. Though he enjoyed her honest opinions and the courage it took to voice them, Xander did not enjoy accusations from a lesser being. He studied the torman girl for a few moments. She had the same defiant stare as the day when he had first met her. Gradually, Xander's frown turned to a smile as he recalled their first meeting.

"I think the next time I walk the streets, I should take you with me," suggested Xander. "That way you people will see that I am capable of sharing a sidewalk. Plus, you could protect me if any danger arises."

"I don't think the prince of Gartol needs a chaperone. Here, take this," and she tossed him a can of soup. "If someone gives you trouble, just throw this at them."

"You know it's lucky that I let you live after that day," jested Xander. "After all, you revealed the secret to toppling a Gartune soldier," and he tossed the soup playfully back to Regan.

At this moment Loras came into the kitchen and saw Xander smiling at his sister. Neither seemed to notice his entrance, so he coughed loudly. Regan glanced at her brother and saw the familiar accusatory look on his face. She met it with a scowl of her own, then turned back to washing the dishes.

"Ah, the brother returns," said Xander.

Loras walked over to the counter, grabbed an apple and stood there eating it while Xander and Regan exchanged looks. There was an awkward silence for a few minutes as Loras stood stubbornly and chewed loudly. It quickly became apparent that he had no intention of leaving the kitchen.

"Well, I think I'll be on my way," said Xander as he turned to Loras and gave him an overly-aggressive pat on the back. "Always good to see you, Loras."

Loras took an extra loud bite of his apple.

"Oh, and you may want to head home a bit early tomorrow," said Xander as he was leaving. "I hear the curfew may be changing."

Loras threw his apple core violently into the sink.

"Don't worry, I'll come by and keep you company," said Xander. He then winked at Regan, gave Loras a mocking little bow, and then turned to leave.

Loras glared at his sister with burning, accusatory eyes.

"What would you have me do?" she whispered under her breath.

Loras just shook his head and walked out of the kitchen, kicking the door on his way out.

Calan knew that isolationism was one of the main deterrents to peace. He sought to bring the Reysene "off their mountain" both literally and figuratively through technology. Reysa's great elevator and the hyper-rail were Calan's attempts to coerce the Reysene to travel outside the safety and familiarity of their city.

- Chapter Three of *The Crescent Wars*, by Nicholas Baston

CHAPTER FIVE
Awake

Dario's proclamation of the accelerated curfew time was received as expected, that is to say not well. His half-hearted attempt to justify the new rule as a safety precaution didn't fool anyone. He hadn't even left his platform at the center of Capital Square before he was assailed with a chorus of boos and even an occasional thrown rock. Luckily, none of the rocks struck Dario, or, gods forbid, one of the Gartune sentries flanking the podium where he made his announcement.

The next day at school, all the students wanted to talk about was their new curfew. Professor Lucan was tired of listening to the teenagers whine, so he decided to change the subject to something more interesting.

"Today we are going to discuss a topic that is shrouded in mystery and controversy. Like many things that are not fully understood, this topic is often feared. But fear is not a justification for ignorance. There are some things that we *do* know about this subject and because it is so important to our history and to our future, I feel it deserves discussion. Today, we are going to talk about the Omegas."

The mention of the Omegas instantly drew the full attention of the class. Even Loras, who had been slowly drifting off into another daydream was jarred to attention when he heard professor Lucan mention the name.

"Now," continued Lucan, "what do we know about the Omegas?"

To no one's surprise, Tinko's hand shot in the air.

"They are the children of the Tormada," answered Tinko.

"But professor," interjected a girl in the back of the classroom, "I thought that the Tormada aren't able to have children."

"You are both correct," answered Lucan. "Like we tormen, the Tormada can mate, but they are not fruitful. They do not give birth. Tormada aren't born, they are *replaced* by The Scales in order to maintain the balance of power. Only after a Reytana or Gartune dies will a newborn Tormada arrive at their city's pool of life.

"However, over the course of history, there have been four exceptions to this rule. Twice in Reysa and twice in Gartol, a Tormada has given birth to a child. These children are the Omegas."

Tinko's hand shot up in the air. His mouth opened before he was called upon. "I heard that only Tormada kings and queens can create an Omega. Is that true?"

In two instances that was true. Octavia and Drohnus were born to royal parents. But the other two were not. Nobody knows exactly what causes an Omega to be created. Some say that the moons must all be in alignment at the time of conception..." As Lucan said this, a group of boys in the back of the room snickered. Lucan pretended to ignore them but talking about sex—especially Tormada sex – was making the professor visibly uncomfortable. He continued anyway.

"...Others say that when two Tormada meet whose auras are identical in nature and of the highest level, then they may conceive a child. But nobody knows for sure. The circumstance of their creation is one of the Omegas' greatest mysteries.

But what else do we *know* about the Omegas?" asked Lucan.

Again, Tinko replied without being called upon. "They have the powers of both the Reytana and the Gartune."

"Correct again, Tinko. Just imagine—the power to harness both sun and stone. They can float like the Reytana and move the ground like the Gartune. They can manipulate solar energy as well as metal and rock. They are the world's fiercest warriors and greatest inventors. And it is because of their awesome power that the Omegas are equally feared by the Reysene and Gartolians."

"Throughout history, different Omegas have used their powers for different purposes. Some used their powers to destroy. Some used their powers to create. The craftsmanship of the Gartune when coupled with the creativity of the Reytana is a powerful inventive force. All of the Omegas created wondrous things, but the greatest of the Omega inventors was Hyperion."

Lucan turned back to the chalkboard and began writing the names of the four known Omegas in chronological order.

"Hyperion is the fourth Omega that we know to have existed. Before him were Calan, Drohnus and Octavia. Octavia and Calan were children of the Reytana; Drohnus and Hyperion were born to the Gartune.

Octavia was the first of all the Omegas. Like the Omegas that would follow her, she was immediately born with her powers—she did not have to wait until her eighteenth birthday to receive her light like a normal Reytana, or her metal like a Gartune. Not much is known about Octavia, for she lived nearly eight hundred years ago. We think that she only lived to be about thirty, although the circumstances of her death are nebulous. It was not until Drohnus that it was discovered how long an Omega could actually live."

Lucan underlined the second name on the chalkboard as he continued. "Drohnus was born to the Gartune. By this time, the Gartune had heard rumors of the Reytana's Omega, so when a child with one golden eye and one violet eye was born to a Gartune princess, they knew they had something special.

"Immediately, Drohnus was trained for combat. The Gartune intended to use him as a weapon, and what a weapon he became. As soon as he was old enough to carry a eüroc, Drohnus was leading regiments of Gartune into battle. His skills in combat were unmatched. Drohnus's battlefield maneuvers became the fighting blueprint that Gartune soldiers use even today.

"For over two hundred years, Drohnus and the Gartolians constantly attacked the city of Reysa. If it weren't for the brave efforts of truly heroic Reytana, the city would have fallen on several occasions. These two centuries were the bloodiest that our planet has ever known. We refer to this time period as the Plague of Drohnus.

"After many years of battle, a curious thing was discovered about Drohnus. The Omega never physically aged. He maintained the physique of a twenty-year-old up until the day he died, or should we say *disappeared*. For, it was said that no Reytana could kill him, and that may have in fact been true. The general consensus is that Drohnus was killed in a rockslide somewhere near Za'Dyn Mountain. All we know is that after two hundred years of leading the Gartolian army, suddenly he was gone. The Gartune tried to muster a few more attacks on Reysa, but without their Omega leading the way, they didn't stand a chance. They retreated, and the Plague of Drohnus was over."

Lucan turned back to the chalkboard and underlined the third name in the list. "And next we come to Calan. Who can tell me something about Calan?"

Before Tinko could answer this one, a boy next to him shouted out, "Calan the Creator!"

"Calan the Unconquerable!" shouted another student excitedly.

"Calan the Uniter!" yelled another.

"Ah yes, Calan the Uniter was born around a hundred years after the death of Drohnus," continued Lucan. "Whereas Drohnus had fought to annihilate his enemy, Calan attempted to unite the two races.

Now, as history had proven, Gartol had no desire to unify with Reysa. But the Gartolians were so afraid of the Omega's powers that they agreed to participate in his unification projects, reasoning that it was better to go along with Calan's requests rather than disobey him and risk angering the powerful Omega.

"What followed was a time of peace, prosperity and invention that had not been known since the creation of the Tormada. Chief among Calan's accomplishments was the creation of the hyper-rail, which you are all familiar with. Prior to its invention, it took days for the fastest Reysene hovercraft or Gartolian speeder to traverse the distance between Reysa and Gartol. Calan combined solar power and magnetism to create the hyper-rail which could transport ambassadors from one city to the other in less than an hour.

"The hyper-rail had a positive effect on the relations between the two cities. No longer did politicians have to wait for days to hear a reply from their counterparts, stewing with impatience and anxiety. Instead, if need be, they could convene within the hour. Tensions eased between Reysa and Gartol."

Lucan pulled down the map of The Crescent and pointed to a point in the middle of the hyper-rail line. "A summit building was constructed exactly halfway between the two cities as a neutral location for meetings. Here, separated from distraction, frequent summits were held to identify ways in which the two races could collaborate for the good of mankind. Each one of these summit meetings was overseen by Calan. Whenever tempers began to flare or old rivalries began to surface, Calan put an immediate stop to them. Such was the respect that he commanded from both races.

"Though Gartol prospered from this collective peace, the city and its inhabitants remained wary of Calan. Reysa's Omega had never shown any signs of hostility towards them, but the

Gartune knew that if he ever had a change of heart, he would pose a serious threat to their city. And so, when a Gartune female was miraculously found to be pregnant, she was immediately hidden and kept secret. No word of her or the Omega that she gave birth to ever reached the ears of Reysa.

"The Gartolians named their Omega, Hyperion. While they were meeting with the Reytana about potential collaborations, the Gartune were training Hyperion to once again bring war to the Reysene.

"But Hyperion was not like Drohnus. He did not have a predisposition to fight. Instead, he chose to build. Though he was raised by the Gartolians, he felt no loyalty towards them and did not share their desire to destroy Reysa. This infuriated the Gartolians, for it was their intention to use Hyperion to assassinate Calan.

"When Hyperion refused to become an assassin, the Gartune made him their prisoner. The Gartune locked him deep within the bowels of their city. To a normal person, this would have been torture, but Hyperion actually preferred the solitude. It was a chance for him to invent, and invent he did.

"It is said that Hyperion fashioned tools from the walls of his cell. He ingeniously created them so that only he could use them. They were so advanced that not even the most skilled Gartune could wield them. Because of this, Hyperion did not worry about the Gartune stealing his creations for their own use.

"Using his custom tools, Hyperion began to create tiny, intricate machines. He would form these machines into any sort of shape or size that he liked. It is said that Hyperion could make a clock in the shape of a key, or a can-opener that looked like a pencil. He used these smaller machines to make bigger machines. Over time, Hyperion's underground cell became a massive laboratory full of mechanical marvels, the likes of which Torma had never seen. But as time went on, Hyperion ran out of things to invent. It was only then that the Gartune convinced him to start making weapons.

Hyperion had one condition—he could not be forced to use the weapons himself. After he created them, he was not responsible for what happened afterwards. The Gartune happily agreed. So Hyperion started inventing.

"This new subject matter inspired his creativity in ways that key clocks and can-opener pencils never did. Hyperion took the eüroc, for example, and refashioned it into a machine within itself. The cruel devices that now emerge from the end of a Gartune's war staff were not always there. Hyperion created them. These eüroc enhancements, or *tre'ances* as the Gartune now call them, have become a point of pride amongst their race. I'm sure that you have seen how the Gartune eagerly brandish them outside in the streets." Several students nodded their heads warily.

"Ultimately, it was one of these *tre'ances* that eventually killed Calan. So, you see, even though he had refused to assassinate his fellow Omega, it was Hyperion that killed Calan in the end."

"Professor," asked Loras, "that was over four hundred years ago. When did Hyperion die?"

"Nobody knows. You see, Hyperion was never known to have left Gartol. For all we know, he could still be hammering away in his cell, creating new and terrible inventions that the Gartolians may use against us."

"There's no way he could still be alive," exclaimed Loras. "Reysa would have been leveled by some bomb in the shape of a pipken by now."

"Yeah," agreed Tinko, "Gartolian technology hasn't made any crazy advances in the past hundred years that would suggest Hyperion is still working for them."

"Oh, they haven't, have they?" Lucan answered as he beckoned out the window. "Some people say that the sun shield is a work of Hyperion, and I agree with them. Just look at the way that it unfolds and then retracts every day... it *transforms*. If you ask me, there is still an Omega alive and well today, even if he is over four hundred years old."

This sparked a lively discussion amongst the students. Half of them believed that Hyperion was still alive, while the other half believed he had died. Lucan allowed the students to discuss this topic for the remainder of the day. Before he dismissed the class, Lucan addressed them one more time.

"I'm sure all of you heard the announcement last night, but in case any of you didn't, the city's curfew has been moved to six o'clock."

"*Dario…*" Loras seethed under his breath.

"I would not count on any leniency being given should you be caught out after this time," Lucan continued. "You had best all head directly home after school from now on." He was looking directly at where Loras, Regan and Tinko were sitting. "Does everyone understand?"

"Yes, professor…" the students grumbled collectively.

"Good. Class is dismissed."

Loras and Regan began to gather their things when professor Lucan called them over to his desk. Tinko gave them a questioning look as if asking whether he should stay or go.

"Your friends will be along shortly, Tinko. Please go wait outside," said Lucan.

The professor waited until all of the other students had cleared the room and then he walked over and shut the classroom door. He turned back to the twins. "I need to have a meeting with the two of you and your parents," said Lucan. "Please tell them to meet here after school tomorrow."

"But they will be at work," said Regan. "They don't have a day off until next week. Can it wait until then?"

"No," said Lucan sternly. "It has to be tomorrow."

Regan looked confused. "But, what is this about?" she asked. She looked at her brother who was staring at the ground guiltily.

"If this is about Loras falling asleep again, why do I have to be here for the meeting?" she asked.

"It's not about that," said Lucan. Loras' head immediately perked up. Now his interest was piqued.

"Then what's it about?" Loras asked.

"Your parents will know. We will talk about it tomorrow. But it *has* to be tomorrow. Make sure they are here."

"But—" Loras tried to interject but Lucan raised his hand to silence him. That was all the information they were going to get out of him today.

"Tomorrow," said Lucan. "Now you two should get going."

Loras and Regan picked up their things and walked out of the classroom. They found Tinko sitting in the hall licking the remains of some chocolate substance off his fingers.

"What was that all about?" he asked.

The twins simply shrugged their shoulders as they walked past the boy. Tinko scrambled to his feet and followed his friends out into the street.

It was half past three in the afternoon and the sun was still shining up above. Loras and Tinko decided to make the most of their remaining thirty minutes of light and so they dropped their backpacks, snatched some tree sticks and resumed their battle from the previous day. Regan decided to go on home without them.

"Go on, you wouldn't want to be late for *him* now would you!" yelled Loras as Regan walked away from the boys. Regan turned over her shoulder and gave Loras a piercing look. Her cheeks were flushed, but whether it was from embarrassment, anger or shame, Loras could not tell. Tinko took the opportunity to sneak in a cheap shot with his stick as Loras watched his sister disappear around the corner.

"You'll pay for that!" yelled Loras as he launched a counter-attack on Tinko. Thrashing his stick like a wild animal, Loras backed Tinko into a corner. He was just about to deliver a stinging blow when the two boys spotted a Gartune sentry walking around the corner. They immediately dropped their sticks and slipped into a nearby alley. There, they watched in silence as another Gartune joined the first one. The boys could hear the two soldiers talking.

"The noise came from over here," said the first Gartune. "It definitely sounded like fighting."

"Let's take a look. It's been a while since I've had some fun with the locals," answered the second Gartune.

The two soldiers walked toward Loras and Tinko's location, inspecting every doorway and alley between them. The boys knew that if they remained where they were that they would be caught and they had a good idea of the sort of "fun" the Gartune had in mind. So, they decided to run.

As the soldiers poked their heads into a nearby doorway, Loras and Tinko sprinted from their hiding place and ran across the street and into a small courtyard that was lined with a row of waist-high bushes. Loras and Tinko crouched behind these bushes as Tinko attempted to catch his breath. The boys sat motionless for what seemed like an eternity, trying desperately to blend in with the bushes. They heard nothing. Finally, Loras decided to take a look under the shrubs to see if he could spot where the Gartune had gone. When Loras bent down to look, he saw two massive boots standing directly on the other side of the bush.

"Well, well, well, it seems that these bushes need a bit of pruning," said the first Gartune as he bent over the shrubs to look at the boys.

"I could hear this one huffin' and puffin' from clear over the other side of the street," laughed the second Gartune. He had the stick that Loras had been using as a sword and he used it to poke the cowering Tinko.

"On your feet, porky" said the second Gartune as he gave Tinko another poke with his stick. This time he drew a spot of blood. Tinko squealed in pain. He instantly regretted his mistake.

The Gartune soldiers both turned their attention to Tinko as they poked and prodded the helpless teenager. Tinko could do nothing but stand and take the abuse. He began to sob, which only made the Gartune increase their badgering. Loras stood with his fists clenched in silent rage. His blood began to boil as he watched the sentries torment his best friend.

Then, something happened.

At first, Loras felt as if his blood was actually on fire. His insides began to burn. His muscles all spasmed simultaneously. Then a blinding white light filled his vision. Suddenly, Loras felt an extreme burst of adrenaline coursing through his veins. It was almost as if his mind had detached from his body and his entire being was now a ball of energy and rage.

Without thinking, Loras hurled himself at the nearest Gartune just as he was about to strike Tinko over the head with his stick. At impact, the shocked Tormada dropped his eüroc and was thrown ten feet into the street. In one deft motion, Loras spun on one foot while he kicked the eüroc up to himself with the other foot. Before the second Gartune had time to react, Loras had swung and landed a mighty blow to the side of his head.

The second Gartune shook his head in confusion as the first Gartune collected himself and charged at Loras.

"Look out!" shouted Tinko.

Loras turned but the rushing Gartune was so close to him that he did not have time to defend himself. Instead, Loras's body made a strange decision. It jumped. Normally, this maneuver would have resulted in Loras being face to face with the taller man before he was pummeled to the ground. But instead, Loras's leap easily cleared the Tormada's head, sending the Gartune clutching at thin air.

When Loras landed, he saw that the two Gartune and Tinko were staring incredulously at him. He did not know how he had just made such a jump. They did.

"Oh my gods…" said the first Gartune.

"It can't be," said the second.

"We need to find Rankin, right NOW." And with that the Gartune sentries turned and ran toward the city's capital building leaving the bewildered Reysene teenagers alone on the street. Overhead, the mechanical arms of the sun shield had begun to unfold. Moments later, Tinko and Loras were in the shadow of the shield.

Loras could not catch is breath. His heart was racing. He didn't even realize that he was still clutching the Gartune's eüroc. Immediately, he let it drop from his hand. His mind still felt like it was detached from his body and his body…. well, something had definitely changed. The heat that he had felt coursing through his veins just a moment ago began to dissipate as the shield unfolded above him, blocking out the sun.

Tinko walked slowly to his best friend, all the while staring at him in disbelief. Silently, he examined him from head to toe. It was like he was some sort of new animal that Tinko had never seen before. Loras didn't like the way his friend was looking at him.

"Wha... what are you loo...looking at?" said Loras, still trying to catch his breath.

"It's your eyes... they're glowing... they're glowing like the sun!"

Loras could feel his mind re-attaching to his body. It made the connection. He had always felt that something lived inside of him. Something more. And now, on his eighteenth birthday—his *actual* eighteenth birthday—Loras had received his light. He was a Reytana.

Loras jumped with excitement. It took him three seconds to come down.

"I told you! Didn't I tell you!" Loras yelled as he hugged his dumbfounded friend.

Tinko stood with his mouth open as Loras proceeded to jump around the courtyard, testing out his new ability. Then, something dawned on him. Instantly, his shocked look turned to fear. He ran to Loras and literally had to pull him down to the ground. He said but one word.

"Regan."

During times of war, whenever an opposing army wanted to lay siege to the enemy's city, they would set up a basecamp as close to that city as possible. In this matter, the Gartolians had a distinct advantage, as they could build their camp right at the base of Reysa. They need only stay out of range of the city's defenses. On the other hand, the closest the Reysene could build their basecamp was at the entrance to the canyon that led to Gartol. That canyon spanned several miles, far too long to enforce any kind of effective blockade of the city.

One time, the Reysene attempted to build their camp at the top of the canyon so that they look directly down onto Gartol. However, this proved to be a costly mistake as the Gartune were able to create several small earthquakes along the ridge of the canyon, causing a large number of Reysene to plummet over the side.

\- Chapter Twelve of *The Crescent Wars*, by Nicholas Baston

CHAPTER SIX
Escape

Regan was doing her homework in the kitchen when Xander strolled in.

"Learn anything interesting at school today?" asked the Gartune prince.

Regan continued reading as if he wasn't there. Xander smiled. *Same old Regan.*

The prince's visits were becoming more and more frequent. It used to be every other week. Now, it was almost every other day. And with each visit, his intentions were becoming more and more obvious.

Xander walked over to the girl and attempted to see what she was reading but she quickly sat on her book. Xander's mischievous eyes lit up as he playfully reached for the book underneath her.

"Now we can do this the easy way or the hard way," Xander said, an impish grin spread across his face. Again, he reached out, but instead of grabbing the book, he reached for Regan's leg. Quickly, Regan swatted his hand away, stood up and walked to the other side of the room, leaving the book uncovered. Still, she said nothing to the prince.

Disappointed that she had given up so quickly, Xander opened the book and found the page that Regan had bookmarked. His eyebrows raised when he saw the subject matter.

"The Omegas, huh? I did not know that they discussed such things in a Reysene school. I think I may have to have a chat with your professor. Surely, there are more important things that you could be studying than old legends and folklore."

Regan didn't answer. She stood with her arms crossed and frowned at the prince from the corner of the kitchen.

Xander regarded the Reysene girl for a moment and considered attempting another playful grab until she spoke to him, but instead he turned his attention back to the book. "Calan the Creator... Drohnus the Indomitable, our ancestors sure had a flair for names." He continued flipping pages. "How come Hyperion doesn't have a nickname? Hyperion the...," he thought for a moment. "Hibernator! That sounds about right."

Regan rolled her eyes, maintaining her silence.

"You know this silent treatment and pouty attitude is not very attractive on you. I think you've been spending too much time around your brother. He's always in a mood."

That did it.

"*I am not Loras,*" Regan whispered through gritted teeth. "But even if I *was,* I'd probably be in a bad mood too."

"I don't know why you're mad at me," retorted Xander. "*I'm* not the one who lowered your curfew."

Xander went back to perusing the textbook. "Ah, the Omegas. The magnificent four. The true offspring of the Tormada. I suppose they've taught you that Octavia could control the oceans and that Drohnus breathed fire? Did you know that someone once told me that Calan could read minds? I wonder why he didn't read the mind of the assassin that killed him? Perhaps he was wearing a special hat."

"Maybe they had special powers, maybe they didn't. Were you there? How can you be so certain of something that you have no personal knowledge of?" asked Regan.

"I have no personal knowledge that your brother farts in his sleep, but I am certain that he does," replied Xander. "Some things you just know."

Regan sighed. "So, you *know* that the Omegas aren't real."

"Do I believe that there have been some Tormada children that have sprung from their mother's womb instead of the river? Yes. Do I believe that they had some magical powers that surpassed all other Tormada? No. They were great Tormada whose legends were enhanced solely because their eyes were two different colors. That's it."

"And what about Hyperion?" asked Regan.

"What *about* Hyperion?" replied Xander.

"There are rumors that he created the sun shield..."

Xander looked at Regan sideways for a few moments. Then his wry smile returned. "Well I can tell you for a fact that those rumors are false... because *I* created the sun shield."

"Oh really," said Regan.

"Yes, your devilishly bright sun was giving me headaches, so I decided to build the shield. It was nothing really."

"I had no idea you were such a skilled machinist," Regan replied.

"There are a lot of things that you don't know about me..." As he said this, Xander slowly approached Regan like an animal stalking his prey. Regan leaned back against the kitchen counter, suddenly cornered, but she did not take her eyes off the prince. Xander placed his hands on the counter on either side of the girl then leaned down to look at her. Regan stared back, unwavering.

"You know," said Xander, "you're quite pretty for a torman..."

"And you're quite rude for a prince," said Regan cooly.

"Do you know how many women back in Gartol would die for a chance to be alone with me in their kitchen?"

Regan leaned back and looked the prince up and down, evaluating him. When she had finished her inspection she gave him a decidedly unimpressed look. "I guess we just have higher standards over here in Reysa," she said.

Xander slammed his hands on the counter and shoved his face an inch from Regan's. His deep purple eyes glared into hers. And then he saw something. Two, faint gold sparks lit up in the center of her irises. Quickly, the sparks began to grow like tiny flames in the twilight. Panic crept over Regan's face and she shoved him backwards. Xander watched in bewilderment as beads of sweat began to blossom on Regan's forehead as her eyes became brighter and brighter until they began to glow.

Just then, Loras and Tinko burst into the kitchen. Seeing the Gartune hovering over his sister reignited the fire inside of Loras. He immediately rushed to Regan's side. Aided by his newfound strength, he easily pushed Xander out of the way. The prince stumbled backwards, dumbfounded. His gaze went to Loras, then back to Regan, then back to Loras again. Loras didn't wait for the prince to regain his composure. He grabbed Regan by the wrist and dragged her out of the house with Tinko running close behind.

Loras was still grabbing his sister by the wrist as he raced down the street.

"Loras, wait!" Regan yelled between breaths. "What is going on?!"

Loras turned and looked at his sister. It was the first time that she had gotten a good look at him since he had charged into the kitchen. Regan immediately stopped running.

"Loras... your eyes," she whispered. "You're a—"

"No," Loras stopped her, "*we're*."

Loras turned his sister toward the window of a nearby building. There, staring back at her, were two sets of glowing yellow eyes.

"Oh no..." she whispered.

"We need to get out of the street," said Loras, urgently. "Two Gartune sentries already know about me, and now that Xander knows about you it won't be long until there is a city-wide search for us."

"Where do we go?" asked Regan, still inspecting herself in the window.

"I... have... an idea," said Tinko breathlessly as he finally caught up to the twins. "We need to go find Professor Lucan. He'll know what to do."

Nobody offered any better suggestions, so they sped off toward their professor's house. Already, Loras could feel his powers growing within him as he ran faster than he ever had before. Three times he and Regan had to stop and wait for Tinko to catch up before they reached Lucan's house.

The professor's house was humble in size but immaculately tended to. Not a blade of grass was longer than it should be. Not a single leaf was out of place in the row of hedges that led to his door. The three teens rushed up to his porch and then stopped, looking at each other. Loras raised his hand to knock, but then hesitated.

"There's no one else," said Tinko. Loras looked at Regan and she nodded her agreement.

Thwap, thwap, thwap. Loras pounded on his teacher's door.

"Professor!" he yelled as loudly as he possibly dared. He did not have to wait long for a response. Lucan cracked open the door just enough to peer outside.

"What are you three do—" Lucan stopped himself mid-sentence when he looked into the faces of Loras and Regan. The professor showed only a second of shock before he ushered his students into his house.

"Get in here immediately! Quick—before anyone sees you."

After they had passed through his doorway, Lucan stepped outside to look around before re-entering his house and locking the door. He then doused the lamp that he had been holding and ushered the teens through the dark house in silence. Loras and Regan had to place their hands on the walls to make sure that they didn't bump into anything. Tinko let out consecutive *oomph's* as he struck a wall, then Regan's backside as she stopped in front of Lucan's cellar door. The professor turned, his face barely visible in the darkness, and waved for his students to follow him. Loras looked over his shoulder at his sister and Tinko before following the professor down the stairs. When they reached the basement, Lucan relit the lamp and addressed the twins in a hushed whisper.

"Has anyone seen you? Does anyone know?" he asked.

"Yes," answered Loras, "two Gartune sentries found me about twenty minutes ago. I attacked them and they ran off." Lucan's eyes looked like they were about to bulge out of their sockets.

"You *attacked* them?!" he asked incredulously.

Loras shrugged, "Well, maybe not so much *attacked*. It was more like I just reacted. To be honest, I can't even really remember what happened exactly."

"He hit one of them in the face!" interjected Tinko, excitedly. Lucan spun on him and Tinko immediately looked down at his feet.

"And what about you?" Lucan now turned to Regan. "Has anyone seen you?"

Regan just frowned with her arms folded in front of her.

"Xander," whispered Tinko. "Xander has seen her. It wasn't more than ten minutes ago."

Lucan's jaw dropped but he did not ask how or why the Gartune prince had seen the girl.

"Then we haven't a minute to lose," said Lucan, quickly regaining his composure. He thought for a moment then quickly walked toward the stairs. "You three stay here and stay quiet! I'll be back as soon as I can."

"But, Professor, where are you going?" asked Tinko frantically.

"To get help," and with that he shut the door to the basement and left Loras, Regan and Tinko in the dark.

The basement was mostly empty, with the exception of a few pieces of dust-covered furniture. Two small windows at the top of the far wall let a small amount of streetlight into the room. Loras walked over to one of the windows and pulled it open a crack. The window screeched in resistance.

"Stop it—they'll hear us!" whispered Regan. Loras put up his hands and mouthed a silent *"I know"* to his sister. He then walked over to a couch that looked like it hadn't been sat on in many years. He wiped off the cushions, sending a cloud of dust floating into the air. Some of the particles caught the faint, orange light coming in from the windows. They began to sparkle as they swam in small circles, falling to the ground. Loras plopped onto the couch, stretched his arms behind his head and closed his eyes.

A few moments later, Tinko wiped off the other side of the couch and sat himself down. The couch groaned and Tinko winced as a spring popped beneath him. He looked at Regan, who was still standing alone in the middle of the basement. She seemed to be deciding whether or not to join them on the couch. Tinko patted the spot between himself and Loras. A small cloud of dust rose from the cushion and he stifled a cough. Regan couldn't help but smile at her friend as she crossed the room and sat down between the two boys.

As they sat in silence, Regan looked at her brother. His head rested comfortably on the back of the couch. His eyes were closed and there was a hint of a smile at the corner of his mouth.

Loras could feel his sister staring at him and he opened his eyes.

"What?" he asked her.

"How can you possibly sleep at a time like this?" she asked.

"He's well-practiced," interjected Tinko.

"I wasn't sleeping, I was just... thinking..." said Loras.

Regan leaned her head back to match her brother and stared at the ceiling. "This is probably the best day of your life," she said with a sigh.

"I don't think hiding from a bunch of Gartune in the basement of professor Lucan's house would qualify as the best day of my life," replied Loras.

"You know what I mean."

"It's definitely... different," said Loras. He lifted his hand in the darkness and inspected it as if it were someone else's. "I feel like the inside of me is fighting with my skin, trying to get out."

"I feel like I'm going to throw up," said Regan. "Everything is spinning."

"Oh, don't worry, that's not just you," said Tinko. "Maybe I'm about to receive my light too. Are my eyes glowing?"

The twins both smiled, their eyes two sets of glowing embers in the darkness.

"No, Tink," said Loras. "I always took you for more of a metal guy than a floater."

"I swear, if I turn into a Gartune, the two of you have my permission to throw me over the cliff," said Tinko.

"We're not that strong yet. Maybe in a couple of weeks we'll be able to lift you," said Loras.

"If we're still alive by then," muttered Regan.

The three teens sat in uncomfortable silence for a minute as the weight of Regan's words began to sink in. The darkness of the room became thicker. Tinko began to squirm. Suddenly, he thought of something.

"Oh, hey guys," said Tinko. The twins looked up. "Happy real birthday. Sorry, but I'm not getting you another present."

"You didn't get me a present three weeks ago," said Loras.

"Yeah, well I'm definitely not getting you one now," replied Tinko.

In truth, Loras had only received one present for his birthday. It was from his parents. Or at least, that's what the card said. Many years ago, Loras had discovered the truth. The present was from Regan, she'd just written their parents' names on the card. To keep up appearances, she always gave herself a present as well. Loras had never thought much about it, but it suddenly dawned on him what it must be like to have to give yourself your own birthday present year after year, just so that your brother could have one as well. He turned his head and looked at his sister. For a moment, he thought about holding her hand... but only for a moment.

While they waited for Lucan to return, a massive thunderstorm gathered outside. With the sun shield up, a thunderstorm in Reysa was different than anywhere else on the planet. Usually, nobody knew a storm was near because they couldn't see the sky. Often, the first sign that a storm was present was the thunderous sound of thousands of raindrops pinging off of the metal saucer.

The steadily building rumble of water meeting steel echoed off the walls in Lucan's basement. Tinko scooted closer to his friends and the three teens huddled together as they listened to the storm above.

"They're probably out looking for us by now," said Regan.

"The rain may slow them down some," suggested Tinko. "They'll probably focus their search on the dry zone first."

The dry zone was the area that was covered by the sun shield during a rain storm. The shield acted like a giant umbrella. If you were unfortunate enough to be caught directly under the edge of the lower part of the shield, you were pummeled by the deluge of water cascading off of the giant saucer. This wall of water separated the dry zone from the rest of the city. At this time of day, the dry zone was about eight city blocks from where they sat. But the zone moved as the shield moved, and it was heading towards professor Lucan's house.

After what seemed like an hour but was in reality more like twenty minutes, the backdoor of the professor's house creaked open and two sets of soggy boots walked through Lucan's kitchen. When the basement door opened, a soaked Lucan came down the stairs, followed by a much taller figure. The teens shrunk back in fear. As the second figure came closer, it was clear that it was a Tormada. The thought of their professor betraying his own students had never occurred to them. *Oh no,* thought Loras. *They caught him. He's brought them straight to us!*

Their fear turned to confusion as soon as Lucan lit the basement lamp. The stranger was the last person they had expected to see.

"*Dario*," exclaimed Loras. "This is the help you brought us? He's one of *them*!"

"Don't be a fool," replied Lucan. "Dario is one of *you*. Moreover, he's the only one that can get you out of the city."

"Out of the city?" exclaimed Regan. "Where are we to go? None of us has ever left Reysa."

"You're about to," answered Dario. "Right now, the city is being torn apart by Gartune search parties. If you stay here, you will be found within the hour."

"But wait..." said Regan, "Xander... he... he kind of... well, he likes me. Maybe if we went to him he could—"

"Xander is leading the search parties," answered Dario.

Loras and Regan exchanged the same look. Loras could tell his sister had been thinking the same thing as him. Leveraging Regan's relationship with Xander had been their only hope. Now, that hope was gone. The little composure that Regan had desperately clung to melted away.

"I don't understand," she said as she wiped a tear from her eye. "How could this have happened? How could we be...?"

"Reytana?" answered Dario.

"It's my fault," said Lucan. "You weren't supposed to receive your light for a few more days. I forgot to take into account the Solstice year. I'm a damn fool." He shook his head in disgust. "We moved your birthdays back on purpose. We didn't want anyone associating you with this date."

"What's so important about this date?" asked Loras.

"I know," whispered Tinko. "Today is the eighteenth anniversary of the end of the Eighth Great War," He looked at his friends excitedly. "You are two of the Fallen Reytana!"

"Wait," said Loras. "The meeting tomorrow—the one with our parents. Did they know too?"

"Yes," said Lucan. "We have all known that this day was coming and had a plan, but now..."

Regan and Loras began to simultaneously speak but were cut off.

"There's no time to explain," interjected Dario. "We have to move."

"Here," said Dario to Loras as he handed him an envelope. "You need to take this to a man named Declin. He lives in the city of Woodhaven at the fork of the Aeil River. He can help you."

"Why can't *you* help us?" exclaimed Tinko. "You're the governor of Reysa, for god's sake!"

"In name only," said Dario. "There is nothing that I can do for you here. You must go to Woodhaven and find Declin. Give him this letter but do not open it yourself. Nobody but Declin can read its contents. Do you understand?"

"I understand," answered Loras.

"Good. Now it's time to get moving."

"But wait!" cried Tinko, "I still—"

"There's no time!" shouted Dario. "You need to follow me. Now!"

Dario led the group upstairs into Lucan's study. He instructed everyone to stay put while he snuck outside to survey the scene. He returned a few minutes later and declared that the coast was clear, but that they had to hurry. Lucan, Loras, Regan and Tinko followed the governor out into the street. The combination of the shield and the storm created an extra layer of darkness in the city. They used this to their advantage as they crept along unnoticed until they reached the edge of the dry zone.

They were about to pass through the wall of water when they saw a Gartune search party emerge on the other side. The leader of the search party stopped his companions when he spied the Reytana through the water wall. As fate would have it, the leader of this particular Gartune search party was Xander.

The two groups stared at each other through the water but did not make a move. Seconds passed. Raindrops dripped off of Regan's stony face as she locked eyes with Xander. This time, there was no bewilderment in his expression.

"Take them," whispered Dario to Lucan. "You know the way. I will hold them off as long as I can."

Dario turned slowly towards the Gartune. He tilted his head slightly toward the ground while staring down his opponents. Sparks began to flicker in his golden eyes until they glowed a fierce yellow. The tired, oft-ridiculed governor that Loras had scorned for years was gone. This new version was a warrior; proud and strong. From underneath his tunic sleeves Dario pulled out two shimmering golden bands which he wrapped tightly around his forearms. He clenched his fists and the bands began to glow. It had been eighteen years since Dario had worn the Reytana adornments. His eyes seemed to indicate that it had been a long wait. But now it was here—the moment when he could again be a Reytana.

They watched as Dario let out a ferocious yell and jumped through the wall of water. Through the shimmering wall they saw a golden beam emit from Dario's right hand and a bright yellow shield form in his left. The Reytana charged at the group of Gartune at the end of the street. Loras would have stayed to watch the ensuing fight, but Lucan grabbed the teens and pushed them down a side street.

"We will have to take the long way," said Lucan.

Lucan, Loras, Regan and Tinko carefully made their way towards the edge of the city. Lucan stopped them at each corner so that he could peer around and look for soldiers. Twice they had to hide in the shadows as a group of Gartune sentries ran past their location. The trip was maddeningly slow. All the teens wanted to do was run, but the professor would take no chances.

Once they had reached the edge of the city's wall, they came to a narrow doorway. Lucan pushed against the old wooden door and its rusted hinges eventually gave way with a loud creak. The teens looked behind them to see if anyone heard, but there was not a soul in sight, so they quickly slipped through the door and through the city wall.

They hadn't taken two steps through the door when Lucan reached out his arm to stop them; if he hadn't, they would have fallen to their deaths. The teens found themselves standing directly on the edge of the cliff. A small path, no more than three feet at its widest, wrapped itself around the mountain. It had been used hundreds of years ago as the only entrance to the city. From a strategic standpoint, it had made the city easier to defend from oncoming invaders. But that was long ago. Now everyone used the lift. No longer needed, the ancient path had been left untended and had grown treacherous, especially with the rain pouring down.

"*This* is how we have to get down?" exclaimed Tinko.

"Won't somebody see us?" asked Regan.

"It's the only way," replied Lucan as he carefully walked to the front of the group and began testing the integrity of the path in front of him with his foot. "Everyone's search efforts are focused in the city or at the lift. Plus, with the rain it will be almost impossible to see us from the ground." He put one hand on the side of the cliff to steady himself and gently tapped the muddy walkway with his foot. Tentatively, he shifted his weight forward. His foot sank slightly in the mud, but the path held. He cautiously took another step. Finally, he turned back to the teens. "It's good. Come on. Just be careful."

The teens and their professor slowly set off on the winding path around the cliff. Wind and rain pelted them relentlessly, but they dared not shield their faces because they needed their hands to grip the rock wall. Several times Tinko slipped and would have fallen off the side if it weren't for the quick reactions of Loras, who was walking behind him. The path snaked back and forth until it eventually reached the ground. For the first time in their lives, the teens set foot at sea level.

At the base of the city of Reysa lay the Gartolian encampment. Over five hundred Gartolians lived here, along with the one hundred Gartune who patrolled Reysa. It was a city unto itself. Meticulous rows of several hundred tents surrounded the command center; a large, circular building at the center of the camp. A steady stream of Gartolians entered and exited the building through its front doors. Their pace was hurried, but not frantic, as if each one knew his duty and was eager to carry it out.

Spaced evenly around the city were the four giant tanks that served as bases for the sun shield's mechanical arms. Each day, at sundown, the arms collapsed back into the tanks. Three of the tanks were on land. The fourth was anchored off the coast in the Delucean Sea, hardly visible due to the rain.

Loras remembered looking down at the tanks from atop Reysa and thinking how small they had seemed. Now, on level ground with the machines, he could see how enormous they really were. Each one was easily the height of four Tormada and over twice as long. Attached to the side of each of the tanks was a large red light. While the shield was up, this light would flash every fifteen minutes to alert anyone nearby that the tank was about to move. In accordance with the position of the sun, the tanks followed a circular path on the ground, thus adjusting the position of the shield above. Years of traveling the same path had produced two giant parallel ruts where the tanks' wheels had dug away at the ground. These trenches had grown to nearly five feet in depth and were currently half flooded with water.

There was more commotion in the Gartolian encampment than normal for a rainy evening. Word of the escaped Reytana had just reached the camp and the Gartolians were rushing to set up a perimeter around the base of the city. The check points were nearly complete by the time Lucan and the teens arrived. The four escapees huddled under a small rock overhang while they surveyed the Gartolian camp.

"You need to move fast," said Lucan. "It looks like there is a hole in their perimeter near the second tank, but it won't be there for long. Go quickly and you can make it."

"But professor," said Tinko, "aren't you coming with us?"

"I am an old man and would only slow you down. Speed is your greatest ally now. Use it!"

As he said this, Lucan shoved his students in the direction of the tank and then, inexplicably, ran off in the direction of a large group of Gartolians.

"What's he doing?!" gasped Regan.

"He's providing a distraction," answered Loras. "We need to use it. Let's go!"

Regan and Tinko watched in horror as their professor ran to meet the armed Gartolian squadron. Loras grabbed them both by the arms and dragged them in the opposite direction until the three of them were sprinting full speed towards the giant tank.

But, when they got there, it was too late. An armed guard appeared at the side of the tank just as the teens were approaching it. Fortunately, Loras saw the guard in time, and threw Regan and Tinko into a nearby tent before they were seen.

"What are we going to do now?" asked Tinko between heavy breaths.

Loras looked around the empty tent. In true Gartolian fashion, it was sparse and perfectly maintained. There was a single bed, a clothes dresser and a lamp. That was it. Loras thought for a moment, then began rummaging through one of the drawers in the dresser.

"What are you doing?" whispered Tinko.

"I have an idea," said Loras. Out of the dresser he pulled a Gartolian military coat. He whipped the coat in the air in front of him and inspected its length. Then he winked at Tinko and threw him the coat.

"This isn't going to end well for me, is it?" grumbled Tinko as he struggled to put on the coat.

Outside, the rain was coming down even harder. The trenches were nearly three-quarters full at this point. The Gartolian sentry was forced to cover his eyes to see the figure walking towards him.

"They sent me to help you keep watch," yelled the oncoming figure. He stood about fifty feet away with his coat pulled over the top of his head to protect him from the rain.

"What?" yelled the sentry. The rain pounding off the tank next to him made it difficult to hear.

"I SAID, THEY SENT ME TO HELP YOU KEEP WATCH!" repeated the newcomer.

"It's about time you got here!" yelled the Gartolian. "There's been no sign of them yet, but I could use an extra set of eyes in this weather!"

The approaching figure slowed his pace. He was about twenty feet from the Gartolian when he stopped altogether.

"What is it?" yelled the Gartolian.

"I... uh, forgot my umbrella. I think I'm going to go back and get it."

"Very funny!" yelled the Gartolian. He motioned to the rear of the tank. "You take that side and I'll keep watch from over here."

"Uh, actually... I was thinking that I would watch this side... if that's ok with you..."

"What are you talking about?" yelled the Gartolian. "Get over ther—"

Suddenly, loud, cranking sounds began to reverberate from the tank. The red light on the side of its shell pulsated brightly as the massive wheels began to inch forward in their ruts. The sound of gears grinding and engines churning was almost deafening.

No longer able to hear what the newcomer was saying, the Gartolian stepped closer. As he did, he could see that something was wrong. For one, the newcomer's jacket was way too small. Moving closer still, he noticed that the man wasn't even a man, but rather a nervous, chubby-faced teen. Panicked, the teen stepped backward, looking frantically from side to side.

"Who the hell are you?!" yelled the Gartolian, his voice barely carrying over the sound of the moving tank.

Tinko's mind raced. for once in his life, he couldn't think of anything to say.

"I... uh... I think I'm going to go back and get my umbrella..." he stuttered as he continued to walk slowly backwards.

"Stay where you are!" yelled the Gartolian.

Tinko stumbled backward and fell into one of the giant water-filled trenches. Before he knew it, he was underwater and gasping for air. He could see the Gartolian soldier looking down at him. Tinko didn't like the look on his face. It seemed that he was trying to decide whether to help him out of the trench or to drown him. The soldier's scowl seemed to indicate that the latter was more probable. Tinko pushed himself up. As his head rose out of the water, his hood fell back, revealing his face. His tan skin and light, blonde hair was unmistakable.

"You're one of *them*," said the Gartolian. Tinko tried to stand up but as soon as he got to one knee the Gartolian soldier leapt into the trench and pinned Tinko back beneath the water.

"Where are the others!?" shouted the Gartolian. Tinko's eyes bulged as he thrashed under the soldier's strong arms. The Gartolian let him up and repeated his question as Tinko gasped for air. When he did not answer, the Gartolian shoved him back into the trench. "Answer or I'll drown you right here and now!" screamed the soldier.

Through the water Tinko could make out the monstrous shape of the tank creeping toward them. Both the water and the ground began to vibrate from the intense sound of the approaching machine. Tinko could no longer hear the voice of the soldier. The Gartolian's watery form began to dim as Tinko's oxygen-deprived brain began to shut down. Suddenly he was yanked out of the water. This time he was too exhausted to gasp for breath. Instead, he hung limply in the soldier's grasp.

The Gartolian began to shake Tinko. "Oh no you don't!" he yelled. "Not yet! Not until you tell me where they are!" The soldier slapped Tinko across the face. For an instant, Tinko's vision came into focus and he could clearly see his attacker's face. He could also clearly see the tank, now only a few yards behind them. The Gartolian was so focused on his prisoner that he hadn't noticed.

Tinko's eyes began to close again and he was abruptly slapped for the second time. It was no use. The little strength that remained in Tinko's body left him. The soldier raised his hand one more time as he screamed a final plea, "WHERE ARE THEY?!"

"RIGHT HERE!" bellowed a voice from above them. The Gartolian turned his head just in time to see Loras leap from the top of the tank. Tinko slipped through the soldier's arms as Loras' foot crashed down on the top of the Gartolian's head, knocking him unconscious.

Loras reached under the water and heaved his heavy friend out of the trench. As he did so, Regan came running out from her hiding place. She had been watching the entire scene, horrified, from behind the tank.

"Is he breathing?" she yelled.

Loras placed his ear to the boy's chest. "I can't tell. I don't know!" Loras began to panic. "What do I do?!" He looked frantically at his sister.

"Move over," she said as she slid in next to her brother. Steely determination now replaced the fear that had seized her while the soldier was drowning her friend. She took her hands and placed them, one over the other, atop Tinko's chest and began to push. The boy's body shook from the weight of each compression, but that was all it moved. Tinko's face remained pale and lifeless. Loras began to shake uncontrollably.

"You're doing it wrong!" he cried. "It's not working!"

Regan continued with her compressions, each one strong and deliberate. Then she leaned down and pressed her mouth over Tinko's and blew. Loras began to sob. "I'm sorry, buddy...I'm s-so sorry. It's all my fault. I should never hav—"

Tinko coughed. Water spewed from his mouth as he turned over on his side and wretched violently. He began to gasp for air as if no amount of it could ever satisfy the needs of his lungs. Slowly, his gasps became shallower. Regan flopped backwards and put her head between her knees.

"You should never have what?" said Tinko weakly. He squinted at Loras through the falling rain. "Used your best friend as bait?"

Loras threw himself on the ground next to Tinko and grabbed his friend's face with both hands. He began to laugh. "Whatever, umbrella boy! I knew you could take him!"

"You're lucky I'm in such good shape," said Tinko and he allowed Loras to help him onto his feet. "Next time, you get to wear the coat."

"Boys!" shouted Regan. "We don't have time for this. Let's go!"

Loras and Regan lifted Tinko's arms and put one over each of their shoulders then ran toward Dellwood Forest. Tinko's feet barely touched the ground as he awkwardly tried to match the pace of the two Tormada. Finally, he gave up and just pulled his legs into his chest like a ball. Loras looked over his shoulder at him.

"Enjoying the ride?" He asked.

"I'd say it's the least you could do after you almost killed me," replied Tinko.

"You're never going to let that go are you?" Asked Loras.

"I can't imagine why I would," said Tinko with a grin. "Oh, and if you two could pick up the pace a bit, that would probably be helpful."

Loras and Regan exchanged wary glances and then increased their trot. Whether they were being chased remained unknown, as they never once looked back.

It did not take them long to reach the outskirts of the forest. Once inside, the undergrowth prevented them from traveling as quickly as they would have liked, but still they pressed forward. The further into the forest they traveled, the denser it became until running in a straight line was basically impossible so they slowed their pace, picking their way around the trees and undergrowth. Eventually, their course began to take them uphill.

After a couple of hours, the rain lightened and the sun began to set over the horizon. A few orange and purple rays of dusk penetrated the forest canopy and painted the wet leaves with a glistening brush. The teens emerged into a small, elevated clearing in the forest. "Wait," said Tinko. "Look back there." Loras and Regan stopped and for the first time looked back from where they had come. Rising out of the top of the trees was Reysa. They watched as the sun dipped behind their home, splashing the tops of the buildings with a parting glow. It was the first sunset they had ever truly seen.

"It's so beautiful," whispered Regan. There was a bit of sadness in her voice; a bit of longing. Now that the sun had set, something inside of Loras felt a little bit empty. He could sense his sister felt it too.

As soon as the last bit of sun had disappeared, the sun shield's panels began to retract into the four arms, which then, in turn, folded down into their tanks. It was quite a different experience watching the process from afar rather than up close. Watching all of the pieces work seamlessly together, and with such rapid speed was, well... awe-inspiring. More than anything else, it served as a stark reminder of the impressive capabilities of the Gartolians; the same creatures who were now pursuing them. An overwhelming feeling of fear and helplessness crept into Loras' heart.

"I'm exhausted," said Loras. "We need to find a place to sleep before it's completely dark."

"We can't stay out in the open," Tinko said. "They might still be chasing after us. We need to find a place to hide." He rapidly began to collect dirt and leaves from the forest floor. "We can cover ourselves in this stuff, like camouflage." Tinko then laid down on the ground and covered himself with the leaves. Loras and Regan grinned at their friend. He looked ridiculous, and was no more hidden now than before, only now he was covered in leaves.

"I've got a better idea," said Loras.

"Yeah, what's that?" asked Tinko.

Loras grinned and pointed to the tree above Tinko.

"Great," said Tinko as he sat up and spit a leaf out of his mouth.

The cities of Reysa and Gartol could not have been any more different. This was because each one reflected the characteristics of their patron deity and, like the unique powers of the two gods, the cities were polar opposites. Reysa was the light; Gartol the shadow.

- Chapter Two of *The Crescent Wars*, by Nicholas Baston

CHAPTER SEVEN
Gartol

Once the sun set, the search parties were recalled to the capitol building. Fifty ill-tempered Gartune stood dripping wet in the meeting chamber. The evening storm had passed, and the first light of the moon shone in through the windows. Xander stood alone, peering out at the sky, while the gaggle of Gartune politicians grumbled around the table. Strapped to the head of the table in his normal seat sat a bruised and battered Dario.

"Basecamp has just reported that a guard was found unconscious near one of the shield tanks," reported a Gartune soldier. "They think it was the twins."

"Pathetic," seethed Rankin. "An entire Gartolian regiment and they can't even stop a boy and his sister."

"They're no longer just a boy and his sister," said Xander. "Now that they have received their light, I would have been surprised if Loras and Regan *hadn't* escaped. A torman is no match for a Reytana, even a young one."

"Still," said Rankin, "if it wasn't for this one's help," he jabbed his eüroc into Dario's stomach, "we would have caught them within the city."

Dario gave a small cough as he was struck in the stomach a second time. He was badly beaten. Blood dripped from the sides of his mouth and from a dozen cuts on his face. His right eye was swollen shut. His left eye glared at Rankin. But there was more life in the old Reytana's one eye than there had been in his entire body for many years. He had fought the Gartune search party valiantly and even managed to upend Rankin. In fact, he probably would have killed him if Xander hadn't stepped in at the last minute and tackled him from behind. Now that Dario had been apprehended, Rankin took every opportunity to inflict his retribution on the defenseless Reytana.

"Which direction were they last seen heading?" asked Xander, still staring out the window.

"They think they were heading for the forest," answered the soldier.

"That makes sense," said Xander. "Dellwood Forest would be the easiest place to hide. But they won't last long. They have no food or shelter and they won't have a clue how to get either one."

"Should we dispatch a search party to the forest?"

"No," answered Xander thoughtfully. "Let's give them a little space. I want to see where they go." Xander gave Dario a knowing look. The Reytana governor frowned back at the prince, but said nothing.

"No need to say anything, old boy," said Xander. "I have no doubt that you pointed them in the right direction. And so, we will wait and watch where they go. Who knows, these two may lead us directly to the hiding place of our lost Reytana."

"The king needs to be notified of this plan," said Rankin, "so that the army is prepared to mount an assault should the Reytana be discovered."

Xander thought for a moment. This would have to involve some tact. The king's wrath was well known throughout Reysa and Gartol alike. News of the escaped Reytana would surely invoke his fury. But Rankin was right, he needed to be told.

"I will tell my father in person," said Xander. "Notify basecamp to charge the hyper-rail. I will travel to Gartol tonight."

"And what do we do with our governor?" asked Rankin.

"Take him down with the others," replied Xander. "It is where he belongs."

Rankin made sure that he got to personally escort Dario down to the cavern cells. He took his time, managing to get in as many kicks and jabs as he could along the way.

"Enjoying yourself?" asked Dario as Rankin pushed him in the back with his eüroc.

"Not as much as I could be," seethed Rankin, "keep talking and you'll find out how much fun we could really be having."

Dario spit a bloody wad in front of him then inspected a loose tooth in his mouth with his tongue. "Oh, I was having plenty of fun with you out in the rain. Maybe someday you and I will get to play again... just the two of us."

"Oh, I very much doubt that," said Rankin smugly. "I'm sorry to say that was probably the last rain you will ever see."

"Rain check, then?" asked Dario, grinning a bloody smile over his shoulder. Rankin shoved him in the back.

"Keep moving, floater."

This time when they arrived at the door to the cavern, the guards immediately let them through without question. One of them winced a little as he made way for Rankin and his prisoner. Dario noticed and grinned a little to himself even though it hurt his face to do so.

Rankin dragged Dario down the dusty stone floor between the two rows of cells and deposited his limp body into an empty cage near the end of the room. Dario crumpled to the floor as Rankin slammed the door shut.

"Finally, you're where you belong," said Rankin.

"For once, we agree," said Dario as he spat blood onto the floor and lifted himself up onto his elbows. Rankin grunted.

"Enjoy your new room, *old boy.*"

Rankin turned and walked back through the rows of cages. Several eyes followed him as he left. Some of them were glowing.

It took two Gartolians to pry open the heavy iron door of the lift so that Xander could enter. The giant elevator could hold up to fifty tormen or half that many Tormada, but Xander stood alone at the center of the platform as it began to slowly lower down the face of the cliff. He looked down at the view below him. It was a clear night and two of the moons were full, so he could easily see the glow of the hyper-rail station as its thrusters began to charge. A Gartolian-operated crane lifted a single passenger car onto the loading dock. A small puff of steam rose from the car as it latched into place. Xander tried to recall the last time he had taken the rail. He couldn't remember.

A group of soldiers nervously waited for the prince at the base of the cliff. "The hyper-rail is charged and ready to depart whenever you are, sir," said one of the Gartolians as Xander exited the lift. The soldier had a rather large lump on the top of his head that he was clumsily trying to conceal.

"What did he hit you with?" asked Xander as they walked briskly toward the rail.

"I think it was his foot, sir," replied the soldier as he struggled to keep up with the long strides of the Gartune. "He jumped off of the tank and hit me from above. I never saw him coming."

Xander nodded. "You know that's their thing, right? They jump so that they can attack you from above." It was clear that the sentry had never seen a Reytana before that night, let alone studied their combat techniques.

"That's all right, chief," said Xander as he clapped the torman forcefully on the shoulder. "I'm sure you'll get him next time."

The sentry took this as a sign to fall out of step with the prince and so he slunk back toward the rear of the escort and tried to become invisible while rubbing the shoulder that Xander had slapped.

A low hum eminated from the hyper-rail car where the magnets between car and rail were interacting. The car itself looked like a bullet. At the front of the vessel was a single window for the occupant to see where he was going, but most passengers chose to shut their eyes during the ride. It was easy to become sick from the view as it sped past with incredible speed.

"We sent a rider ahead to alert Gartol of your arrival," said the Gartolian in charge of the hyper-rail.

Well, there goes the surprise, thought Xander as he climbed into the car. He leaned back against the single captain's chair and closed his eyes as the outer door was shut and locked. The magnetic hum intensified from beneath the car and then, as if shot from a cannon, the car catapulted down the rail.

After the initial jarring start, a hyper-rail trip was fairly comfortable (assuming you kept your eyes closed). Xander thought about what he was going to say to his father as he zoomed along the flat stretch of land known as the Battle Plains. This barren desert composed the majority of the space between Reysa and Gartol. It was here that most of the great wars were fought. It would not have taken much digging in the ground to come across a smashed eüroc, some broken hovercraft or parts of a Gartolian tank. However, very few people ever traveled over this land; at least on foot. The history that had unfolded here made the Battle Plains sacred ground. Other than the occasional hyper-rail passengers, the only time that anyone crossed it was when they marched to war.

Xander looked out over the moonlit plains as they sped past. His stomach began to turn, so he shut his eyes and thought about the destination ahead. It had been two years since Xander had last seen his father and double that since he had last been to Gartol. It dawned on him that Reysa was now just as much his home as Gartol. Five years ago, he would not have believed that possible, but there it was. He wondered what kind of reception awaited him, both from his peers and his father. Would they welcome him back, or see him as an outsider? Truthfully, he had never really cared what his fellow Gartune had thought of him, but try as he might, he could not say the same about the king. His opinion mattered.

The smooth, humming vibrations of the hyper-rail car eventually began to calm Xander's nerves, so much so that he was almost asleep when he felt the car slow down as it approached the mouth to Hadrian's Canyon. He was almost home.

Hadrian's Canyon was a massive valley that stretched a thousand feet wide at its base. Through the center flowed the southern branch of the Aeil River. The river escaped the canyon at its mouth and skirted around its base as if searching for a home until it finally emptied into the Delucean Sea.

The canyon had not always been called Hadrian's Canyon. Previously, it had been Tendrel's Canyon, Plutarch's Canyon and Drohnus's Canyon. It was Gartolian custom that the canyon be named after the current king of Gartol. That way, a visitor always knew who awaited him at the end of his journey.

The hyper-rail car slowed as it swerved through the snake-like path of the canyon. Xander knew these turns by heart. As he felt the car come around the twelfth turn, he opened his eyes to watch the immense city of Gartol appear before him.

Gartol was more of a fortress than a city. Over half of it was built into a giant cavern in the side of the canyon. Because of this, only a small portion of Gartol was ever hit by the sun's rays. This was, of course, by design. If ever Reysa decided to attack Gartol, they would have to do it in the shade.

The city was encompassed by a massive outer wall that was one hundred feet high and made of solid iron. It stretched all the way from one side of the canyon to the other, enclosing the entire city. Only the upper levels of Gartol could be viewed behind the height of the wall.

The Gartolians' mechanical prowess was visible throughout the city. Tiny contraptions performed thousands of different tasks in thousands of different locations. The city was alive with the hum of spinning gears, pulleys and levers. It was a fortress that was constantly in motion.

Though it was a dark and cold city, Gartol did have a certain beauty to it. Chief amongst its beautiful elements was the Aeil River which careened over the top of the western canyon wall. The tall and stormy waterfall collected in a glossy lake at the base of the city. The Gartolians called this Moon Lake because of the way that it reflected the moons of Torma on clear evenings. From here, the water of Moon Lake emptied out through Hadrian's Canyon and spilled into the Delucean Sea.

Many years ago, the Gartolians built a large marina along the edge of the lake. Today, the marina was filled with hundreds of Gartolian war ships—ships that were rarely used but available in case a sea battle was necessary. The portion of the marina nearest to the waterfall was walled off, and only Gartune were allowed within. This was where the Gartune infants were collected after their eggs came tumbling over the waterfall. The Gartune believed that it was the treacherous conclusion to their incubation journey that hardened Gartune babes and separated them from the Reytana, who enjoyed a relatively peaceful path to existence from Za'Dyn Mountain to Reysa's own pool of life.

The hyper-rail car slowly pulled into the Gartolian docking station. Xander exited his car and was greeted by several Gartune soldiers. Amongst the faces were several old friends he had not seen in many years. They exchanged the traditional Gartune handshake, wrapping their fingers around each-others' forearm, just above the wrist, in an excruciatingly tight grip. It was a sign of weakness to be the first one to break the handshake and so some of them could go on for several minutes. However, when shaking the hand of a superior, the subordinate Gartune was expected to break the handshake first.

Xander spotted his old training partner, Belkore, talking to a group of Gartune next to the hyper-rail platform. He made his way toward the group, but before he could reach them, he was stopped by a stern-faced Gartolian in a royal guard uniform.

"The king is expecting you," he said.

Well that didn't take long.

Just before he turned to follow the guard, Xander caught Belkore's eye. His friend gave him a quick acknowledging nod and then went back to his conversation. "Humph," Xander snorted to himself. *Nice to see you too, old friend.*

The soldiers' compound was the first area of town that one must pass through as they entered the city of Gartol. Like everything else in the city, this was by design. The might of the Gartolian army was in full display in this compound, and it was an intimidating spectacle for any outsider.

Four stone-paved courtyards contained the barracks for the Gartolian infantry. Here, several regiments of torman infantrymen trained under the watchful eye of a daunting Gartune drill-sergeant. The Gartolians preferred to train at night. Darkness was their ally and the more experience they Gar'onered battling in the dark, the better.

The basic rank and file did not practice with eürocs; those were reserved for the Gartune. No, their armaments were of a much simpler nature; just steel swords and shields. Xander watched as a young Gartolian accidentally dropped his sword while practicing a maneuver. No sooner had the weapon hit the ground than the drill sergeant was on top of the soldier administering several punitive blows with his eüroc. The Gartolian stood tall and accepted his punishment with barely a wince. Once his beating was over, he quickly retrieved his sword off the ground and continued with his maneuvers as if nothing had happened. *Good for him,* thought Xander.

At the center of the four infantry yards was a large, raised platform. This was the place where the Gartune trained. On this particular evening, young Tormada (the product of the last war's fallen Gartune) were being trained on one of their most fundamental maneuvers, the *bodong*. Like most maneuvers, this one had been perfected by Drohnus and was specifically intended to combat the powers of the Reytana. In battle, the Reytana would charge by jumping high into the air and attacking from above. The Gartune did not have the Reytana's jumping abilities, so they had to come up with a way to meet the Reytana at their height. Thus, the *bodong* was invented.

The *bodong* consisted of two movements that had to be executed in perfect timing for the maneuver to succeed. First, a Gartune in full sprint tilted his eüroc and brought it down in front of him with a sharp strike. This strike caused the ground in front of him to ripple and pile up into a small hill. Depending on the strength and accuracy of the eüroc's strike, the hill could be between five and twenty feet high. The second, most difficult part of the maneuver consisted of the Gartune using his planted eüroc as a lever to vault himself through the air and land directly on the hill in front of him.

It was a very difficult maneuver to perfect. The timing had to be precise and it had to be done in one fluid motion. Run. Strike. Plant. Jump. Land.

Xander watched as young Gartune struggled to create the mound of dirt in front of them, and then went flying over their hills. He smiled. These Tormada had only received their metal in the last day or two, and their inexperience with the eüroc was evident. One, in particular, got so frustrated that on his next pass he smashed his eüroc too hard into the ground and created a twenty-foot wall of dirt directly in front of him. He proceeded to slam into the mound at full speed.

I remember those days, thought Xander. Though he had been one of the more gifted young Gartune in his class, he had still struggled with the *bodong* like everyone else.

Elsewhere, metal-fresh Gartune were custom-fitting the tips of their new eürocs. This was a tradition that Gartune dreamt of from the time he or she was young. Each Gartune was allowed one customization to their eüroc. It was referred to as it's *tre'ance*. A *tre'ance* was a hidden weapon within the weapon. Each one added an extra deadly dimension to the eüroc, and accordingly, required that the Gartune train in that *tre'ance's* specification.

Xander watched one young Gartune fill the tip of his eüroc with explosive powder. There was a deadly gleam in his eye as he poured the black dust into a secret compartment within the staff. He would need to be trained in alchemy and pyrotechnics in order to take full advantage of his chosen *tre'ance*.

A second Gartune eagerly screwed several retracting spikes into his staff. He would be trained in long combat. A third loaded his eüroc with a sharp, disc-like projectile. When he pressed a button in his staff, the projectile went flying through the air faster than a bullet. It is said that a similar device killed the Omega, Calan, hundreds of years ago, and because of that it was a popular choice among young Gartune when they outfitted their eürocs. It was not the most practical of *tre'ances* because after the projectile was launched, it must be retrieved or a new one had to be fashioned, during which time the eüroc was without an added advantage. But, boys like to shoot things.

Xander laughed to himself, remembering how he had almost chosen that *tre'ance* for himself before his father forbade it. *No son of mine will go wielding such a superficial weapon. If you want to shoot things, get a slingshot.*

Xander's actual choice of *tre'ance* had raised a few eyebrows. It was a customization that was rarely ever chosen. In fact, ever since his specialization training ended, Xander had never once activated it, not that he had been presented with many opportunities.

Xander passed through the training compound and entered the city via its main gate. The "front door" to Gartol was ten feet thick and one hundred feet high. It consisted of several ten-foot by ten-foot iron blocks that could move independently of each other. This way, the entire door did not have to open in order to let someone through. Sections of the gate could open by themselves in order to let normal pedestrian traffic pass. When the Gartolians controlling the front door saw Xander approach, they threw a switch and a series of screws that were inlaid into the gate began to turn, causing a ten foot section of the door to slide open. No sooner had Xander and his escort passed through the opening than the iron slid back into place, sealing the gate shut.

In the lower half of the city, tucked into the shadow of the wall, it was always nighttime. Where Reysa was lit by thousands of glowing tubes, the streets of Gartol were illuminated by fire. Torches in ornate iron castings were everywhere; along the sidewalks, attached to street posts, flanking every door and entryway. The ever-present darkness accompanied by the flickering firelight made the lower half of Gartol feel like an open-air dungeon.

Several Gartune sentries strutted up and down the streets, occasionally poking or tripping a passing torman with their eürocs. Another difference between Gartol and Reysa was that the tormen in Gartol did not go out of their way to avoid the Gartune. Rather, they walked briskly past the oncoming Tormada with their heads bowed, hoping to be ignored. Sometimes they were. Sometimes they weren't. But, the occasional jab or poke that they received was nothing compared to the punishment they would incur if they intentionally avoided their Tormada masters. Such disrespect was not tolerated in Gartol.

Xander traveled up through the layers of the city's outer streets until he reached the king's royal apartments. In the front courtyard he came upon several armed soldiers sparring with a single Gartune. The single combatant's skill was impeccable. One after another the soldiers charged, only to be dealt a crippling blow. Eventually, they all tried to attack at the same time, but the result was no different. No matter how they approached the Gartune, they were rebuffed by a violent kick, a smash of the shield or a thump from the eüroc.

Finally, the soldiers threw down their staffs and yielded. Most bent over either from pain or breathlessness. The solitary warrior had barely broken a sweat. Xander smiled.

"You're taking it easy on them, sister" said Xander.

Septa's long, jet-black hair spun around her as she turned to face her brother. Her purple eyes were almond-shaped, slanting slightly toward a pointed nose. Like her brother, she had dark, chiseled features, but where Xander's face glowed with irreverence and mischief, Septa's face was the epitome of seriousness. She was beautiful, but she was also terrifying.

"Perhaps you would like to step in, brother?" answered Septa. "I have not had a good fight in years. Or have the floaters made you soft?"

"I wouldn't want to embarrass you in front of your friends," smirked Xander.

"Some other time then," said Septa.

"Indeed. Now, where is father?"

"I will take you to him." She turned to Xander's escort. "You are relieved."

Septa led Xander through the royal apartments, though he did not need a guide. He had spent his childhood running through these hallways and playing in the courtyards. Septa was thirteen years older than Xander and had chosen to spend most of her youth with their older brother, Lex.

Xander's two older siblings had been inseparable. The Scales must have released some of the same Gartune's aura when the two of them were formed. They had the same steely cold temperament, the same drive for perfection and the same knack for intimidating all those around them. Day and night the two of them could be found sparring together, perfecting their battle craft. When Xander was young, he tried to join them, but they would have nothing to do with their younger brother. It wasn't that they were worried that they might hurt him; for his well-being was not a concern of theirs. They simply did not want to waste their time sparring with an opponent that offered no challenge. "You'll just embarrass yourself," they had said. "Come back when you aren't so weak!"

Xander was five.

Eventually, Xander gave up on trying to fit in with his older siblings and learned to entertain himself, much to the chagrin of the palace staff. The poor torman maids and butlers came to rue his daily pranks and schemes.

At first, Xander thought that his actions would Gar'oner some attention from his father, but the king had no interest in disciplining his son. He had servants for that. Xander quickly realized that if he couldn't hold a eüroc, he was of little interest to his father, and no amount of bad behavior would change that.

Rather than sulk in his loneliness, Xander discovered freedom in his neglect. He could do whatever he wanted, and nobody would care; at least nobody important enough to concern him. And so, he continued to act out, knowing there would be no consequences to his actions. Though he had matured into a powerful Gartune, the mischievous child had never truly left Xander. That is why when an old Gartolian maid spotted him walking down the hall, she quickly ducked off into a side compartment after realizing who had returned.

Septa and Xander found the king in the war chamber, where he spent most of his time. When they entered, their father was conversing with Morlo, a commander in the Gartune army. Both men appeared agitated.

"Every time I hear from you, you're further and further behind schedule," said Hadrian to Morlo. "I'm starting to think that this job is more than you can handle. Perhaps I should find you a position that is more equated to your abilities."

"But, your highness, the ground has proven to be—" answered Morlo but the king cut him off.

"No more excuses. Either catch up or I will find someone else to do your job. And trust me, you will not like the next job I find for you."

"Yes, your highness. I will not fail you," answered Morlo, bowing deeply before the king.

At nearly nine feet tall, Hadrian was large even for a Tormada. He showed no signs of his age, though he had just turned eighty-three. The only wrinkles on his body were battle scars. His hair and pointed goatee were still as black as the day he received his metal. The years may not have betrayed his body, but they had most certainly lessened his patience.

"Well, at least he's in a good mood," whispered Xander to his sister. Septa made no response. Hadrian looked up from his conversation and saw his children standing in the doorway.

"So, what is so urgent that you felt the need to abandon your post?"

"There is a... situation," answered Xander cautiously, "that I wanted to discuss with you in private." Xander waited for Hadrian to order Septa and Morlo out so that they could converse privately. Instead, the king simply stared impatiently at his son.

"Say what you've come to say," said Hadrian. Xander could sense a smirk creeping onto Septa's face.

"Earlier this afternoon, two Reytana were discovered within Reysa," said Xander.

"Good," replied Hadrian. "I expected they would try something soon. I'm assuming you interrogated them before you came here."

"Not exactly. They escaped."

Hadrian stared hard at his son. His violet eyes darkened. Xander did not look away, choosing instead to accept the malignant look the king sent his way.

"Of course they escaped..." said Hadrian in a low growl. "Why would I have thought that you had actually done your job?" Hadrian's voice grew with every word he spoke. "You never did take anything seriously. And now you've let two rogue Reytana infiltrate the city. We don't know their mission or who sent them or even who they are!"

"Actually, I know who they are. It was a brother and sister, and I can guarantee you that they weren't sent into the city with a mission."

"And how do you know that?" exclaimed Hadrian.

"Because they didn't know they were Reytana until today. They just received their light."

"CHILDREN?! You let children escape!"

"They had help," answered Xander. "Dario and their school professor."

"*Dario*," seethed Hadrian. "We should never have let him live. It was weakness. So, how many search parties have you sent out after the *children*?"

"Father," replied Xander. "Hear me out. The escape of these two Reytana may be a blessing in disguise. I am certain that Dario provided them with some information to help them once they escaped. It is very possible that he may have even sent them to meet up with the hidden Reytana. If we capture them now, we will never know. But if we allow them to continue their journey, they may lead us to the Reytana's hiding place."

Hadrian turned his back to his son and stroked his goatee thoughtfully. Nobody said a word. The king began to slowly pace. He disliked indecision because it was inefficient, but he absolutely abhorred rashness, especially when it came to important decisions. Given the choice between being fast and being right, he would always choose to be right. This philosophy was one of the reasons why he was still alive today. It was also why he was such a master tactician. And this was a decision that required some thought.

"Father," Septa said, breaking the silence, "let me track them. If they lead me to the lost Reytana I will call for the army, and if they don't then I will strike them down in cold blood."

Hadrian regarded his daughter in silence for a few moments before answering. "No. Xander, this mess is your responsibility, so you will clean it up. Take some Gartune with you. You have one week. After that time, I expect to have heard one of two things from you; either you have found the Reytana's hiding place or that you have killed the escapees. In the meantime, Morlo, I want you to mobilize the army. If we discover their hiding place, I want to be ready."

"Yes, your highness," answered Morlo.

"They should be prepared to move at a moment's notice. Do you understand?"

"Yes, your highness. It will be done."

Hadrian turned back to his son. "One week! I had better not hear news of your failure or there will be consequences, Xander."

"Understood," replied Xander.

The prince bowed to his father and exited the war chamber. Septa followed close behind. When they were out of earshot of the king, Septa turned to her brother.

"Take me with you!" she demanded.

"You heard him," answered Xander. "This is my mess to clean up, not yours."

"You know I can fight better than any of those lumbering idiots down in the courtyard. He needs to see that I am worthy, especially if a war is coming. Damn it, Xander—take me with you!"

"Rain check," said Xander.

And with that, Xander turned and left his sister alone in the hallway. Septa slammed her eüroc into the ground, splintering the granite beneath her feet and sending cracks up and down the walls of the corridor.

The hyper-rail was built as a single line, which may seem strange seeing as how a single line could only, theoretically, transport cars going in one direction, otherwise they would crash into each other. However, this isn't the case. The hyper-rail can, in fact, simultaneously transport cars going north and south at the same time. When they meet, the cars begin to rotate along the rail and corkscrew around each other as they pass. A brief alarm is sounded in the cars before the corkscrew begins, alerting the passengers to buckle up in their seats. It has become a tradition for experienced riders to 'forget' to inform first-time passengers what the alarm means and watch as they tumble over themselves while the cars corkscrew.

- Chapter Three of *The Crescent Wars*, by Nicholas Baston

CHAPTER EIGHT
Embark

Xander found Belkore at the training compound scolding a pair of infantrymen. Based on the look on the two Gartolians' faces, they were not entirely sure what exactly they were being berated for. They looked at each other nervously, trying to figure out what to do next as the menacing Gartune hulked over them.

"Now prove to me that you understand what I just told you!" shouted Belkore. The two tormen sprang into combat stances and began to awkwardly swing their swords at each other, unsure as to which maneuver their Gartune instructor wished them to perform. What resulted was a spastic, flailing dance between two terrified soldiers. Belkore was about to lay into them again when Xander approached the group.

"What a fine example of military precision!" exclaimed Xander. "Belk, you definitely have found your calling. Why, these are some of the finest-trained soldiers I have ever laid eyes on!"

Belkore addressed his trainees while scowling at his old friend. "You two get back to your barracks. If your skill has not improved by this time tomorrow, you will find that I will not be so lenient." The two Gartolian soldiers quickly bowed and ran away in the direction of their barracks. Just before they were out of view, one of them tripped over his own boot and face-planted into the ground. His companion just kept on running.

"Truly impressive," said Xander.

"*Tormen*" grunted Belkore. "They shouldn't be allowed near a sword. Hauling gear is all they're good for."

"Perhaps they just lack proper motivation," quipped Xander.

"Oh, I've given them plenty of motivation."

"Yes, I can see that," said Xander. "And it's working marvelously."

"Perhaps I should pat their heads and bake them a cake when they fail. Isn't that what they do in Reysa?"

"Pretty much," said Xander.

"And how does that work out?"

"Deliciously."

Belkore snorted again. His face relaxed for the first time. "I must admit, there have been a few times when I've missed that smart mouth of yours."

"Just my mouth?"

Belkore pretended to size up the rest of his companion. "The rest of you I could probably do without. It looks like that floater food must agree with you. Not a lot of exercise to be had in Reysa, then?"

"Well, we have our weekly tormen chases, of course, but they just don't run as fast as they used to."

"*Tormen chases,*" laughed Belkore. "That sounds like something we should suggest to your father."

"It *does* sound like his type of sport, doesn't it?" responded Xander.

"So, what brings you back to the city? Other than to bother me," asked Belkore.

"I'm forming a gang. You interested?"

"What type of gang?" asked Belkore.

"Oh, you know, the usual. A tough brood of thugs to spread intimidation and mayhem. There might also be singing."

Belkore rolled his eyes. "Seriously, what are you doing here?"

"I'm forming a gang!" repeated Xander. "Ok, well maybe more of a search party. But I thought 'gang' had an edgier ring to it. I was thinking you and the old tracker. What do you say?"

"I can't just leave. I have my training duties to attend to," said Belkore.

"Yes, and I'm sure that you will be sorely missed. Now come on, we're leaving." Xander turned and started walking towards the hyper-rail station but Belkore stood still.

"They're hopeless, Belk!" shouted Xander over his shoulder as he continued walking. "Come and do something useful with your time."

Belkore frowned. He grumbled to himself then went to catch up with the prince.

Through the windows of the hyper-rail car, Xander could see that the city had already begun to prepare for battle. Several Gartolians were loading supplies and weapons onto transport vehicles. Monstrous iron tanks emerged from hidden caves in the side of the canyon, smoke billowing from their backs. These iron beasts were the same as those that had been outfitted to support the shield in Reysa. In the space where the shield legs would have been there were giant turrets capable of firing a shell ten feet in diameter. Instead of long, protruding cannons, the shells were fired out of concave holes in the turret. This gave the tanks a squatty, turtle-like appearance.

Xander watched the tanks roll into formation. Because of their great size, they moved very slowly. It would take them over two weeks to travel from Gartol to Reysa. *If those make it to the front steps of Reysa, it won't be much of a battle,* thought Xander. Even if the hidden Reytana return, without any solar energy to power the city's defenses it would be a lopsided affair. Reytana are no match for Gartolian tanks.

"So do you really think the old man is going to go for it?" asked Belkore as he leaned back against the window of the hyper-rail car. "Word is that he's retired. Nobody has even seen him or those idiot kids of his for a long time."

"So maybe he'll just need a little convincing," replied Xander. "Besides, Aefort is the best tracker in The Crescent. We'd be doing ourselves a disservice if we didn't at least try to get him to join our little gang. But if you don't mind, I'll try talking to him first. If that doesn't work, you can hit him with that Belkore charm."

Belkore grunted then closed his eyes and crossed his arms on his chest. Outside, the last remnants of the city disappeared from view as the hyper-rail car shot around the first bend of Hadrian's Canyon.

From her regal apartment at the top level of Gartol, Septa had the best view in the city. She often came out onto her balcony at night. It was peaceful and it was quiet; a good place to think. Lately, her thoughts had been as black as the city below her.

Because it was built into an enormous cavern, Gartol was always dark, but the night gave it a particularly ominous feel. Light from a thousand torches flickered on the walls of the alleyways, pushing the shadows back into dead ends and corners. Hardly any citizens were out at night. There wasn't a curfew per se, but the thought of meeting a Gartune alone in the dark was enough to keep the residents in their homes.

Septa watched her brother's hyper-rail car speed away through the night, the moon glistening off of the top of the car's metallic surface. She knew that Xander had selected Belkore to accompany him; a choice made more for companionship than competence. Should they actually capture their prey, which she thought unlikely, there was a good chance that they would let them escape again. Septa's anger smoldered inside of her.

"I should have been in that car. I should have been leading the whole damn search!" she said aloud to herself.

"What's stopping you?" said a voice from behind her.

Septa turned and saw Morlo emerging from the shadows of her room.

"I thought I smelled your stench, *Commander*. I don't remember inviting you into my quarters," said Septa.

"Forgive me, Princess," said Morlo. "But I thought perhaps you could use some friendly counsel."

"And yet I see no friends of mine here," replied Septa.

"A truth which I hope to someday remedy, Princess," said Morlo. "I think you may find me to be a useful ally, especially in the days to come."

"I think my father may have something else to say about your usefulness."

"Your father is a great man, but we do not always... see eye to eye. I think that is something you and I have in common."

Septa's scowl lessened slightly. "You heard what he said. My brother must clean up his own mess."

"That's not what really bothers you, is it?" said Morlo as he walked slowly toward the Gartune princess. "You think that your father sees you as less capable than your younger brother." It was as if Morlo had looked straight into her heart.

"Only because I'm a woman!" shouted Septa.

"I have seen you in the courtyard," continued Morlo. "That is no mere woman fighting out there. That is a soldier of Gartune. I know that *I* would not want to face you on the battlefield." His voice was cool and calculated. His eyes never made direct contact with the person that he was talking to unless it was the king, and the way he walked could best be described as reptilian.

"What does it matter?" answered Septa. Morlo's words dampened the fire inside of her, but she was still frustrated. "Even if we go to battle, father will keep me off of the front lines, just like the last time."

"Yes," Morlo said carefully, "what happened during the war was... regrettable. But if it doesn't matter, then why do you train every day?"

"To show him! To show him that I am strong—stronger than the soldiers he sends in front of me—stronger than Xander! To prove that he should have sent me last time! All I need is an opportunity."

"Then make your own opportunity!" replied Morlo. "Go and find these Reytana fugitives before Xander does. Bring them back here and claim the glory for yourself. The king would not be able to ignore you then."

"You would have me disobey the king?"

Morlo bent over so that he was inches from Septa's ear, and he whispered, "Sometimes, in order to get noticed, you must break the rules."

Septa did not like how close the commander was to her. She could feel his breath on her ear as he lingered by her side. For a moment, she considered reminding the commander of his place; a reminder that he would feel for the next several days. However, his words had some truth to them. The thought of going out on her own had already occurred to her, and Morlo's suggestion only reinforced that idea. But why did Morlo care what she did? His mannerisms could have been perceived as seductive, but Septa did not sense any sexual intent from the older Gartune. Even he knew better than to make advances towards the king's daughter. *Then why the serpentine behavior? And why was he still standing so close?*

Septa shoved the commander off her shoulder. Morlo gracefully shuffled backwards with his head bowed. "My apologies, Princess," said Morlo humbly. "You may, of course, do as you wish. I only hoped to lend some friendly council."

"What are you really doing here, Morlo?" asked Septa. She walked slowly towards the bowed commander, tapping her eüroc on the floor as she approached him. "You take a big risk saying such things. If my father knew of your 'council,' he would not be pleased. And you are not my friend. So, I ask again, why are you here?"

Morlo kept his head bowed and lowered his voice to a whisper. "You're right, we are not friends. But we share something. Your father looks at us both the same way. In his eyes we are weak, we are *less than*. He does not believe that we are capable of greatness." Morlo began to raise his eyes towards Septa. "But he is wrong. About us both. I know that I have the capacity for greatness inside of me and I intend to prove it to the king! I just assumed that you were the same."

Sparks flickered in Septa's dark purple eyes. Morlo's little speech still seemed like it had an ulterior motive, but she did not care. Her heart had been a smoldering fire and Morlo's words had been the gas she needed to ignite it into a blaze. She would do it. She would find the Reytana and bring them back to her father. *He will not be able to ignore me anymore.*

Now that she had a mission to focus on, Septa stormed out of her apartment at a determined pace. It took her only a few minutes to reach the castle's armory. The guards did not dare question the princess as she stalked past them. They feared her almost as much as the king himself. Septa shoved a few weapons and provisions into a bag and then headed directly for the hyper-rail.

When Septa arrived at the hyper-rail station, she found a group of Gartolian engineers standing over one of the docks, arguing.

"What is going on here?" she snapped.

The Gartolians immediately stood at attention. "Apologies, Princess," said one of the engineers. "We did not see you there."

"Well, you see me now. I want a car loaded onto the dock for immediate departure."

The engineers looked at each other uncomfortably. Finally, one of them gathered the courage to speak. "Of course, Princess. There's just a small thing that we need to fix first. One of the primers did not detach properly when your brother's car departed earlier. It will need to be replaced before we can launch another car from the station."

"And how long is that going to take?" Septa replied, her eyes narrowing.

"We've already sent someone to the engineering bay. He should be back with the new primer shortly. After that, it shouldn't take more than an hour—two at the most—to install it. Don't worry! We'll have you on your way in no time."

"Two hours is hardly 'no time,'" said Septa. "Very well…" She turned and looked out over Moon Lake towards the canyon that Xander had departed through. Part of her wondered if he had something to do with the primer not detaching properly. *Did you know I was coming after you, brother?* She hoped that he had. It would make the chase more interesting.

It is much less common for a Gartune to live outside of their city than a Reytana. Several Reytana, in their older years, chose to make their homes in Dellwood forest or on the banks of the Crescent Mountains, choosing to live out their remaining days in peace with nature. The Gartune, however, would 'dig in' as they aged and formed little isolated nooks in the cavern of Gartol. Here they would remain, alone, until their days ran out. For it was a disgrace to be seen in such a weak, fragile condition.

- Chapter Six of *The Crescent Wars*, by Nicholas Baston

CHAPTER NINE
Aefort

There was only one stop along the hyper-rail line where a passenger could disembark between Gartol and the Summit. This unmanned weigh station was at the mouth of Hadrian's Canyon. Originally, it was built because from time to time, the river flowing through the canyon would flood and submerge the hyper-rail line. If this happened, a passenger heading for Gartol could exit at the weigh station and walk a rather treacherous cliff-side trail for the remainder of their journey. The Gartolians had since figured out how to stop the canyon's flooding, so now the only reason that someone got out at the weigh station was if they wanted to travel into the woods.

Once they had reached the mouth of the canyon, Xander slowed the car to a stop and the two companions exited the hyper-rail. The moons provided enough illumination for

Xander and Belkore to easily find the forest trail. They followed it for several minutes, walking quietly under the moonlight. As the trees became larger, the sounds of the forest increased until the canopy was alive with the nighttime songs of the woodland animals.

"I don't know how anyone could sleep with all of this noise," grumbled Belkore. "How much farther?"

"Don't know. Never been here," replied Xander.

"What if he's asleep?"

"Then we wake him up," said Xander.

"If you ask me, anyone who would choose to live out here instead of in the city, has officially lost their mind," said Belkore.

"Oh, I don't know," said Xander as he pulled back a tree branch that was blocking the path. "I think it would be kind of fun." As he said this, he let go of the branch and sent it springing back towards Belkore who just barely managed to duck underneath it.

"Are you ever going to grow up?" said Belkore.

"I certainly hope not," replied Xander. Then he held up his hand. "Wait a minute. Did you hear that?" Both Gartune stopped walking. The birds were quieter now. Xander looked around slowly.

"I swear to the gods, if I walk into some crazy Aefort trap, I'm going home," said Belkore.

"Quiet!" whispered Xander. "I think somebody is watching us."

"You smell," said a voice from above. Belkore and Xander looked up. In the tree above them, hunched on a large branch, was a grey-haired Gartune. His bare feet curled over the tree branch and his knees were pulled up to his chin. To his side he held a eüroc, planted in a notch in the branch.

"I think he was talking to you," whispered Xander to his friend.

"I was talking to the both of you!" replied Aefort. "I could smell you the minute you got off your little train."

"And what do we smell like?" asked Xander.

"Idiots," replied Aefort as he jumped out of the tree and landed softly next to the two Tormada. "You smell like idiots. And you," he poked Xander in the stomach with his eüroc, "smell like a floater."

Belkore sneered at his friend. "And what does a floater smell like, master tracker?" asked Belkore.

"Smugness… and fire," replied the old Gartune.

"Hmm," said Xander, his eyebrow raised. "So you know their smell. That could come in handy where we're going."

"I assume by 'we' you mean the two of you, because I ain't going nowhere," replied Aefort.

"But you haven't even heard our offer yet," said Xander. "I'm told that I can be very persuasive. Perhaps there is somewhere that we could go and talk?"

Aefort studied the two Gartune for a few moments. His grey, bushy eyebrows halfway concealed his violet eyes, but even so, Xander doubted that those eyes missed much. Eventually, Aefort grumbled something to himself, then turned and walked into the forest. Xander and Belkore took this as a sign to follow, so they silently fell in line behind the old tracker.

Aefort's pace never slowed, even though the path he chose contained several obstacles to traverse. With casual sweeps of his eüroc, the old 'Mada brushed away hanging vines, scraggly bushes and tree branches, paying no mind to where the impediments rebounded, which tended be at Xander. Belkore laughed from behind as Xander dodged several swinging branches. "Not so funny now, is it?" he laughed. Xander didn't respond; he was too busy avoiding a heavy vine that came swinging his way.

Eventually, they came upon a clearing in the woods. At the center, stood an old wooden shack that couldn't have contained more than one room inside. Puffs of smoke rose from a rusted chimney on the roof and the smell of cooking meat wafted towards the Gartune.

"Ah, good. I'm starving!" said Belkore.

Aefort frowned at him. "Then I suggest you go catch something to eat." Belkore's face dropped.

"Don't be rude, Belk. You can't just invite yourself to a man's table. After all, he has a family to feed. Speaking of," said Xander. "Are your children home? I've heard so much about them and I would very much like to meet them."

The side of Aefort's lip curled into a smile. "Then say hello."

Xander hesitated a moment, shrugged, then put his hands to his mouth and shouted at the cabin. "Hello there!"

Muffled laughter came from behind Xander. But it wasn't Belkore. Xander spun. Standing just five feet behind him were two young Gartune; a boy and a girl. And they were identical. *Twins,* thought Xander, musing at the chances that The Scales would have allowed two sets of Tormada twins to occur at the same time. *What are the odds? That must have been a particularly violent battle eighteen years ago for The Scales to be overwhelmed so quickly.*

The brother and sister were not much more than six feet tall. Xander could tell by the color in their eyes that they had just recently received their metal. Soon they would be as tall as him, but for now they looked like normal tormen, if you didn't look at their eyes.

"This is Damnar and Damina," said Aefort. There was a hint of pride in his voice.

"How long have you two been back there?" asked Xander.

"Pretty much the whole time," said Damnar. He had a big grin on his face.

"Impossible," grunted Belkore. "We would have heard you."

"I liked it when he almost hit you with that branch," said Damina. "It was funny." Belkore's jaw dropped.

"It looks like there's more than one master tracker in these woods!" said Xander. "Your father has trained you well." He turned to the old Gartune. "Very impressive, Aefort. You should teach a class in Gartol. I hear they are in need of good instructors." He glanced sideways at Belkore, but his friend was too busy scowling at the twins to notice Xander's insult. Aefort, however, appeared to pick up on the slight and he cracked a smile.

"Who are you anyway?" asked Damnar.

"This is the prince of Gartol," said Aefort.

Xander raised an eyebrow. "I wasn't sure that you recognized me."

"It's been awhile, but you haven't changed that much. I saw you once or twice before the king sent you off. Besides, who else would smell of Reysa?"

"Well, it's an honor to formally make your acquaintance," said Xander, extending his arm to Aefort. The old Gartune paused for a moment before extending his own arm. The two Gartune grasped each other's forearms for several moments, then, surprisingly, Xander broke off first.

Aefort studied the prince with those sharp, eyebrow-covered eyes then finally nodded. "Well, come on inside, since you're here. There may be a bit extra in the pot for ya."

Xander, Belkore and the twins followed Aefort into the small house. Once inside, the five Gartune nearly filled the entirety of the space. There was a small, cracked table in the center of the room surrounded by three wooden chairs. There were a couple of well-stocked cupboards and shelves, but no furniture other than the table and chairs. An iron pot hung over a small hearth at the end of the room.

"Where do you sleep?" blurted Belkore as he looked around the room disapprovingly.

"We sleep where we want!" exclaimed Damina.

"Why would anyone want to sleep indoors when you could be outside with the stars and the animals?" added Damnar.

"And what if it rains?" asked Belkore. The twins just shrugged. Belkore shook his head and began to take a seat at one of the chairs but Xander quickly shot him a glance that made him stand back up. Aefort grunted as he stirred the concoction bubbling inside the pot.

"So, let's have it then," he said as he continued to stir. "The sooner you tell me why you're here, the sooner you can leave."

The twins sat down in their seats at the table and eagerly watched Xander as if he was about to tell them a story.

"Well, you see," began Xander. The twins looked up at him excitedly. It was obvious that they hadn't had many visitors. They were hanging on his every word. "There's been an incident in Reysa. A couple of Reytana have escaped into the forest and they need to be found."

"So why aren't you searching for them yourself right now?" Aefort dipped a spoon into the pot and tasted the stew, then went back to stirring.

"Excellent question!" said Xander. "I would expect nothing less from such a seasoned tracker. Your reputation indeed precedes you." Aefort shot Xander a glance that very clearly said 'get to the point or get out.' So he continued.

"I suspect that the escapees are going to join up with the Lost Reytana. So I gave them a bit of a head start, knowing that, with your help, we could easily pick up their trail later and follow them to their destination."

"Which you assume to be the hideout of the Lost Reytana," said Aefort.

"Correct," said Xander.

Aefort sipped his stew again, this time approving of the result. He began to ladle the steaming spoonfuls into bowls. Belkore watched greedily as the old Gartune placed a bowl in front of Damnar and Damina, and then sat down at the table to join his children. Belkore's head immediately dropped. The old tracker enjoyed a couple of bites while he watched Belkore pout silently, before he eventually relented and nodded at the pot for him to help himself.

"So you think that you'll be able to find the single most sought-after location in the entire Crescent?" asked Aefort as Belkore shoveled the remainder of the stew into a bowl.

"No, I think that *we* will find it!" exclaimed Xander. Belkore rolled his eyes at his friend's exaggerated excitement but the twins were eating it up just as fast as they were eating their stew.

"Then you're a fool," said Aefort, turning his attention to his own bowl. "Even if you did find their lair, which even your own father hasn't been able to do, what then? Do you expect to take on the entire Reytana army by yourself? Do you think they will just let you leave and go tell the king their location? No, if you find them, then you're dead. And if you don't find them, well… I don't want to be the one to tell Hadrian that you have failed."

"You're assuming that the only way to find the lair is to get caught," said Xander. "Well, I don't plan on getting caught. This mission is strictly reconnaissance."

"What if you find the escaped Reytana before they lead you to the hideout?" asked Aefort.

"Ok, not strictly reconnaissance," said Xander. "If we find the fugitives and they don't lead us to the hideout, then we're taking them prisoner."

"Just like that?" asked Aefort. "You don't think they'll fight?"

"You are awfully concerned about fighting," grumbled Belkore. "You may be old, but you're still a Gartune. We don't shy away from a fight!"

Aefort slowly looked up from his bowl. Xander shook his head. He knew that any chance they had of Aefort joining them had just vanished.

"There's that old Belk charm," said Xander.

"You two should be going now," said Aefort.

Xander patted Belkore's shoulder and led him out of the house. "Come on, we'll just have to track them on their own. How hard can it be?"

The two Gartune hadn't taken ten steps outside of the house when they heard a voice shout, "Wait up!" from behind them. Damnar came rushing out of the shack. He carried a eüroc with a small bundle tied to the end of it.

"Take me with you!" he exclaimed.

"Me too!" came another shout from the shack. Damina burst through the door, tying a similar pack onto her own eüroc as she did so.

The twins stood eagerly in front of the prince, awaiting his orders. They looked as if they wanted to salute, but were unsure as to the proper form, so they simply stood at attention with their arms straight at their sides. Xander looked past the brother and sister towards the house behind them. Standing in the doorway was Aefort. He wore a disapproving look on his face, but he gave Xander a small nod anyway.

"Well, it looks like we have our gang after all," said Xander to Belkore. "Let the hunt begin!"

Belkore scoffed and then turned towards the forest but Xander held him back. "Why don't we let these two lead the way."

Belkore sat by himself in the corner of the hyper-rail car and stared reproachfully at the twins as they scampered around the compartment, inspecting every nook and cranny. It was obviously their first time on the hyper-rail.

Twins were a rarity amongst Tormada and often occurred during times of battle. This was because The Scales sometimes became overwhelmed with the incoming auras of dead Tormada and occasionally let too much of the aura spill into the river. This occasionally resulted in twins. Twin children were considered blessings in both the Reytana and Gartune culture, because The Scales only regarded the twins as one child. Thus, a twin constituted a "bonus" Tormada and a few bonuses could turn the tide of a battle.

Chances are, Damnar and Damina would not be responsible for turning the tides of any battle.

It was shortly after the end of the Eighth Great War that Aefort decided to adopt the twins. Actually, decided may be the wrong word. He was persuaded to adopt them. Aefort had no interest in being a father and was perfectly content to live a solitary life. But, at nearly two hundred years old, that solitary life was nearing its end. The Gartune—and in particular, Hadrian—decided that before he returned to The Scales, he would need to impart his wisdom to a new generation of Gartune. For, Aefort had a particular skill set that was unequaled among the Tormada. He was the best tracker in The

Crescent. The Gartune would not let his skills die with him, so they insisted that he adopt children and impart his knowledge on to them. Enter Damnar and Damina.

Just because Hadrian had mandated that Aefort become a father didn't mean that he was required to be a good one. He fed and clothed the children, as was his responsibility, but that was about the extent of his parenting; until the twins turned ten. For some reason, Aefort decided that ten was the proper age to become a tracker.

Since he had never trained anyone before, he didn't exactly have a blueprint for the most effective method for teaching his craft. He just did the first thing that came to mind. One day, he took the twins out into the middle of Dellwood Forest, and left them there. They had no gear and no instructions, just the remains of their own tracks to follow back home.

Once he had left, it began to rain. After three days and no sign of the twins, Aefort began to rethink his decision to abandon them in the forest. However, that afternoon Damnar and Damina stumbled through Aefort's front door; wet and hungry but smiling ear to ear. It was then that Aefort knew they were naturals.

He began to actually teach, and the twins soaked up his knowledge with a ravenous thirst. They started to take weekly trips out into the woods. Aefort would blindfold them and then leave a trail to follow home. Eventually, that became too easy for the twins, so he began to leave false trails as well. One day, he decided to lead them directly into a mendkin hovel. Fortunately, the beasts had already eaten that week, so the twins were able to escape unharmed, but they learned their lesson and that was the last time they were fooled by a false trail.

Soon, the twins' skills began to rival those of their father. News of the two young trackers spread throughout Gartol, even reaching the ears of Xander in Reysa. Still, Xander's first choice had been Aefort. But if he couldn't have the master, then he would take the apprentices. However, the idea of chaperoning two adolescent Gartune as they grew into

Tormada was not what Belkore had in mind when he agreed to join Xander's search party, and he made no effort to hide his displeasure.

"I would put that down before you hurt yourself," said Belkore to Damnar as he clumsily twirled his new eüroc in his hand. The young Gartune frowned but acquiesced to the older 'Mada. It was unwise to get on Belkore's bad side this early in the journey, so he sat back in his seat and pouted. Next to him, Damina fidgeted quietly with the button on her eüroc that triggered her chosen *tre'ance*—a tiny saw blade that spun rapidly as it went up and down the top half of her staff. Her eyes gleamed as she watched the devious device whiz up and around her eüroc. Belkore shook his head disapprovingly. "Kids..." he grumbled to himself.

"You know, maybe if you two are lucky, old uncle Belkore here will show you how to use those things," said Xander.

"Not bloody likely," replied Belkore. "You chose those idiotic contraptions. You figure them out."

"You'll have to forgive him," added Xander. "He's more of a traditionalist when it comes to *tre'ance* choices."

"Yeah?" asked Damnar. "What did you choose?" he asked, pointing at Belkore's staff.

Belkore tapped a hidden button on his eüroc and a large, gleaming scythe popped from the end of his staff. Simple, deadly, and incredibly intimidating. The twins eyed it with equal parts fear and admiration. Damina glumly retracted her saw blade and looked down at her feet.

"Hmmmph", snorted Belkore as he retracted his scythe with a satisfied smile.

"Don't worry about it, kid," said Xander. "It's not the size that matters."

"What's yours?" asked Damnar, beckoning towards Xander. Belkore began to laugh.

"Yeah, Xan. Why don't you show the kid yours?" chuckled Belkore.

"Maybe some other time," said Xander.

"*Speaking of dumb choices...*" Belkore whispered to himself, loud enough that everyone heard, though Xander pretended not to. The twins looked disappointed, but they didn't press the prince to show them his *tre'ance*. The four companions sat in awkward silence for several minutes before Damnar broke the air.

"So, are you going to tell us what we are hunting?"

"Yes, I suppose that would be helpful, wouldn't it?" said Xander. "We are tracking two Reytana and their Reysene friend. They escaped Reysa earlier this afternoon and were last seen heading towards the forest. As fate would have it, they are all about your age, so maybe you can lend some insight into what two eighteen-year-old Tormada twins are thinking."

The twins glanced at each other. Xander tried to decipher the looks on their faces, but they were unreadable.

"Well?" asked Xander. "Any ideas?"

"If they were me," started Damnar, uncertainly.

"They'd what?" demanded Belkore, leaning forward in his seat.

"They'd be..." Damnar stammered nervously, looking at his sister for assistance.

"Spit it out!" shouted Belkore.

"They'd be hungry!" said Damnar and Damina together. Belkore shook his head and leaned back in his seat. Xander chuckled. He opened up a compartment next to his chair and threw a couple of wrapped sandwiches to the twins. Their eyes lit up appreciatively and they tore into the sandwiches while the hyper-rail car sped through the night.

The hum of the magnets beneath Septa's hyper-rail car began to decelerate as it slid to a gradual stop at the weigh station. She had been traveling at maximum velocity ever since she left Gartol and the sides of her vessel were almost too hot to touch as she stepped out onto the dusty platform. In the dust were two distinct sets of footprints; one leading away from the platform, and one returning. She noticed there were more footprints in the tracks that returned to the platform. *You went and got help. Maybe you're not as dumb as I thought. Still, going all the way back to Reysa to start your search is a mistake. You will follow from behind while I will cut the fugitives off from the front!*

Septa looked out over the horizon. To her left she could faintly make out the tree line of Dellwood Forest. To her right was the coast of the Delucean Sea. And spread right before her was the vast Battle Plains. She turned to her left and set out at a determined trot. *I will show them*, she thought as she ran. *This is the last time that they will underestimate me.*

It was very early in the morning when Xander and his three companions arrived at the Gartolian encampment at the base of Reysa. They stretched their legs and yawned as they exited the hyper-rail car. It was not a long trip, but sixty minutes was a long time for a Tormada to sit in one place.

"I still think that we should have gotten off at the Summit," grumbled Belkore.

"We could not track them from there," answered Damnar. "We have to start where the tracks start, and that's here."

"You said that when they left it was raining," added Damina, "which means the ground was soft. They will have left an obvious trail."

"Chances are they went towards the river as it is their only source of fresh water," said Damnar. "If we follow the river, Damina and I should be able to find their tracks."

"And what happens when we find them?" asked Belkore, looking at Xander.

"We capture them. Alive. Do you understand me?" Xander's face was all seriousness. His companions nodded, though they didn't seem pleased with the order.

Whereas the Battle Plains has been a veritable "no man's land" over the years, Dellwood forest has served as a zone of neutrality where both the Reysene and Gartolians could interact without fear of attack. There is a reason for this - the waifs. The woodsmen serve as a buffer between the two races, and they have learned how to profit mightily from this unique position.

- Chapter Four of *The Crescent Wars* by Nicholas Baston

CHAPTER TEN
Lem

Tinko and the twins spent the night among the branches of a large tree. It had been Loras' idea to climb high into the forest canopy so that they might avoid being detected by any search parties as they slept. It was a good idea, in theory. However, none of the branches were wide enough to allow a person, let alone a robust one like Tinko, to comfortably lie down without fear of rolling over the edge. And so, the companions spent most of their night drifting in and out of sleep as they struggled to keep themselves from falling.

The morning sun was almost ready to peek over the horizon when they heard a noise in the forest. It wasn't a loud noise, but rather a large noise, like a hundred small twigs breaking simultaneously. The three teens held tight to their branches and looked in the direction of the sound. Again, the sound of hundreds of branches breaking reverberated through the forest; this time significantly closer. Their tree branch shuddered, causing the teenagers to scramble to hold on. Tinko lost his grip and began to slide off off the side of his branch. His arms flailed as he struggled to grasp onto anything that would prevent his fall.

"Help!" he screamed. He reached for something—anything—but his fingers closed around empty air. Suddenly, two strong hands grabbed his forearm and held him in mid-air.

"Quiet!" whispered Loras. He adjusted his grip, trying to get a better hold on his heavy friend.

They heard the sound again, this time directly below them. They looked down into the darkness, unable to see the forest floor as it was hidden by a dense black haze. They felt a giant, rumbling exhalation as a puff of warm, moist air rose into the tree. Then, they heard it again; the same crunching sound of hundreds of pieces of wood breaking as something attempted to emerge from the woods below.

The trapped teenagers froze with fear. Tinko could feel Loras' fingernails digging into his arm, breaking the skin, but he was too frightened to cry out in pain. Slowly, a shape emerged from the darkness below. A great shaggy mound rose up to the spot where Tinko was hanging from the tree. The pungent smell of wet fur filled Tinko's nose, nauseating him. He began to dry heave. Suddenly, two giant eyelids opened from the face of the giant, furry mound. The glowing orbs that they revealed were like two moons shining in the darkness. They were solid white. Even without pupils to indicate the direction of the beast's gaze, Tinko could tell that the eyes were staring directly at him.

For a full minute, nothing happened. Nobody moved. Nothing breathed. The giant eyes didn't blink. Tinko tried to will his heart to pump more quietly. It sounded to him like each beat was echoing off the tree branch. Regan sat motionless and attempted to silence her breathing. Inhale. Exhale. Measured, slow and steady.

A large drop of sweat hung on the tip of Tinko's nose. He watched it quiver as it grew in size. Finally, it dropped, falling in slow motion until it splattered on a leaf, breaking the silence. It might as well have been a crack of thunder.

The creature blinked. It let out a large exhalation and a burst of warm air blew through the tree branches. The moon eyes began to slowly survey the rest of the tree's inhabitants. The way its eyelids bent slightly gave an indication of where the eyes were pointing. They inspected Loras, who was splayed out on the branch above the hanging Tinko. Then the eyes moved to the branch where Regan was sitting motionless. Another puff of air. Another blink. But this time the eyes did not re-open. The shaggy mound of hair descended back into the darkness of the forest floor, breaking the few remaining branches that had survived its ascent. The teens listened as the crunching of the creature's footsteps slowly carried him out into the forest.

"Pull me up already!" grunted Tinko after he had judged that the coast was clear. Loras gave one hearty yank and his friend belly-flopped next to him on the tree branch. Both boys rolled onto their backs with exhaustion. Tinko began to laugh.

"What was that thing?" asked Loras.

"You don't know?" said Tinko, continuing to laugh.

"It was a mendkin," said Regan as she climbed over to where the boys were laying. "Had to be. Nothing else that big lives in the forest."

"Says the expert who has spent a grand total of one night in the forest," replied Loras.

"Ok, genius, then what was it?" said Regan.

"Oh, it was definitely a mendkin," interjected Tinko before Loras could respond. "Did you see how its eyes filled its entire face? And it had no pupils. Definitely a mendkin. Perfectly harmless beasts when they aren't hungry."

"I guess we were lucky it wasn't hungry then," said Regan.

"Maybe it wasn't hungry, but I'm starving," said Loras.

"How can you think of food after what just happened?" asked Regan incredulously.

"I guess saving Tink's life works up an appetite!" said Loras as he began to jump down from the tree. Regan watched him, dumfounded.

"Truth be told, I am a little hungry myself," said Tinko.

"I... I don't even..." started Regan, but then she just shook her head and began to slowly follow her brother down the tree.

Loras had read a book once about hunting and saw no reason why he shouldn't be able to easily kill some lazy woodland animal. So, he set off into the forest in search of breakfast. He quickly found out that hunting was not as easy as it seemed, and he spent the better part of an hour hurling sticks at annoyed, but perfectly safe, nimbers and pipkens. Fortunately, Regan spent this time gathering wild mushrooms and berries while Tinko devised a rather ingenious net out of tall grass and used it to catch three fish from the river.

However, since nobody knew how to start a fire, they had to eat the fish raw. It turned out to be a rather unpleasant meal for everyone.

As they were choking down their last bits of raw fish, Tinko noticed something about his companions. "You two must have grown at least two inches overnight," he said. "We're only going to be able to pass you off as very tall tormen for a few more days. After that, there will be no hiding the fact that you are Tormada. You'll stick out like a sore thumb."

"Then that gives us three days to find this Declin person," said Loras.

"And give him Dario's letter," added Regan. "You still have it don't you?"

"Yes," replied Loras.

"You haven't opened it, have you?" asked Regan, her eyes narrowing suspiciously at her brother.

"No. But why shouldn't I? If there's something in there that can help us, wouldn't you want to know what it is?"

"If it was something that could help us, Dario would have told us to read it," answered Regan. "I knew you wouldn't be able to resist opening it. Why don't you just give it to me so that you're not tempted?"

"It's my letter! Dario gave it to me, not you!" answered Loras. "If he would have wanted *you* to have it, he would have given it to *you*."

"I have an idea. Why don't you give it to me," suggested Tinko.

The two Tormada frowned down at their friend. Their new height made Tinko seem a lot shorter than he used to be. "Or... you could just keep it," said Tinko sheepishly.

"Fine, you keep it," said Regan. "Just promise you won't open it."

"I promise," answered Loras.

"I'm serious," replied Regan.

"I'm serious too."

"Ok, good."

"Fine."

"Soooo," interjected Tinko. He had seen these sibling squabbles go on for many minutes. "We should probably get moving. Woodhaven has to be somewhere along the river, so if we just follow along the bank for long enough then eventually we'll hit it."

"Won't the river be the exact place that the Gartune will be searching for us?" replied Regan.

"Do you know any other way to get to Woodhaven?" replied Loras. Regan didn't reply.

"No? Then I agree with Tinko. We follow the river, but we stay under the cover of the trees."

"And if we're spotted?" asked Regan.

"I don't know, I'll think of something," replied Loras.

"Nice plan."

"Thanks. I just thought of it."

"All right, here we go!" yelled Tinko as he started off toward the river. It was going to be a long day.

Tinko and the twins followed the river all morning, staying hidden within the tree line. There was a well-worn path near the bank of the river that would have sped up their journey, but they decided to stick to the woods instead. During this time, they saw two tormen walk past them on the path. Judging by their clothes, the travelers were not Reysene or Gartolians. They were waifs; woodsmen.

Long ago, when the torman race was choosing sides, those who would not swear complete loyalty to either Rey or Gar'on were forced to live in the woods. There, they had remained for hundreds of years. Though the waifs had not benefitted from many of the advancements of the Reysene or the Gartolians, they had also not suffered through eight centuries of war. The woodsmen took no sides and were generally left alone.

Whenever they saw a waif approaching on the path, Tinko, Loras and Regan ducked behind a tree so as not to be spotted. After the second waif had passed, Tinko suggested that perhaps they should ask one of them for the way to Woodhaven. Loras and Regan immediately shot this idea down. The waifs were a wild and covetous race and could not be trusted. During wartime the waifs were notorious for selling information about troop movements to both the Reytana and the Gartune if it meant a handsome reward. Though they remained neutral, the waifs did not hesitate to profit from anything of value that turned up in their woods. And the location of two lost Reytana was definitely a valuable piece of information.

When a third waif was spotted approaching on the path, Tinko and the twins again threw themselves underneath some nearby forest bushes. They all held their breath as the waif slowly approached.

The waif's right foot was bent awkwardly inward and he walked with a noticeable limp. He carried a walking stick to help take pressure off of the gimp foot. After a sufficient amount of time had gone to allow the waif to pass, Loras peeked out from his hiding spot. There, standing directly in the middle of the path was the waif. He was peering in their direction. Immediately, Loras ducked his head back down but the quick movement drew the attention of the waif.

"You der, show yerself!" yelled the waif. Nobody moved. "I seen you jump back der; there's no use hidin!"

"Why don't we just go talk to him?" whispered Tinko. "There's only one of him and three of us. What's he going to do?"

"Quiet," whispered Regan. "If we stay put maybe he'll go away."

"All right, have it yer way," yelled the waif. Instead of continuing down the path he began to walk towards their location. He swung his walking stick to clear the brush in front of him. The teens crouched in silence as they listened to the approaching waif.

"Do something!" whispered Regan to her brother, but when she turned to look at him, he was gone. The waif was nearly upon them. Tinko looked around for Loras but couldn't find him anywhere. It was just him and Regan. He knew he had to do something so he mustered every bit of courage he had, and with a rabid yell, came crashing clumsily out of his hiding place. The waif turned to face the oncoming boy. He watched with a half-bewildered, half-amused face as the clumsy youth came stumbling towards him with clenched fists swinging from his sides.

Once the waif had turned to face Tinko, Loras came out from his new hiding place. As Tinko approached from the front, Loras approached from the back, but with much less noise. When Tinko was only a few feet from the waif, he tripped and tumbled to the ground. At this same moment, Loras lowered his head and closed the remaining distance between him and his target. Suddenly, without turning around, the waif thrust his walking stick behind him. The tip of the stick caught Loras right between the ribs, knocking the wind out of him. With Loras disabled, the waif then turned and smacked the heaving boy over the back of the head with his stick. Loras crumpled to the ground, unconscious.

The waif turned back to meet Tinko who was now frozen with terror. The boy's heart would not let him retreat but his mind would not let him advance. Clearly, he was no match for the woodsman. Tinko's only chance was to use his size and rush directly at the man. After a second of internal debate, Tinko's heart won out, and he jumped up and ran at the waif.

Wearing the same amused look, the waif deftly side-stepped the charging Tinko and struck him on his backside as he passed. This caused Tinko to fall forward and he landed directly on top of the unconscious Loras. Huffing and puffing, Tinko gathered himself as quickly as he could and turned to begin another charge at the waif.

"Easy der, big fella," said the waif. "Yer not gonna win dis one unless you got more floaters hidin in da woods."

As the waif spoke, Regan arose from her hiding place. The waif immediately turned to meet her. Regan walked calmly toward her brother with her hands held above her head in surrender. The waif looked at her with but did not attack. Tinko couldn't decipher the man's expression. It was part surprise and part bewilderment. When she had reached Loras, Regan knelt down by his side, all the while keeping her hands held above her and her eyes fixed on the waif.

"What did you do to him?" she asked coolly with a hint of accusation in her voice.

"He'll be ok, just got his bell rung a bit," said the waif, the confused expression leaving his face. "Are there any more of yas out there?"

"No," said Regan. "Please, we don't want any trouble."

"I think dis one might've wanted a bit o' trouble," said the waif as he poked Loras with his walking stick. Loras let out a low groan as his eyes flickered and he rolled over toward his sister.

"See, told yas he'd be ok."

Loras sat up on his elbow and rubbed the back of his head. Regan moved his hand so that she could inspect his wound. A large lump was already beginning to form.

"Nice plan," she said to her brother. Loras moaned.

"What are two floaters doin' out 'ere in da woods?" asked the waif.

Loras and Regan looked at each other. They couldn't tell if the waif had known they were Reytana from a distance, but now that he stood in front of them, there was no hiding their true identities. Their eyes gave them away.

"We're trying to get to Woodhaven," answered Tinko. Loras and Regan gave him the same glaring look.

"What's in Wood'aven?" asked the waif.

This time Tinko kept his mouth shut. He knew he had already said too much. The waif looked at Loras and Regan but neither would answer his question.

"Well, do any of yas know how to swim?" The teens all shook their heads. "Cause' yer never gonna make it to Wood'aven if you can't swim. Dat is, unless, you had a boat."

"It wouldn't just so happen that you have a boat, would it?" asked Regan suspiciously.

"S'pose I might have somethin', but it ain't free."

"But we don't—" said Tinko before he was interrupted by Loras.

"We can pay! But only after you get us to Woodhaven. We will pay you once we get there," said Loras.

The waif pondered this for a moment. "You wouldn't be thinkin' of pullin' a fast one, now would ye? 'Specially seein' as how friendly I've been to yas even after yas tried ta attack me."

"Attack *you*," said Tinko, incredulously. "We were just—" but Regan cut him off.

"We have money," interjected Regan. "But it's in Woodhaven. That's why we need to go there. Will you help us?"

The waif walked over to where Loras was laying and offered him a hand up. "Aye, it's a deal." Loras cautiously accepted the hand of the waif who pulled him off the ground with surprising ease.

"Ya should'a jumped," said the waif.

"What?" said Loras as he dusted himself off.

"When you was chargin', you should'a jumped. Wouldn't 'ave hit you 'den," said the waif with a wink.

Loras gave the waif a confused look then he, his sister and Tinko followed the woodsman back up the river from where he had come. The waif refused to trudge through the woods and so they reluctantly kept to the path. They walked in silence, keeping their eyes and ears open. Several times Tinko thought he heard something behind them but each time he looked around, there was nothing there. "Easy, big fella," the waif would say each time without turning his head. Eventually, Tinko realized that if something was truly pursuing them, the waif would know before anyone else did.

Only once did they come across a traveler who, fortunately, took no extra notice of them as they passed. But Tinko noticed that the waif's grip on his walking stick had shifted slightly as the stranger approached.

They walked all day without stopping to eat or drink. Nobody, not even Tinko, protested. Their fear of being caught was greater than their hunger, and they decided that the more room they could put between them and Reysa, the better. Also, they had no clue how far it was to Woodhaven and the woodsman would not tell them. He simply would say "It's up 'ere aways. You'll hear it before ya see it."

Finally, evening came, and the waif instructed that they find a place to sleep for the night. The teens explained how they had spent the previous night in a tree, to which the waif gave an amused laugh.

"It was to hide us from—" Tinko began but was quickly cut off by Loras.

"Animals," said Loras as he shot Tinko a look that said you're not allowed to talk for the rest of the night.

"We were afraid that some animals might attack us while we were sleeping," added Regan.

"Ain't no animals gonna attack you," said the waif, "'sept for maybe a mendkin, but dats only when dey're real hungry. And if a mendkin finds ya, der ain't no tree dats gonna keep you from him." The teens looked at each other warily.

The waif led the group into the forest where they found a gathering of small, tangled trees whose overgrowth formed a small canopy. Loras and Tinko went about building a wall out of twigs and leaves to conceal their location while the waif went in search of firewood. When he returned, he had two dead pipkens and a nimber slung over his shoulder. Within minutes, the woodsman had dinner cooking over a neat little fire. Regan watched him like a hawk as he slowly turned the skewered meat over the flames. The waif noticed her watching him and he returned her stare. The two of them locked eyes for several seconds, as if each was attempting to read the mind of the other.

"So how big is your boat?" asked Tinko as he eyed the roasting nimber ravenously. He had never been on a boat before and the thought of riding on one made his stomach a bit queasy.

"What boat?" said the waif.

"Your boat," replied Tinko. "The one you told us you had!"

"Never said I 'ad a boat," said the waif as he turned the nimber over the fire.

"You said you had a boat to get us across the river!" added Loras.

"I said I 'ad somethin' to get ya across da river, but I never said it was a boat." The waif winked at Tinko as he grabbed the smoking hot nimber off the fire with his bare hands. He then tore off half and tossed it to Regan. "Ladies first." Regan let the smoking meat fall into her lap to cool. The waif then tossed the other half to her brother who caught it one-handed, never breaking eye contact with the waif.

"No need fer dat look of yers, my young floater friend. I says I would get yous across da river and so I will. Yous just make sure dat you keep yer end of da bargain."

Loras continued to stare at the waif, but he said nothing. After a few moments, he took an extra-large bite of the steaming-hot nimber. It burnt his mouth terribly, but he tried not to show it. Only after water began to pool in his eyes did Loras break eye contact with the waif. The waif gave an amused snort as he skewered the remaining two pipkens and placed them over the fire.

Tinko still had nothing to eat. Regan and Loras had been so hungry that they had totally forgotten about their friend. Tinko watched miserably as his companions tore into their dinners. All the while the waif slowly turned the spit and grinned at the hungry boy. Tinko could see that it had not been by chance that the twins got their dinners first.

"Yous needs to learn to control yourself a bit der big fella. "

"Excuse me?" said Tinko. "You don't even know me. You have no id—"

"Right der, dat's what I mean. You just start spoutin' uncontrollable from yer mouth without thinkin' first, just like ya run at me in da woods today." Loras and Regan looked up from their meals, their mouths full of meat. "Yous don't want to let people know what you're thinkin' or doin' all the time. Makes ya an easy target." As he said the word target, the waif took one of the sticks off of the fire and flung the end of it toward Tinko. The pipken flew off and hit the boy directly in the stomach, juices squirting everywhere. Tinko didn't care. He tore into the meat with both hands and ate greedily.

The waif looked sideways at Loras while he nodded at Tinko. Loras simply shrugged his shoulders and went back to his own dinner.

"Who does this guy think he is anyway?" said Tinko with a mouthful of meat. "We don't even know his name."

"That's true," said Regan. "What should we call you?"

"Yous can call me Lem if ya need ta," said the waif.

"Well, *Lem*," replied Regan suspiciously, "I am Re—" Loras stopped her.

"We shouldn't tell him our names!" he whispered. "What if he decides to double-cross us?"

Lem looked incredulously at the twins and then at Tinko. "He knows I'm right 'ere, right?"

Tinko just rolled his eyes. "He's not the brains of the operation," said Tinko through a mouthful of pipken meat.

"I suppose we don't have any choice but to trust him," said Regan, not trying to hide her voice from their companion.

"Besides, if he sells us out then there will be no money for him."

"Aye, dat's the spirit," said Lem.

"Mr. Lem, my name is Regan. This is my brother Loras and our friend Tinko. It is nice to meet you," said Regan.

"I'm glad ya got to meet me too," said Lem with a toothy smile. Tinko chuckled. Even Loras grinned a bit. Everyone's mood began to improve, as usually is the case when you have food in your belly.

There are three moons that orbit Torma; Castion, Lemure, and Ramala. Castion is the closest and appears the largest in the night sky. However, due to its small orbit, it is also the least seen of the three. But when all three moons are visible, there is very little difference between day and night on Torma.

Even though the three moons combined provide nearly as much light as Torma's sun, they do not provide the same benefits - mainly, the Reytana cannot draw any power from them and their light does not charge Reysa's lotus.

\- Chapter Two of *The Crescent Wars* by Nicholas Baston

CHAPTER ELEVEN
Moonlight

Moonlight cascaded through the shifting openings of the forest canopy as Loras and Regan lay next to each other, staring up at the stars. Above them, several flying animals glided from branch to branch. The twins watched the creatures, transfixed, as they floated effortlessly between trees.

"The whirls are out tonight," whispered Regan. "I don't remember seeing any last night, do you?"

"No," replied Loras as a whirl unfolded its crescent-shaped wings and spun through the air. Its feathers were a glossy black and they reflected the moon's rays when it hit them, painting the nearby leaves with slivers of light. The effect was mesmerizing.

"They must not live that close to the edge of the forest. We're quite a ways in now," continued Loras.

"It's like a whole different world out here, isn't it?" said Regan.

"It's definitely different," replied Loras.

Regan sighed contentedly. "I've missed this view," she said.

Loras rolled over to look at his sister. "You've missed it? That implies you've seen it before."

"I have," said Regan, continuing to look up at the night sky.

"Liar," said Loras. He rolled back over on his back.

"You may think you know everything, but you don't," said Regan. "And that includes everything about me."

"You and me both know that you've never been out of the city," said Loras. "Hardly anybody has left since the Gartune took over."

"People have left," replied Regan.

"Who?"

"Dario has left."

"That's different."

"How?"

"He has to do… political stuff… I don't know," said Loras. "He doesn't count."

"I'm pretty sure professor Lucan has left," said Regan.

"Teacher stuff…" said Loras. "Doesn't count."

"If you say so."

"The point is, you haven't left. The lift is guarded every hour of the day and night. They don't let anybody out unless they're escorted. Wait…" Loras rolled back towards his sister. "You went with *him* didn't you?" His voice started to raise.

"Keep your voice down," said Regan. "We're supposed to be hiding, in case you forgot."

"So what was it? Like a little date? Just you and the prince of Gartol, strolling through the woods holding hands?"

Regan raised up on to her forearm and confronted her brother. "You need to calm down."

"*You* need to stop telling me what to do!"

"Why are you so angry all the time?" asked Regan.

"Why do you think?" exclaimed Loras, not heeding his sister's suggestion to lower his voice. "Maybe it has something to do with being a prisoner my entire life. I would have thought you felt the same way. But apparently, flirting with the guards comes with privileges!"

Regan rolled her eyes and lay back down. "Xander never took me outside of the city."

"Then who?"

"It's none of your business."

"You're seriously not going to tell me?"

"No."

The two lay in silence for several minutes. Loras kept fidgeting, unable to regain his composure. His sister always knew how to push his buttons and this time was no different. How could she lay there so calmly with everything that was going on? It infuriated him. But that had always been her nature. Nothing phased her. Nothing angered her—not even the Gartune. The only time she ever got upset was when she disapproved of something he did. It wasn't fair.

"How do you do it?" asked Loras, his voice returning to an acceptable volume.

"Do what?" replied Regan.

"Not be angry?" said Loras.

"I get angry. I get angry a lot, actually. I've just learned that it's better not to show your emotions to people. That way, they can't use them against you."

"But you're never scared. Like ever. Even around the Gartune, you never flinch. And don't tell me you're just concealing your emotions because I've seen you around them. You might as well be talking to Tinko or me."

Regan thought for a moment before responding. "You're right, I'm not scared of them. I don't think they will do anything to me. Not as long as Xander is around. But I am *terrified* of what they will do to you or Tinko. That's what you don't understand about me. It's not *me* that I'm worried about. It's the people I care for. So when you see bad things happening to me and I don't react, that's because they're just happening to *me* and I'd rather have that than something happen to the people I love. Does that make sense?"

"No."

Regan sighed. "Someday it will. I hope."

Off in the distance, there was a small clearing in the woods. Unblocked by trees, the moons illuminated the clearing as if it were daytime. Too tired to continue arguing, Loras watched a group of harbits graze on the dew-covered grass at the center of the space when a figure emerged from the side of the woods. Loras poked Regan to get her attention and she lifted up onto her elbows. The figure casually approached the group of long-legged animals. One of them lifted their head, while the others continued to graze, unconcerned. Harbits were normally benign in nature, but when provoked, the crown of antlers that protruded from their foreheads could serve as a formidable weapon. The stranger didn't seem worried as he approached the group. The harbit that had raised its head left the pack and walked over to meet the newcomer.

"Is that Lem?" whispered Loras. As if on cue, the waif turned towards the twins' location. He was too far away for his face to be recognized, but the walking stick that he held in his hand gave him away. It was definitely their mysterious travel companion.

"What's he doing out there?" asked Loras.

Regan stared at the waif, her brow furrowed, but said nothing.

Lem peered around the clearing as if looking to see if anyone was watching, then leaned over the Harbit's head. He appeared to whisper something in its ear.

"Please tell me our guide doesn't think he can talk to animals," said Loras. Regan continued to watch intently but said nothing. Lem still had his hand cupped over the harbit's ear and little white puffs of mist blew from the beast's nose as their conversation continued. The harbit appeared to nod its head at something Lem said.

"Yep. He's definitely talking to that thing," said Loras. "Actually, come to think of it, this is pretty on par with what we know of him so far. I mean why wouldn't he talk to animals?" That got a small smile from Regan, or at least her look relaxed a bit. It was hard to tell in the dark.

Eventually, Lem and the harbit separated, each going back the way they had come. Lem disappeared into the woods while the harbit rejoined his group and grabbed a mouthful of grass as if nothing had happened. Loras flopped back on to the ground but Regan continued to stare at the spot where Lem and the harbit had conferred.

"So what do you think?" said Loras. His sister continued to stare off at nothing.

"Hey," he repeated, this time poking her in the side. Regan frowned but then snapped out of her trance.

"What do I think of what?" she said.

"Of Lem," said Loras. "Do you think we can trust him?"

"I don't know that we have much of a choice at this point," said Regan.

"That's not exactly the answer I was looking for."

Regan turned to her brother. "I don't know if we can trust him, but I don't think he's going to hurt us if that's what you mean. He could have done that a long time ago." Loras rubbed his ribs, reminded of when the waif had struck him at their first encounter. Regan was right. He definitely had the upper hand then and could have done what he wanted with the frightened teens. But he didn't. Loras guessed that was something at least.

"Still," Regan continued thoughtfully, "we should watch what we say around him. Only tell him what he needs to know."

"I'm pretty sure there isn't much he needs to know from us, other than where our money is," said Loras. "Speaking of..."

"Yeah, we'll cross that bridge when we come to it," said Regan. "For now, we'll have to follow him and trust that his greed is his main motivating factor at the moment."

"And if it isn't?"

"Then we need to find out what is."

Spirea was originally a prison colony for Gartol. For hundreds of years, the worst criminals in Gartol were sent to the woodland outpost to serve their sentences. However, the colony eventually became overcrowded and the Gartolians decided that it took too many Gartune to police the prison, so they closed it, thinking that their limited Tormada were needed more inside of Gartol.

Nobody told the prisoners.

It did not take long for the inmates to realize that the guards had left. At first, they thought it was some sort of trap, so they remained in their cells. But hunger and curiosity eventually won out and they began to creep out of their cages. When they realized that they were truly free, they did a curious thing. They stayed.

Perhaps it wasn't so curious, seeing as how they really had nowhere to go. They couldn't return to Gartol and Reysa would not take them in, so they decided to build their own little city. And that is how the prison colony of Spirea slowly transformed into a city.

- Chapter Six of *The Crescent Wars* by Nicholas Baston

CHAPTER TWELVE
Spirea

It had taken almost no time for Damnar and Damina to find the set of tracks left by Loras, Regan and Tinko. As Damina had predicted, the tracks led straight to the river and then onwards from there. The Gartune trackers' eyes never left the ground as they quickly made their way through the forest. Xander and Belkore did their best to keep pace with their guides but it wasn't easy. The twins were fast. Very fast. They spent the entire first day traveling at a half jog through the forest. They made good time, stopping only occasionally to take a drink from the river. At the pace they were going, they thought they might even catch up to the teens by nightfall.

But night came, and the tracks continued on. It appeared that the teens had pushed themselves hard during that first day. Fear must be driving them, thought Xander. He remembered his father telling him when he was a child what a great motivator fear was. The fact that three lost teenagers had evaded him thus far seemed to validate his father's theory.

The moon shining through the trees provided enough light for the Gartune twins to continue tracking the footprints in front of them, although the light wasn't really needed to follow the trail. The tracks were obvious. The teens had apparently been more concerned with speed than covering their footprints. Finally, Damnar stopped in a small clearing in the forest. All around were broken branches and trampled undergrowth. There were footprints everywhere, but they were sloppy and unorganized.

"Something happened here," said Damnar.

"It looks like a fight," said Damina.

"Do you think they were killed?" asked Belkore with a hint of disappointment.

"Not unless the dead can walk," said Damnar, pointing to a new set of tracks that led towards the river.

Back on the trail, he followed the footprints until he reached the worn path that ran along the riverbank. "Whatever happened back there convinced them that they didn't need to hide in the forest anymore. Look—the tracks go right along the path now. And there is an extra set of footprints. They've gotten help."

"They must have found a Reytana!" said Belkore excitedly. Just a minute ago he worried that his search had been prematurely cut short, but now it looked like he might actually get to fight a real Reytana.

"No, those aren't Reytana footprints," said Damnar. "They're too small. And one of them doesn't look right." Xander walked up to where Damnar was standing and inspected the footprint that he was pointing to. He was right. There was something wrong with the right footprint. It was pointed inward at an awkward angle. A brief memory flashed through Xander's mind but was gone before he could make any sense of it. Still, there was something familiar about that foot.

"It's getting late," said Damina. "These tracks aren't going anywhere. Why don't we pick them up in the morning?"

"No," said Xander. "Now is when we gain on them. You can sleep once they've been captured. Keep moving! Damina sighed. "What was that?!" snapped Xander.

"N-nothing," stammered Damina who was unaccustomed to the prince's serious tone.

"What's your deal, Xan?" asked Belkore. "Did something happen back in Gartol that we don't know about? Daddy giving you a hard time again?"

Xander turned slowly towards his old friend. "What did you just say to me?"

Belkore took a few steps towards the prince. He made sure to lift his chin up and swing his eüroc casually as he sauntered forward. "Must be tough being the son of the king; getting everything you want all the time, nobody ever messing with you. And on top of all of that, landing a cushy position ruling over the floaters. I can see how it might put you in a mood."

Xander's eyes were barely more than black slits. The little violet that did show burned with intensity. For several seconds, the two Gartune stared at each other in silence. Damina stepped forward to break the tension, but her brother immediately held out his arm and stopped her.

Slowly, Xander's familiar grin spread across his face. "I've missed you, Belk."

Belkore grinned back. "Ahhh. For a second there, I thought I was going to get to thrash you like old times."

"Oh, don't worry," said Xander. "There's still time. Bring my father up again and you may get your chance."

Belkore laughed. "I thought for sure that would have done it. I guess the floaters really have made you soft."

Xander stretched. "Not soft. Just out of practice. It's good to be out doing something productive again. Now, if nobody else has anymore objections…" Xander looked over at the twins who shook their heads in unison.

"Good. Then we keep moving," said Xander as he brushed past Damnar and took the lead. Now that the footprints were on the river path, it did not take an expert tracker to follow them. Xander set the pace as the Gartune hastily made their way west under the moonlight.

Septa had been trekking non-stop through the woods since she departed the hyper-rail the previous night, but she was not tired. Her determination was all the fuel she needed. The moons were at their zenith when Septa entered the woodland city of Spirea. People said that Woodhaven was for the cast-outs of The Crescent. If that was true, then Spirea was for the cast-outs of Woodhaven.

The city lay in a shallow ravine, surrounded by large, overhanging trees on all sides. The canopy of trees served to keep the city cool, but it also trapped a large amount of moisture in the ravine, giving the city a constant smell of mildew and rot. Spirea's pungent bouquet greeted Septa as she entered the city.

Spirea, the armpit of Dellwood Forest, she thought. In truth, the city was more of a blemish on the face of the forest than an armpit. From above, it looked like a small brown and red circle festering in the center of a lush, green face. Nothing in Spirea contained the natural green colors of a forest. Everything was the color of rust. From the dingy tin roofs of the buildings to the rotten smoke that was emanating from their chimneys, everything was a mixture of brown and red. Even the dirt on the ground had a reddish tint, as if it had been mixed with blood for many, many years.

Spirea had but one street, and it ran straight down the middle of the city. On the north side of the street was a hodgepodge of mercantile stores, butchers, barter shops, skilled (and un-skilled) tradesmen and a post office that looked like it had been closed for years. That side of the street was dark and lifeless. Everyone had moved to the south side of town. For it was nighttime, and the south side of the city consisted entirely of saloons, hotels and gambling halls.

A cacophony of sounds emanated from these buildings, and the street reeked of lewdness and debauchery. Septa glanced into some of the dirt-smeared windows as she slowly strode down the main thoroughfare. Inside she saw drunk waifs smashing bottles against the walls for no apparent reason. Fat-fingered piano players pounded out songs on out-of-tune instruments as ladies (in the loosest sense of the word) sat on mens' laps and sang bawdily as the drunkards groped them up and down. Septa watched one woman drag the man whose lap she had been roosting on up the stairs to the second floor. The man stumbled behind her, his tongue hanging out of his head like a rabid nimber. The smell of spilled beer and urine rose from the ground. Everything was covered in a sticky, wet film. Septa's boots actually began to stick to the dirt street. She didn't know how that was even possible.

Spirea was the polar opposite from the immaculate paved roads and polished marble walls of Gartol. But Septa did not feel the least bit homesick, even though this was the first time she had been outside of her city's gates in many years. Nor did she feel pity for the citizens who had to live in this squalor. No, the only thing she felt for these people was contempt. But it was more than that. She hated these dirty little forest waifs, and she intended to let them know how she felt before her visit was through.

Several waifs stumbled by Septa as she walked down the street, but none of them paid any attention to the towering Gartune. This she found odd. It wasn't that they were too drunk to notice her. Several even had the temerity to look up and make eye contact with her! But they just kept on walking as if... as if they were used to seeing a Tormada in their street. *Perhaps coming here wasn't a waste of time after all*, Septa thought. Could this be the place that the high-and-mighty Reytana have been hiding this whole time? No... this city is too small to hide hundreds of fully-grown Tormada. Still, these people have seen them. She was sure of it.

Septa decided that it was time to make her presence known. She entered one of the larger saloons, expecting the room to become immediately silent as she walked through the door. If anything, the noise escalated. Two drunks were wrestling on the floor in front of her. She deftly stepped over them with one, giant stride, making sure to prod the fellow on top with her eüroc as she walked over him. A waif at a nearby card table saw this and actually tried to reach out and grab her staff.

No sooner had the waif reached out his hand than it was lying detached on the floor. Septa had removed it with one swipe of her eüroc, having first transformed the end of her staff into a large blade. Before the first drop of blood fell to the floor, she pressed a small button on the top of her eüroc and the blade retracted with a quick snap. The waif didn't make a sound. He simply held his bloody stump in his good arm and looked up at the Gartune, his face a mixture of surprise and sadness. It was as if he fully expected to lose his hand at some point in his life, he had just hoped to hold onto it a little longer. The waif then turned back in his seat and resumed his card game, struggling to pick up his cards with his one good hand.

After Septa's performance, the crowd became a bit more subdued. The piano player continued his song though he pounded the keys a little less forcefully. Septa thought it sounded better. She walked over to the bar at the far end of the saloon. This time, nobody tried to grab her eüroc as she passed.

The bartender was an ugly man, even for Spirea. His hair was long and shaggy, with one or two patches missing. A massive scar stretched from his forehead to his jaw, passing through an empty left eye socket. Septa thought it interesting that he chose not to wear a patch to cover the gruesome hole where his eye had been. She liked the decision. It gave him a more imposing look, which was probably an advantage for anyone running a bar in this town.

The bartender spoke to her without looking up from pouring his drinks. Septa appreciated the lack of eye contact, which was appropriate for a torman addressing a Gartune. Maybe this one has learned better, she thought.

"I haven't seen you here before," said the bartender.

He said you, *not* your kind, noted Septa. *I was right. There have been Tormada here.*

Septa minced no words. "Tell me where they are."

Septa could see that the bartender was weighing his next words carefully. He grabbed a dirty rag and slowly began to wipe the bar in front of him, all the while keeping his head down. Septa waited patiently. *This man is smart*, she thought. *Whoever took his eye did not come by it easily.*

"If I tell ya, are you going to kill them?" asked the bartender.

"If you don't, I may kill you," answered Septa coolly.

The bartender continued to wipe down the bar slowly and steadily. "I believe that," answered the bartender. "I think I'm damned either way, though. 'Cause I'm sure that they would kill me for telling you where they were."

"Then you have a choice to make," answered Septa.

"Aye, so I do," said the bartender. He continued to wipe the bar until he had cleared every spot of liquid from its surface. Once he finished, he looked up at Septa with his one good eye. "You ain't worried what they may do to you?" said the bartender. "They outnumber you."

Septa leaned down so that her face was directly in front of the waif's. He did not budge. Her fierce purple eyes stared directly into his. "Do I look worried?" she replied.

The bartender looked past Septa toward the severed hand that still lay on the floor. Then he looked back at her. He made his decision.

"Next building down. Room twelve." As he said this he returned his attention to the bar, grabbed another rag and began to wipe off a stack of dirty glasses. *He bet on me against the Reytana*, thought Septa. The idea made her smile. She turned and walked out of the saloon.

The saloon next door was much like all of the others—damp, dirty and full of loud drunkards. This time Septa did not go to the bar, but rather straight up the stairs to room twelve. She considered kicking the door down but thought better of it. She did not know what awaited her on the other side. It could be the twins that escaped from Reysa. It could be a host of Reytana soldiers. The bartender at the previous saloon could have sent her into a trap, although it was unlikely. He seemed smarter than that. Still, she had to be cautious. Lightly, she placed her ear against the door and listened. She heard muffled voices and laughing. There were also female voices; female torman voices. *This is no trap*, thought Septa. She turned the doorknob, expecting it be locked. It wasn't. Without thinking twice, she burst through the door.

Sitting in the candle-lit room were three faces that Septa hadn't seen in many years. Their jaws all dropped simultaneously as Septa came through the door.

"Rankin," seethed Septa as she addressed the closest of the three Gartune men. Each one of them had a scantily-clad waif woman sitting on their knee and a large stein of ale in their hand. One of the Gartune dropped his glass while the other shoved his girl off of his lap. Only Rankin did not budge.

"Septa," replied Rankin, "it's been a long time. What are you doing here?"

"I am looking for the Reytana fugitives. And you three fools—why aren't you in Reysa?"

"We were but then we—" started one of the Gartune but Septa quickly smacked him across the head with her eüroc.

"I wasn't talking to you," she said, keeping her glaring violet eyes fixed on Rankin.

"Your brother ordered that we come here to look for the fugitives as well," answered Rankin. He had no sooner finished his sentence than Septa slammed her eüroc into the floor, splintering the wood planks.

"LIES!" shouted Septa. "I was with Xander AND the king when he ordered Xander to search for the escapees, alone."

"If that's true, then why are *you* searching for them, Princess?" asked Rankin as he slowly got to his feet, pushing the terrified waif off of him at the same time. All three women took this as an opportunity to run for the door and they quickly vacated the room.

Septa's fury was palpable as she locked eyes with Rankin. Sensing a fight may be imminent, the other two Gartune arose from their chairs as well. Unfortunately for them, they had carelessly set their eürocs on the fireplace mantle, a good ten paces from their chairs. They dare not try for their weapons. For a few moments, the four Gartune stood in silence, waiting for someone to make the first move. Then, Septa spoke.

"You pathetic swine. You come here to defile yourselves with drink and women and then dare to question me? You disgrace all Gartune."

"But your brother—" stuttered one of the soldiers but Septa quickly silenced him.

"My brother has made you soft! Reysa has made you soft! Someone needs to remind you of your metal."

Suddenly, one of the soldiers made a motion for his eüroc. With stunning speed, Septa smashed hers into the floor. The wooden floorboards buckled and piled onto themselves as they raced towards the fireplace. The pile of wood reached the mantle at the same time as the Gartune and it smashed him into the wall before he could grab his staff. Septa then swung around and smacked the second Gartune in the head with her eüroc before he had a chance to even think about reaching for his own. He crumpled to the floor in a heap. With his companions unconscious, Septa turned her attention to Rankin, who still had not moved.

"Wait," said Rankin holding up his hand. "I do have some information. Information about the Reytana. I will gladly tell you if you spare me the sting of your staff."

"You always did have a flair for politics, didn't you, Rankin?" replied Septa. "I see your time playing with my brother in Reysa has only encouraged that character flaw. How about this; you tell me what you know, and I'll decide if it warrants a greater or lesser beating."

"Of course, of course. It's only that... I haven't had time to follow up on it myself, you see. But there is a man here who knows something. They say he's been helping the Reytana. He might even know where they're hiding. All of them, not just the runaways. You go and ask him. You'll see."

Septa stepped closer to Rankin. She had not decided if she would beat him or not. "Where is this man? And if you tell me

'I don't know' you might as well just start bleeding right here and now."

Rankin took a small step back. "He's just next door. The bartender. We were going to go question him... after we were done."

Septa swung her staff to the side of Rankin, stopping it a fraction of an inch from his ear. He flinched. When he realized that he had not been struck, Rankin bowed his head in shame. Septa then ran her eüroc through the handle of the beer stein sitting on the end table and doused him with the contents. "You're done," she said and then stormed out of the room, leaving the Gartune captain dripping.

Septa's anger had been building since she entered the city, and now it was at its peak. To think that she had been led astray by a torman, and a waif at that, was maddening. She splayed the swinging doors of the previous saloon open with such force that she ripped them off their hinges. This time, the piano player stopped playing. Every conversation came to a halt. The only sound was that of Septa's boots marching straight towards the bar.

There stood the bartender, wiping down his grimy glasses just as he had been when she left him. He did not look up when she approached.

"You made a dangerous mistake, bartender."

"Did you not find them?" he replied.

"Right height, wrong color," replied Septa.

The bartender continued cleaning his glasses. Septa's patience had ended. She swept her arm across the bar sending the glasses crashing onto the floor. The bartender didn't look up, he simply grabbed another rag and began to wipe down the bar where the glasses had been.

"I know you know where they are," whispered Septa directly into the bartender's ear. "This is your last chance. Tell me where the floaters are. Now!"

"I... I know where dey are... or at least where dey might be..." said a quivering voice. It came from a man at one of the card tables. And it wasn't just any man. This one had a crude bandage wrapped around a bloody stump where his hand used to be. Septa turned to face him.

"Speak," she said as she pointed her eüroc directly at him. The waif recoiled at the site of her staff. There was blood on the end of it. His blood.

"Der's a man in Wood'aven. He goes in and out of Reysa, carryin' messages and such. Dey say he talks directly wit da governa'. Dey say he knows where da floaters is hidin'!"

"What's his name?" said Septa as she approached the man until she was directly over him with her staff inches from his throat.

"D-d-declin. His name is Declin."

"Very well," said Septa. She lowered her eüroc. The waif breathed a sigh of relief. Now that he didn't have a eüroc shoved in his face, he gained back a bit of confidence. He looked at his severed hand still lying on the floor, then back at his bloody stump. His brow furrowed as a thought crept into his dull waif brain. And then he made one, final mistake. He couldn't help it. He was a waif, after all.

"So, do I get anything fer dat valuable information?"

Septa turned on a dime. She grabbed the cowering waif by the collar and drug him out of his chair.

"Wait! I was just kiddin'! No comper'sation necessary!" gasped the waif.

"Oh yes there is," said Septa as she continued to drag the man across the floor and out into the street. A crowd, including the bartender, followed them wordlessly into the cool night air. Nobody did anything to stop Septa. The stench of stale beer and urine was just as strong outside as it was in the bar. Septa shoved the man into the muddy street, face first. The crowd formed a circle around them. The waif got to his knees, holding his bloody stump pathetically in his hand as if to say "haven't I been punished enough already?" The look on Septa's face indicated that he hadn't.

"You ask for compensation, and so I will give you the greatest gift that I can think of." Septa was speaking to the waif, but she was really addressing the crowd. "I grant you freedom from this pit of defilement that you call a city. I free you from your drink and your gambling and all of your other maladies." She raised her eüroc above her head and pressed the button. The bloody blade sprung from its tip. "I release you."

In a second it was over. The waif's limp body crumpled to the ground. No one said a word. Septa looked around at the blank faces of the crowd. She saw no emotion. No anger. No fear. No pity. Nothing. Septa's anger rose once more. The students required further teaching. Septa addressed the crowd.

"This man was a coward. And this is how cowards die—on their knees in the street!"

She looked around at the crowd. Still nothing. It was as if they agreed with her; like it had just been a matter of time before this particular waif ended up dead in the street. His death had not been a punishment, merely a formality. They still had not learned their lesson. The students required further teaching.

"There is only one thing worse than cowardice," Septa continued as she scanned the crowd looking for a particular face. She found it. "And that is defying your masters!"

She pulled the bartender out of the crowd. This time, a couple of people gasped. Everyone's face showed concern. *Good*, she thought. The bartender allowed himself to be drug into the center of the circle. He did not fight when Septa shoved him down next to the dead waif. Septa looked back into the crowd. This time, she had their complete attention. *They're learning.*

"You people think that because you live outside of the walls of Gartol that you do not have to abide by its rules? You think that you can disrespect and lie to your Tormada masters and that there will be no consequences? Let this be a lesson to anyone who thinks that they can deceive a Gartune!"

Another audible gasp arose as Septa lifted her eüroc again into the night sky. She paused a few seconds for dramatic effect. As she did, she looked down at the bartender. He raised his head, his one eye staring directly into hers. She waited a few more seconds, allowing them to share this moment. *Good for you*, she thought as she swung the death blow, separating his head from his body. His torso crumpled over the remains of the one-handed waif. The two of them lay on top of each other, their blood mixing with the mud of the wet, dirt road.

Lesson over.

Shortly after Rey and Gar'on created the Tormada, they created Lyse. Not quite animal and not quite torman, Lyse was an elemental - a sapient, spirit-like entity that lived in the waters of Torma. Her main purpose was and is to ferry and protect the Tormada newborns as they travel from Za'Dyn Mountain, along the Aeil river to their chosen city. For, the Tormada babes are extremely vulnerable during their journey, and the gods didn't want some hungry mendkin to reach in and eat the infants before they reached their destination.

Over the centuries, Lyse has become very protective of her domain. Not only does she protect the Tormada newborns, but also every living creature that dwells under the water. The waifs, and even the woodland animals, know to take care when approaching the Aeil, for it does not take much to draw the ire of its motherly elemental.

- Chapter Eight of *The Crescent Wars* by Nicholas Baston

CHAPTER THIRTEEN
Fishing

Xander woke later than he had intended. Sleeping in late had become habitual for the prince while he lived in Reysa. After all, he was the prince and princes woke at their leisure. Most mornings he didn't rise until everyone had already eaten breakfast and gone about their day.

But now that he was on a mission where time was of the essence, he had planned to wake before the sun rose and continue his pursuit of the escaped Reytana. Unfortunately, his internal clock betrayed him. In fact, if it weren't for the sound of two quarreling pipkens wrestling for a nut, he would have probably kept on sleeping for another hour or two.

Xander rose to his feet and groggily brushed some leaves off of his tunic. His back ached from sleeping on the ground and his stomach turned with hunger. *Maybe they're right. Maybe I am getting soft,* he thought to himself. He looked around for his companions, but they were nowhere to be seen. *There's no way they left without me. No way.*

But, thinking more about it, he realized it was entirely possible that he had been left behind. Damnar and Damina didn't need him to track the Reytana. They could do that perfectly well on their own. However, they wouldn't have dared to disobey the prince of Gartol. Unless... Belkore. He could have convinced them to leave Xander. But why?

Xander closed his eyes and listened to the forest. The gurgling of the Aeil River made up the majority of the early morning sounds, but he thought he heard movement coming from a clump of trees not far down the river path. He turned one ear in that direction and concentrated on the sound. There it was again, this time unmistakable; the sound of muffled voices, and familiar ones at that.

I knew they wouldn't leave me. Xander opened his eyes, relieved. Internally, he admonished himself for even considering the possibility that his companions would abandon him. He was the prince of Gartol and betraying him would have had dire consequences.

Fueled by a renewed sense of self-worth, Xander's mischievous side returned and he decided to sneak up on his companions. Softly, he tip-toed through the trees until he had reached the location where the three Gartune were huddled. They were undoubtedly trying to conceal their voices as they spoke in hushed tones. Xander decided to eavesdrop a bit before surprising them. He crouched down in the brush just a few yards away and listened to their conversation.

"I'm telling you, he won't do it," whispered Belkore. "I've known him longer than you two have, and it's obvious that something has changed. Living in that damn city has made him weak. I can see it in his eyes."

"Even if he has changed, he'd never risk crossing the king... would he?" asked Damina nervously.

"Xander isn't dumb. He knows what will happen if he sends those Reytana back to Gartol. And he knows what will happen to *us* if we let them escape. That leaves only one option; and I know him—he doesn't have the stomach for it."

"But we can't just—" started Damina.

"Yeah," interjected Damnar. "What are we supposed to do?"

"You leave that to me," said Belkore. "When the time comes, you'll know it."

"And then what?"

"Then, you'll have to make a decision."

Xander crouched motionless in the bushes, processing what he had just heard. He thought for a few moments before slipping out of his hiding spot and returning to the campsite. A few minutes later, Belkore and the twins returned to find the prince stoking the ashes of the small fire they had concocted the night before.

"Ah, there you are," said Xander pleasantly. "I've been thinking about it, and I feel bad about pushing you all so hard yesterday. There's no need to rush. You're right—the Reytana are clueless. We'll probably catch them by midday at the latest. What do you say to a nice breakfast before we head off? My treat."

Damnar and Damina exchanged confused looks while Belkore frowned at the prince. Xander merely smiled back at them with a disarming grin. Suddenly, a puff of smoke rose from the ashes Xander was prodding. "Ah, there we are!" he shouted happily. "I'm assuming you two can hunt animals as well as people?" he said, pointing to the twins. "Why don't you see if you can wrestle up a few nimbers while me and grumpy here put together a spit."

The twins nodded silently and then hurried off into the woods. Once they had gone, Belkore sat down across from Xander and stared at the prince. The fire between them began to crackle and burn. Through the rising flames, Xander looked back at his old friend. The two Gartune sat, unblinking, while sparks of red and yellow reflected in their dark, violet eyes.

Two days had passed and still, Loras, Regan and Tinko had not reached Woodhaven, although Lem kept assuring them that it was "just up a'ways." It had been two days of non-stop walking with the occasional duck into the forest to avoid an oncoming traveler when the twins got nervous. Lem thought they were being childish for doing so, but he grudgingly joined them in hiding while the travelers passed.

They ate in the morning and at night. That was all. Nobody mentioned anything about missing lunch, although Tinko became noticeably irritable during that time of day.

The sun was still new in the sky on the third day when Loras, Regan and Tinko were woken by the smell of roasting meat. Lem had caught two fresh pipkens earlier that morning and was cooking them on the spit he'd built the night before. With his mouth watering, Tinko grabbed at one of the pipkens like a wild animal. The meat was too hot to hold, however, and he ended up with a burnt hand and nothing to show for it.

"Easy der, big fella'," said the waif to Tinko. "It'll be done soon enough and den you can share wit da rest of us." Tinko rubbed his blistered hand as the teens waited patiently for their breakfast to finish cooking. Once it had cooled down, they ravenously tore into the greasy meat. Lem watched them in amusement as they gnawed every last bit off of the bones. A pipken did not yield a large meal as it was only slightly larger than a rat, but its meat was lean and tasty. So tasty, in fact, that pipken were one of the most hunted prey amongst forest animals and woodsmen alike.

"You'd best learn ta catch these on yer own if ya plan on being out here in da woods for any 'mount of time," said Lem. A thought dawned on Tinko for the first time. What if they *were* going to have to be in the woods for a long time? What if they were going to have to hide here forever? They had been so focused on getting to Woodhaven and finding Declin that they hadn't thought of what would happen next. They had just assumed they'd be returning to their homes in Reysa. But what if *this* was now their home? Suddenly, Tinko wasn't so hungry.

"So how long before we reach Woodhaven?" asked Loras.

"Shouldn't be no later dan dis afternoon, assumin' we don't have no trouble. Best dat we stay off da path from here on out. You two are gettin' a might tall."

He was right. Loras and Regan had grown at least two inches each night. They now stood nearly six and a half feet tall. It would not be long before their size would reveal their true nature to the world.

The group finished breakfast and started out through the forest at a faster pace than the day before. Even with his gimp foot, the waif seemed to travel more swiftly over the uneven ground of the forest than he did on the flat path by the river. He used his walking stick as though it were a third leg, and the teens, even Loras and Regan, often found themselves struggling to keep up.

They traveled on without a word for the entire morning, pushing right through to the afternoon. Tinko, realizing that he was facing the prospect of a third consecutive day without lunch, began to grumble to himself. When nobody paid attention to his muffled complaints, he began to grumble louder and louder about how hungry he was. Finally, he sat down and refused to move.

"Get up and stop acting like a child," said Loras.

"I can't. I'm too hungry," whined Tinko.

"We're all hungry," said Regan. "But we can't slow down now. We don't know who might be behind us."

"I'm sorry, but I've never walked this much in my life. I need to refuel, or I won't be able to go any further. Can't we just eat something real quick?"

Loras stomped angrily toward Tinko. "Get off your ass right now or I'll—"

"Enough!" said Lem. "I can catch somethin' quick enough for us to have a snack, if dat's what it'll take to get 'em movin. Yous all stay here."

"I can help," said Loras. "Let me come with you."

"No, you stay here wit da other two."

"You said yourself that we needed to learn how to provide for ourselves. Why don't you teach me?"

"No time. You'd only slow me down. You stay."

"But—"

"I said stay!" It was the first time the waif had raised his voice since they had met him. While his tone made it clear that the conversation was over, he still turned and disappeared into the woods before Loras could argue any further. He hadn't been gone for more than two minutes before Loras announced that he was going hunting.

"He said to stay here," said Regan. "What if someone comes while you're gone?"

"We haven't seen anyone all day," answered Loras. "Besides, you have Tink here to protect you."

"Funny," said Tinko.

"Seriously," said Regan, "he'll be back soon and then we'll need to get moving again. What if something happens to you?"

"Nothing is going to happen to me," said Loras. It was clear that his mind was already made up. "If it makes you feel better, I'll just go down to the river, so you'll know where I am. If I'm not back in fifteen minutes, you can send Tink to come get me. Deal?" Arguing was useless once Loras had his mind made up, so Regan let him go.

"Fifteen minutes," she said. "Then I'm sending Tinko. And you better hope that nobody comes down that path in the meantime."

"You'll be fine," said Loras with a grin and he bounded through the brush in the direction of the river.

On his way to the river, Loras surveyed the forest, looking for something that he could use as a spear. He spotted a fallen tree branch that looked promising as it had already been stripped of any off-shoot limbs. He grabbed it, gave it a few test jabs through the air, and after skewering a sufficient amount of make-believe fish, he continued towards the sound of running water.

When he arrived at the river, Loras found a broken rock whose edge had not yet been worn down by the river's current. Loras stepped cautiously into the water and used the rock to sharpen the end of his branch into a jagged point. Once Loras had waded to a knee-high depth, he saw several brightly-colored fish swimming around his legs. *This is going to be easy,* he thought. Loras picked out a large, orange-banded fish that was swimming in a small bed of rocks. *Time for lunch.* Loras lifted his makeshift spear above his head. As he did so, the current intensified behind him and pushed him slightly off balance. He flung the spear in the direction of the fish. It missed by three feet.

"Gods, damnit!" said Loras aloud. He swam over to retrieve the stick before it was swept downstream. The current was running faster, making it a bit more difficult to see the fish under the water. After about a minute of searching, Loras spotted the same orange-striped fish swimming among a group of seaweed, totally oblivious to the fact that it was being hunted.

"This time, you won't be so lucky, my friend," said Loras. He once again raised the spear above his head, his eyes squinting with concentration. Once again, a rush of water surged behind him the moment he released his spear, throwing it well off the mark.

"Seriously!?" Loras looked around to see if anyone was watching him, but there was nobody there. As he retrieved his spear for a second time, he looked down and spotted the same fish swimming slowly around his right leg. This time Loras didn't raise the spear above his head. Instead, he quickly jabbed the stick under the water and planted it into the riverbed. This time, the spear found its mark. Wriggling on the end of the stick was the orange-striped fish.

Loras was too transfixed with his catch to notice the wave forming at his back. Within seconds, a wall of water several feet tall was rapidly bearing down on him. He didn't hear it until it was only a few feet from his back. As he turned to face it, his right foot caught fast between two rocks, trapping him. He held his breath as the wave came crashing down, knocking him flat onto his back and pressing him against the river bottom. His foot remained jammed between the rocks. He struggled to lift himself off of the floor, but the current held him down. Three times he tried to push himself out of the water and three times he was knocked back down. On the fourth try, Loras managed to shove his face above the surface. He gulped for air, but, instead, ended up sucking down more of the river. He coughed violently and yanked on his foot as hard as he could, but it remained stuck between the rocks. Upstream, another, larger wave was building towards him.

How are there waves like this in a river? Loras thought, frantically, to himself. *This doesn't make any sense!* He yanked on his leg and could feel the rocks' grasp begin to loosen, but he wasn't able to pull his foot free fast enough. With the wave now only a few feet off, Loras closed his eyes and braced himself. When it hit him, he knew that this time he wasn't coming back up.

The force of the water crushed him back down into the riverbed. The water churned over him, simultaneously lifting his body off of the ground and slamming it back down like he was a rag doll. Loras didn't even have a chance to sit up on his elbows, such was the force of the angry water above him. He figured he had about ten, maybe fifteen more seconds of oxygen left before everything would go dark. He had enough time and strength left for just one more push. Loras mustered all of his remaining strength and pushed off of the river bottom. His lungs burnt inside his chest as he strained for the open air. This time, his head didn't even come close to surfacing. The river level had somehow risen two feet in the past minute. It was as if the river was trying to kill him.

Just before he lost consciousness, a set of strong hands grabbed Loras under his arms and lifted him up with incredible strength. Loras' head surfaced. All of his senses were instantly overwhelmed. The sound of the rushing water was deafening. The glare of the blazing sun was blinding. His body was void of strength, and he fell limply below the waves once again. But the hands did not let go. One more violent yank and Loras' foot was free of its trap. Loras felt himself being pulled toward his rescuer's chest, registering in the back of his mind that they were moving toward the shore. Once on dry ground, he was dropped with a thud.

Loras spent the next minute lying limp on the riverbank and sucking in as much air as his body would permit. His head was spinning. His eyes refused to focus on anything, so he squeezed them shut. He could hear the river's current gradually slow to its normal pace. A new sound took its place—a continuous stream of garbled curse words and intermittent coughing coming from the man beside him.

"Yer da dumbest floater I'd ever... *cough*... can't do a damn... *cough*... stubborn sonnuva...*cough cough*"

Loras turned over on his side to see the wet and disheveled figure of Lem sitting next to him. He didn't think he'd ever seen anyone look angrier.

"You stupid... *cough*... good-fer-nothin... *cough*... shoulda just let ya drown...*cough*"

Loras finally felt strong enough to speak. "What the hell was that? Rivers aren't supposed to do that, are they? It was like... it was trying to kill me!"

"She *was* tryin to kill ya, ya stupid floatin' sonnuva—"

"Loras!" Regan and Tinko came running out of the forest and flopped right down next to their wet companions. "What happened to you??"

"The river... it... it tried to kill me!" panted Loras.

"It what?!" exclaimed Regan. She turned her gaze from her brother to the waif and back again.

"It weren't da river," said the waif. "It were Lyse."

"Who is Lyse?" asked Loras.

"I know who Lyse is!" exclaimed Tinko. *Of course he did,* thought Loras. "She's the mythical goddess of the seas! She rules over all of the oceans, rivers and streams. I read about her in a book once."

"First off, she ain't *mythical*—she's real," said the waif. He was beginning to become annoyed with Tinko. "And second, she ain't no goddess. She's an elemental, and a vengeful one at 'dat. All da fish an' critters of da sea is her children, an' she don't take kindly to tormen, or *Tormada*," he looked hard at

Loras, "poachin' her family. That's why ya don't never see no woodsman spear fishin' in da river. Like I said, she's vengeful, she is."

"But wait," said Loras. "Tink caught some fish yesterday and he wasn't nearly drowned for it."

"How did he catch 'em?" said Lem.

"With a net I fashioned out of some long grass," said Tinko proudly. "It was actually quite clever what I did, you see I tied some knots—" Lem raised his hand to cut him off.

"Der's a way to do 'tings and a way not to," said Lem. "Animals get caught and eaten. Dat's da way of nature. But he did it da civilized way." Lem spit on the ground in front of him. "*You* did not."

"How is it that we've never heard of this Lyse," asked Loras, addressing his question to Tinko as much as the waif.

"Because all yous Reysene and Gartolians care about is your own damn gods. Every'ting is *"Rey" dis* and *"Gar'on" dat*. Yous never paid no matter to what happens outside those fortresses yous call cities. But let me tell yous some'ting," and he leaned close to the teens, "der is more to da world dan you learn from yer fancy professors and books... a lot more," he was looking directly at Loras now. "Yous best learn dat quick if yous gonna survive out here."

There was silence for a few moments as the teens digested the waif's words. Tinko squirmed in his seat the way he did when he had a question, but professor Lucan refused to call on him. Finally, he couldn't hold it in any longer.

"So you can't hunt the fish but you can hunt the pipkens and nimbers? Won't the god... er *elemental* of the forest get pissed that you're eating *his* children?"

"Ain't no elemental of da forest, dummy. Who ever told ya dat?" Tinko's mouth hung open in bewilderment. Loras let out a grunt of laughter. Someone had finally stunned Tinko into silence.

There is no logical reason why the city of Woodhaven should exist where it does. There are plenty of more suitable locations along each branch of the Aeil river that would have provided firmer land and calmer waters. The fork of the Aeil is one of the most tumultuous waterways in all of The Crescent, causing the shores on both sides to constantly erode and deteriorate. It is a non-stop effort for the citizens of Woodhaven to keep their city from falling into the river.

So why build there?

It is said that the first settlers were 'drawn' to the location by a mysterious force. Some tormen claim that they still get a 'feeling' when approaching the city, but it is most acutely felt by the Tormada. It could be the proximity to Za'Dyn Mountain and The Scales. Nobody really knows. But this 'feeling' is most likely what persuaded the first citizens of Woodhaven to build their city at such a precarious spot.

- Chapter Five of *The Crescent Wars* by Nicholas Baston

CHAPTER FOURTEEN
Woodhaven

Lem had not had a chance to catch anything before he rushed off to save Loras from drowning, so the four of them continued on without lunch, after all. Nobody complained. Even Tinko held his tongue.

As they continued on along the river path, Loras could hear the river surging upstream. The current got much stronger the further they went, and the river itself seemed to have doubled in size from shoreline to shoreline. The louder the river roared, the more uncomfortable Loras became. The memory of being crushed into the riverbed sent a shiver down his spine.

"Are you alright?" asked Regan.

"I'm fine," said Loras, trying to control his shivering.

"You don't look fine," said Regan.

"Well, I don't suppose you'd look great either if you had just nearly drowned," said Loras.

"Oh, I don't know about that," interjected Tinko. "I actually *did* drown a couple of days ago, and I think I actually look better." The twins glanced sideways at their friend but he just sauntered past them whistling a little tune to himself as he went.

"Where did *that* come from?" said Loras as he watched his friend incredulously.

"Oh forget about Tink. He's just proud that he was able to catch some fish and you were…less successful. Give the guy his little victory."

"Little victory indeed…" grumbled Loras under his breadth. "It's just some stupid fish."

"Snap out of it!" exclaimed Regan and she gave her brother a shove with her shoulder. "We don't have time for your pouting. There are bigger issues for us to deal with."

"Like what?"

"Like I think we're going to get to Woodhaven soon and we need to form a plan of what to do when we get there."

"The plan is simple," said Loras. "Ditch the waif. Look for this Declin guy."

"I don't think either of those things is going to be as simple as you think," said Regan.

"Maybe. Maybe not. I guess we won't know until we get there," said Loras.

"So you don't want to come up with some strategy first?"

"Why? Strategies hardly ever go like you think they will. And when they get screwed up, then you're left scrambling. Better to go in with no strategy at all. That way we're not thrown off our game when stuff doesn't go our way. Besides, if things get really bad, we can fight back now." As he said this, Loras gave his newfound muscles a little flex.

"Same old Loras," sighed Regan. "When in doubt, just punch something."

"You have to admit," said Loras, his eyes glowing as he continued to flex, "that plan is a bit more effective now than it used to be."

"It's not always the strongest that wins, Loras."

"No, but they definitely have the advantage."

Regan just shook her head.

The group trudged on for two more hours until the midday sun was directly overhead. The sound of the river's rushing water was so deafening that it was difficult to hear anything else. Through the trees ahead, they could spot the place where the river forked. Loras felt a peculiar sense of nostalgia. This was the place where eighteen years ago the river had borne him and his sister to the left, towards Reysa. He did not want to think about what their lives would have been like if the river had carried them to the right.

Before the river forked, it became a single massive stretch of whitewater and foam. Off in the distance, rising up from the river itself, was the faint outline of Za'Dyn Mountain. Loras gazed at the famous peak. Professor Lucan had described the mountain before and Loras had pictured what it looked like in his mind, but Lucan's description did not do it justice. Back in class it had just been the Tormada's mountain—something he couldn't relate to. Now he had a new appreciation for it, as it was the place where he had been created.

Za'Dyn Mountain's sides were impossibly steep and too treacherous for any torman or even Tormada to scale. A few had tried, but none had succeeded. Staring up at the mountain, Regan whispered to her brother. "I can't believe anyone would even consider climbing that thing. I don't care what is on the top of it."

"I'll bet an Omega could make it to the top," said Loras.

"You mean like Drohnus?" added Tinko. It was rumored that Drohnus had died trying to scale the mountain, but his body was never found. However, a large pile of boulders at the base of the mountain marked the location where he presumably met his end. For, on the day he had planned to start his ascent, there was a massive landslide; the only one ever recorded on the mountain. It was as if the gods had spotted the intruder and threw him back.

"Maybe he did," answered Loras. "Maybe he's up there staring at us right now."

Standing on the forest floor, one could not tell that the peak of the mountain was flat, but everyone knew that was the case. The top of Za'Dyn Mountain was the most famous place in all of the world, for it was there that stood the Scales of Torma, the legendary regulator of Tormada life.

Water that was collected all along the Crescent Mountain range funneled into an arched aqueduct that connected the Crescent Mountains to Za'Dyn's solitary peak. Amazingly, the water flowed *up* to the peak as if it were summoned by The Scales. From there, the water crossed Za'Dyn's flat plateau and came tumbling down the eastern side of the mountain in a massive, foaming waterfall. The pool at the bottom of the falls fed the Aeil River.

The fork of the Aeil was a magical place. The water, the trees, even the air was different than in the city. Everything was alive. Loras felt a sudden surge of exhilaration within him. *Maybe this is what Drohnus felt like before he tried to scale that thing,* thought Loras. He could start to understand how someone might consider the climb.

The intoxicating energy that filled Loras was quickly dashed when the group approached the bank of the river. Laying between them and their destination were three hundred feet of swirling, gushing whitewater. Even with a boat, there was no way that they could cross the river. But, cross they must, for on the other side was the city of Woodhaven.

Woodhaven was actually two cities bisected by the mouth of the Aeil River. The buildings were a hodge-podge of straw huts, log cabins, metal lean-to's and multi-level tree houses. Most of the structures looked like a strong breeze could blow them down. They were impossibly lopsided and ill-constructed. Several buildings leaned on adjacent structures, each propping the other up. It was a crude, makeshift city, but charming in its own way. The laws of physics in Torma would tell you that there was no way Woodhaven should be standing, but there it was, flanking the banks of the gushing river in stubborn defiance.

For centuries, Woodhaven had served as a way station for travelers from both Reysa and Gartol. This was due, in part, to its location midway between the two great cities. Elements of both cultures were visible in Woodhaven's architecture and technology. There were several light tubes running along what appeared to be the main streets of the city. Little bits of solar light flickered inside of them—just enough to periodically illuminate the bottoms of the nearby buildings. It created an eerie effect. A rusty conveyor belt ran through the second-story level of the city. Traveling back and forth along the belt were several rudimentary machines, each one designed to perform a single function. The teens watched as one of the machines stopped and collected an overflowing trash bin that was hanging out of a window. Another was pouring some glowing liquid into a light tube that had gone out. A third robot attempted to fix a crooked window by wildly swinging a hammer at it. Eventually, the window fell off its frame and crashed into the street below. The robot, seeming satisfied, retracted its hammer and zoomed down the conveyer belt in search of something else to fix.

Tinko pointed out two Gartolian scooters and Loras thought he could see the remains of a broken-down hovercraft. All of these things may have been gifted, borrowed, or stolen over many years. But more than likely, they were rewards for waif spies. Loras wondered what valuable bits of information had won those prizes.

"I've never seen anything like it..." an awestruck Tinko said as they surveyed the city across the river.

"Truly amazing," added Regan.

"Little different dan what yer used to?" asked Lem. He then leaned in close to Loras and whispered in his ear. "Like I says before... ders more to dis world dan what can be found in Reysa. About time ya came down and had a look fer yerself"

"You've got to be kidding me," cried Tinko, his attention turned to churning water in front of them. "How does anyone cross this?" The waif smiled and pointed up.

The teens hadn't noticed until now that running up above them were a series of thick zip lines that spanned the entire width of the river. At the ends of the zip lines were wooden huts of different sizes. These huts were attached to large trees on either side of the riverbank. In one of the smaller huts, a waif was being strapped into a harness that connected to the zip line above it. Once he was secure, another waif inside of the hut began turning a large crank. Gears turned, raising the hut along the tree trunk that ran through its center. After it had risen about thirty feet, the harnessed man began to slide down the zip toward the hut on the opposite side of the river. The zip line dipped under the waif's weight to the point where his feet skimmed the water as the line bowed at its center. The Reysene teens watched the man nervously, expecting him to plunge into the angry water, but the zip line had been calibrated perfectly. The man sped along until he eventually made it to the other side of the river where he was caught by a waiting man in a similar hut.

The larger huts were connected by a much thicker zip line. Instead of individual harnessed riders, these zip lines held large metal cages that could fit about ten people inside. The process was the same. Once the passengers were loaded into the cage, two men turned a large crank inside of the hut and it rose until the cage began to slip down the zip line.

Tinko watched the passengers zipping across the river with an uneasy look. "*That's* what you had in mind?" said Tinko. "That's worse than a boat!"

"Don' worry, big fella," said Lem. "We won't be takin da zips. Sure to be spotted if we do. Plus, I dunno if dey could handle da weight." The waif patted Tinko on the stomach.

"Then how are we going to cross?" asked Regan.

"Dis way. We ain't der yet."

Lem waved at the teens to follow him and they traveled along the river bank for about a mile. They passed the fork and followed the eastern branch of the river, the one which led to Gartol. Maybe it was the shade of the trees, but Loras thought the water seemed darker on this side of the river.

The waif stopped at a large pile of rocks about fifty feet from the shoreline. He circled the rock pile twice as if inspecting it, then once he was satisfied with what he saw he started moving some of the boulders around.

Loras watched Lem, impatiently. He whispered to his sister, "I don't get it. We stopped here so that he could play with some rocks?"

"Give him a minute," said Regan. "He's led us this far, hasn't he?"

"Yeah, he led us to Woodhaven... and then walked us straight past it! What are we doing here?"

"Look," said Tinko, joining the conversation. "Look at the rocks."

The teens inspected the rock pile that Lem was working on. Eventually, they began to see that there was a method to the way that the waif was shifting the stones. It was as if each rock had two places where it fit perfectly—its current spot and the spot that the waif moved it to.

After a few minutes, Lem beckoned to the teens. When they walked over to where Lem was standing, their jaws dropped. There, in the side of the rock pile, was a perfectly shaped rectangle, large enough for a man to fit through. the Hole was totally undetectable if you were looking at the rock pile from any direction other than directly in front of it. The teens had been standing only five feet away from Lem as he created the Hole, and they had not seen it.

Tinko peered incredulously down into the cavity. The path beyond it appeared to slope down and underneath the river. It was extremely dark. "I think I'd rather take the zips," said Tinko.

"In ya go!" yelled Lem as he gave Tinko's backside a kick and the Reysene boy went tripping into the tunnel.

Loras, Regan and Lem followed him in. Once Lem had entered the tunnel, he turned towards the entrance and pulled on a small, wooden lever that protruded from the side wall. Immediately, all of the rocks that he had previously moved fell back into their original places and covered the door.

The tunnel was now pitch black. Loras held his hand up in front of his face but couldn't see it. Suddenly, he felt a hand on his shoulder. It was his sister's.

"Here," said Lem as he placed Regan's other hand on Loras' shoulder. "Keep a hand on da person in front of ya and don't let go." He then took Loras' hand and dragged him forward, following the sound of rapid, shallow breathing until he found Tinko. The waif then put Loras' hand on Tinko's shoulder and moved Tinko's hand onto his own.

"All set now, here we go!"

Lem led the teens down under the river. Their pace was slow. Loras used his free hand to reach out and touch the wall of the tunnel. Occasionally, he felt gaps in the wall. The air was different in these gaps. *Tunnels. Lots of them.* In fact, he counted at least a dozen other tunnels branching off of the one they were currently in. All of them were pitch black.

Lem led his little train of blind teenagers through the silence for about ten minutes. The darkness made it difficult to gauge the distance they had crossed. Loras knew that Woodhaven was about a half mile away, but he couldn't tell if they were near it or still underneath the river.

"Ok, so once we get there, how are we going to find this Declin person?" whispered Loras to his sister.

"Oh, *now* you think we should make a plan?" whispered Regan back to him. Honestly, Loras just wanted something to take his mind off of his surroundings and the feeling of dread that was growing in his stomach.

"A small plan couldn't hurt," said Loras.

"We stick out too much to look for him ourselves. We'll have to send Tinko out to search for him while we stay hidden somewhere," answered Regan.

"Good plan," said Loras.

"Thanks."

"Do you think we're nearly there?"

"It can't be long now."

But another ten minutes of silent walking passed, and they had not reached the city. Then another twenty. During this time, Lem made several turns, and they were now traveling in a side tunnel that ran off of the main one. Loras had no idea how to get back the way they had come, so he silently continued to follow the waif through the darkness. On more than one occasion, he swore that he heard a noise coming from one of the tunnels that they passed. He was sure Lem heard it too. Whenever it came, the waif would stop briefly, turn his head and listen. Then, after a few moments, he would continue on, leading at the same steady pace.

With every minute that passed, that sense of dread grew larger in Loras' stomach. They should have reached Woodhaven long ago. Had Lem betrayed them? It occurred to Loras how easily they had placed their trust in the stranger. A few roasted pipkens was all it had taken. How *naïve* they had been. The waif could be leading them straight into a trap, or to Gartol itself. It did not take a genius to imagine the bounty that could be claimed if the young Reytana were handed over to the Gartune. Lem didn't seem like that type, but he *was* a waif... One thing was for certain. Lem wasn't taking them to Woodhaven.

Other than the sound of their soggy footsteps trudging through the damp tunnel, there was complete silence. Nobody said it, but after over an hour of walking in the darkness, Loras knew they were all thinking the same thing. There was no more questioning it; Lem had betrayed them, and there was nothing they could do about it. If they challenged him now, he would surely kill them right then and there in the tunnel. And even if they could overpower him, they were totally and utterly lost. They had no chance of escaping this underground labyrinth on their own. There was nothing to do but continue following the waif toward whatever fate awaited them.

As if being blindly led to an uncertain fate wasn't enough, Loras was beginning to struggle for breath. He had never been prone to claustrophobia in the past, but now the darkness of the tunnel seemed to suffocate him. An emptiness formed within Loras' chest the further along they went. Eventually, that emptiness filled with cold and he began to shiver. Loras could feel his sister's frozen fingers digging into his shoulder as she followed him through the darkness.

After another thirty minutes of dips and turns, Loras could finally make out a faint light up ahead. It was the first light that he had seen since they entered the tunnel. As they got closer, an outline of a door began to appear. *This is it*, he thought. Their fate waited for them behind this door. At least now he could stop guessing as to what terrible situation lay ahead of them. They would soon face it, and the fearful anticipation would end. If nothing else, at least he would be out of the tunnel, or so he hoped.

"Is... is-s this W-w-oodhaven?" stammered Tinko.

"Oh, I think ya know better dan dat, big fella," said Lem. Tinko took his hand off of the man's shoulder and slumped backwards, huddling with his friends. Lem then took his walking stick and knocked three times on the tunnel door. Nobody answered. There was a faint murmur of commotion on the other side. The waif knocked three times again, this time louder. After a few moments, there came another three knocks from the other side of the door.

"Who goes?" thundered a deep voice from the outside.

"Special delivery!" yelled Lem.

"Who goes?" repeated the voice.

"Just open da bloody door," replied the waif.

"Who goes?"

"Oh fer god's sake, it's Declin! Now open up ya big galoot!"

CHAPTER FIFTEEN
The Hole

When the door opened the light was blinding. After walking for hours in the darkness, it took the teens' eyes several seconds to adjust to what they were seeing. Even after their vision cleared, they couldn't believe it. They climbed out of the tunnel and emerged into a gigantic cave. It appeared that some of the cave had been formed naturally, but its area had definitely been expanded past its original size. Half of its walls were smooth and natural, but the other half looked dug out by hand. Running all along the walls of the cave were tubes of light—the same tubes that ran throughout Reysa. But where the city's tubes merely twinkled, these tubes were so bright that you couldn't look directly at them without hurting your eyes.

The cave was full of Reytana.

"Welcome to the Hole," said one of the Reytana as he helped Regan out of the tunnel door. "My name is Gracien." He smiled warmly and offered his assistance to Tinko next. Tinko reached out with a shaky hand and grasped the Reytana. "You're safe now, friend," said Gracien as he helped him out.

"You're the Lost Reytana!" exclaimed Tinko.

"And now you've found us," said Gracien with a warm smile. Loras exited the tunnel last and joined his companions. He didn't even seem to notice the Reytana but rather went directly to the waif.

"*You're* Declin," he said.

"At yer service."

"You mean this whole time—"

"But you said your name was Lem" said Tinko.

"No, I said yous can call me Lem if ya like," said Declin. "And it seemed dat you liked it, so I didn't stop ya."

"But the whole point of us coming to Woodhaven was to find you," said Loras.

"Aye, I figured dat were da case. Last I talked to Dario, he said I was to bring you here, so dat's what I did. In fact, I was on my way to pick yous up in Reysa when I found ya in da forest. Saved me a day's walk, ya did. Much 'preciated."

The teens exchanged a flabbergasted look.

"Declin is a friend to the Reytana," explained Gracien. "He has been helping us send messages back and forth to Dario for many years now."

"Loras, give it to him," said Regan. Loras was still confused. He was having a hard time processing this overload of information. He didn't budge until his sister nudged him with her elbow. "It's *him*," she replied, more forcefully this time. "You promised."

"Aye, if yous got somethin' fer me you'd best hand it over," said Declin.

Loras took Dario's letter out of his pocket and reluctantly handed it over to the waif. Declin unfolded the paper and read its contents. Dario must not have written much, because only a few seconds passed before he re-folded the letter. Then, he stared hard at the twins, as if he was looking for something that wasn't there. Without saying a word, he handed the letter to Gracien.

"Wait!" shouted Loras. "Dario told us that you were the only one allowed to read that letter! We weren't even allowed to look at it!"

"And did you?" asked the waif. His tone was serious as death. Gracien finished reading the letter and looked up at the twins as well. He repeated Declin's question.

"Did you? Answer us true," said Gracien. "Did you read the letter?"

"I didn't. I promise," answered Regan. She looked at her brother. "Loras? You didn't, did you... Loras?"

Loras' eyes darted between his sister, to the waif and then to the Reytana. He didn't know what was going on and he was starting to get upset. "No! I didn't read the damn letter! Why? What does it say? We have the right to know!"

Gracien folded the letter and placed it in his pocket. As he did so he let out a relieved sigh. He then bent down and whispered something to Declin who, after receiving the message, turned and walked away from the group.

"Wait. Where's he going?" shouted Loras. "What's going on? Tell me what the letter said!"

"Now is not the time," said Gracien and he walked over and placed a hand on Loras' shoulder. His grip was incredibly strong. "Be patient, young warrior. All will be known when it needs to be. "

"But—" exclaimed Loras as he unsuccessfully tried to shrug off Gracien's hand.

"Look at me," said Gracien. He, too, studied the young Reytana's face as if he were looking for something. It made Loras uncomfortable and he refused to look the older Tormada in the eyes.

"Loras, look at me," Gracien repeated. Loras finally gave in and looked into Gracien's unblinking golden eyes. He saw warmth and concern in the Reytana's gaze. "I know you have many questions," said Gracien, "and rightfully so. Much has

happened to you in a short period of time. Just receiving your
light is traumatic enough; add in everything else that has
happened... Anyone would be overwhelmed and frustrated.
But know this. We have been waiting for this moment for a
long time. There is a plan—one that you will be part of. But
for right now, you need to trust me. Do you trust me, Loras?"
Loras held Gracien's gaze. The older Reytana's hand had not
left his shoulder. Eventually, Loras nodded his head. "Good,"
said Gracien. "Now, if you'll follow me, I will show you the lay
of the land, if you will."

By this time, several other Reytana had come over to inspect
the visitors. When they saw the golden eyes of the twins, an
excited buzz began to grow in the crowd. More and more
Reytana joined the group as Gracien showed the newcomers
around the cave. Tinko looked at the group of giants that were
happily following them.

"Look!" whispered Tinko to Loras excitedly, "they're all
wearing the bands! It's just like in the books." He pointed
towards the glowing bands of light that were wrapped around
the Reytanas' forearms.

"I know," answered Loras. His frustration was slowly
dissipating and excitement was taking its place. "They're just
like the pictures, except brighter!"

Gracien led a slow pace through the cave, allowing the teens
to soak everything in. It was hard to tell who was more in awe;
the newcomers or the surrounding Reytana. The group of
towering Tormada whispered to each other while they
motioned towards Loras and Regan. Loras tried to pick up
what they were saying, but to no avail.

"the Hole has long been a haven for the Reytana," explained
Gracien. "Declin claims that it was his ancestors who originally
built it, hundreds of years ago, in order to 'hide things.'" Loras
and Regan exchanged sideways glances. "At some point, the
waifs struck a deal with the Reytana and allowed us to use the
location for our own needs."

"I wonder how much that cost them," whispered Tinko to Loras. Loras didn't seem to notice. He was too busy looking around at everything, trying to take it all in.

"It's okay to blink, you know," said Regan to her brother.

"How are you not freaking out right now?" exclaimed Loras. "Look… just *look* where we are. All these years. This is where they've been hiding. It's amazing!"

Regan just shrugged and followed along with the group.

"Some people are just hard to impress," said Tinko.

"More like some people are just dead inside," responded Loras.

"Ah, if only everyone was blessed with your passion for life."

Loras smacked Tinko on the back of the head.

Gracien continued, "Before the Eighth War, we used the Hole to conduct business with the woodsmen. The tunnels you have traveled through connect to the forest cities; Woodhaven, Arsdale, Spirea—all of them. the Hole has also been used to hold prisoners, triage injured soldiers and, most recently, hide Reytana from the Gartune."

This last part struck a nerve with Loras. "Why have you been hiding all this time? Why not come out and fight? The Gartune have taken over our city. They *live* in *our* city! What are you waiting for?!" Some of the Reytana who had joined the group began to whisper amongst themselves uncomfortably. A few looked away so as not to catch the gaze of the teens.

"I understand your frustration, young warrior," Gracien replied calmly, "but we have had no choice. The shield was a major blow to our defenses. As long as it is up, we cannot defeat the Gartune. To expose ourselves would have been suicide."

"So are you just going to hide in here forever and let the city suffer?" asked Loras.

"Not forever," replied Gracien. "We have waited eighteen years for the right time, and that time is nearly here. Look over there." He pointed to the center of the room where a beam of sunlight was streaming down from a small hole in the ceiling of the cave. the Hole couldn't have been more than a foot in diameter. Directly underneath the Hole was a large, glass orb full of shimmering, liquid light.

"An energy orb! " exclaimed Tinko.

"Yes," replied Gracien. "And it's nearly full. It's taken us all this time to fill it because we get such a small amount of sunlight each day. Some days we have to cover the Hole altogether if we think there might be Gartolians in the area."

"But how did it get here?" asked Regan.

"We smuggled it out of Reysa right before it fell to the Gartolians. Only the Reytana knew that this second energy orb existed. It was meant as a back-up; a reserve in case the lotus was depleted. Unfortunately, both orbs had been drained during the attack on Reysa, and once the shield was raised, they could not be replenished. King Atholos knew this. He knew that it was only a matter of time before the city fell. And so, he ordered me to take the remaining Reytana and flee to the Hole with the empty reserve orb. I protested—we all did—but he would not be dissuaded. The night that he went to fight the Gartune alone, we snuck out of the city." The teens could hear the regret in Gracien's voice as he told this last part of the story.

Tinko nudged Loras. "Look how embarrassed they are," he whispered to his friend. And it was true. The other Reytana could no longer make eye contact with Tinko or the twins. They bowed their heads and remained silent as they walked on through the cave.

"And so, we have lived here since the war," Gracien continued. "Declin brings us news from the city when he can so that we know what's going on." Loras could detect a hint of anger in the Reytana's voice now. "Know this," continued Gracien, "the Gartune will not walk the streets of Reysa for much longer."

Loras was stewing. A hundred questions rattled around in his head, and he struggled to choose the one to ask first.

"There *is* a plan," answered Gracien before Loras could speak. "That will have to suffice for the time being. But now, you need your rest."

Gracien led them into an offshoot of the main cave. They entered a long hall that contained hundreds of cots lined up in two perfectly straight rows. The beds were bunked three high. Each one was perfectly made; not a sheet unfolded or a blanket wrinkled. Gracien led the teens to the end of the hall and assigned them a stack of cots. "I'm sure you must be very tired," said Gracien. "Rest here for the evening and we will talk more in the morning."

"But we're not tired!" said Tinko. It was true; they were too excited to sleep and had several more questions that needed answers.

"You can't expect us to sleep after all of this," added Loras.

"Loras, you are a Reytana, a guardian of Reysa. You may do whatever you please. But you may find that you are more tired than you think. And you will need your strength in the days to come. That, I can promise you." With that, he turned and began walking back towards the main cavern. "Even Tormada need to sleep, young warrior," he added over his shoulder as he walked out of the barracks.

"He's right," said Regan. "We haven't slept much in the past four days. Besides, after sleeping in the forest, these beds look pretty good." She climbed into the lower bunk and pulled the covers over her. Within a minute of closing her eyes, Regan was asleep.

"Well, maybe I am a little tired," said Tinko as he crawled into the middle bunk. He yawned once and was out before he could even slip under the sheets.

Loras looked toward the main cave for a few minutes, deciding what he wanted to do. A wave of exhaustion hit him as he was thinking. "Ah, screw it," he said, and he jumped effortlessly up into the top bunk. When he landed, the stack of beds shook. Tinko gave a muffled snore but did not wake up. Loras stared at the ceiling of the cave until his eyes became too heavy to keep open. It was not long before he was matching snores with Tinko.

CHAPTER SIXTEEN
Claustraphobia

"The tracks stop here," grunted Belkore. Frustration was thick on his voice. This mission had taken much longer than he had planned. By all accounts, he should have already been on his way back to Gartol with prisoners in tow. But ever since that first night, when Xander had ordered that they continue the search without breaking for camp, something had changed. Now, every time that they appeared to be closing in on the Reytana, Xander had inexplicably delayed the pursuit. Suddenly, Xander was very concerned that his companions were properly fed and rested. They had already stopped to eat three times that day. They even found time for a mid-afternoon nap. It didn't make any sense.

The group had been following the tracks along the river for the entire day. They were surprised to see that the trail continued on past Woodhaven, but they continued to follow its lead. Eventually, the tracks ended at a peculiar grouping of rocks. Xander joined Belkore in inspecting the spot where the footprints disappeared.

"Astute as always," replied Xander. "The tracks have indeed stopped here."

Damnar and Damina snickered, having finally started catching on to the prince's humor. Belkore had insisted on taking over the tracking earlier that day because he said that their pace was too slow. Everyone knew that Xander was the cause for the slow-going with his insistence on stopping to eat and nap every couple of hours. Since nobody would openly blame the prince for the delay, Belkore chose to blame the twins for not tracking fast enough. Damnar and Damina had been sulking ever since their demotion, but now they were relieved to see someone else roasting on the spit. Belkore could sense their amusement and shot them a piercing look.

"You two find something funny? Why don't you start moving those rocks and then tell me how funny that is?" snapped Belkore. Damnar and Damina looked to Xander for advice, but the prince merely raised an eyebrow and nodded towards the rock pile. The twins grudgingly walked over to the pile and began to toss the rocks out of the way.

They labored for over ten minutes on the mound of rocks but made little progress. It was strange. Each time they moved a rock, another slipped right into its place. Though the pile was becoming shorter, the face of it was still perfectly level. The twins became frustrated. Each new rock that slid into the Hole left by the previous one was a perfect match for the vacated space, so much so that there was little room for the Gartune to wrap their fingers around the edges to pry the new rocks free. It was maddening.

Eventually, the rock pile was no longer a pile. Instead, it was flat like a patch of cobblestone street that was flush with the riverbank. Each rock was nestled perfectly against the next. There was no room in between them and no way to extract any more. Xander inspected the rock floor that they had created as he tapped it with his eüroc. It was perfectly solid.

"Well *that* is something," he said in awe. This time there was no sarcasm in his voice. He looked genuinely impressed. "Well, now we know two things. First, they obviously crossed the river here to avoid detection. Most likely, they're somewhere in Woodhaven by now. And second..." he tapped the rock floor one last time just to make sure there wasn't a stone loose. "Whoever is helping them is rather clever. This could be fun."

"I wouldn't call spending thirty minutes moving rocks around for no reason, 'fun,'" replied Damnar as he wiped sweat off of his brow.

"No? Well, let's see if we can find something to better entertain you." There was a glint of mischief in Xander's eyes.

Back inside of the Hole, Loras awoke from his slumber and began to toss and turn in his cot. He had only gotten a few hours of rest and his body begged him to sleep more, but he couldn't. Something inside of him was restless.

Loras had never been prone to claustrophobia before, but now it seemed like the walls of the cave were closing in on him. Also, a coldness had begun to grow inside his chest. Well, maybe not a coldness, but a decided lack of warmth. It was as if something was missing. He had felt the same when Declin was leading them through the underground tunnels. It was an entirely new sensation to Loras, and he didn't like it. All of the sudden, he had an insatiable need to get above ground.

Loras climbed out of his top bunk, making sure that he didn't arouse Tinko and his sister. He wandered out of the barracks and back towards the main chamber. Even at this late hour, there was still plenty of activity inside of the cavern. Off to one side, several Reytana were sparring with each other. Their fiery swords threw sparks as they collided with shields made of the same glowing material. Loras was transfixed. He had previously only seen depictions of the Reytana's weapons but seeing them in person was nothing like he had imagined. It was as if the swords and shields grew right out of the Reytana's hands; like they were a part of them. In reality, their weaponry sprung from small devices in their palms. These devices connected to the Reytana's wrist bands. The light energy that lived inside each Reytana flowed through their bands, into the palm devices where it was shaped into a sword or a shield. It was one of the many ways that the Reytana were able to transform and manipulate solar energy.

Sparks flickered in the golden eyes of the warriors as they swung their glowing weapons through the air with ferocious speed. Loras lost track of time as he stood watching what he had previously only seen in his dreams. He only snapped out of his daze when a friendly hand patted him on his shoulder.

"Is it like you imagined?" asked a familiar voice from behind Loras. Loras turned to see Gracien standing behind him, smiling.

"It is... but it isn't," replied Loras. "I mean, I knew how the weapons worked, but I just never knew how they *worked*."

Gracien laughed. "I remember when I first saw a ray blade. It was my father's. I remember thinking that I had never seen anything so terrifying and yet so wonderful at the same time. The light hurt my eyes, but I couldn't look away."

"I know the feeling," said Loras as he turned his attention back to the sparring Reytana. *His father showed him his first ray blade... his father was a Reytana, like mine should have been.* Loras thought about what it must have been like to grow up *knowing* that you were a Reytana. Even before he received his light, he would have been trained on how to use a sword and shield, how to jump and fight; how to be a Tormada. Eighteen years. Eighteen years had been lost. His entire life.

"When will I get mine?" he asked.

"Patience, young warrior. It takes time to master our weapons. We will begin your training once you are rested. Speaking of which, I thought you had decided to get some sleep?"

"I tried, but I can't," replied Loras. "Something about this cave is making me uneasy. It's like it's pressing down on me or something."

"I know the feeling," sighed Gracien. "Reytana were not meant to live underground. You learn to deal with it after a while, but it never feels natural. When the ceiling is open, it helps," he pointed to the Hole in the ceiling which was now covered up for the night, "but it's not the same as being above ground where we can absorb the full energy of the sun. It is our lifeblood. It feeds us. Our bodies need it, which is why yours is now craving it."

"So how do you feed that hunger when you're underground?" asked Loras.

"You never really do. You can supplement it with other things. You can distract your mind with training and with work. But that is only temporary. That is why we all must travel above ground every now and then, even though it is extremely dangerous for us to do so. If we didn't, we would die."

"How?" asked Loras. "How do you go above ground without being detected?"

"Through the tunnels. Some of them lead to empty spots in the forest where we can emerge for a few hours to recharge. We always take a waif with us to scout the area first. Declin and his people have been an invaluable resource and have put themselves in great danger by doing so."

"Can Declin take me out to one of these spots? I need to get out of here. Just for a few minutes. I feel like I can't breathe in this cave," pleaded Loras.

"Declin has gone and won't be back until tomorrow. Besides, the sun is setting. There is nothing out there that can feed the hunger inside of you. You must wait."

"I can't wait!" exclaimed Loras, becoming frantic now. "I need to get out of this cave! I know the sun is down but just a few breaths of fresh air—that's all I need. Then I'll come right back, I promise!"

Gracien placed his hand back on Loras' shoulder. Loras swatted it away. Gracien's kind face became stern as he returned his hand to the teen's shoulder, more forcefully this time. Loras felt like his collar bone was being crushed. "I have given my answer and you will obey it. It is too dangerous for you to go outside, especially at night." Gracien's grip loosened on Loras' shoulder and his brow unfurled slightly. "Why don't you go back and try to get some sleep. You will feel better if you do."

"I told you, I can't sleep," said Loras as he wriggled his way loose of Gracien's grip. "Can I at least just walk around and watch for a while? Maybe that will help."

"Loras, you are a Reytana, a guardian of Reysa. You may do what you wish."

"Except leave this cave," quipped Loras.

"Except that," said Gracien with a smile as he walked away, leaving Loras to admire the training Reytana. Loras sat and watched for another thirty minutes or so, but this time he was not interested in the combatants. His eyes scoured the cave searching for an exit. The only one he saw was the door they had arrived through that afternoon, and it was guarded by two Reytana.

Frustrated, Loras decided to go for a walk. He paced the perimeter of the cave, acting as if he was giving himself a self-guided tour of his new home. In reality, he was looking for anything that could be an exit. *There has to be some sort of hidden door or passageway here,* thought Loras. He ran his hands slowly over the sides of the cave's walls but could find nothing out of the ordinary. Eventually, he came to a small alcove at the far end of the cave. It couldn't have been more than thirty feet deep, a mere dimple in the side of the cavern. The back of the alcove was completely dark. Loras took one step in and was immediately overcome by a crushing sense of claustrophobia. The darkness from the back of the alcove rushed at him, engulfing him in blackness. He couldn't breathe. Immediately, he stepped back into the light. Once he was out of the darkness, he regained his breath and the claustrophobia dissipated.

Loras looked back into the alcove. Something had caught his eye an instant before his panic attack. There was a hint of light at the back of the room. He wasn't sure what it was, but he knew that he wanted a better look at it. Fighting off his fear, Loras stepped back into the recess. His body became cold the instant he left the light of the main cave. Again, the blackness enveloped him. Loras held his breath and squinted. There it was again; a tiny shaft of light running in a thin line at the base of the room. Loras could feel the walls closing in on him but he decided to take another step forward. The light became stronger. Loras exhaled loudly and gulped down another gasp of air. He took another step forward, and then another. The light at the back of the room became brighter. With each step, Loras could feel the blackness around him thinning. It became easier to breathe. Loras was now only a few feet from the light. He held out his hands in front of him, groping in the darkness, searching for the back wall. Two more steps brought him to it. The thin, horizontal line of light was now directly in front of his feet. His hands met the wall, but, instead of a jagged, rocky surface like he had expected, the stone was smooth and polished; cool to the touch. Loras ran his hands along the wall until he found what he was looking for. A latch.

He tried to move it. Nothing. He tried harder. Again, nothing. Loras shoved his whole body against the door and pushed as he tried to turn the latch. It did not budge. Frustration and panic overtook Loras. He kicked the door as hard as he could. Instantly, he regretted that decision. White-hot pain shot through Loras' foot and into his leg. His toes felt crushed inside of his boot. Loras collapsed onto the floor of the alcove and held his damaged foot as he rocked back and forth in agony. *You moron,* he thought to himself. *Who kicks a stone door?*

Loras sat by himself for a good ten minutes until the pain eventually began to subside. His mind began to clear. The pain in his foot had distracted him from his claustrophobia. The walls were no longer collapsing onto him and he could breathe normally, but it was still pitch black and this made him feel cold inside. He had just decided to leave the alcove and return to his bed when he heard footsteps approaching. Trapped, Loras had only one option. He scooted away from the door and huddled near the side of the room.

The silhouette of a Reytana appeared at the mouth of the alcove. Loras could not see his face, only the shape of his body. The figure stopped for a moment, looked behind him, and then proceeded directly toward the door in the back of the room. Loras pulled his feet tightly to his body as the Reytana walked past him in the darkness. When the Reytana reached the back of the room, Loras heard a faint scratching sound, then a series of clicks. The door slid open. Suddenly, the alcove was awash in soft, golden light and Loras was no longer hidden by darkness. He was visible for anyone to see—a frightened teenager huddled in a ball. Loras imagined the punishment that was sure to be doled out to him. He closed his eyes, anticipating a beating. But none came. Loras opened one eye just in time to see the shadow of the Reytana moving along the wall of the corridor beyond the door. The door —it was still open, although swinging shut quickly. There was no time to lose. Without thinking, Loras jumped up and stuck his arm through the opening in the door before it could close. The door was incredibly heavy, and it took all of Loras' strength to shove it back open so that he could squeeze through. A week ago, he would not have been able to hold the door open, but his newfound Tormada strength served him well. He slid his body through the opening and collapsed onto the dirt floor of the corridor. The door shut behind him with a *click*.

Loras looked up. The tunnel was lit by a series of torches spaced every ten feet along the walls. Even with the heat from the torch-fire, the tunnel was decidedly cool. But the air was fresher than inside the cave. *Open air must be near,* thought Loras. He crept up onto his feet. Ahead of him, he could faintly hear the Reytana walking through the tunnel. Tip-toeing as quietly as he could, Loras
followed the footsteps in front of him.

CHAPTER SEVENTEEN
Zips

The moon shone off the frothy, churning water of the Aeil River, giving it an even more ominous appearance than usual. Xander, Belkore, Damnar and Damina studied the zip lines that crossed over the angry river. All but two of the platform huts that connected the zips were closed for the evening. One was a single rider platform and the other a larger, multi-occupant platform. Each had torches flickering in them and a half-asleep waif lounging on the floor.

The Gartune approached the hut of the multi-occupant zip line. Damnar and Damina eyed the rusty steel cage that hung off the zip line overhead, then looked down warily at the rushing water below. Looking back at the cage, it was clear that this mode of transport was obviously not made for Tormada. Xander watched his companions as they tried, unsuccessfully, to hide their anxiety. It amused him.

"What's the matter?" asked Xander of his young companions. "I figured two adventurous youths such as yourselves would jump at the chance to take a ride in one of these."

"Errr.. do you think they're safe?" asked Damina.

"I think they're here," answered Xander. "You're free to swim across if you would rather do that."

The twins eyed the moonlit rapids and then re-assessed the zip lines.

"But do you think that we'll all fit?" asked Damnar.

"Only one way to find out!" Xander yelled up to the half-sleeping waif on the zip platform. "You there—oh, master of the crossing! We seek passage on your finest vessel!"

The waif jumped at the sound of Xander's voice. He looked down from his raised platform and was startled to see four Gartune hailing him. As fast as he could, he began cranking the wheel that controlled the height of the platform and lowered himself to ground level.

"Permission to come aboard!" cried Xander with a mock salute. He was really enjoying himself. His companions... not so much. The waif could see the uncertainty on their faces as they climbed into the hut. With their added weight, the smaller torman labored greatly to crank the platform back up to departure height. None of the Gartune offered any assistance and he didn't dare to ask them for help.

"What's your name there, master cranker?" asked Xander.

"Cy... Cyrus," gasped the waif as he threw his entire body weight into the crank to get it to revolve. Sweat poured from his brow and he had little breath to spare for speaking. So, naturally, Xander decided to start a conversation with him.

"You probably don't see too many of our type around here, do ya, Cy?" asked Xander.

"No, sir," panted Cyrus as he cranked.

"What about your fellow crankers? You all must talk to each other—share trade secrets and such—any of them seen a Tormada around here lately?"

"No sir... not... in... many... years," replied Cyrus. Each word was exhausting.

"Well then this must be your lucky day!" said Xander as he clapped Cyrus on the back.

"So these things have never transported a Tormada?" asked Damina. There was an obvious touch of fear in her voice. Belkore glared at her. Even Damnar, who shared her worry, gave her a dirty look. Gartune did not show fear, especially in front of a lowly waif.

"She'll hold... 'fer certain... she'll hold," panted Cyrus as the platform finally reached its departure height. In front of the platform, dangling from the zip line overhead, was the rusted-out cable car. The twins entered first, testing each step cautiously as they went. Belkore, eager to show he was not nervous like his companions, shoved the twins inside the car and followed behind them. The cage dipped heavily from the weight of the three Gartune. It now hung a good two feet below the platform. The zip line above creaked with disapproval, but it held.

"Thanks for the lift, Cy. I'll tip ya once we get to the other side," said Xander as he jumped into the cage. The cage dipped another foot. Snapping noises sprung from the tethered line above them but it did not break. Xander grinned at Damina.

"See, isn't this fun?"

"Wonderful," Damnar responded as she grasped one of the cage's rails and frowned through the bars at the river below.

Cyrus reached up and released the cable car's brake. Immediately, the car began to zoom down the line and over the thrashing water below. The waif was correct, the cage was fully capable of carrying the Gartune's extra weight. However, the height of the zip line had been calibrated to transport normal-sized tormen, not Tormada.

The cage dipped lower and lower as it approached the middle of the river. Waves began splashing over the sides of the compartment. The zip line dipped further until the bottom of the cage was quickly submerged. Water rose from the Gartune's ankles to their knees. The cage slowed, eventually coming to a complete stop in the middle of the river. White water crashed over the sides and sprayed the Gartune in the face. Damina swallowed a big gulp of water and began to cough. Her brother closed his eyes and spit out some of the river that he had just nearly ingested. The spray hit Belkore right in the face as he stood, arms crossed and dripping from head to toe. Damnar looked terrified. Xander was having a blast. He watched his friends struggle with the rushing water while he, himself, stood calmly with one arm wrapped around the corner of the cage, letting the river's spray wash over him like a soft summer breeze.

Upon seeing that the cable car had gotten stuck in the river, Cyrus frantically began cranking his wheel again. For thirty agonizing seconds, the platform began to rise, and the zip line with it, until finally, the cage was pulled out of the river.

Cyrus collapsed onto the platform, exhausted. The Gartune were now the problem of the waif on the other side of the line. From down below, Xander yelled, "this is coming out of your tip!" as the cage continued flying down the line.

The cage and its passengers arrived dripping-wet at the platform on Woodhaven's side of the riverbank. The attending waif rushed to open the cage door and help them onto dry ground. Belkore shoved the twins out of the way so that he could exit first, then proceeded to shove the waif into the ground as well. Damnar and Damina exited next but paid no attention to the waif. Xander exited last and helped the waif off of the ground.

"Hell of a ride you've got there," he said to the waif, an impish smile still on his face. The waif nodded but did not say a word. Once the Gartune had exited the car, the waif immediately went to cranking his platform's wheel, rising up into the sky and out of reach.

Xander caught up with his companions who were already trudging towards the city. He swung his arms over the twins' shoulders and fell into step with them. "I don't know that I've ever witnessed such bravery," said Xander. "It was truly inspiring. Promise me this, when you are back in Gartol telling the story of how you were almost swallowed whole by the river, don't leave out the part about Belkore getting spit in the face."

"So glad to be of entertainment, my prince," sneered Belkore.

"Not as glad as I!" replied Xander cheerfully. "Now what do you brave warriors think about finding something to eat?"

"As long as it has a fire," grumbled Belkore as he unclipped his cloak and began wringing the water out of it.

CHAPTER EIGHTEEN
The Tavern

A particularly loud snore caused Tinko to rouse from his slumber. He rolled on to his back and kicked the bed above him.

"Loras! You're snoring again!" There was no answer.

"That wasn't Loras, it was you Tink," said Regan from the bunk below.

"Nonsense," grumbled Tinko as he pulled the covers back over himself. "I don't snore." He hadn't quite fallen back to sleep when he heard another throaty gurgle. This time he knew it came from him. He faked a cough in a vain attempt to cover up his snore but ended up dislodging something in his throat which caused a violent hacking episode.

"Are you dying? You sound like you might be dying," said Regan.

Tinko eventually got his hacking under control. "It must be this damp cave air," he said.

"There definitely is something about the air in here," said Regan. "I can't sleep."

"Sorry," said Tinko. "I'll try to breath through my nose... or something."

"It's not you," said Regan. "I just can't sleep. My mind won't turn off. You ever have that problem?"

"Me?" said Tinko. "Nah. When I need to go to sleep, I just say 'mind—off' and it's out like a light. Now turning it back on is a different story. That can be a bit trickier."

Regan chuckled. "That's why I love you, Tink. Even with everything that's going on around you, you never change."

"Oh, I don't know about that. I think I've changed quite a bit in the last few days, actually. I mean, I slept in a tree. I caught a fish. Oh, and there was that one time when I was almost murdered by a Gartolian sentry. Nothing jumpstarts your personal development like a little drowning, I always say. Granted, I haven't gained superpowers and grown almost a foot, but I still think I've changed."

"I didn't mean it as an insult," said Regan. "Staying true to yourself is a good thing. And yes, I agree that you have changed in these past few days. We all have."

"Yeah, well some more than others, I suppose."

"Yes," whispered Regan to herself, "some more than others."

Tinko rubbed his eyes. "Well, I guess if you're not sleeping then nobody is sleeping. That includes you too, Loras!" He kicked the bed on top of him. No sound. Tinko kicked it again, harder this time. Still nothing. "You up there?" he called. When he got no reply, Tinko pulled himself up and peered over the top of Loras' bed. It was empty.

"Looks like you're not the only one who can't sleep," said Tinko. "He's gone."

"Why am I not surprised?" asked Regan with a sigh.

"I don't know what's wrong with you two," said Tinko. "We've been trudging through the woods for days and we finally get a warm bed to sleep in and now you can't sleep? Do you prefer sleeping on the wet ground or in some prickly tree?"

"Actually, right now I think I would prefer that, yes," answered Regan. "Just anywhere outside sounds better than being in this cave. It's so... cold in here."

"If by 'cold' you mean pleasantly warm, then, yes, it's very cold in here," said Tinko sleepily as he laid back down onto his bed and slipped underneath the covers. "But if you need out, then why don't you just go ask someone to let you outside. I'll stay here."

"What if they don't let me outside?"

"Why wouldn't they? We're not prisoners here," replied Tinko.

"Are you sure about that?" said Regan.

"I'm pretty sure," said Tinko.

"Well, I still feel like we're trapped. Maybe not prisoners, but we're definitely being guarded."

"Is that such a bad thing?" replied Tinko. "I'm sure Xander has some Gartune out searching for us right now and I, for one, could use a little guarding. And I would prefer it be by three hundred Reytana."

"Fine," replied Regan curtly. "You stay here in bed. I need to get some fresh air. Maybe I can find Loras. I'm sure he wants out too; if he isn't already." Regan got out of bed and walked away. Tinko watched as she strode down the long row of bunk beds. He tried to close his eyes and go back to sleep but to no avail. The warm cloak of sleep had lifted from him.

"Hold on!" yelled Tinko as he hopped clumsily out of his bed. "If you're going then I'm going too."

Loras followed the Reytana through the woods for a good thirty minutes. He made sure to keep his distance so that he wouldn't be detected. It was slow going. The Reytana made a point to stop and listen every five minutes or so. Loras hoped that this was a trained behavior and not an indication that the Reytana thought he was being followed.

Loras didn't mind the stopping and starting. He was happy just to be outside breathing the fresh air. There was still a coldness inside of him, but the claustrophobia from the cave had subsided, and that was a relief. Curiosity was now at the top of his mind. Where was this Reytana going in the middle of the night? Surely, he wouldn't venture into Woodhaven by himself, and yet, Loras felt that was the direction they were heading.

Something touched Loras' arm and, instinctively, he jumped. The Reytana in front of him stopped and turned his head. Loras knelt down just as the Reytana turned towards him. He tried to peer through the tall grass to see if he had been spotted. Thirty seconds passed. Then a minute. The Reytana did not move. A small, pulsing light reflected off the grass in front of him. Loras looked down at his arm. He had been so transfixed on the Reytana that he had forgotten about the thing that spooked him in the first place. A large, translucent moth, sat calmly on his arm, flapping its wings slowly. Each time its wings flapped, a small pulse of light emanated from its body. Loras turned his arm slightly so that he could get a better view of the creature. A long, thin snout delicately prodded his arm as if searching for something. Then, Loras felt a small prick as the snout punctured his skin. A small trickle of light flowed up the moth's snout and into its body. The next time that its wings flapped, the glow in its abdomen was brighter.

I know what this is... it's a wapa, thought Loras, surprised he had remembered such a small detail from one of professor Lucan's lectures. Greedily, the wapa pricked Loras' arm again and sucked up another stream of light. His stomach began to glow more. Suddenly, a dozen small, glowing bodies began to appear out of the darkness. All around him, things began to glow. He looked up and saw a swarm of wapas hovering above him amongst the trees. They began to circle his location as they slowly descended. Loras realized now why he had remembered Lucan talking about the wapas; why he had found them so interesting. *They eat light.*

Frantically, he shook his arm in an attempt to throw the wapa off of it, but the moth's grip was strong. Three tiny claws dug into his arm and his snout went in for a third plunge, this time digging well past the surface of his skin. Loras looked up. The swarm of wapas was only a few feet overhead and getting closer by the second. Panicked, he began to stand up to run but then instantly remembered why he had crouched in the first place. The Reytana. He hadn't moved. Suddenly, the Reytana spoke.

"Hail," said the Reytana. Loras' eyes widened. *Maybe he's just testing to see if anyone will answer.* Forced to choose between revealing himself or being sucked dry by a swarm of glowing moths, Loras decided to remain silent. It was the right decision, because moments later he heard another voice off in the distance.

"Hail yerself," said a familiar voice. Loras straightened slightly out of his knelt position and saw his old waif companion emerge from the woods in front of him. *What's he doing here?* Loras stood up a bit more. As he did so, he heard a tiny *smuuck* sound from his arm. The wapa had detached itself and began to fly in the direction of the other Reytana. Above him, the swarm of glowing moths followed their friend towards what they must have thought to be a larger meal.

Declin spoke with the Reytana for a few moments. All the while, the Tormada swatted, annoyed, at the circle of glowing moths that surrounded him. Loras strained to hear what they were talking about, but he only caught a stray word here and there. The conversation was brief, and after it ended, Declin disappeared back into the forest. The Reytana then turned and began walking straight back towards Loras' position. He strode quickly, trying to outrun the pack of wapas behind him. It did not take long before he had outdistanced the swarm. Loras pressed himself flat on the ground and then crawled as quickly as he could behind a nearby clump of bushes. He peered through the leaves and listened to the rapidly approaching footsteps. Loras' heart began to race as he flashed back to a recent situation when he had tried to hide in a bush from a

Tormada. This time, his concealment was a success. For the second time that evening, the Reytana passed within a few feet of Loras without notice.

Loras waited until he could no longer hear the Reytana's footsteps before slowly rising from his hiding spot. He was careful not to make a sound. After all, Declin could still be in the area, and that waif was sneaky. He could be watching right now and Loras would never know it. Loras slowly scanned the forest. Beams of moonlight shooting through the canopy above created random white shapes on the forest floor. Other sections were in complete darkness. If Declin was out there, he was undoubtedly in one of the dark areas.

Loras had two choices. He could turn back and try to follow the Reytana back into the Hole, or he could go in Declin's direction and see if he could find his way to Woodhaven.

The city had captivated Loras from the moment he laid eyes on it. It was like no place he had ever seen. Granted, that wasn't saying much since the only place he had ever known was Reysa. He longed to explore, and more than that, he dreaded the thought of returning to the cold cave with its oppressive walls.

Curiosity, compounded by the fact that he was ravenously hungry, made his decision an easy one. Only halfway through his growth spurt, he could still pass as a tall torman if he slouched... and if nobody looked him in the eyes. He would have to be careful.

Loras quietly picked his way through the forest in the direction Declin had gone. He made sure to give a wide berth to the swarm of wapas circling lazily nearby. For a while, he stopped every five minutes to listen behind him like the Reytana had done, but the chorus of forest animals squawking their nighttime songs made it difficult to hear anything out of the ordinary. Eventually, Loras gave up trying to listen for followers and continued on without stopping.

For over an hour, Loras made his way through the forest, using only the sound of the distant river for navigation. The Aeil was his compass. Once he found the river, he could find Woodhaven. Eventually, the sound of rushing water became louder and more distinct. Loras made out a faint orange glow up ahead between the trees. He had found Woodhaven.

Carefully, Loras crept to the tree line that marked the city's edge. A dilapidated fence surrounded Woodhaven. It was full of gaping holes and there were even sections where it had fallen down altogether. Entering the city would not be a problem. Entering the city as a *torman* would require some skill.

Loras pulled the hood of his cloak over his head and headed towards one of the Holes in the fence. He stepped through and looked around. *That was easy*, he said to himself. The buildings here at the outskirts of the city were mostly dark and quiet. A few ominous-looking alleys led toward the center of the city. Loras chose the nearest one then, after taking one more look around, walked towards it, trying his best to look like he belonged.

In Woodhaven, there was not much of a difference in size between the main streets and the side alleys. Both were extremely tight—no more than nine or ten feet across at their widest points—and very dimly lit. Reysene light tubes ran across the walls of most of the buildings, but only about one in five gave off any illumination. Torches provided the majority of the light during the evening. Fortunately for Loras, only a few of each were lit in the alley he had chosen.

From under his hood, Loras peered through the grimy windows that flanked the alley. Each one told a similar story. Drunken waifs yelled loudly at each other and threw goblets against the walls while scantily-clad ladies (in the loosest definition of the word) tried to garner their attention. Waif musicians pounded away on a variety of crude instruments. A group of young men gleefully danced in front of them, hoisting their mugs in the air as they circled arm-in-arm. There was laughter. There were fights. It was loud and it smelled. Loras loved it.

He passed several waifs as he made his way down the alley. None of them paid him any attention. This gave Loras enough courage to enter one of the buildings. He found one that smelled like it served food and he decided to investigate further. As soon as he walked in, his senses were overloaded. Instead of an individual piano or lute player, this particular establishment fielded an entire band of musicians. The song they were playing must have been a crowd favorite, because the majority of the patrons were singing along and sloshing their mugs together during the chorus. The smell of roasting meat met Loras' nose and he could hear his stomach growl over the music.

Not long after he had entered, a woman with huge breasts and a lazy eye grabbed Loras' arm from behind and swung him around to face her. "Hey 'der, shoog," she said as she raised her hand to lift the hood off of Loras' face. Loras smacked her hand away before she could touch him. Frightened, he looked around to see if anyone had seen him strike the woman. Nobody had noticed. Or if they had, no one had cared.

"Fine, ya bastard! Have it yer way!" said the woman, feigning offense. "Was just tryin' to be friendly. Now yous don't get any of Miss Molly." She formed her lips into a pout, then turned and stuck her rump out at Loras as she waddled away.

Loras looked around. Luckily, his little interaction with Miss Molly did not seem to have garnered any extra attention. *That was close,* he thought. He quickly found an empty table in the corner of the tavern and sat down. Slouching over the table, he pulled his hood further over his head; far enough to shadow his face but not so far that he couldn't spot someone approaching. In fact, he hoped someone *would* approach him; someone offering food, not... whatever Miss Molly was offering.

Loras waited for a few minutes, but nobody came to his table. His stomach was roaring, and at this point he considered getting up and walking to the bar to order something to eat. But, before he did, a man in a dingy apron with a dirty towel slung over his shoulder approached his table. He was the ugliest man Loras had ever seen. He only had hair on one side of his head. The other side was marred by a gruesome scar that must have opened his skull at one point. Loras didn't know how anyone could have survived an injury that would have caused a scar like that. The answer may have been in the man's eyes. They were an impossibly bright shade of blue and conveyed an animalistic fierceness. Loras was both in awe and terrified of this man.

"Ya gonna sit 'ere all night or ya gonna order somethin'," said the waif.

"What do you have to eat?" asked Loras without raising his head.

"Food," answered the waif. Loras considered asking for a more detailed menu but thought better of it.

"That sounds good. I'll take it."

The waif grunted and then went into the kitchen. A few minutes later, he re-emerged with a plate of steaming meat. There were also a couple of lumpy vegetables that Loras didn't recognize and a hunk of crusty bread. Loras could smell the meal as the waif approached. His mouth began to water. The waif began to set the plate in front of Loras and then pulled it back.

"Ya got money?" he asked.

Loras' stomach immediately stopped churning and turned into a pit of stone. He hadn't even considered money. His hunger had clouded his brain. Unfortunately, he was pretty sure that this waif didn't take credit. He also got the sense that the waif wasn't going to take that plate of meat back without exacting some sort of payment for his time and effort.

The only thing for Loras to do was to make a run for it, but he could see that the waif was just waiting for him to make a move. His electric blue eyes were almost daring Loras to jump from his seat. Then, suddenly, two coins dropped onto the table in front of Loras.

"Fer his, and one 'fer me too if ya be so kind, Miles," said a voice from behind Loras. The waif gave a familiar nod to the man standing behind Loras and then dropped the plate unceremoniously on the table before returning to the kitchen.

"Der's no doubt about it now. You are absolutely da *dumbest* floater I've ever known," said Declin as he plopped down next to Loras.

"You've mentioned that before," said Loras, a little relieved that he hadn't been struck on the back of the head by the waif's walking stick.

"What the 'ell are you doing out of da cave?"

"I couldn't stay in there. It was too hard to breathe. I just needed to get out."

"Well dat's da floater in ya, dat is. Yer gonna 'ave to learn to live wit dat like da others 'ave. Better to suffer a bit of discomfort 'dan to be spotted out 'ere by someone lookin' to make a profit," Declin leaned in close to Loras' hooded face, "and 'dey are *all* lookin' to make a profit."

"And what about you?" asked Loras. "Aren't you looking to make a profit?"

Declin grinned and took one of the pieces of meat off of Loras' plate. "Always," he said as he pulled the meat from the bone with his teeth. "But my compersation ain't no concern of yers."

"Why wouldn't it be?" asked Loras. "You, yourself, admit that everyone out here can be bought. Why should we trust you? What's in it for you?"

"Let's just say dat my motivations lie in 'tings other than money," said Declin as he took another bite. "And you've got bigger problems dan dat to worry 'bout right now."

"I know," said Loras dejectedly. "Can you help me get back to the Hole? Maybe Gracien won't find out that I've left."

"Dat's not yer problem," replied Declin. He pointed to the door. "Dat is."

Loras looked up. There, having just entered the tavern, stood Xander with three dripping-wet Gartune.

Loras instinctively began to get up but Declin grabbed his arm before he could rise from his chair. "Don't move," said Declin. He continued to chomp away at Loras' food as if he hadn't a care in the world. "Dey 'aven't spotted ya. Just act natural and keep yer 'ead down. Here," he slid the plate over to Loras. "Eat somethin'."

Loras reached for a piece of meat, but his hand was shaking so terribly that he pulled it back and hid it under the table. He suddenly became very aware of how much light was in the room. He slouched further down in his chair.

"What are they doing?" whispered Loras.

"Dey just sat down at a table across 'da room. Looks like dey are 'ere to eat too. What a bit o' luck, eh?"

"Luck? You think it's lucky that they happened to come into the same place as me?!"

"Na, I 'tink its lucky dat dey are 'ere fer dinner and not fer you."

"So what do we do?" whispered Loras.

"Nothin' we can do, 'sept to wait fer dem to go." At this point, Miles returned with the second plate of food Declin had ordered. He dropped the plate on the table and gave Declin a knowing look while nodding in the Gartune's direction. Declin nodded back but said nothing. Miles returned to the bar.

"He knows who I am, doesn't he?" whispered Loras at a volume that he immediately regretted.

"'Course he knows," replied Declin.

"Then we have to get out of here before he turns us in!"

"He ain't turnin' no one in."

"How do you know? Isn't he looking for... compensation?"

"Oh he's lookin' for compersation all right. Him more 'dan most. But it's a different sort of 'compersation dat Miles is lookin' fer." Loras was confused but decided not to press the issue.

Loras and Declin sat in silence for the next twenty minutes, eating their dinner. Loras eventually calmed down enough to the point where he could grab his food without shaking. His stomach thanked him for his bravery. As his hunger subsided, he calmed a bit more. It was obvious that the Gartune were not interested in anything other than their own food and drink. A few of the less mannish-looking ladies purposefully sauntered past their table. It wasn't long before two of the

Gartune had a lady bouncing on each knee. Xander watched his companions and smiled.

An hour passed before it looked as if the Gartune were ready to leave. Xander instructed the two Gartune with the lady friends to say goodnight to their companions. They did, reluctantly. One irritated Gartune gulped down a last mug of ale and stood up from the table. As soon as they got up, they froze. Something at the door had captured their attention. Xander had his back to the entrance, so one of the Gartune tapped him on the shoulder. As the prince turned, his eyes immediately widened.

Back at the table in the far corner of the tavern, Declin poked Loras in the side to alert him. Loras looked up from his meal and choked.

There, in the doorway, stood Tinko and Regan.

CHAPTER NINETEEN
Trapped

Loras felt his heart sink into his stomach. He watched in horror as his sister and Tinko quickly spotted the group of Gartune sitting next to the door. They froze as Xander rose slowly in his chair, a smile growing on his face.

"See, Belkore, I told you that this was the best tavern in the city," said Xander. "Absolutely, *everyone* comes here."

"Indeed," replied Belkore malevolently.

Loras began to panic. He didn't know what to do. Sensing, probably, that the young Reytana was about to do something foolish, Declin placed his hand on Loras' arm. "Stay put," he whispered. Loras obeyed.

Tinko and Regan began to slowly creep back toward the door behind them. Belkore laughed.

"*Please*, try to make a run for it," Belkore sneered. "I've been waiting for some fun." Tinko and Regan stopped their retreat.

Nervously, they began to scan the tavern, searching for something that could help them. Regan found the huddled shape of her brother sitting in the corner of the room. Their gazes met for an instant, then she quickly looked away. But in that instant, Regan's eyes had betrayed her. Xander saw the look of recognition on her face. With his eyes locked on Regan, he waved over his shoulder to Loras' table.

"Why don't you come join us, Loras," shouted Xander. "You've been anti-social long enough. It's time to join the party." Loras' heart sank further into his stomach. *He knew I was here the whole time.* "Bring your friend too," said Xander. His eyes were still locked on Regan.

Cautiously, Loras and Declin rose from their table and walked over to the Gartune. The few patrons left in the tavern were silent. The music had stopped. The only sound was the slow tap of Declin's walking stick as he approached the grinning Gartune.

"Well now," said Xander. "You two left the city so abruptly that I haven't had a chance to talk to you since your... *discovery.* Kind of rude, don't you think? After all, I thought we were friends." Though his tone was thick with sarcasm, Loras thought he detected a hint of sincerity in the last part.

"Friends don't send out search parties to capture their friends," responded Regan. Belkore took a step toward the Reytana girl, but Xander waved his eüroc in front of his companion's chest.

"Careful," said Xander to Regan. "We are not in your kitchen in Reysa. And Dario is not here to help you."

Dario, thought Loras. The image of the Reytana governor charging into Xander's search party flashed in Loras' mind. It was the first time that he had thought of the governor since they had left Reysa. So much had happened since then that their time with Dario seemed like an eternity ago, even though it was only a few days past. He wondered if the old governor was still alive.

"What happened to him?" demanded Loras. "Did you kill him?"

"Would you have liked that?" asked Xander. A few days ago, Loras would have. Much had changed since then. "No, he's not dead... at least he wasn't when I left him," continued Xander. "Although I fear that the man in charge of his incarceration does not share my affinity for the old boy. Reysa may soon be in need of a new governor."

Loras' blood began to boil. The same heat he had felt when he first received his light began to permeate throughout his body. He clenched his fists at his sides as sweat began to bead on his forehead.

Damnar and Damina could see the rage building in the Reytana teen and they both clutched their eürocs, sensing that a fight was imminent. Belkore turned to face Loras as well, his violet eyes gleaming with anticipation.

"You better learn to control that fire inside of you, Loras, before it gets you in trouble." said Xander, coolly. "I don't want your sister to have to watch you bleed."

"Stop it! Both of you," shouted Regan. "Nobody is going to fight, ok. You've got us. You won. Now what?"

"Now," said Xander, "we take you back to Gartol." Damnar and Damina quickly glanced at Belkore, who responded with a quick shake of his head.

"Why?" asked Tinko. It was the first time he dared to speak. "Why not take us back to Reysa?"

"Because, my robust little friend, the king wishes to speak with you."

"But we haven't done anything wrong!" pled Tinko. Xander bent down to look the panicked teen right in the face.

"You don't really believe that, do you? I thought you were the smart one."

Tinko tried to answer but Xander had heard enough from the Reysene. "No more questions from you," said Xander and he shoved Tinko over to Damnar's grasp. "We have a long trip ahead of us and you're already giving me a headache.

"You—" Xander pointed at Declin. "You're coming with us too." As he said this, he reached for the gimpy waif but, to his surprise, the waif deftly side-stepped his grasp.

"I'm gonna have to disagree with ya 'der," said Declin calmly.

"It was not a request!" shouted Belkore as he stormed toward the waif. This time, Xander did not stop him. Belkore reached out with both hands but again, Declin showed surprising quickness for a man with a gimp leg and side-stepped the oncoming Gartune. As he did so, he swept his walking stick under Belkore's back foot, sending him tripping into the table behind him. Glass and porcelain burst into hundreds of sharp pieces and the contents of the table went flying all over the floor. Belkore immediately collected himself and turned around furiously. But as soon as he did, he was tackled to the ground by a charging Loras. Once on top, Loras began swinging wildly at the Gartune pinned beneath him. He landed a few glancing blows before Belkore threw Loras off with a ferocious shove. Loras went tumbling backwards and was caught from behind by Xander, who grasped Loras' arms behind his back in a painful lock. Loras struggled, but it merely made Xander's grip tighter. He continued to squirm only to show Xander that he would not relent, but Loras knew that he was caught. Meanwhile, the other three Gartune began to circle Declin.

"If you're smart, you'll tell your friend to surrender before he gets hurt," said Xander in Loras' ear.

"I think it might be the other way around," responded Loras, still squirming in Xander's vice-like grip.

"Ha," laughed Xander. "I guess we're about to find out."

Declin stood calmly at the center of the circling Gartune. Their eyes were fixed on the unassuming waif. They would not be out-manuevered this time. Damnar made a quick jab toward the waif to try to get him to jump back, but Declin stood still. Then Damina rushed a few steps forward to see if Declin would react, but again, he did not move.

"I told ya's before," said Declin calmly. "I ain't goin with ya. You's can keep dancing around all ya like, but it ain't gonna change 'tings."

"You may be quick with your little stick, old man. But you're no match for the three of us," snarled Belkore.

"Nope," replied Declin, "but 'dey are."

Declin's gaze shifted towards the tavern door where Regan and Tinko were still standing. The Gartune had stopped paying attention to them ever since Declin sent Belkore sprawling. Now all four Gartune looked back at the same time. Tinko and Regan were still there, but they were not alone. Standing behind them was Gracien and six other Reytana.

Before the Gartune had time to react, ray blades sprang from the palms of Gracien and his companions. The Reytana then leapt over Regan and Tinko. Gracien landed in front of Xander and quickly swiped at him with his fiery blade. Xander barely reacted in time, blocking the swing with his eüroc, and in doing so, freed Loras from his grasp. Two other Reytana landed on top of Belkore, pinning him to the ground. The other four Reytana landed smoothly in a circle around Damnar and Damina. With the tables now turned, the twins leaned up against each other back-to-back in a defensive position.

Meanwhile, Xander regained his composure and began sparring with Gracien. Sparks flew from Gracien's sword as it collided with Xander's staff. Several times Gracien nearly landed a devastating blow to Xander's body but was deflected by a quick defensive maneuver. An equal number of times Gracien was nearly struck but managed to avoid the blow. The two danced through the tavern, colliding with chairs, tables and the occasional waif as they each tried to gain the upper hand. However, it was not long before Belkore was restrained and Damnar and Damina were overpowered by the remaining Reytana. Once his companions were subdued, Xander could see that the fight was lost. He swore bitterly and held up his hands in surrender.

"Nice to see you haven't gotten rusty during your vacation," said Xander as he allowed Gracien to tie his hands behind his back. "We should continue this sometime, just you and I."

"Make sure their restraints are tight," said Gracien as he tied off Xander. He then began barking orders at the other Reytana.

"You three scout the nearby buildings to see if there are any other Gartune in the area. You two stand guard over the prisoners. I don't want to hear a sound out of any of them." Gracien looked directly at Xander when he said this. Xander, in turn, gave him a little mock bow.

"And somebody go find Miles," ordered Gracien.

The Reytana grouped the four Gartune in the corner of the tavern and made them sit against the wall while Gracien waited for the bartender to return. Loras ran to his sister and Tinko and embraced them.

"What are you two doing here?" he exclaimed as he wiped a stray tear that had somehow leaked from his eye.

"We came looking for you! What are *you* doing here?!" replied Regan.

"I thought we were gonna die!" interjected Tinko.

"I... I was hungry... and then I saw Declin..." stammered Loras. "Wait, how did you get out of the cave?"

"Well, when we couldn't find you, we went and found Gracien," replied Regan.

"I thought we were gonna die!" repeated Tinko, clearly in a daze.

"Wait – you *told* on me?" said Loras.

"We thought you were in danger!"

"I can't believe you told on me!" exclaimed Loras.

"You're lucky she did," said Gracien as he walked over to where the teens were huddled. "If she hadn't, you would have been on your way to Gartol right now."

Loras could see that Gracien was more than a little annoyed. He expected to get another firm hand on the shoulder from the Reytana, but this time he got a finger jabbed into his chest. "Several people have risked their lives in order to bring you here, Loras." Gracien's normally calm voice rose with every word. "More people than you know. And you would throw away all of their sacrifices, why? Because you couldn't sleep? Just because you have no regard for your own life doesn't mean that you can be so careless with it! It is time that you grew up and started thinking about somebody other than yourself. You are no longer a child. You are a Reytana. Your life is valuable and it's time that you learned that."

Loras bowed his head in shame. He knew that Gracien was right. Even though the reprimand hadn't really been directed at them, Tinko and Regan bowed their heads as well. The three teens sheepishly sat down at a table and kept to themselves while Gracien sought out Declin.

"Once again, we are in your debt," said Gracien, upon locating the waif.

"I'm keepin' count, ya know," replied Declin. ""Dis is goin on yer tab."

Gracien smiled for the first time. "I have no doubt. Thank you, old friend."

Declin mumbled something to himself as he walked over to join the teens at their table. They were too embarrassed to look him in the eye. They knew that Declin was one of the people that had risked their lives for them, and on more than one occasion. Declin gave a tired sigh, smacked Loras on the back of the head and then slumped down in a chair next to him.

"Did you know that we had been spotted?" whispered Loras to Declin.

"Not fer certain, but I had a feelin'," answered Declin. He nodded in the direction of Xander. "'Dat one may play sometimes, but he's no fool. I reckon he spotted you's the minute he walked in."

"Then why didn't you say something?" asked Loras.

"I did. Just not to you," replied Declin.

"*The bartender*..." said Loras. "You sent him for help."

"Ay, but lucky for you, help was already on da way." He grinned across the table at Regan and Tinko. "You two needs to do a better job of lookin' after 'dis one. Ol' Declin ain't always gonna be here to pull his ass out of da fire."

"No," said Loras. "It's not their job to look after me. Gracien is right. I need to be more careful." He looked at his sister and Tinko. "I'm sorry. Honestly, I am. Things have just been happening so fast and I haven't been thinking straight."

Regan and Tinko were dumbstruck. Loras had never apologized for anything in his entire life and he could see that his sudden display of maturity had staggered his companions. Eventually, their astonishment subsided and Regan moved to sit beside her brother.

"It's ok. Just promise me that from here on out we stay together."

"I promise," answered Loras.

"And promise to be more careful!" added Tinko. "I thought we were gonna die!"

"I promise, Tink" said Loras, smiling at his friend. Suddenly Miles the bartender appeared from behind the bar.

"'Dat's good, because 'tings are just startin' to get interestin'. Word has spread tru da city. Everyone knows a bunch of diggers and floaters just had it out in my bar."

"Then we need to get moving," said Gracien.

"Dat may be a bit tricky," said Miles. "She's here."

Declin moaned and rubbed his temple with both of his hands. Loras was confused.

"Who is here?" he whispered to Declin.

"Da sister," he replied.

"Whose sister?" asked Loras.

Declin pointed a finger at Xander.

CHAPTER TWENTY
Snare

Septa disliked Woodhaven only slightly less than Spirea. It had the same smell; the same texture. There was the same overarching theme of avarice mixed with poverty. Yet, the waifs in Woodhaven were different. Or, at least they acted differently when they saw her. Whereas the citizens of Spirea hadn't given her a second look when she entered their city, the waifs in Woodhaven were actively avoiding her. More than a dozen had crossed to the other side of the street or ducked in a nearby building when they saw her. Several doors and windows had shut as she approached. Taverns fell silent when she entered.

It appears that word travels fast in these woods, thought Septa. *Perhaps these waifs will not require any lessons in obedience. That should make finding this Declin all the easier.*

Septa entered several taverns before she came to the one run by Miles. She had interrogated each bartender she had met, and each one had regurgitated the same story without needing coercion. There was a fight somewhere at the end of town. They didn't know who was involved, but they heard there may have been Tormada. That was the extent of the town folk's knowledge. When she had asked about Declin, everyone knew the man but wasn't sure of his current whereabouts. Septa had accepted their stories. The unmistakable fear in their voices was all the verification that she needed.

Methodically, Septa inspected each bar, brothel and tavern as she moved towards the edge of town. The hostess at the previous establishment was all too eager to inform her that Declin often frequented the place next door, and that Septa should go there immediately.

When Septa entered Miles' tavern, it was empty except for the ugly waif behind the bar. She walked directly to the bartender. Miles was quietly and deliberately wiping down some empty beer glasses. He did not look up at the Gartune standing in front of him. Something about his behavior reminded Septa of another waif bartender she had recently met.

"Do you know why I'm here?" asked Septa.

"Aye," said Miles without looking up.

"And do you know what I do to those who lie to me?"

Miles gritted his teeth together. "I've heard."

"Good. Then I'm only going to ask this once. Where is Declin?"

"Don't know who dat is," answered Miles.

Septa smiled. *Finally,* she thought.

"How long have you lived in Woodhaven?" she asked as she slowly walked around to the other side of the bar.

"Long as I can 'member," answered Miles as he continued to clean the glass in front of him. It was the same one he had been working on since Septa entered the room.

"Interesting," said Septa. She now stood directly next to the waif. "You've lived here that long and you don't know who

Declin is? Every other waif that I've talked to in this town seems to know him. How is it that he has escaped your acquaintance?" Miles didn't answer.

Septa placed the tip of her eüroc under Miles' chin and slowly lifted the bartender's head. "You know what I think?" she asked coolly. Miles did not answer. "I think you're lying to me, waif. And there's only one reason that you would lie to me. You know where he is."

Again, Miles said nothing.

"And, you know what I do to waifs that lie to me." Septa pressed the button on her eüroc and a blood-stained blade sprung from the tip of her staff. She pressed the blade up against Miles' neck. The bartender closed his eyes and held his breath. Septa waited. Miles began to shake. Finally, he couldn't take it anymore.

"Wait!" cried Miles. "I'll tell ya where he is. Just put dat 'ting down."

"You're not as brave as you look, bartender. But maybe you're smarter. You're not going to tell me where he is. You're going to *take* me. Then I will decide how much punishment you require."

"Aye," replied Miles as he let out a deep breath. Septa removed the blade from underneath the bartender's neck and the two of them walked out of the tavern.

Miles slowly led them through the city with Septa following two strides behind, the tip of her eüroc pressed to the small of his back. The streets were deserted. These waifs knew when to hide. Occasionally, she saw a little head peek around a darkened window as they passed, but then immediately ducked out of site when she looked in that direction. It didn't take long for the two to reach the gap in the city fence that led to the forest. Septa pushed Miles through first, then, after taking a cautious look behind her, followed the waif into the woods.

The forest was pitch black except for a few places where the moonlight penetrated the canopy above. But even in the darkness, Miles navigated the woods with ease. He and Septa walked in silence for nearly twenty minutes. Every once in a while, she would poke the waif with her eüroc just to let him know that she was still behind him. That, and she enjoyed making him squirm.

"I'm going to give you a chance to lessen your punishment," said Septa. "On my way to your tavern I heard someone talking about a fight between some Tormada. You wouldn't happen to know anything about that would you? Remember—I know when you're lying."

"Aye," replied Miles.

"'Aye, what?" said Septa.

"Aye, der was a fight," said Miles.

"Was it between Tormada?" asked Septa.

"Aye, it was" replied Miles.

Septa reached out with her eüroc and stopped the bartender in his tracks. "Which color were they?" she asked.

"Both," said Miles.

"There were *Reytana* in the city?!"

"Aye," said Miles.

"You're positive," said Septa.

"I know my colors." said Miles. "There was four of your kind and den 'bout half dozen floaters showed up."

"And you know this, how?" asked Septa.

"'Cause dey were in my bar."

Septa picked the waif up by the neck and shoved him against a tree. "You fool! You thought you could keep that information from me and I wouldn't find out?!"

"No," coughed Miles as he struggled for air. "Was just 'waitin."

"Waiting for what?!" yelled Septa.

"Fer 'dis,"

Septa's legs suddenly swung out from underneath her and were pulled over her head. A rope tightened around her feet as it pulled her up into the air. Septa's eüroc fell to the ground as she hung upside-down, suspended from a tree branch. She flailed her arms wildly as she grasped for the waif, but he was a good three feet below her reach.

"Dat should just about do it," said a voice from behind the tree. "Just let me tie dis off real good, 'den we can have a bit of palaver." Two arms reached around the tree and tied off the end of the rope to secure the swinging Gartune. Once that was done, Declin stepped out in front.

"You 'ave any trouble bringin' 'er 'ere?" asked Declin.

"Nah," said Miles. "Went about as we tought it would. Da funny 'ting was 'dat she was actually lookin' for *you*."

"*Fer me?*" Declin looked incredulously up at the Gartune swinging above him. "You's got a bunch of floaters an' diggers tearin' up da city and you's came lookin' fer *me*? Who da 'ell woulda told her about me? Wait..." he turned to Miles.

"Ya better watch what ya say next," said Miles as he bent over to pick up Septa's eüroc, "before you goes accusin' a dead man of what you knows he didn't do."

"Ay," said Declin. "I knows your brotha better 'dan dat, rest his soul." Declin gave Septa an accusatory look. "He wouldn't 'ave sold me out. But I'll bet ya somebody else in dat damn city bent their tongue." Declin yelled up at Septa. "So, what'd it take? A few coins? A lady for da night? How much to sell out ol' Declin?"

"Oh, it was cheaper than that," said Septa as she slowly swung above the two waifs. "It only cost him his hand... then his head."

"Ha," grunted Declin. "Don't seem like a very fair deal."

"I don't hear him complaining," said Septa.

"Ya, he wouldn't would he," grumbled Declin. "And on 'dat subject, I believe da two of you's have some business to discuss. So I will leave ya to it. You's can take it from 'ere?"

"Aye," said Miles as he patted the eüroc in his hand. "I'm good. You goin' to meet up with da rest of dem floaters?"

"Yar. Looks like I 'ave to now dat DA WHOLE WORLD KNOWS ABOUT ME!" he yelled above him.

"Well, have fun wit dat," said Miles.

"You too," said Declin with a wry grin. "'Member she's a lady now and should be treated as such."

"Oh I'll treat her as she deserves," replied Miles. Declin winked at his friend and disappeared into the forest, leaving Miles alone with Septa. Miles circled his suspended prey a few times, patting the eüroc curiously as he did so. The tree branch creaked slightly under the weight of the Gartune swinging slowly beneath it.

"You will be punished severely for this, waif," said Septa. "I was going to kill you quickly, but now I am going to take my time."

"Seems to me like you ain't in no position to be offerin' threats at da moment," said Miles. He prodded the eüroc searching for the special button that sprung the blade. Then, with a click, he found it. "Ah, der it is!" exclaimed Miles with delight. "Quite da contraptions, 'dese sticks of yours. I'm not sure if I'd rather 'ave one of 'dese or light shootin' out my ass like da floaters." He twirled the staff between his two hands in a clumsy figure eight motion. "I 'tink I like 'dese better."

He stomped the staff into the ground. Nothing happened. Septa laughed mockingly from above. "Stupid waif," she said. "You think a torman can make the ground shake like a Gartune? That staff is useless in your hands."

"Not entirely useless," said Miles. He waived the eüroc in front of Septa's face. The blade came inches from cutting her. Septa's violet eyes glared down at the waif.

"Do that again and it will be the last thing you do."

"Again wit' 'da threats from someone hangin' upside-down," chuckled Miles. Then his face turned serious.

"'Ave ya figured out who I am, yet?" he asked.

"You're a dirty little waif that runs a dirty little bar in a dirty little town."

"Aye," replied Miles. "It just so happens dat I 'ave a brotha who is a dirty little waif dat runs a dirty little bar in a dirty little town not far from 'ere."

"Why am I not surprised," said Septa. "I'm guessing your whole family runs a string of dirty little bars all over these woods."

"Nah, just da one," replied Miles. "'An' he don't run dat one no more."

"On account of him drinking all of his profits?" said Septa.

"On 'count of you choppin' his 'ead off!" screamed Miles. As he said this, he swung the eüroc violently at Septa. But he was not toying with her this time. This swing had but one purpose—to avenge his brother's death.

Septa was ready for the attack. She quickly raised her head to avoid the blade, then spun around in the air and grabbed the eüroc as it sliced through her hanging hair. Jet-black hair fell onto Miles' upturned face. Septa let out a yell as she hacked through the rope that was suspending her from the tree, flipping through the air and landing on her feet in one fell swoop. Miles stumbled backwards in shock. The turn of events had taken only seconds.

"I told you if you tried that again, it would be the last thing you did," said Septa as she strode menacingly toward the waif. "Do you know what the difference is between me and you, waif?"

Miles did not answer, so Septa did for him.

"*I* do not lie."

Moonlight reflected off of metal for an instant as Septa's eüroc sliced through the night air. A second later, Miles' lifeless eyes were staring up at her from the ground. His body was three feet away.

"Ah, now I see the family resemblance," said Septa as she used one of Miles' pant legs to wipe the blood off her eüroc.

CHAPTER TWENTY-ONE
Revenge

It is not easy to traverse a forest with a bag over your head, as Damnar and Damina were quickly finding out. Without any direction or word of guidance, the twins stumbled ahead of their captors through the dense maze of trees. If they stopped, they received a stern "keep moving!" and a prod in the back with a stick. They mumbled to themselves under their hoods, but not loud enough to elicit any further reprimands from their Reytana guards. And so, the bound twins trudged through the forest, hitting tree after tree and tripping over root after root; not knowing where they were going or when they would get there.

Belkore fared slightly better. He, too, struck many a tree and bush, but he insisted on plowing through them in a forceful straight line rather than tentatively trying to avoid them like the twins. He scraped off tree bark with a loud grunt; stubbed his toes over and over again, but he did not let that hinder his pace.

It was as if the forest was his enemy now and he was battling every combatant that got in his way. The only time Belkore had to stop was when he finally hit a tree squarely in the face and was unable to scrape off of its side. Instead, he took two wobbly steps backward, lowered his head and kicked the base of the massive tree as hard as he could, then emitted a yowl that sounded more animal than man. A swift prod in the back and a "keep moving!" set Belkore walking forward again.

"You'll have to excuse him," said Xander as he plodded forward in the middle of the group. "You know how they say when some people lose one sense, their others are enhanced to compensate? Well I'm afraid it's the opposite with Belkore." Belkore grunted then hit another tree.

"Always with the jokes," replied Loras. "Doesn't your mouth ever take a break?"

"Is that you, Loras?" asked Xander. "I'm sorry but I can't hear too well with this bag over my head. Perhaps you can come over and remove it so we can have a proper conversation."

"How stupid do you think I am?" said Loras.

"I'm assuming that was rhetorical?" replied Xander.

Loras started to turn towards Xander's direction but Tinko held him back. "He's just trying to get under your skin," said Tinko. "And you're letting him."

Loras scowled at Xander, who, of course, could not see him. Then he fell back in line with his companions. They all had to wait a second for Damnar and Damina to gather themselves after a particularly knobby tree root claimed both of their ankles.

"Cheer up, Loras," Xander continued. "You should be happy. Things could have gone much worse for you back there. Learn to enjoy the upper hand. You will soon find that it doesn't last for very long."

"If yer referrin' to yer sista, I'm 'fraid I 'ave some bad news for ya," said a winded Declin as he emerged from the trees behind the group.

"How did it go?" asked Gracien.

"'Bout as ya thought it would," replied Declin. "She showed up not long after you's all left. Went straight fer Miles, and you's shoulda seen da face dat he put on. Oooh boy! He had 'er sold from da moment she entered da bar. Led 'er straight out to our little trap, he did."

"So it's done," said Gracien.

"Ya, by now it oughta be."

"What do you mean it *oughta be*?" said Gracien.

"Well I left Miles to 'ave a bit o' fun wit 'er. After all, he had some compersation to collect for 'is brotha."

"You left him alone with her?" Gracien stopped walking and looked directly at the waif. Xander began to laugh underneath his hood.

"I have bad news for you my little gimpy friend," said Xander. "That bartender is dead. And soon, you will be too, seeing as how you've led her straight to us."

"You were supposed to take care of her before you returned!" said Gracien who was whispering now but in an angry tone.

"Relax, you giant pipkin," said Declin. "When I left 'er she was swingin' from a tree and Miles 'ad 'er weapon in 'is 'ands."

"Then those hands are probably no longer attached to his body," quipped Xander.

"Quiet!" whispered Gracien. "Everyone, get down and be still!" He motioned with his arms for everyone to get low. Damnar, Damina and Belkore were abruptly pulled to the ground. Nobody made a sound. Gracien listened intently as he scanned the forest but all he could hear were the nimbers and pipkins chatting away in the trees.

"If she doesn't want you to hear her, you won't hear her," said Xander. Nobody moved. Everyone looked at Gracien to see what their next move should be.

"We're almost to the Hole," whispered one of the Reytana to Gracien. "Why don't we just make a run for it? It's not like she's going to attack the entire base by herself."

"I wouldn't be so sure of that," said Xander.

"No," replied Gracien. "We cannot reveal the location of the base. If she's out there, she's probably following us right now, hoping that we lead her to our hideout. No... we have to find her. And we have to find her now."

"But I told ya—" started Declin but he was cut off.

"If she's dead then we have nothing to worry about," said Gracien. "But we have to assume she's still alive. I want you to go back to where you left Miles and find out for sure."

Declin frowned but acquiesced. "If dats what its gonna take to quiet your little pipkin 'eart, den so be it." He turned and set back out toward the direction he had come from. Gracien shouted after him.

"Be careful, Declin. She's not like these ones."

"Ya, I know, I know," and Declin disappeared into the forest.

"Now, the two of you—" Gracien pointed at two of the Reytana soldiers, "Tie the four of them together around that tree. You will stand guard here with Loras, Regan and Tinko."

"Let me come with you!" pleaded Loras. "It's my fault that we're all in this mess. At least let me help get us out of it."

"You are helping," said Gracien, "by guarding the prisoners."

"How am I supposed to guard them without a weapon? What if his sister comes? Am I just supposed to throw rocks at her?"

Gracien thought for a moment then unraveled the armband off of his right forearm. At the end of the band was a small pad that he placed into Loras' palm. He then wrapped the band several times around Loras' arm. Once it touched his skin, the band glowed with an intense golden light. Gracien raised his eyebrows, impressed. The light traveled the length of the band until it reached the pad in the palm of Loras' hand. Loras pulled his hand back as if he had been shocked.

"It's energized," said Gracien. "You'll get used to the sensation. Now, clench your fingers over the pad and make a fist, as if you were squeezing a ball." Slowly, Loras closed his hand over the pad. As soon as he began to squeeze, a small circle of light shot out from his fist. The harder he squeezed, the larger the circle became until it formed a full, glowing shield of light energy.

"*Wicked,*" exclaimed Tinko. "Do I get one?" Both Loras and Gracien gave him a look.

"Just kidding..." said Tinko sheepishly. "I guess I just have to wait until I get *my* light... randomly... in the street... three weeks after I turn eighteen..."

Loras unclenched his fist and the shield disappeared. He walked over and clapped his pouting friend on the shoulder. "You never know," Loras said as he smiled at his friend. It wasn't the cocky, sarcastic smile that Loras had flashed so many times in the past at Tinko. It was a genuine smile. One that said *I really do hope you receive the light someday.*

"Don't you want to see what else it can do?" said Gracien to Loras.

"*The ray blade!*" exclaimed Loras as his eyes lit up.

"This one is a bit more difficult," said Gracien. "Here, give me your hand." He took Loras' hand and brought the tips of his thumb and index finger together. He then curled the rest of his fingers to match the arc of the index finger. "Hold your hand up and pretend like you're doing a pull-up, but with one hand."

Loras held his hand up in the air. He felt slightly foolish, grasping at nothing, but was too excited to care.

"Now," said Gracien, "tap your pinky finger to the pad." Loras did so and a beam of light shot out of his hand so fast that he nearly fell down. A couple of Reytana chuckled. Gracien smiled. "And that is why I always have the rookies hold their hand up in the air the first time," he said. "If you would have been pointing that the wrong way, you could have put a hole in yourself." Loras looked over at Tinko, his eyes full of wonder.

"Still want one of these, Tink?"

"I think I'll let you hold onto that one for me," replied Tinko. "I'm good."

"I wish I could give you some training, but there is no time," said Gracien. "Only use that if you absolutely have to. Do you understand?"

"Yes, sir," replied Loras. He let go of the pad with his finger and the ray blade disappeared into thin air.

"Good. Now, the rest of us are going to fan out and look for Septa." Gracien motioned to the other Reytana. "If any of you find her, do not attempt to engage her by yourself. Call for help and we will be there as soon as we can. Understood?"

"Yes, sir," they all replied.

"The rest of you," he nodded back at Loras and the prisoners, "stay down and stay quiet. If we don't return in one hour, head straight for the Hole and don't look back. We'll meet you there."

"Yes, sir," replied the other two Reytana.

Gracien's group disappeared into the woods as the remaining Reytana finished up tying the four Gartune prisoners to the base of the tree. Damnar and Damina slid to the ground and let out a sigh of relief now that their blind journey had ceased. Belkore and Xander remained standing. Belkore struggled stubbornly with his restraints while Xander leaned casually against the tree trunk.

"Seeing as how we aren't moving and are in no danger of seeing your secret lair, do you think we could take these hoods off?" asked Xander.

"Gracien didn't say we could take them off," answered one of the Reytana.

"He didn't say you *couldn't* take them off either," replied Xander. "Come on, just for a few minutes. The big guy here is about to suffocate." Belkore continued to struggle with his restraints and the fabric around his mouth was indeed pocketing in and out quite quickly now.

"It's okay, you can take them off," said Regan. The Reytana guards looked like they were about to protest, but the look she gave them somehow convinced them to do as she said. Tinko watched, dumbfounded, as the Reytana obeyed Regan and removed the bags over the prisoners' heads.

"How did you do that?" whispered Tinko to Regan. She just shrugged. Meanwhile, Loras practiced summoning the ray blade and shield to mixed results. Sometimes he would summon a shield only a few inches in diameter. Then he would press the pad in his palm too hard and a ten foot shield would spring to life, burning a groove in the ground in front of him and slicing tree limbs overhead.

"I think we all would feel a lot safer if you gave that weapon over to your sister, Loras," said Xander. "We all know that she's the brave one in the family. Did she ever tell you about the day we met?"

"Nobody knows that story," said Regan, speaking for the first time since they left Woodhaven.

"Not even your brother?" asked Xander with genuine surprise.

"What story?" asked Loras.

"It's nothing," said Regan.

"I wouldn't call the toppling of an armed Gartune sentry *nothing*," replied Xander.

"You did *what?*" said Loras.

"He exaggerates," replied Regan.

"I do nothing of the sort," said Xander. "One of my sentries was mocking her by stepping on one of her groceries. She walked straight up to him, reached under his foot and pulled out the can that he was standing on. He was so surprised that he nearly fell over backwards. It was the bravest thing I've ever seen from a torman."

Loras looked incredulously at his sister. "Is that true?" Regan rolled her eyes but nodded.

"I told you," said Xander. "She's fearless."

"I was terrified," said Regan. "I'm no braver than anyone else here. And the last thing I want is that stupid ray blade."

"Hah," snorted Belkore. "Some warrior she is. Afraid to even carry a weapon."

"That's where you're wrong," replied Xander. "Some people need a sword in their hand to feel courage, but the bravest of all do not."

"Bravery is just an excuse to do stupid things and to hurt people," said Regan. "Perhaps if people weren't so *brave* then we wouldn't have so many wars."

"I agree, we should all lay down our weapons. Loras, you first!" said Xander.

"Over your dead body," replied Loras.

"And therein lies the problem," said Xander, turning back toward Regan. "Nobody will ever be the first to lay down their sword. That's just the way it is. It's the way it's always been. It's the reason the Tormada were created; why you and me and even Loras exist. The only real way to deter violence is with the threat of greater violence. The Gartune and Reytana are Torma's system of checks and balances. It's the way that things stay even."

"Funny," said Tinko, "things haven't seemed so even lately. And I'm pretty sure there's a giant shield over my home so that it stays that way."

"Ah, to be eighteen years old and to know everything," sighed Xander. "Tell me, since the shield has been up, how many Reysene have you seen killed?"

"What does that have to do with anything?" replied Tinko.

"Just answer the question," said Xander.

"Fine. None," said Tinko.

"Well that's strange," said Xander. "Because before the shield was up, I saw hundreds of Reysene killed. I also saw hundreds of Gartolians murdered. Tell me, have you ever seen a person get a hole burnt clear through their chest? Have you ever held a person in your arms only to have them disintegrate into thin air? Because that's what happens when a Tormada dies. Their aura evaporates into the sky and they literally disappear. Imagine your best friend, Loras, is standing right next to you one minute, and the next minute he is gone forever, leaving no trace behind that he had ever existed. No body to bury. Nothing to say goodbye to. Just gone. Have you ever seen anything like that?" Tinko didn't answer.

"No, of course you haven't. And do you know why? Because the shield is up, that's why. Because there's order. You may call it oppression, but the result is the same. So, go ahead, complain all you want about how horrible it is to live under the shield, but keep in mind that for your entire lives you have known nothing but peace, and that is more than any of the rest of us can say."

Nobody said anything for a few minutes. Eventually, Belkore started struggling with his ties again, earning him a swift kick from one of the Reytana guards. Loras began practicing with his light weapon again, changing it from sword to shield and back again. He started to get the hang of it. One of the Reytana called him a natural.

"Careful, his head might explode," said Tinko.

While the Reytana showed Loras a few tricks with his ray blade, Regan crept over to Xander's side of the tree and sat down across from him.

"What was his name?"

"Whose name?" asked Xander.

"You know who," she said. "Your friend that you watched die." Xander didn't answer right away. Finally, he sighed.

"His name was Lex," he said.

"When did he die?" asked Regan.

"On the first day of the war. A hovercraft's solar cannon hit him and ten others right in front of us. Only Belkore and I survived the shot." From the other side of the tree, Belkore grumbled something incoherent.

"Wait, you were in the war?" asked Regan. "But you hadn't received your metal yet. You couldn't have been more than seven... eight years old?"

"I was five," said Xander. "My father insisted that I *be present* during the battle. He didn't want me fighting... no, I was far too young for that. But he wanted me to watch; to witness the battle. He said the earlier I got a taste of war, the better."

"And your friend, was he also just there to watch?"

"No. He was older. A full-grown Gartune and one of the best." Xander's voice had lowered as he continued to speak until it was barely above a whisper. "And he wasn't my friend. He was my brother."

"I'm... I'm sorry," said Regan. She looked like she wanted to put her hand on his knee, but then thought better of it.

"My father told me to 'watch Lex if I wanted to see how a true son of Gar'on behaved.' I was to carry his gear and learn. That was it. It never even occurred to me that he could die. He was the best warrior I had ever seen. Even Septa couldn't defeat him.

"He was next in line," continued Xander. "He was supposed to command Reysa after the war, not me. You should consider yourself lucky. He did not share my congenial nature. He was much more like my sister. The two of them were inseparable."

"Was Septa there when he died?" asked Regan.

"No," replied Xander. "Just me. Father would not let her on the front lines, and it's probably best that she wasn't there."

"Why? As horrible as it might be, I know that if it were me and Loras was the one dying, I would want to be there. I would want to be with my brother."

"You don't understand. Septa did not take Lex's death *well.* Like I said, they were close. So close that I think she has been trying to avenge his death every day since he died. But, no. She did not see what I saw. The last thing I remember about my brother is his body dissolving between my fingers. It's an image that is forever burned into my brain. If Septa had been there to see Lex die, there wouldn't have been any army strong enough to keep her from throwing every man, woman and child over the cliffs of Reysa."

"And after all of that, you still think that war is a good thing?"

"I think it's a necessary thing," said Xander. "Only the naïve and foolish think otherwise, and you are neither."

"Right. I'm *brave.*"

"Bravery is an admirable quality. Why do you deny it in yourself?"

"I told you, bravery is overrated. I would rather be kind and tolerant than brave and intimidating," said Regan. Xander laughed and shook his head.

"Well, when the reign of Queen Regan begins and the enemy is at your gate, you can throw compliments and blow kisses at them. Let me know how that turns out."

"Maybe if I didn't *provoke them,* they wouldn't be at my gate," replied Regan.

"Tell you what," said Xander, "if we ever get back to Reysa, I will give you a shot at governor. Politics was never really my thing anyway. It'll be perfect; I get a vacation and you can put your 'hugs and butterflies' governing philosophy to the test. What do you say?"

"I say that for a minute, I thought there was more to you than a wise-cracking brute, but I guess I was wrong!" Regan stood up and stormed off to join Loras, Tinko and the other two Reytana.

"Lover's quarrel?" said a low, snake-like voice. It came from behind the tree that Regan had been sitting in front of.

"How long have you been there?" whispered Xander. There was a hint of fear in his voice.

"Long enough. It's so cute that you think you're the only one burdened with the memory of Lex's death. Well, I have news for you brother. I *was* there! I snuck out to the front lines when father wasn't looking, and I watched the whole thing! I know what *really* happened, coward! It is lucky that you have been in Reysa all these years. If I had known you were spreading these lies about our brother's death, I would have killed you a thousand times already!"

"Well then here is your chance!" said Xander. "I am defenseless! Avenge our brother's death!"

"Don't tempt me..." said Septa.

"Is that Septa?" whispered Belkore from the side of the tree. "It's about time! Cut us loose already!"

"Here," said Septa as she threw a sharp rock at Belkore's feet. "Cut yourself loose. I have work to do."

Septa emerged stealthily from her hiding place and crept up behind the spot where Regan and Tinko were standing. The two teens were watching Loras spar with the other two Reytana. He was a quick learner, so much so that he almost got the better of one of the older Reytana, a Tormada named Tao. Loras nearly side-swiped him with an outlandish jumping attack, but Tao quickly pivoted and deflected the younger Reytana, sending him sprawling on his back. Loras lay on his back, beaming ear to ear. "I almost had you!"

"Almost," smiled Tao as he lent a hand to lift Loras up off the ground. "But look where it landed you. Your move was creative, but risky. 'All or nothing' maneuvers like that can easily get you killed. It is better to be patient and let your opponent make the mistake rather than trying to land the death blow yourself."

"But what if there is no time to be patient?" asked Loras, dusting himself off.

"There is always time. Even when there isn't," replied Tao. Loras cocked his head sideways and gave the Reytana a bewildered look.

"Oh, that's going to throw him for a loop," whispered Tinko to Regan as they watched the pair square off again.

Meanwhile, Belkore quickly freed himself and the twins then he went to work on Xander's restraints while Damnar and Damina searched for their eürocs. As soon as he was free, Xander quickly crawled towards the sound of the Reytana sparring. Not far in front of him, he saw his sister doing the same. She crouched among the brush like a werkin stalking an unsuspecting nimber. Slowly, she closed the gap between her and the Reytana without making a single sound. Fifteen feet. Now ten feet away. Now five. She stopped and lifted her eüroc into an attack position. Her thumb slid to the base of the staff where she found a familiar button and pressed it. *Click.*

It was just loud enough.

Tinko turned around to investigate the sound and let out a quick gasp before he was struck on the head by the blunt end of the staff and immediately knocked unconscious. Regan screamed as her friend crumpled to the ground. As she bent down to try to catch Tinko, the blade side of Septa's eüroc swung centimeters over her head with a *swoosh*. Septa quickly recovered and planted her left knee into the chin of the kneeling Regan. Her limp body fell on top of Tinko.

"Spread out! Make a circle!" yelled Tao as he and the other Reytana separated in an attempt to surround Septa. Loras saw his sister fall and instinctively ran to her.

"Leave her!" yelled Tao. "Take the flank! Don't let her out of the middle!" Loras hesitated for a moment, but when he saw his sister's eyes flutter open, he stopped and took up his position as the Reytana had instructed.

Loras and the other two Reytana began circling Septa in a slow, clockwise pattern. The glow of their ray blades reflected off of Septa's eüroc as she spun it menacingly in the middle of the circle.

"I will give you all a choice," said Septa. "Reveal the location of your base or die. You have three seconds to decide. Three."

"We will nev—" cried one of the Reytana. Before he could finish his sentence, Septa struck the ground with her eüroc and sent a shockwave that threw him against a tree. He slid to the ground with his head drooped over his shoulders.

"Two." She grinned at the remaining two opponents.

"Just wait," said Tao. He at least got to finish his sentence before he was slammed against a tree by another shockwave.

"One," said Septa as she sneered at Loras who was gripping his ray blade with both hands and shifting his weight from one leg to the other as he looked from side to side.

"Don't be a fool, Loras," said Xander as he, Belkore and the twins walked up behind Septa. "Give us the location of this hidden base. Live to fight another day."

Loras' eyes burned with golden fire as he stared down the Gartune prince. "You were right," said Loras. "It *is* easier to be brave with a sword in your hands!"

Immediately, Septa stomped her eüroc into the ground, but, having watched the same thing happen to his two companions, Loras was ready for the shockwave that shot towards him. He jumped up into the air, swinging his sword above his head. The shockwave went barreling underneath him until it hit a tree and split it directly in half. Loras landed three feet in front of Septa, who was still for just a moment, surprised that her shot had missed. This gave Loras the opportunity he needed to strike at the Gartune princess. He swung his ray blade down with all his might, but Septa casually side-stepped the oncoming blow. Loras' sword cut through the fabric of Septa's cape and lodged deep in the soft dirt of the forest floor.

Loras lifted his pinky finger and retracted the ray blade. He then rolled on the ground just in time to avoid Septa's sweeping eüroc. Quickly, he spun, got up to his feet and turned around to face the Gartune princess. He tapped the pad in his right hand and his ray blade sprung from his grip.

"Impressive..." said Septa. "You move well for someone so young. Too bad that talent will be wasted when I send you back to The Scales."

"It is *you* that will be visiting The Scales, not me!" cried Loras. He charged full speed at Septa with his sword once again raised above his head. The princess waited patiently for the oncoming teen, a deadly smile on her face.

Just before he reached Septa, a body flew in from the side and knocked Loras to the ground. It was Regan.

"Stop this!" she shouted with her arms held out in front of her. "You have us defeated! There is no need to fight. We surrender."

"Coward!" seethed Septa. "At least *that one* had the guts to face me!"

"Yes, and you have bested him," pleaded Regan with her hands still held out in front of her. "There is nothing to prove. You have us outnumbered. We give up. Please..." She got down on her knees while looking Septa straight in the eye, "I beg of you... show some mercy."

Septa walked slowly to where Regan was kneeling. She hovered over the young Reytana. "Mercy is reserved for those who have earned it in battle. I will show your brother mercy. But you... you have chosen a different fate."

"Noooo!" cried Loras but he was too far away to reach his sister. He watched in horror as Septa raised her eüroc into the air.

Regan turned her head towards her brother. Her face was perfectly calm. "It's okay," she said, raising a hand to stop her brother from approaching.

Then, suddenly, a ripple shot through the ground towards Septa. When it struck her feet, she was sent flying backwards through the air. Xander stepped in front of the stunned Regan and watched as his sister deftly collected herself in mid-flight and landed softly on her feet.

"Traitor!" yelled Belkore. "You will answer to the king for this!"

"No..." whispered Septa. "He will answer to *me!*"

Xander crouched into an attack position and his sister did the same; an exact mirror image. Simultaneously, they shot at each other as if thrown from a catapult. They met with a crash as their eürocs collided violently between them.

"I've been waiting for this for a long time, brother," exclaimed Septa through gritted teeth.

"Looks like you've finally gotten your rain check," said Xander as he shoved his sister backwards. The two began to circle each other. Septa feinted a step forward to see if Xander would react but he just kept pacing in his little semi-circle. He grinned. "I'm not one of the little sparring buddies that father sent to play with you. Tell me, do you really think they were trying their hardest against you? The princess of Gartol? What do you think would have happened if one of them actually wounded you?" Septa's scowl cracked just a bit. "They would have been thrown in prison, or worse!" continued Xander. "I hate to break it to you, sis, but you haven't had a true challenge your entire life. Father made sure of it."

Septa couldn't help herself. She let out a scream full of anger and frustration then bolted towards Xander who waited with his ready. When they met, the crack of their eürocs echoed throughout the forest. Septa wailed on her brother. Blow after blow she thrashed at him while spit flew from her mouth like a rabid animal. All Xander could do was hold up his eüroc to block her barrage of strikes.

The onlookers could do nothing to intervene. This fight was between Septa and Xander. Gartune and Reytana alike formed a circle around the two combatants. They knew that it was pointless to fight amongst themselves. The victor of this fight would determine how the rest of this evening unfolded. And so, they watched as brother and sister battled each other in the moonlight.

"I always knew your heart was false!" said Septa as she sent a shockwave flying past Xander's feet. "I tried to tell Father, but he refused to believe it. But now he'll know who you *really* are!"

"Who I *am* is someone who doesn't kill an unarmed woman!" said Xander as he blocked a furious wave of jabs from his sister. "You care more about killing than you do about honor. THAT is why father never let you in real battle!"

"DO NOT SPEAK TO ME OF HONOR, COWARD!" screamed Septa. Her rage had fully overtaken her. She sent four lightning-fast jabs at Xander. He somehow managed to block the first three but the fourth one sent him to the ground. Septa immediately stomped on his chest and kicked his eüroc out of his hand.

"Get it over with," wheezed Xander. Septa's boot had knocked the wind from his lungs. "It's what you've been waiting for."

Before she could reply, a bolt of light shot from the sky and struck Septa's side. Her cheek sizzled and her limp body crumpled to the ground. The smell of burnt flesh filled Xander's nose. He looked down to see his sister lying motionless. Acrid smoke was rising from her body. The left side of her face and torso was charred to the bone.

Overhead, a large floating vessel emerged from the trees. Spotlights shone down from its hull, illuminating the forest. Xander covered his eyes to keep from being blinded. The craft slowly floated over his location while several shapes jumped over the sides and landed next to him. Eventually, Xander's eyes adjusted to the brightness and he looked around. He was surrounded by Reytana. At least thirty had landed and more were coming off the ship every second. About twenty yards away, Belkore and the twins were being put into restraints. Belkore briefly escaped and got a few steps into the forest before he was tackled by several Reytana. While all of this was happening, Loras, Tinko and Regan huddled together under a group of trees and watched in stunned silence. Regan had tears running down her face. She was staring directly at Xander.

Xander's gaze returned to his sister. He could not tell if she was breathing. It didn't look like it. Wisps of white smoke rose from her charred face. He started to move towards her when a familiar voice addressed him.

"Stand up and put your hands behind your back," said Gracien.

Xander offered no resistance as he got to his feet, but his eyes remained on his sister. "Why didn't you let her kill me?"

"We saw what you did," said Gracien as he tied Xander's hands behind him, "for the girl."

"And yet you're still taking me prisoner," said Xander.

"'Live to fight another day,'" whispered Gracien.

After he finished tying the knot above Xander's hands, Gracien took his prisoner to join the other Gartune. Before he reached them, Regan ran over and grabbed Xander's arm.

"Wait!" she said. "What are you going to do with him?"

"Regan, he is our prisoner," said Gracien. "We're taking him back to the Hole just the same as before."

"But he saved me! Can't we let him go?"

"You know that we can't do that," answered Gracien. "He knows too much. He must come with us."

Regan turned back to Xander. She looked up into his face. There were still tears in the corners of her eyes.

"I'm sorry..." she said. Then she looked over to where Septa was lying. "Your sister... is she..."

"No," said Xander.

"How do you know?" asked Regan.

"Can you still see her?"

"Yes," said Regan.

"Then she's not dead."

"But she—"

"Regan," said Xander, before she could finish. "Go back to your friends."

Regan started to say something but then changed her mind as Gracien pulled Xander along with him toward the hovercraft. She watched as he walked away from her, his once proud and effortless gait now reduced to a slow, stumbling stride. Before he stepped onto the ship, Regan shouted at him.

"Xander!" she yelled. Xander turned his head halfway in her direction. "Thank you."

A gleam of wetness shimmered in Xander's eye. Without looking at her, he gave a slight nod and then stepped up into the hovercraft.

CHAPTER TWENTY-TWO
Loss

Gracien leaned over Septa's body and cautiously turned her over onto her back. Her remaining eye was wide open, fixed in an unwavering stare. The rest of her body was as stiff as her gaze. Her left side, from her chest to her face was charred black. Thin wisps of smoke still rose from her smoldering flesh. The smell was awful. Gracien placed his hand on the side of Septa's neck and felt for a pulse.

"Is dat it 'den?" asked a voice from behind Gracien. Declin emerged from the woods and bent over to examine the body.

"She will begin her transition soon, I think," said Gracien, releasing his fingers from her neck. "The wound is too much to recover from."

"Hmmm..." said Declin. He frowned as he poked the side of Septa's body with a stick, to see if she would react. Her body remained motionless.

"What of your friend?" asked Gracien.

Declin shook his head. "Aye, it was as ya thought."

"I'm sorry," said Gracien. Declin merely shrugged.

"Is she... dead?" called Regan from behind the two men. She was still huddled with her brother and Tinko near the hovercraft. Gracien and Declin blocked her view of the body.

Gracien shook his head. "Not yet. But soon."

Regan looked back inside the hovercraft and saw Xander seated on a bench, slumped over with his head bowed and his cuffed arms dangling between his legs. "Can't we take her with us?" she called back to Gracien. "There has to be something we can do! We could take her back and keep her as a prisoner. Wouldn't having her as a hostage be valuable?"

Gracien did not answer, but Regan could tell that he had no intention of bringing her back to the Hole.

"You're just going to leave her there?" said Regan, her voice choked with emotion.

"She will not be here for long," replied Gracien. "The Scales aren't far from here. I would not extend her journey needlessly."

"I can stay with 'er," said Declin. "You's all need to get out of da open and back to da cave. Sun will be up soon and it'd be a miracle if you's haven't been spotted already." Gracien eyed the waif with hesitation. "I know, I know," said Declin. "It won't be like last time. I promise ta stay wit 'er."

"And if she wakes," said Gracien staring hard at the waif.

"Den' I will finish da job, fer good dis time." Declin picked up Septa's eüroc off the ground and released the blade with a quick snap. His eyes told Gracien everything he needed to know.

"Very well," said Gracien. He turned and walked toward the hovercraft, leaving the waif alone with the body.

Loras put his arm around his sister. She couldn't bear to look at Septa's body any longer, so she buried her head in Loras' chest and began to sob. Tinko joined them, putting his arms around his friends. The three of them huddled together for a time before Gracien told them that they had to start moving.

"It will be morning soon," said Gracien. "We need to get you all back to the Hole before someone spots us out here. We've made enough commotion for one night." So, the three teens fell in line behind Gracien and the remaining Reytana. When they climbed onto the vessel, Regan selected a seat on one of the benches across from Xander. The prince was flanked by two Reytana, although the guards seemed unnecessary. Their captive could not have been less of a threat as he slumped in his seat with his eyes closed.

The hovercraft slowly rose through the trees and headed towards the mountains. The journey home was short and silent. Nobody said a word until they were safely inside the confines of the Hole.

The scene inside the cavern was much different than when they had left. The movements of the Reytana had become militaristic. Whereas before the Reytana roamed casually through the cavern, they now moved in regimented groups. Everyone had a purpose.

Several tubes had been attached to the energy orb at the center of the cave. A glowing stream of solar energy pumped through them to a circle of docked hovercraft. The electric hum of the vessels energizing filled the void while the sharp bark of orders being shouted echoed off the cave walls.

"What's going on?" asked Tinko.

"They are preparing for war," replied Loras. He tried to hide the excitement in his voice. After the previous night's adventures, he was sure that his friends were wary of anymore fighting. And everything around them said that a battle was imminent. Still, the energy in the cave was palpable and Loras couldn't help but get caught up in the moment.

"Is this because of us?" asked Regan.

"I'd say there's a good chance we had something to do with it," said Loras.

"Look!" said Tinko. He pointed over to where a group of Reytana were escorting a shackled Xander through the cave. Xander's head was down. He was totally oblivious to his surroundings, only paying attention to the patch of dirt directly in front of his feet as he walked.

"I want to see where they're taking him," said Regan.

"Why? They're not going to let you near him. He's a prisoner," said Loras.

"He saved my life! And he saved yours too," replied Regan. "Doesn't that mean anything to you?"

"He's still a Gartune, Regan," said Loras sternly. "I don't care if he saved our lives or not, he's still our enemy." Regan looked at her brother incredulously. Then she shook her head and brushed past him. Loras did not try stop her.

"She has a point," said Tinko.

"Oh not you too," said Loras. "It's like everyone has suddenly forgotten the past eighteen years."

"Things change, Loras," replied Tinko. "Take a look in the mirror."

Loras was suddenly reminded of the armband that Gracien had given him. He lifted his forearm up to admire it. Waves of golden light flowed through the lace as it wrapped itself around his arm.

"You should really get someone to teach you how to use that thing," said Tinko. "Especially if a battle is coming," Tinko looked over Loras' shoulder where three Reytana were mounting a solar cannon on to the back of a hovercraft, "...and a battle is definitely coming."

"That's not a bad idea," said Loras as he continued to inspect his armband. "I think I'll go and see if I can find Gracien."

"And what am I supposed to do while you're out learning how to be a Reytana?"

"I don't know. You're smart. Maybe they could use your help with the hovercraft. Who knows, maybe if you ask nicely someone will teach you how to fly one!" Loras smiled over his shoulder at his friend as he left to go find Gracien. Tinko stood for a moment, thinking, then walked over to a group of nearby Reytana who were connecting a light tube to a solar cannon.

"Need a hand?" he asked. One of the Reytana grinned and waved him over. There was a little extra pep in Tinko's step as he jogged over and grabbed one end of the light tube.

Regan caught up with the soldiers just as they escorted Xander into an empty room at the far end of the barracks. Once he had been locked inside, two Reytana posted up on either side of the door. One of the Reytana was Tao, the soldier who had been sparring with Loras in the woods earlier that night. The other was a female Reytana that Regan did not recognize. The female guard gave Tao a small wink, which he warmly returned. Regan noticed that they both wore matching golden bracelets on their right wrists.

Both Reytana looked at Regan with understanding, but she could tell by the way that they guarded the door that they could not let her inside to speak with the prisoner. So, she just stood in front of the cell, trying to decide what to do next. She could not go in, but something inside of her prevented her from leaving. Then, the female guard took a small step to the side and nodded towards a thin window in the cell door. Regan looked at her, questioningly. The guard gave her a small nod, as if to say, "it's ok," then gave a knowing smile to Tao, who also took a small step to the side. Regan approached the door. She wiped a thick layer of dust off the glass and peered inside. There, in the corner of the room sat the prince of Gartol. His legs were flopped straight out in front of him and his shackled hands lay on his lap. His head leaned tiredly against the wall and his eyes were closed.

Regan watched the Gartune's chest slowly rise and fall with each breath. She thought back to the arrogant creature that had so often strutted around her kitchen in Reysa. It resembled nothing of this being that sat defeated on the floor in front of her.

Eventually, as if he knew someone was watching him, Xander barely raised one eyelid and lifted his head slightly off the wall. He met the two golden eyes peering at him through the smudgy window in the door. The two Tormada stared at each other in silence for a few moments without so much as a blink. Regan couldn't help it. Her shimmering eyes released a solitary tear that slid down her cheek. Xander let out a tired sigh, leaned his head back against the wall and shut his eyes.

CHAPTER TWENTY-THREE
Training

For the next few days Loras, Regan and Tinko were left to entertain themselves as the Reytana went about their preparations for their return to Reysa. It was clear that they would be moving out soon and there was a quiet mix of anticipation and excitement in the air. After eighteen suffocating years in the Hole, the Reytana were going home.

Tinko, never being one to need assistance in order to entertain himself, chose to pass the time with an unlikely companion. Several times a day, the Reysene teenager chose to visit the cell of Belkore. Emboldened by his present situation, and knowing that he would probably never have this opportunity again, Tinko spent hours torturing the Gartune captive with a continuous barrage of jests, witty observations about prison life, and jokes that generally were not funny.

The two Reytana guards posted to guard Belkore had started to expect Tinko's visits and, though their demeanor remained steadfast, seemed to enjoy the entertainment. At the moment, they were struggling to maintain their stoic appearance.

"You know what I find funny about this whole situation," mused Tinko as he sauntered outside of Belkore's cell.

"What," sighed Belkore who was leaning against the back of his cell and rubbing his temples.

"The fact that you Gartune love being underground, and the Reytana hate it. And yet here you are, imprisoned in a room that very well could be a comfortable residence in Gartol. This is like home away from home for you isn't it? I think these guards out here may actually be suffering more than you. Although that could just be because you haven't showered in days. Do they have showers in Gartol? That's not an insult; I'm being serious. Ok, the first one was an insult. But I'm genuinely curious about the shower situation. Is it like a group bath type of deal? Do you use water or just rub dirt on yourselves? You see, this is my first time out of Reysa so I'm trying to soak up as much knowledge as I can before I go back.
"

"When you go back…" whispered Belkore. "What exactly do you think is going to happen when you *go back*?"

"Are you asking what the attack plan is going to be? Well, I've only been invited to a few of the strategy meetings, but from what I gather it is going to involve two mendkins, some deceptive dancing, a large boomerang and… Wait! I shouldn't be telling you this! I guess that's why they stopped inviting me to the meetings. Damn my big mouth." One of the Reytana guards let out a quick snort but then quickly collected himself.

"Keep talking, tubby," said Belkore. "Enjoy it while you can."

"Oh, I am," said Tinko. "I really am."

"Good," said Belkore, "because the longer you talk, the longer I will draw out your death."

"There it is!" yelled Tinko happily. He looked at the guards. "How long has it been? Twenty minutes? Who had twenty minutes before he threatened me? Was it you?" He pointed to the guard on his left who had tears welling in his eyes. "It *was* you wasn't it. Well fair is fair. Here you go." Tinko took a coin out of his pocket and made a show out of slapping it into the hand of the guard. "Don't go spending that now before I have a chance to win it back from you tomorrow," said Tinko. The guard gave him a sideways wink.

"Well, I have to be off," said Tinko. "Lots of important things to do. I think Gracien is going to teach me how to drive a tank. Ta ta for now my violet-eyed friend."

Belkore grunted.

As it turned out, Gracien was already busy with another job; teaching Loras how to fight.

"Keep your balance," said Gracien as he easily side-stepped a clumsy lunge from his new student. "Every time you swing you lose your balance. Stop reaching."

"If I don't reach, how am I supposed to hit you?" asked Loras between heavy breaths.

"Let your enemy come to you. If you are prepared for the attack, then you will have the advantage once they open themselves up. But you have to maintain your balance at all times so that you can react to any maneuver.

"Here, look at your stance and now look at mine." The two Tormada squared off at each other, their knees bent slightly. A glowing shield covered their left arm while a flickering sword of light rose from their right. "There is your problem," said Gracien. "Your feet are too close together. And you're leaning forward. You look like a nimber about to pounce. Don't tip your hand. Your enemy should never know if you are about to advance or retreat."

And how do I do that?" asked Loras. "Half the time I feel like you can read my mind."

"Stay even," replied Gracien. "Get your weight off of your toes and bend your knees more. That's it." Gracien adjusted Loras' stance slightly and then reset himself against him.

"Now, be patient. Let your enemy come to you." Gracien took one quick step towards Loras and then stopped. Loras flinched. "Patience," Gracien repeated. This time he took two steps towards Loras before stopping. Loras held his stance. "Good," said Gracien.

"But if I wait too long to react, you'll be on me before I can defend myself," said Loras.

"That's why you work on your quickness," said Gracien. "Speed is a great advantage in combat. You must learn speed just as you must learn patience. Once you can master them both, there won't be an adversary that you cannot defeat. Here, I will show you. Attack me, but keep your balance."

Loras took a quick step forward and then jumped to the side. Gracien did not move, but his eyes were locked on the young Reytana. Loras took two more quick zigzag steps toward his teacher, then backed away quickly, recoiled and jumped into the air while raising his ray blade above his head. Gracien did not move until Loras was almost on top of him. Then in an imperceptibly fast movement, Gracien swung his shield across his body and stung Loras on his chin right before he would have landed on top of him. Loras flew back and landed in a heap. He slowly got up onto his elbows and glared warily at his instructor. The Reytana captain gave a small smile.

"That was an interesting maneuver," said Gracien.

"Apparently not interesting enough," said Loras as he spat onto the ground and was not surprised to see it was tinted red. "Was that really necessary?"

"Was it necessary to strike you like that? If I had more time to train you, I would say no, it wasn't necessary. But since our time is limited, I needed you to learn the point as quickly as possible." Gracien walked over to his student and lent him a hand up. "And you, Loras, are not always the quickest learner," said Gracien amicably.

"You must have been talking to my sister," said Loras. "She says the same thing. So does Tinko. Actually, so does everyone. I guess you're wasting your time on me."

"Relax, young warrior," said Gracien as he patted Loras on the shoulder. "There are other things that are just as important. Like courage and loyalty—both of which I can tell you have in abundance. It may take you a while to learn the ins and outs of hand-to-hand combat, but when the moment of truth arises, like it did back in the forest, you rise to the occasion... and *that*, more than anything I can teach you, is what makes you a warrior."

Loras blushed and looked at his feet. Gracien studied the young Mada and rubbed his chin, thoughtfully. "I think I might have something that can help you with your training. Stay here, I'll be right back."

Gracien walked back to the end of the cave that held the barracks and left Loras to practice his maneuvers alone. The young Reytana slowly and deliberately went through his defensive and offensive positions, concentrating on his footwork and maintaining balance. The stances that Gracien had taught him were not easy. Loras' movements became increasingly staggered as his frustration grew. His feet tangled and he almost fell to the floor when the Reytana captain returned.

"I'm never going to be able to fight like you," said Loras dejectedly.

"Here, try this," said Gracien as he unraveled a golden ribbon from his hands. He then walked behind Loras and carefully tied the ribbon around his forehead. When he had finished, he turned Loras to face him so that he could inspect the headband.

"What is this thing for?" asked Loras.

"It's for shooting fireballs out of your head," said Gracien.

"It's for *what?!*" shouted Loras as reached up and tried to take off the ribbon. Gracien laughed and stopped his hand.

"Wait... did you just make a joke?" asked Loras.

"Why? Was it funny?" said Gracien, still chuckling to himself.

"Hilarious," said Loras. "You and Tinko should team up." Loras looked around the cave and noticed that some of the Reytana had started to notice Loras' new headpiece. They too, were smiling at him. Loras felt his cheeks begin to flush.

"So what is this thing really for?" asked Loras.

"It's to help you focus your light," replied Gracien.

"Why isn't anybody else wearing one?"

"Does it look like anybody else needs help focusing?" asked Gracien with an amused look on his face.

"I suppose you're right," said Loras. "But it still feels weird. And people are looking at me." More Reytana had taken notice of Loras and were pointing and smiling at him.

"Don't worry about them," said Gracien. "Try it out. Take your stance, guardian of Reysa, and defend yourself!"

Gracien's sword met Loras' and the two Reytana traded swings as they slowly circled the cave. Sparks of light danced off of his shield and sword. Occasionally, Gracien shouted a command or compliment, but they never stopped their dance. Loras began to breathe heavily, but he continued to fight, concentrating on keeping his balance as the larger and stronger Tormada relentlessly charged. Eventually, Loras' clumsy gait began to improve. His legs were steadier; his reactions quicker. A small cloud of dirt began to rise from the ground as the two combatants quickly shuffled their feet back and forth. Their eyes gleamed. The golden ribbon around Loras' forehead began to glow a fierce yellow. Determination and confidence began to show in Loras' face. A group of Reytana gathered around to watch. Loras didn't notice. He was in heaven.

Meanwhile, Regan could not deny it any longer. She tried to keep herself occupied, spending her time helping the Reytana pack gear onto the many hovercraft docked in the cave. Even so, her mind constantly wandered to him. Finally, after three days of pretending he wasn't there, Regan went to see Xander.

Tao and his wife—Regan had determined that they were married—once again stood guard outside Xander's cell. Further down the hall, Tinko stood outside of Belkore's cell. She could only hear bits and pieces of what he was saying, but she could tell that her friend was thoroughly enjoying himself.

"... *so two Gartune walk into a bar...*" said Tinko from down the hall.

Regan frowned in Tinko's direction and then approached Xander's cell. The guards silently stepped aside so that she could look through the window. Other than his pristine goatee sprouting a few stray whiskers, Xander looked exactly the same as the last time she saw him. He was leaning against the wall of his cell with his eyes closed when Regan approached the small window in the door. A tired smile crept across Xander's face.

"I was wondering if you would come back," said Xander with closed eyes.

"I tried not to."

"Why?" asked Xander.

"I didn't know what good it would do," said Regan. "There's nothing I can do for you."

"Ah, but there you are mistaken," replied Xander. His voice was tired. "There is something you can do."

"What?" asked Regan. She started to get nervous.

"You're doing it right now," said Xander and he opened his eyes for the first time to look at the girl with the golden eyes. "You can talk to me. A friendly voice can do a lot for a person."

Regan relaxed. "Ok, I can do that."

"That's all I ever wanted, you know," said Xander.

"What?" said Regan.

"To talk," said Xander.

Regan thought back to the last time she and Xander had been in her home. She remembered the look in his eyes as he hovered over her while she sat on the kitchen counter. "Somehow, I doubt that," she said.

"You're referring to the last time we were in your kitchen," said Xander. "I admit, I overstepped some lines there. But things were different then. *You* were different."

"Different how?" asked Regan.

"Well for one, you weren't seven feet tall." Xander laughed dryly as he straightened himself up against the wall.

"So, it was ok to come on to me when you thought I was a torman?" asked Regan, coolly.

"Regan, I am the prince of Gartune," said Xander matter-of-factly. "I could have done whatever I wanted to you or anyone else and nobody would have batted an eye." Regan looked away, disgusted.

"But that's not why I came to your house time after time, and you know that," said Xander. "Regan, look at me. You know me." Regan looked back at the captive Gartune. Her brow was still furrowed.

"I came to visit you because I liked you. You were interesting. You weren't afraid of me. Do you know how rare that is? Nobody else in that entire city looked me in the eye, let alone spoke their mind to me. You were *different*. And now that you've received your light—now that we are the same—you are afraid to talk to me. I don't understand."

"We may both be Tormada, but we are not the same," said Regan, her voice hardly more than a whisper.

Xander leaned his head back against the wall and sighed. "We are more alike than you think. Maybe someday, I will show you that is true."

Laughter echoed from down the hall. The guards stationed outside of Belkore's cell were holding their stomachs while Tinko attempted to finish his joke.

"... *he says... he says... 'you're gonna have to dig your way out of this one,'*" Tinko and Belkore's guards doubled over, their chests heaving. "*Get it?... You're gonna have to DIG your way out...*" Suddenly, the ground shook, causing dust to fall from the walls of the cave. The tremor had come from Belkore's cell. Tinko and the guards immediately stopped laughing and looked inside.

"It sounds like old Belkore finally had enough of your friend's jokes," said Xander.

"He can do that?" asked Regan. Apparently, the guards outside Belkore's cell were not concerned with what they saw inside. They went back to their posts, motioning for Tinko to be on his way. He grudgingly walked down the hall toward Damnar and Damina's cells.

"But we took away his eüroc," said Regan. "How did he shake the ground?"

"The staff is just a tool, just like your armbands are tools. They do not create power; they merely shape it. A Tormada's power is always there, inside of him... or *her*." He opened one eye and directed it at Regan.

"So, you mean to tell me that you can cause your little earthquakes without your eürocs?" Xander smiled. Then he flicked the ground next to him with his index finger. The floor cracked. A small fissure grew along the stone and traveled from his finger all the way to the door. Regan's eyes widened. "*You could break out of this cell if you wanted to...* " she whispered.

"Of course, I could."

"Then why don't you?"

"Because I don't particularly feel like fighting through three hundred Reytana at the moment. Besides, the accommodations here are surprisingly comfortable." As he said this, he stretched his arms behind his head and yawned. There was an uncomfortable silence that lasted about a minute before Regan dismissed herself, saying that she had promised to help with dinner that night. It was, of course, a lie. She turned and began to walk away when Xander called to her.

"Regan," he said.

"Yes."

"Will you come talk to me tomorrow?"

Regan thought for a moment before answering. "I'll think about it," she said.

"I hope you do," said Xander. His voice was tired.

Regan walked away.

CHAPTER TWENTY-FOUR
Fight

"I need to see the king!" shouted Morlo as he came rushing up to the guard stationed outside of King Hadrian's bedroom. It was early in the morning but Morlo knew the king would be awake. Hadrian was not one to sleep in.

"Wait here and I will tell him you wish to see him," said the guard.

"You will open this door right now and get out of my way!" said Morlo.

The guard raised an eyebrow but did not stop Morlo from shoving past him as he opened the door. If Morlo wished to risk entering the king's bedchamber unannounced, then he accepted the consequences if the king was not in the mood for visitors.

Hadrian was clasping the last button on his dark violet tunic when Morlo came rushing in. Had he been a few seconds earlier, he would have caught the king half-dressed, and that would have been unfortunate for everyone. Luckily, Morlo's unannounced entrance only earned an annoyed glare from Hadrian.

"What?" said Hadrian as continued dressing himself.

"It's your daughter," said Morlo. The words almost caught in his throat before he could speak them.

"What has Septa done now," Hadrian asked with a sigh. He straightened the metal wristbands on his forearms so that they were perfectly symmetrical.

"She found the Reytana," said Morlo, this time rushing his words before they could catch in his throat. Hadrian looked up for the first time.

"Where..." he said, his voice barely above a whisper.

"They were in the forest outside of Woodhaven," said Morlo. "There was a fight. Septa..." this time the words caught. "She... she's..."

"Spit it out!" shouted Hadrian.

"She's been hurt."

The weight of Morlo's words hung on the king. He knew that "hurt" was not what he meant. Septa didn't get hurt. This was something else.

"Where is she?"

"She's in the infirmary, but you—"

Hadrian stormed past Morlo and was out the door before he could finish his sentence.

The king's cloak billowed behind him as he stamped through the halls of the royal palace, down through the city and to the infirmary. Everything about the block stone building was cold and sterile. From the worn, granite floor that had been stained with blood and then wiped clean countless times over centuries of war, to the empty walls with their small, frosted windows so that nobody could see in or out. The smell of disinfectant hung in the air, as permanent a fixture as the iron-framed lights that were molded into the ceiling. When he entered the building, Hadrian immediately knew something was wrong.

There were several Gartune standing around the anteroom, but nobody spoke. They all parted silently to make room for Hadrian as he slowly walked across the annex toward a door in the back. When he reached the door, he paused for a second, preparing himself for what he was about to see. Then, he pushed it open with both hands.

The first thing that he noticed was the smell. It was a mixture of charred flesh and antiseptic fumes. A large metal table was in the center of the room. Above it hung a flickering lamp that was slowly swinging back and forth. A Gartune surgeon in a white coat leaned just under the swinging light. His torso covered the top half of the motionless body lying in front of him.

Hadrian stood silently in the back of the room and watched the doctor as he worked on his patient. There was a large cylinder of strong-smelling gel on a stand next to the table. The doctor dipped his hand into the cylinder and grabbed a large glob of the clear gel. He gingerly applied it to the body, which still lay hidden from Hadrian's view. Suddenly, the doctor pulled back his hand from the area he had just touched. At the same time, he jerked his head right into the lamp above him, sending it swinging again. The doctor cursed under his breath and flung the remaining gel off his hand and onto the floor. The glob on the floor was no longer clear, but red.

Hadrian stepped forward, making his presence known to the doctor, who quickly turned. Upon seeing who it was, the surgeon instinctively blocked the king's view of the patient.

"Your highness," said the doctor. "I am still—"

"Move," said Hadrian with a raise of his hand.

The doctor bowed his head and slowly moved away from the table, revealing Septa's body.

Hadrian took two slow steps toward the table, then stopped. The swinging lamp illuminated what was left of his daughter. The wavering light combined with the translucent gel made it look like Septa's skin was boiling. Hadrian reached up to stop the light from swinging. He gripped it so tight that he crushed the hood of the lamp.

Septa's one eye was still wide open, like she was staring down an invisible enemy on the ceiling. The left side of her body, from her face down to her hip, was a bloody mix of burnt flesh and medicinal gel. Hadrian unclenched his hand from the lamp and laid it on his daughter's arm. It felt cold to the touch.

"The gel is meant to—"

Again, Hadrian raised his hand to silence the doctor. He did not need a medical explanation to understand what he was seeing. Relieved, the doctor retreated to the corner of the room and sat down. Hadrian kept his eyes locked on his daughter. His face was like a stone. He scanned her body from feet to head, eventually stopping on her face. A clear breathing tube ran from Septa's nose to an accordion-shaped machine next to her. The steady sound of the bellows rising and falling filled the room.

Friends of the king, or at least those close enough to risk the question, used to ask Hadrian why he had chosen to adopt Septa. After all, he already had Lex.

It was uncommon for a Gartune to adopt more than one child, especially when they already had a son. But for Hadrian, there was no questioning whether Septa would be his.

Two weeks before the great waterfall bore Septa into the bay of Gartol, a famous Gartune had died. Next to Hadrian, he was Gartol's most glorified warrior. He was also a masterful builder, a respected politician and one of the most influential Gartune in the city. But, Septarian was known for one thing above all else—he was the king's only rival.

Septarian and Hadrian disagreed on almost everything, but where other Gartune were afraid to speak against the king, Septarian openly defied him. Publicly, Hadrian denounced Septarian as a traitor and an enemy of Gartol. However, privately, he embraced the antagonist because he respected Septarian more than any other Tormada.

Septarian and Hadrian's arguments were the stuff of legend. It could be something as small as the meal choice for a state dinner, or as significant as the king's philosophy on leadership.

Septarian objected to everything that Hadrian said or did as a matter of principle. Often, these disagreements culminated in a fantastic duel between Gartol's two finest warriors. These duels always ended in a stalemate. All but the last one.

Hadrian remembered the insult that had pre-empted this final battle. Septarian had accused the king of being a negligent father to his son. At that time, Lex was still a young boy, barely old enough to hold a eüroc, so he was of little interest to the king. The boy's education and training were handled by the court's assigned masters, as was the custom. The king rarely saw his son, except on his mandated testing days where Lex had to prove that he was advancing in all areas, or else the Gartune in charge of that particular discipline was replaced. Lex never disappointed, but all he ever received from his father was a satisfied nod.

When Septarian pointed out that Hadrian should pay more attention to his young son, the king erupted with anger. Perhaps it was because he knew Septarian spoke the truth. But nobody told the king how to raise his own child. This time, when they inevitably came to blows, Hadrian had an extra measure of fire in his belly.

Septarian immediately knew he was in trouble. It was all he could do to fend off the barrage of strikes that Hadrian threw his way. After almost an hour of fighting, Septarian was bloodied and bruised. Hadrian, still fueled by a seething hot anger, was as fresh as when they had begun. The exhausted Septarian could see in the king's eyes that there would be no stalemate this time. So, rather than prolonging the inevitable, he dropped his defenses right as the king threw a savage blow with his eüroc. The king struck Septarian so hard in his chest that his ribs punctured his heart.

Immediately, the fury in Hadrian's eyes was gone. Shock and confusion filled its place. Septarian crumbled to the ground, holding his chest in his hands. Blood seeped through his fingers. He looked down at his chest and then up at Hadrian standing above him. "Prove me wrong," were his last words.

As the defeated Gartune lay on the ground breathing his last breath, Hadrian looked at him as he now looked at his daughter. Full of anger. Full of regret.

"You have his fight," whispered Hadrian to his daughter. "That was why I picked you."

Hadrian moved his hand from Septa's forearm to her hand. He continued to look at her. His face still as stone, his eyes dry and clear. Then, something happened. He felt a slight squeeze in his hand. Septa's eye turned slowly to her father. The two looked at each other in silence, and then Hadrian squeezed his daughter's hand and gave her a satisfied nod.

"Fight!" he whispered. Then he gave her hand a squeeze before he turned and walked over to the doctor.

"Who brought her back?"

"He's in the mess room, your highness," answered the doctor.

"Good. I want to talk to him," said the king.

The doctor escorted the king through the infirmary and into the cafeteria. There, at one of the tables, sat a small man ravenously finishing off the last of a sandwich. His head was bowed so the king could not see his face. Morlo sat at a table behind him, watching closely as he ate.

"A *torman* saved her?" said the king in amazement.

"He says he dragged her here all by himself," said Morlo. "Although he must have had some help. He probably double-crossed the others right before he arrived so he could keep the reward all to himself."

"The *reward?*" said Hadrian, his eyes widening as he looked to where the torman was sitting. The torman lifted his head.

""Figured der might be a bit of coin in savin' da princess," said the torman. "If not, I'll be on my way."

The king's face relaxed a bit and a small smile of recognition crept across his face. "Now there's a voice I haven't heard in many years," said Hadrian. "Hello, Declin."

"Your 'ighness." replied the waif.

CHAPTER TWENTY-FIVE
Orders

"So, it was you that carried my daughter all the way here from Woodhaven?" asked Hadrian.

"Aye," said Declin.

"Impossible. You can hardly walk as it is!" said Morlo. "There's no way you carried her here without help."

Declin shrugged. "I've carried larger 'dan her, further 'den here," he said.

"And what were you doing in the forest when Septa was attacked?" said Morlo.

"Just 'appened to be walkin' by when I heard a racket," said Declin.

"Just *happened* to be walking by?" said Morlo suspiciously.

"Aye, dat's what I said."

"Well, that's awfully lucky," said Morlo.

"Lucky fer da princess, I suppose," said Declin as he took a bite of his sandwich. Morlo took two angry steps toward the waif but Hadrian stopped him.

"Enough, Morlo," said Hadrian.

"With all due respect, your highness," said Morlo. "How do we know he wasn't with the Reytana when Septa was attacked? He could be playing both sides. He's a waif, after all. It's their way."

"Because Declin learned long ago the consequence of choosing the wrong side," said Hadrian coolly.

Declin's hand unconsciously went to his lame leg. "Aye," said Declin. "Ain't no profit in defying da king. No one knows dat better dan I."

"Then tell us what you were doing in the forest!" shouted Morlo.

"I live in da forest! Where else was I s'posed to be?!"

"I said enough!" said Hadrian. "Morlo, your presence is no longer required. Go see to the preparations. The Reytana have shown themselves. They must be close to returning home. Mobilize the army."

"Yes, your highness," said Morlo.

"Oh, and Morlo," said Hadrian. "Your *project* had better be completed by the time they get there."

"It will be," said Morlo.

"Good, then go," said Hadrian. Morlo exited the infirmary cafeteria leaving the king alone with the waif. Once the Gartune captain had gone, Hadrian turned slowly to Declin, his gaze fierce.

"What are they planning?" said Hadrian.

"What are who plannin'?" asked Declin.

"I will ask you one more time," said Hadrian as he bent over the much smaller torman. "What are they planning?" This time Declin did not answer. He began to rub his gimp leg nervously. The king grunted. "You play a dangerous game, waif. I wonder how you keep it all straight; switching your loyalties whenever its most profitable for you? I'll give you this, you must be very clever, or you would have been dead long ago."

"Your 'ighness, you've got me wrong," said Declin. "I know better dan to go against Gartol."

Hadrian slowly circled the seated waif. "Do you know the only thing I like about a waif? It's that you're all predictable. Greed is predictable. I don't doubt that you brought Septa back here because you were hoping to earn a reward. I also don't doubt that you were helping the Reytana who attacked her. What did they give you? Coin? The promise of a position in Reysa when they reclaimed their city? Or was it just that they made you feel important?"

"Your 'ighness, ya don't—" Hadrian stopped him.

Hadrian slammed his hand down on the table, squashing what was left of Declin's sandwich. "I'm going to give you one last chance. Normally, I would just kill you, but since we're such old friends, I'm going to give you a chance to earn the most valuable reward I can offer. Your life."

Declin gulped and nodded his head slowly.

"Go back to the Reytana," continued Hadrian. "Find out how and when they plan to return to Reysa. I want details; do you understand? Very. Specific. Details." He emphasized each of the last three words with three sharp pokes to the waif's ribs. "Do that," said Hadrian, "and you will have earned your life back. Until then, it is mine. Do you understand?"

"Aye, your 'ighness," whispered Declin.

"Good. You have one week to return with my information."

"I will be back in one week, yous can count on 'dat," said Declin.

"No, you won't be coming back here. In seven days, you can find me in Reysa. I trust you know the way."

CHAPTER TWENTY-SIX
The Note

Eventually, Belkore began to realize that if he just ignored the taunts of his snarky visitor that the boy would eventually go away. Tinko tried and tried to get a reaction out of the suddenly stoic prisoner, but the only response he got was an occasional chuckle from his guards. After two days of telling jokes to a silent audience, Tinko finally bored of visiting Belkore and decided to seek his entertainment elsewhere.

Loras and Regan had been mostly absent of late. Loras spent the majority of his time with Gracien learning how to master the ray blade and shield. Tinko occasionally would watch them train. It was almost disturbing to see how rapidly Loras' skills had developed. The more he watched them, the more Tinko knew that his days of sparring with tree sticks in the alleyways of Reysa were over. He had never been much of a match for Loras, but now he might actually get hurt if he tried to spar with him. That knowledge made Tinko sad and homesick, and so he stopped sitting in on the training sessions.

Regan had, at first, made an effort to spend time with Tinko. The mismatched pair had gone on walks through the cavern and lent a hand with the army's preparations whenever they could. But Tinko felt a distance between him and Regan, for while she was there in body, he could tell that her mind was always on Xander. Over the past couple of days, she had begun to visit the Gartune prince more and more frequently and so Tinko was left to entertain himself.

The Reytana were polite to him, but they never seemed interested in anything more than small talk. Understandably, they were very busy. But, Tinko wasn't sure if they would have been keen on his companionship even if they weren't preoccupied. He wasn't one of them. And with Loras and Regan now full-grown Tormada, Tinko, for the first time in his life, felt small.

One day, after a short sulking session, a very lonely and very bored Tinko decided to stop feeling sorry for himself and went to explore the sections of the Hole that were off limits to him.

The far end of the barracks housed the living quarters for the Reytana officers. These were actual rooms as opposed to the rows of ubiquitous bunk beds where the rank and file slept. Gracien and his lieutenants slept in the rooms, although, as of late they had not been doing much sleeping at all. This meant that the rooms were almost always empty, and they were never guarded. No one saw the need. A simple warning not to enter had seemed sufficient to dissuade any of the newcomers from exploring this restricted area. But today Tinko was bored.

When Tinko entered the barracks, he was relieved to find that they were empty. He nonchalantly walked past the rows of bunks, then, after a quick peek over his shoulder, trotted over to the doorway that led to the officers' quarters. He was not surprised to find the door unlocked. After all, if the Reytana didn't feel the need to guard the rooms, why would they need to lock them?

Tinko slid inside the first room, which just so happened to be Gracien's. The room was small and dark, with a bed that was only slightly larger than the cots outside. Next to the bed, a nightstand and lamp accounted for the entirety of the room's furniture. *I guess when you wear the same thing every day, you don't need a dresser,* thought Tinko.

Having found nothing of interest in the room, Tinko considered leaving. But then, his eye was drawn to a familiar slip of paper on top of the nightstand. *The note that Dario had written for Declin,* Tinko thought. It was too much to resist. Tinko knew how much Loras had wanted to read the note and, admittedly, he had been curious as well. Perhaps if he knew its contents, he could regain the attention of his old friend. It was worth the risk.

Tinko cracked open the door and peered out to make sure that nobody was coming, then he went back to the nightstand and opened the piece of paper. The message was shorter than he expected.

The twins wear the rings.

That was it. One sentence, and nonsense at that. Tinko knew for a fact that neither Loras nor Regan wore any jewelry. What rings could Dario possibly be talking about? And moreover, Dario had not met the twins when he wrote the letter; so how could he know about their fashion habits? It didn't make any sense. Still, Tinko knew that Loras would want to know the contents of the note. He decided to go find his friend, hoping that maybe Loras would know what the cryptic note meant.

It was easy to guess where Loras would be. When Tinko arrived in the main cavern, he was happy to see that Loras had just finished his training session for the day. Gracien seemed pleased with his pupil and patted him on the shoulder as Tinko approached.

"Ah, you're back! I haven't seen you in a couple of days" said Gracien. "I was going to find someone to teach you some maneuvers, if you're interested."

"I appreciate the offer," said Tinko, "but I don't think I'll be receiving my light anytime soon, so I think your efforts may be wasted on me."

Gracien smiled. "Even though you can't wield our weapons, there are still some tricks you could learn. It will be useful for you to know how to defend yourself, especially in the days to come."

"I'll keep that in mind," said Tinko, hoping Gracien would take the curt response as his cue to leave so that Tinko could talk to Loras in private.

"Very well," said Gracien. "If you change your mind, just let me know," and with that he turned, leaving the two teens by themselves. Tinko waited until Gracien was outside of earshot before turning excitedly to his friend.

"What's with the headband?" asked Tinko.

"It's for shooting fireballs," replied Loras.

"Oh. Cool. Hey, so I've been doing some exploring and found something interesting," said Tinko.

"Oh yeah? Are they hiding the good food somewhere in the back?" said Loras as he wiped the sweat off of his face with a towel.

"I'm sure that they are, but that's not what I found," said Tinko. He waited to see if Loras would ask him, but his friend didn't seem very interested. "Ok, I'll tell you," said Tinko excitedly. "I found the note."

"What note?" asked Loras.

"What do you mean, 'what note?'!" exclaimed Tinko. "How many super-secret notes from the governor of Reysa did we smuggle out of the city and deliver to a name-changing waif in the middle of a Reytana hide-out!?"

"Oh, that note," said Loras. "I had actually kind of forgotten about it."

"Well fine," said a frustrated Tinko. "Then I guess you don't care what it said."

"Not particularly," said Loras. Tinko's jaw dropped. He stared up at his now-gigantic friend in disbelief. Loras could only keep a straight face for a few moments before he cracked.

"Of course, I want to know what it said, you mendkin!"

Tinko closed his mouth. "You know, for a second I thought Gracien had brainwashed you during all of this training you've been doing."

"Oh, he's tried. Luckily, I'm a little slow on the uptake," said Loras. "So, tell me. What did it say?"

Tinko looked around to make sure nobody was listening. Then he beckoned for Loras to bend down so he could whisper to him.

"The twins wear the rings."

"What?" said Loras.

"That's it. The twins wear the rings," said Tinko.

"What is that supposed to mean?" asked Loras.

"I thought you might know," said Tinko disappointedly.

"Does it look like I wear a ring?" said Loras.

"No, but—"

"Have you ever, in your life, seen me wear a ring?" exclaimed Loras.

"No," said Tinko who was growing irritated, "but how should I know what you do in the privacy of your own home?"

"Funny," said Loras.

"So, you don't know what it means?" asked Tinko.

"No idea."

"Well, it must mean something, or Dario wouldn't have gone to all the trouble of having us deliver it to Declin," said Tinko.

"That's it!" said Loras. "Declin must know what it means! We should go find him and ask."

"But I haven't seen him around in a few days," said Tinko. "He must be outside of the Hole"

"That's ok," said Loras quietly. "I know a way out."

"Oh, not this again," said Tinko. "Have you already forgotten how well things went the last time you ventured outside?"

"Well, last time I didn't have you with me!" said Loras. He grabbed Tinko's arm and began to quickly shuffle him across the cavern.

"Wait!" said Tinko. "Shouldn't we tell Regan about this? It concerns her too." Loras stopped. His eyes narrowed. He was aware of how his sister had been spending her time lately, and he did not approve.

"You know we have to tell her," continued Tinko. "Maybe she knows something about the note's message that we don't."

"I'm thinking," said Loras, his brow still furrowed.

"Well that's never solved anything," said Tinko and he began walking toward the prison cells. "Besides, you know I'm right."

Loras waited a moment and then caught up to his friend with a couple of long strides. "All right, all right I'm coming," he said.

Tinko and Loras found Regan exactly where they thought she'd be—leaning against Xander's cell door. She was peering down with a small smile on her face and her cheeks had a slight blush to them.

"I hope we aren't interrupting anything," said Loras as he walked up to his sister. Regan jerked her head up. Whatever smile had been on her face was replaced with an annoyed scowl, and the slight pink that had garnished her cheeks turned into a deep red.

"You aren't interrupting," said Regan. She tried her best to sound blasé but couldn't hide the tinge of embarrassment in her voice.

"Yes, you are!" crowed a voice from inside the cell.

Loras stormed up to Xander's door and pressed his face against the small window. Xander was sitting in his regular spot in the corner of the room. He grinned at the fiery, golden eyes peering in through his door.

"Can you come back in a few minutes?" said Xander. "Your sister and I were just planning my escape."

"I wouldn't be surprised if you were," said Loras, giving his sister a sideways look. "Your scheming will have to take a break while I talk to my sister. Is that ok with you, your highness?"

Xander twirled his hand in front of him and nodded, then leaned his head back against the wall, shut his eyes and smiled. Loras turned back to his sister and Tinko.

"Prison life appears to agree with him," said Tinko.

"Even locked up, he's an ass," said Loras to his sister. "I still don't know why you waste your time on him."

"Because I'm pretty!" came another shout from inside the cell.

Loras grabbed Regan and Tinko's arms and dragged them away from the door so as not to be heard. Once they were out of earshot, Regan yanked her arm free of her brother's grip.

"What do you want?!" she said in an angry whisper.

"Tell her," said Loras to Tinko. Tinko looked over his shoulder to see if anyone was around. He started to talk then stopped and looked over his other shoulder. Regan rolled her eyes at him.

"So, I was doing some... um, exploring... earlier today," began Tinko, "and I happened to come upon the note."

"What note?" said Regan.

"Are you kidding me?!" shouted Tinko.

"Keep your voice down!" hissed Loras.

"You mean the note from Dario?" asked Regan.

"I mean seriously—how many notes could I possibly be talking about?" said Tinko incredulously. Both Regan and Loras just stared at him with their arms crossed, so he continued.

"Yes, the note from Dario," he continued.

"And how did you get it?" asked Regan.

"It doesn't matter," interrupted Loras. "Just tell her what it said."

"It said..." Tinko stopped to look over his shoulder again. "The twins wear the rings."

"What rings?" asked Regan. Both Tinko and Loras let out a small groan.

"What rings indeed..." sighed Tinko. "We thought you might know."

"I don't wear any rings, Tink," said Regan.

"Yes, apparently neither does anyone else in your family," said Tinko as he put his hands on his head and stared at the ceiling.

"Declin might know what it means," said Loras.

"Maybe," said Regan. "But Declin has been gone for days."

"We're going to go find him," said Loras. A mischievous smile grew on his face.

Regan's eyes widened and her fists clenched. She was about to lay into her brother when a shadow appeared on the wall behind them. They spun around to find Gracien looking down at them.

"Find who?" asked Gracien. His arms were crossed but his face gave no indication as to how much of their conversation he had overheard.

"Uh..." stammered Tinko, "We were going to find someone to teach me how to fight, like you said before. I changed my mind. I think it might be a good idea."

"It *was* a good idea, but unfortunately, it will have to wait," replied Gracien. "We're moving out."

"When?" said Loras excitedly.

"Tonight. We leave for Reysa tonight," said Gracien. The teens could tell he had been waiting a long time to say those words. "You all should get some rest. I will come get you when it is time."

Loras and Tinko exchanged excited glances. They were finally going home. It was hard to believe it had only been a couple of weeks since they escaped Reysa, but it seemed much longer. Especially since they didn't know if they'd ever return. But now, not only were they returning, but they were going to have to fight their way back in.

As this realization sank in, the excitement left Tinko's face and was replaced by worry. Loras' excitement, on the other hand, only grew stronger. He thought back to all the times he sat daydreaming in professor Lucan's class. He remembered charging across the Battle Plains with an army of Reytana at his back and jumping higher than he ever thought possible while swinging a sword made up of pure light. It was all surreal then. Just a dream. But not anymore. Loras looked down at the golden wristbands wrapped around his forearms. He clenched his fists and little wisps of golden light shimmered through the bands. *My time has come,* he thought.

"What is going to happen to them?" Regan nodded towards Xander's cell.

"The prisoners are coming with us," replied Gracien. "We might need them."

"Need them?" asked Tinko. "You don't think they'd actually help us, do you?"

"He means we might need them as hostages," said Loras. "Because that's what they are." He stared straight at Regan. She met his gaze without blinking.

"What we use them for is not your worry," said Gracien. "Now, I will suggest again that you try to get some sleep before we leave. There may not be many opportunities for rest in the days to come."

"Fine. We're going," said Regan. She led Loras and Tinko in the direction of the barracks. As they were about to turn the corner, Loras looked back and saw Gracien standing in front of Xander's door. He could not tell if he was talking to the prisoner or just looking at him, but he could tell that something was bothering the captain.

Before he could turn and look where he was going, Loras ran square into a wall with a thud. Or, at least, he thought it was a wall until the wall started cursing at him.

"I swear to da gods, you are da dumbest floater I have *ever* met," said Declin as he got up off the floor and brushed himself off.

"Declin!" shouted Tinko. "Just the guy we were looking for!"

"Yeah... why is dat?" said Declin suspiciously.

"Where have you been?" asked Regan.

"Yeah," added Loras as he inspected the shoulder that had just rammed into Declin's head. "You've been missing for days."

"Missin'?" replied Declin. "Can't be missin' if there's nowhere I have to be. I come and go as I please here, master floater," said Declin. He gave Loras a mock bow.

Regan lowered her voice as she bent down to Declin's level. "Declin, we need to talk to you."

"Sorry, m'lady," replied Declin, continuing with the fake humility, "but ol' Declin has some other business to attend to at the moment." He started to peek his head around the corner, but Loras pushed him back in front of the group. Both he and his sister towered over the waif. They took a step closer to emphasize the size difference. Declin did not appreciate the gesture.

"Well, will ya look at da two of you," sneered Declin. "All grown-up and full of demselves now dat they got da light flowing through dem veins." He nodded curtly at the golden wisps flowing quickly through Loras' wristbands. "If ya 'tink dat I still couldn't take da two of you without breakin' a sweat, den you be 'tinkin wrong."

Loras laid a hand on Declin's shoulder. "I haven't forgotten my lesson in the forest, master waif. But this is important."

Declin shoved Loras' hand off his shoulder with a *humph*. "Later," he grunted, and once again started towards the hall leading to the prison cells. Loras blocked his path and refused to budge.

"Let him go," sighed Regan. "We can ask him later."

Loras looked down at the waif. The waif looked up at him, waiting for him to move. Finally, Loras leaned back and made room for Declin to pass. The waif brushed past Loras, making sure to jab him in the hip with his walking stick as he did so. The teens watched as their old companion limped hurriedly down the hall. It looked to them as if his limp had increased since they had seen him last.

Gracien was still standing in front of Xander's cell when Declin approached him. Whatever Declin asked Gracien seemed to irk the Reytana captain. He pulled the waif away from the prison door and bent to whisper something in his ear. Something about the way they were talking seemed... off to Loras. Gracien looked like he didn't want to continue the conversation, but the waif was persistent. As their agitation increased, the volume of their conversation began to rise to the point where Loras could almost hear what they were saying. He tried to listen, but then Regan reminded him, as only a twin sister can, that time was wasting and they had better get some rest. Loras watched Gracien and Declin for a few more moments.

"Loras!" shouted Regan from up ahead.

"Coming," replied Loras and he ran ahead to catch up with

his sister and Tinko.

CHAPTER TWENTY-SEVEN
Testing

The Gartolian basecamp at the foot of Reysa had grown to three times its normal size since Loras, Regan and Tinko had escaped. Now, nearly a thousand Gartolian soldiers, as well as the majority of the Gartune regiment camped out in front of the city. It was as if all of Gartol had emptied and relocated to the foot of Reysa.

Hundreds of newly-built tents stood in precise, evenly-spaced lines. Patrols of Gartune soldiers marched up and down the rows, occasionally peeking in a flap of one of the smaller tents. The larger dwellings, those built for the Gartune, were left alone.

Inside the command center, Hadrian, having just arrived in camp the previous day, met with his commanders. Reysa's newly-appointed governor was also in attendance. Ever since Hadrian had reinstalled him, Rankin had been insufferable; ordering people around and flaunting his power at every opportunity. Now he stood haughtily next to the upper echelon of the Gartune ranks as they went over their plans. A map of The Crescent was laid out on a table in front of them.

"They will arrive through Octavian's Pass, I guarantee it," said Rankin smugly.

"You guarantee it, do you?" said Hadrian as he sized up the governor, "What happens if they come through the Battle Plains or somehow by sea? Will you *guarantee* that you will resign your new position if you are mistaken?"

"They couldn't come by the sea... they have no boats," replied Rankin, suddenly feeling less sure of himself.

"The Reytana didn't have any boats when they left. That doesn't mean that they don't have any now. Eighteen years is plenty of time to build an armada of ships," said Hadrian.

"Your highness," interjected Morlo, "the pass does seem to be the most logical route. It would provide them with cover until the moment they arrived. It is also the most direct route from their last reported location near Woodhaven. If I had to guess which way they would choose to come," he continued cautiously, "it would be Octavian's Pass."

"Well I don't *guess*," growled Hadrian as he pounded the table in front of him. "Where's that waif!"

"What waif?" asked Rankin.

"Declin," said the king.

"The one who brought Septa back?" asked Morlo. He immediately regretted mentioning the king's daughter.

"Yes," said Hadrian, giving Morlo a hard stare. "He should have been here by now."

"Your highness," said Rankin, "if I may suggest an alternative... the prisoners have received their light. They are ready—"

"No," said Hadrian, cutting him off, "the prisoners stay in their cells until I say otherwise. If all goes according to plan, we won't need them."

"But your highness—" started Rankin.

"They are not to be released! Do I make myself clear?"

"Of course, my king." replied Rankin, his head bowed.

Hadrian took a few moments to compose himself, then continued. "I trust that the rest of the prison is ready for its new inmates?"

"Yes, my king. Preparations are complete" said Rankin. He started to lift his head proudly but ducked it slightly when he saw that the king was not as impressed with the achievement as he was. "We are finishing it just today. It would be my honor to escort you for an inspection."

"Very well," said Hadrian. "But first," he looked at Morlo, "what is the status of *your* project? Is everything in place?"

"Yes, your highness. The project is complete. We are ready."

"Good. Then the trap has been set." Hadrian smiled and addressed the entire room full of Gartune. "Find whatever glory you seek in the battle that is to come, for this will be the last of the Great Wars, and it will be a short one at that!" He turned back to Rankin. "Come! Take me to the prison. I want to see what eighteen years of Reysene labor looks like." The two started for the door. As they went through, Hadrian shouted over his shoulder, "And, Morlo, if that waif ever does show up, bring him to me!"

"Of course, my king," replied Morlo with a low bow.

Lucan clasped his hands behind his head and leaned back against the cold, steel bars. The remnants of that day's meal sat between his legs on a metal tray. Everything about his life was now made of metal or steel. Everything was cold. Everything was hard. Even so, he had started to adapt to his new environment. Though he had only recently been caged, he had felt like a prisoner for many, many years; a prisoner in his own city. But he had learned to adapt to that life, and now he would learn to deal with this one as well. He would endure. He would go on. The simple clarity of these goals gave him a degree of solace. His cellmate, on the other hand, was not doing as well.

It was harder for a Reytana. Every ounce of their being yearned for the sun. It was their lifeblood. Being stuck underground for weeks without a single glimpse of the sun was slowly killing Dario. They both knew it, but they didn't speak of it. There was no need.

Even if Dario had started his incarceration in perfect health, he would still be ailing after all the time spent away from the sun. As it was, the ex-governor of Reysa entered captivity battered and bruised, and his wounds had not healed. If anything, they had gotten worse. Lucan offered to help, even though he knew there was little he could do. Each time Dario simply brushed him away. And yet, the old Reytana had not given up. Neither of them had. Perhaps if they had each been alone in their prison, they would have resigned themselves to whatever fate awaited them. But all they had to do was look out at their fellow prisoners and they had all the motivation they needed to continue to fight on; to continue to eat and sleep and breathe—to continue to live so that when the time came, they would be ready to do what must be done. They would be ready to fight.

A loud bang rang out from the cell two doors down from Lucan and Dario. Then a low moan and another loud bang, followed by a slightly louder moan.

"Thumper is at it again," said Lucan. "Poor guy just can't help himself."

"Don't call him Thumper," replied Dario stiffly as he rolled over to look at the cell where the bangs were coming from. A pale Reytana youth, clad only in a dirty loincloth, was rubbing his head while inspecting the ceiling of his cell a few inches above him. His golden eyes glowed angrily as he bent his knees in preparation of another jump.

Suddenly, Dario raised his hand. The youth stopped to look at the old Reytana, still frozen in a crouch, ready to spring. Dario locked eyes with him and slowly shook his head. The youth's shoulders slumped, and he slid down to sit on the floor, putting his head between his legs. Tears began to stream down his dirt-covered cheeks, but he did not make a sound.

Dario turned back to Lucan. "Don't call him Thumper."

"You're right," Lucan sighed. "But they should have names. They aren't animals, they're Tormada. Tormada have names."

"Their parents will give them their names," said Dario, "just like always." Lucan gave a small smile and nodded. Further down the row of cells, another bang rang out. And then another.

"They get more restless by the day," said Lucan. Prisoner after prisoner began to get up and make a commotion in their cell. Some grabbed their cell bars and pulled back and forth as hard as they could. Others paced the tiny perimeter of their cage, back and forth and back and forth. Still others were imitating Thumper and banging their heads against the ceiling. Even though they had only inches of space above them, they still insisted on jumping. The need to jump was stronger than the pain of hitting their head. The only Reytana that remained calm was the one directly across from Dario and Lucan. He crouched at the front of his cage clutching the bars with both hands. His wide-eyed face was pressed hard against the bars. The boy watched Lucan and Dario's every move without blinking.

"We should give him a name at least," said Lucan, gesturing toward the crouched Reytana across from them. "We may as well be his parents."

Dario studied the youth. *He's one of the bigger ones. Although, I've never seen him stand up so it is hard to tell. But he looks strong.* The boy's eyes were always probing, always searching them for something. In a room full of emptiness, this Reytana was trying to absorb as much as he possibly could. Dario thought he knew why the boy didn't blink. It was because he was afraid he might miss something.

"That one would chew his way through those bars if we asked him to," said Dario.

"If *you* asked him to," corrected Lucan. The youth shifted his stance slightly, his gaze locked on Dario. "He knows you're talking about him."

Dario looked into those searching eyes for a long time. "Would you like a name?" he asked solemnly. The youth blinked.

"Well if that wasn't a *yes*, I don't know what is," chirped Lucan. The youth blinked again, excitedly this time.

"Very well," said Dario. "I'll have to think about it. You deserve a good name."

Just then, the sound of a door sliding open came from the far side of the cavern. Everyone immediately became silent and looked in the direction of the sound. Lucan and Dario both stood up and looked at each other, confused. There was only one door in this place, and it was on the other side of the room.

Two shadows began to grow on the wall across from where the new door had opened. The familiar sound of a eüroc tapping on the ground echoed as the shadows became larger. Tap... tap... tap. The origins of the shadows revealed themselves as two Gartune appeared around the last prison cell and walked toward the wall at the back of the cavern. One of them held a torch. The prisoners in the cells nearest to the light shielded their eyes with their arms and cowered in the back of their cages.

"You said it was done," said Hadrian as he stared at the blank wall at the back of the cavern. "This doesn't look done to me."

"I thought I would leave you the honors," said Rankin, gesturing toward the king's eüroc.

"Hmmm...." the king smiled, then turned to face the rest of the prison for the first time. Rows of shining golden eyes locked on to his every move. As if in a trance, those that were sitting stood up and those that were standing moved closer to the front of their cells to get a better view of the king. His sheer presence overpowered them. They could not look away. A few reached out through the bars, reaching for him.

"Look at them," whispered Lucan. "They can't resist." Another pair of arms grasped longingly for the king as he walked toward Lucan and Dario's cell. "Plucking those two from the river before they could reach him may be the greatest thing I've ever done," said Lucan.

"Quiet!" whispered Dario.

"Is that you, governor?" said Hadrian as he sauntered over to Dario and Lucan's cell. "I heard you were down here." Dario straightened himself the best he could but a quick squint of pain in his eyes betrayed him.

"It's been a long time, Hadrian," said Dario with a labored breath.

"That's *King* Hadrian!" shouted Rankin as he swung his eüroc at the bar that Dario was gripping. Dario did not remove his hand from the bar to avoid the blow, choosing instead to slide his hand just an inch below where Rankin's staff struck the cage at the last instant. He winked at Rankin.

"Still got a bit of fight left in you, I see," said Hadrian while holding back an enraged Rankin with one hand. He looked Dario up and down, noticing the cuts and bruises that covered his body. "Looks like you might be a bit out of practice, though."

"Yeah," said Dario with a grunt. "Well, you should see the other guys."

"Oh, I have. They are currently back at Gartol training to be real soldiers."

"You might want to consider sending a few more back," said Dario. "I've seen them exercising in the courtyards for many years and I've got to say... I'm not impressed."

Once again, Hadrian had to hold Rankin back. "Maybe you can size up my new army for me then," said Hadrian as he waved his free arm toward the prison cells. "You've been down here a while. You've watched them grow. That couldn't have been a pleasant thing to witness; a Reytana receiving their light while trapped in a cage. They seem to have all made it through, though. What do you make of them? Would they fight if they had to?"

"Oh, I don't doubt they would fight..." whispered Dario. He looked past the king and into the cell behind him. Standing, for the first time, was their inquisitive friend. His eyes were still locked onto Dario whereas everyone else was fixated on the king. He leaned his head forward slightly, as if he was about to pounce. His eyes searched Dario's face, searching for an order. Dario gave a quick shake of his head and the young Reytana crouched back down into his familiar position.

Hadrian looked around to see who Dario had motioned to. The crouched Reytana did not look up at the king.

"Interesting," said Hadrian. He thought for a moment. "Open that cage. Bring him out."

The youth jumped to his feet as Rankin removed a large keychain from his belt and unlocked the cell door.

"What are you going to do with him?" shouted Lucan.

"Back to your corner, torman," cracked Rankin. "This doesn't concern you."

Lucan looked around frantically but there was nothing he could do. Dario raised his arm halfway towards his cellmate in an attempt to calm him but Lucan was all out of sorts. He started stammering to himself as he paced back and forth in the back of the cell.

Hadrian shook his head. "See what happens when you put your faith in the weak, Dario? You end up sharing a prison cell with them."

Lucan shot the Gartune king a piercing glare but he kept pacing back and forth.

"He's stronger than a lot of tormen I know," said Dario and then he glanced at Rankin. "And more than a few Tormada as well."

Rankin ignored the slight and flung open the cell door so hard that it clanged loudly against the metal bars of the cage. The sound amplified as it echoed off the walls and all of the prisoners covered their ears in pain and began to moan. All except one.

The young Reytana plastered himself to the back of his cell as Rankin entered. His eyes darted back and forth between Dario and the approaching Gartune. Rankin dragged the youth into the hall and threw him at the feet of the king. Dario couldn't help but think that the anger behind Rankin's unnecessary show of force was directed toward him, not the terrified youth on the floor. He glared at Rankin but kept his mouth shut, not wanting to inflict anymore punishment on the innocent boy.

"Now we'll see if they will fight," said Hadrian. He held his eüroc in front of him and motioned for the prisoner to take it. Again, the young Reytana's eyes darted back and forth between Dario, Hadrian and the staff that was being offered to him. Dario gave a cautious nod and the youth slowly grabbed the eüroc then took two quick steps backward. "A little skittish," said Hadrian, "but I guess that is to be expected. Let's see how much light this one has." He motioned to Rankin.

"No!" shouted Lucan from the back of his cell. Dario raised his hand to silence him. The frightened Reytana took another two steps backward as Rankin approached while twirling his eüroc in his hands. Dario didn't need to see Rankin's face to know that he was grinning. The young Reytana looked at Dario. The older Reytana stared straight back at him and did not blink. He gave another small nod. A touch of fire began to glow in the young Reytana's eyes. He stopped retreating and faced his opponent.

Rankin laughed and threw a light jab at the prisoner's stomach. The eüroc struck him just under his ribs. The Reytana coughed but he did not step back. Rankin laughed again and threw another jab, this time slightly harder. It caught the Reytana right under the chin, forcing his head backward. Still, he did not step back. The glow in the young Tormada's eyes grew fiercer.

"Here we go..." said Hadrian.

Rankin's smile transformed to a scowl as he took two quick steps forward while raising his eüroc over his head. Just before he could bring it down on the prisoner, the Reytana lifted his own eüroc over his head and blocked Rankin's attack. The clang of metal on metal reverberated throughout the cavern. A few gasps came from some of the cages. Rankin's eyes widened as he looked through the crossed eürocs in front of him and saw pure fire emanating from the unwavering stare of the young Reytana. Suddenly, the Reytana disengaged from Rankin, bent down, and swung his staff behind the Gartune's legs and sent Rankin toppling backward. The surprised Gartune dropped his eüroc and it rolled over to the front of Dario and Lucan's cell. Rankin lifted himself onto his elbows and frantically crawled backward as the Reytana advanced upon him. Rankin stopped when he reached Hadrian's feet. Hadrian delivered a sharp kick to his back. The now terrified Gartune looked up but he found no aid in the face of the king. Suddenly, the Reytana swatted Rankin across the face with his staff. The prisoner was about to deliver another blow when Hadrian caught the eüroc as it sliced through the air. As soon as the Reytana met the king's cool, violet eyes, his fire left him.

"Good," said the king, reclaiming his eüroc from the prisoner. "Very good." The prisoner lowered his eyes and backed up against the outside of his cell. "It's ok. You can go back in," said Hadrian. He motioned toward the cell door. The Reytana looked back at Dario for approval and he received it with another nod. He slid back into his cell, crouched down and grabbed the prison bars with his hands. Once again, he was a frightened Tormada in a cage.

Hadrian casually closed the cell door. Then he removed the keychain from the lock and threw it at Rankin with disgust. The embarrassed Gartune stood quickly and brushed himself off with as much dignity as he could muster, then returned the keychain to its place on his hip.

Dario watched the crouched Reytana in the cell across from him. The youth was rocking slowly back and forth on his heels. Instead of looking at Dario like usual, he was staring at the floor.

"So, what now," said Dario.

"Now, nothing," said Hadrian as he looked approvingly at the cells full of Reytana. "And, if all goes to plan, it will continue to be nothing. More than likely, none of you will ever see me again." Hadrian walked over so that he was standing only inches from Dario's cell. Rankin's eüroc sat at the base of the cage. Hadrian toed it while staring Dario directly in the eyes and then kicked the staff up to himself. "But it's nice to know," said Hadrian with a smile.

The king's violet cape whipped around him as he turned and walked back to the far end of the cavern. Rankin came shuffling up behind him, being careful not to pull abreast of the king.

Hadrian stopped when he came to the foot of the wall. He looked back over his shoulder and shouted, "You're going to want to see this, governor. After all, it was your people that made it happen." Hadrian slammed his eüroc into the ground and the rock immediately cracked in front of him. A fault line zig-zagged up the wall until it reached the ceiling. Dust and small rocks fell from the crack for a few seconds, then a low rumbling started. The rumbling became louder until the entire cavern began to shake. Suddenly, the entire wall collapsed upon itself. Dario and Lucan watched in horror as the dust settled, revealing another, larger cavern behind it. It was lined with cages stacked on top of each other; hundreds of empty prison cells awaiting their occupants.

A few Reysene laborers with shovels and pick-axes wandered throughout the cavern. Dario thought he saw Loras and Regan's parents among the group, but he couldn't be sure. Once they saw Hadrian and Rankin, the Reysene quickly disappeared around a corner in the back of the room, leaving the newly-revealed prison empty.

Hadrian scanned the prison and then turned to Rankin with a satisfied look on his face. "Like I said, *this* will be the last war."

CHAPTER TWENTY-EIGHT
Time

Xander couldn't sleep. It wasn't that the cell was uncomfortable. In fact, quite the opposite. It was cool, dry and it even had a small cot in the corner to sleep on—a luxury that surely wasn't found in the prisons of Gartol. On most nights—or days—it was hard to tell when you were underground, Xander had slept rather well. But tonight was different. His mind wouldn't stop racing. And it wasn't just the knowledge that they would soon be moving out, or that a great battle was most likely on the horizon. No, the majority of his thoughts surrounded one subject. Regan.

Her visits had been the highlights of his days. Not that there was much to compete with. And that's not to diminish the companionship of an overly friendly rodent who had made the habit of frequenting Xander's cell, usually around meal time. *I'll miss you too, Reggie.* But now that his time in the Hole was coming to an end, Xander found that for the first time in his life, his thoughts didn't revolve around himself and his own future. They revolved around Regan's. She had no idea what waited for her. None of them did.

Outside his cell, a familiar shadow approached. He smiled. She had become like clockwork. But his smile vanished when the back of the prison guard's head suddenly stepped in front of the little window in his door.

"No visitors today, Regan," said the guard, blocking her path.

"Why?" Xander could hear the annoyance in Regan's voice. "I won't stay long. I just wanted to say goodbye before we left."

"I'm sorry," replied Tao. "The prisoners are about to be moved and the captain didn't want anybody to speak to them before that."

"Moved where?" asked Regan. Xander could see the guard's head nod towards something down the hall.

"So, they're flying out with us?" Regan asked. The guard nodded. A small wave of relief sprouted in Xander's stomach. He hadn't really thought that the Reytana would leave him imprisoned after they left for battle, but he wasn't sure until now. He wondered if all four of the prisoners were being taken, or if it was just him. The fates of his companions had not been high on his list of worries but he hoped that they would be coming as well. At least Damnar and Damina, anyway. They were mostly innocent in all of this. Belkore could sit and rot in his cell forever, as far as Xander was concerned.

"When will the rest of us know what ship we're on?" asked Regan.

"That is up to the captain," replied Tao.

"Any idea where he might be?"

"I would imagine he's in the main hall. There is a meeting with the other officers to finalize the plans, but it should be over soon."

"Thanks, Tao," replied Regan. There was a brief silence. Xander hoped that the guard might shuffle to the side so that she could at least say goodbye. But after a few moments, he heard Regan's footsteps walking away from his cell.

The look he gave her made it very clear it was time for her to be on her way so Regan turned around and walked back toward the main cavern, making sure that her brother and Tinko were still asleep as she passed the barracks.

She found Gracien talking to two other Reytana next to a large hovercraft at the center of the cave. The massive ship hummed with light energy and slowly bobbed up and down as if an invisible line tethered it to the ground. Small groups of soldiers conversed around the craft. It appeared that their meeting had just broken up. Regan patiently waited for Gracien to finish giving instructions to his two lieutenants, then she cautiously approached the Captain.

"I figured it would have been Loras who chose not to sleep," said Gracien amicably.

"I know. I tried, but I just couldn't," said Regan.

"I don't blame you," said Gracien. "Come; walk with me." He put his hand on Regan's shoulder, which was now level with his own. For a while, the two walked in silence. All around them, the final preparations were being completed.

Small energy orbs were being filled from the main orb in the center of the cavern and then loaded onto the ships. Some of the hovercraft were testing their take-offs, presumably because they hadn't been used in many, many years. The giant vessels hummed as solar energy flowed from the energy orbs into the various compartments of the ships. Impossibly intricate wings began to unfold from the sides of each vessel. The wings consisted of several shimmering feather-like segments that interwove seamlessly with each other. When they moved, the fluidity was organic, as if they were the wings of a giant bird. Each time the wings flapped, a wave of solar energy pulsed from the bottom of the hull and lifted the ship slightly off the ground. As more and more ships began to energize, the light in the cavern increased. The room was brighter than Regan had ever seen it, and the brighter it became, the warmer she began to feel inside. She could see that it was having a similar effect on everyone else. All the Reytana had an extra glow in their eyes as they went about their tasks.

Gracien led Regan through the fleet of hovercraft, casually inspecting them as he walked by. Finally, he broke the silence. "You are worried about what will happen to the prince," he said.

"I am worried about what will happen to all of us," replied Regan. "But yes... him too. He saved my life back in the forest. And I—"

"You feel you owe him something?" Gracien said with a raised eyebrow as he stopped and turned to face Regan.

"I just don't want to see him killed. And I don't think he will be a very useful hostage."

"Why is that?" asked Gracien.

"You know the Gartune better than me," replied Regan. "Do you think they would take him back after what he has done?" Gracien did not respond.

"I think the moment he saved my life, he gave up his own. It all just happened so fast, I don't think he even realized what he was doing."

"He knew what he was doing," said Gracien. He took his hand off of Regan's shoulder and looked her in the eyes the way a father might.

"I never got to say goodbye to him," she said in a voice barely above a whisper. "I'm afraid I might never see him again."

Gracien sighed. "Why don't you ride with him," he said. Regan tried to restrain her smile but she could not hide the look in her eyes. Gracien took a step closer to her and lowered his voice. Still locking eyes with Regan, his tone was deathly serious. "I won't pretend to know the extent of your relationship with the prince, nor will I tell you how you must act around him. You are a full grown Reytana now and those decisions you must make for yourself. But know this. No matter what he tells you or how he looks at you, Xander is dangerous. He is an animal looking for a way out of his cage. Don't think that he won't use you, or any one of us for that matter, to free himself."

Regan gave a slight nod. "I understand, Captain."

Gracien regarded the young Reytana in front of him for a few moments. "You have changed quite a bit since you arrived here, Regan. And I'm not just talking about your height. You are stronger—more sure of yourself. And I think perhaps your visits with Xander may have had something to do with that. Whatever happens next, I don't want you to lose what you have gained these past days."

"I won't," said Regan.

"Promise me," said Gracien.

Regan mustered up the strongest look she could manage. "I promise," she said.

"Good," said Gracien. "Now go wake up your brother and Tinko. It's time."

CHAPTER TWENTY-NINE
Octavian's Pass

Octavian's Pass was a tree-lined valley that skirted the base of the Crescent Mountains from Woodhaven to Reysa. Many years ago, a river had flowed through the center of the valley making it a convenient trade route for waifs looking to barter with the Reysene. But the river had long since dried out and filled in with dense forest.

Several massive shadows in a "V" formation swept over the forest canopy as the Reytana fleet gracefully floated through the valley. The tips of the trees gently bent and swayed as ship after ship flapped just a few feet above. Other than the rhythmic whooshing from their wings, the hovercraft were completely silent—an impressive feet for such a large armada of machines. It was a testament to the ethereal craftsmanship of the Reytana. The Gartune may have been known as the "builders," but the Reytana also had plenty of engineering prowess.

Aboard the lead ship, Loras closed his eyes and tilted his head back. He let the warm breeze flow over his face, soaking as much of it into his body as he could before it rippled through his hair. Waves of golden light gently pulsed through the ribbon around Loras' forehead. Behind him, a pale-faced Tinko leaned over the deck's railing. His white-knuckled hands clutched the bar as hard as they could, but they could not prevent his hefty frame from swaying back and forth with each flap of the hovercraft's wings. Frequently, his cheeks would puff up, followed by a muttered "sorry" and then a wipe of his mouth.

"Who are you apologizing to?" asked Loras, his face still tilted toward the sky.

"The ship. The trees. Whatever is living in the trees," mumbled Tinko.

Loras laughed. "Aren't you empty by now."

"Not quite yet. I swear I just saw a nimber shake his fist at me," replied Tinko.

"Maybe he was just waving," continued Loras.

Tinko wiped his mouth again and attempted to stand up straight, leaving one hand on the railing for support. "Well, if somebody kept throwing up on me, I would like them to apologize."

"Fair enough," replied Loras.

"I see at least one of you is enjoying the ride," said Gracien as he strode up the hovercraft deck and joined the two friends.

"Oh, it's a lovely ride. Just lovely," said Tinko. Then his cheeks puffed up again and he quickly leaned over the railing. "Sorry," he muttered.

"It's amazing," said Loras. "I feel like I'm being fueled."

"You are," said Gracien. "We all are. Reytana are meant to be outside in the sun, not trapped underground. That life is for the Gartune." Gracien nodded toward the two cages on the far side of the deck. Inside, Damnar and Damina had the same queasy complexion as Tinko.

"This life is for us," Gracien said.

"I don't know how you did it for so long," said Loras. "Why did you stay hidden for so many years? What were you waiting for?"

Gracien thought for a few moments before he answered. "For the right time," he said.

Loras opened his eyes and turned toward the captain. "And now is the right time?"

"Now is the time, young warrior." Gracien placed his hand on Loras' shoulder, as he was so apt to do, while tilting his own head up to the sky and closing his eyes. "Now is finally the time," he repeated softly. The two Reytana took a few minutes to soak in the sun's rays together, side by side. But, even in the peaceful sunlight, something nagged at the back of Loras' mind. It had been bothering Loras since they left the Hole. He wasn't sure if it was his place to bring it up, but he decided to anyway.

"Aren't you worried that someone has spotted us?" asked Loras.

"Not really," replied Gracien.

"You're not?" asked Loras. "Shouldn't you be? I mean look around. Twenty giant hovercraft are pretty hard to miss. I mean somebody down there has to have seen us."

"Oh, I'm sure somebody probably has," replied Gracien, still unconcerned. Loras looked at him, confused.

"Then why aren't you worried?" asked Loras.

"Look down," said Gracien. Loras leaned over the hovercraft's railing and looked down at the trees zooming past them. "Nothing in this world moves faster than we are moving right now, except for the hyper-rail. If some woodsman spotted our ships, it would not matter. We will be at Reysa far before any word of our coming has reached the city."

"But what if somebody spotted us a week ago in Woodhaven?" said Loras, suddenly feeling very guilty.

"Yes, I suppose somebody could have seen us then," said Gracien. Loras searched for any hint of blame in the Reytana commander's voice and was relieved to not hear any.

"And you're still not worried that the Gartolians could be waiting for us?"

Gracien opened his eyes. They were glowing. "I hope that they *are* waiting for us!" Loras was taken aback by the captain's sudden change of demeanor, and a little scared too. Gracien saw the worry in the young Tormada's face. "There's something you will soon come to understand about Tormada, Loras. It is not in our nature to back down from a fight. It is not in our nature to retreat. And it is especially not in our nature to abandon those that we swore to protect. All of those things happened eighteen years ago when King Atholos forced us to retreat to the Hole. You have no idea how hard it has been on all of us since then. We weren't suffering because we had to live underground, away from the light. That, we dealt with because we had to. It was the *guilt* that caused us to truly suffer. The guilt from abandoning Reysa has been a festering wound. And now, finally, we get a chance to redeem ourselves. To heal. It does not matter if we face one Gartune or the entire Gartolian army tomorrow. At last, we will be given the chance to make things right."

Loras thought about that for a while. "Yeah, well given the choice," said Loras, "I think I would rather face just one Gartune rather than the entire army."

Gracien smiled. "We don't always get to choose the playing field. But we still have to play."

"So, we attack tomorrow?" asked Tinko, rejoining the conversation. "But at this speed, we will be at Reysa by tonight."

"We will wait for the morning," replied Gracien. "Reytana do not fight in the dark unless we absolutely have to."

"Riiiight," said Tinko. "Because you need the sun to fuel your weapons." Gracien nodded. "Well, I have some bad news for you, Captain. I know you've been gone a long time, but there's been an *addition* to the city since you left."

"I know of the shield," said Gracien.

"So, you know that all of the city's weapons are blocked from the sun and chances are, you'll be fighting in the shade as well," said Tinko.

Loras began to panic. He had forgotten about the shield. There was no way that the Reytana could defeat the Gartolians while the shield was up. They needed the city's defenses activated if they were to have any chance.

Gracien nodded toward the rear of the ship, where the massive energy orb from the Hole was tied. "That will reactivate the city's defenses," he said.

"But for how long?" asked Tinko.

"For as long as it takes us to defeat the army on the ground," replied Gracien.

"So, it's a race..." said Loras warily, "we need to defeat the Gartolian army before the orb runs dry."

"That's one way to think about it," said Gracien.

Tinko started doing some calculations in his head. He didn't seem to like the results. "Assuming that Reysa's defensive shield is fully activated and the solar cannons along the city's walls are still functional, how long do you suppose we will have before we are out of juice?"

"Somewhere between seven and eight hours," replied Gracien calmly.

"That's it?!" exclaimed Loras and Tinko simultaneously.

"It will be enough," said Gracien. "And if it is not, then I will disable the Gartolian sun shield. "

"How?" asked Tinko. "You've never even seen it. How do you know how to disable it?"

"I know more about it than you think," said Gracien. "Even though I've been away, I have not been totally cut off from what was happening in the city. Dario sent news whenever he could. We were not unaware."

"Ok, so then you know that you can't just blow the shield up," said Loras. "It would fall onto the city and kill everyone. "

"Correct," said Gracien. "It has to be retracted."

"And you know how to retract it?" asked Tinko.

"I know how to retract it," replied Gracien.

Both Tinko and Loras stared at the captain, waiting for him to tell them how it was done, but Gracien said no more.

"I'll bet there's a button," whispered Tinko sarcastically to Loras. "It probably says 'down.'"

Gracien laughed in spite of himself. "In fact, there is a button. The problem is getting to that button."

"It's on a tank, isn't it," said Loras. Gracien nodded.

"Which tank?" asked Tinko. Gracien looked at Loras for the answer.

"It's on the one in the water, isn't it" said Loras, glumly. He thought back to the time in the river when he had invaded the realm of Lyse. "How are you going to get there?" asked Loras. "That... elemental... doesn't like us in her water."

"No, she doesn't," agreed Gracien. He did not seem to be sharing Loras' concern.

"Then how are you going to get to the tank?" Loras asked again.

"I'm going to swim," replied Gracien, smiling.

"She won't let you," said Loras.

"I'm a very good swimmer," replied Gracien, still smiling. He winked at Tinko. Loras was dumbfounded.

"Why don't you just take a hovercraft?" asked Tinko.

"I'd be spotted," said Gracien. "They can't know that I'm coming to disable the shield. They might lock it... or worse."

"*They might blow it up,*" whispered Tinko to himself. Gracien nodded.

"And what if you fail?" asked Loras, still struggling to process the plan. "What if you aren't able to disable the shield?"

Gracien glanced over at Tinko. "Then we fight in the shade," he said calmly. Loras sighed. It was all becoming very real now. No longer a daydream in Lucan's classroom. Loras began to feel the weight that all soldiers felt on the eve of battle. More likely than not, that battle was going to be against a large Gartolian army that was prepared for an attack. He shook his head.

"We're going to be outnumbered, aren't we," said Loras to nobody in particular.

"Probably," said Gracien.

"It's not fair," interjected Tinko. "There are always supposed to be an equal amount of Reytana and Gartune. That's why the Scales exist! So that the sides are even. So that nobody gets slaughtered!"

"I don't suppose we're stopping to pick up the Fallen Reytana somewhere here in the forest," said Loras to Gracien. There was a bit of hope mixed in with his sarcasm.

"I'm afraid not," said Gracien. Loras pounded his fist on the railing and looked down into the forest below as if he hoped to discover a camp of one hundred and fifty Reytana.

"If only we knew where they were, this could be a fair fight," said Loras.

"We know where they are."

Loras spun around to face Gracien, his eyes wide.

"Say that again?" said Loras.

"We know where they are," repeated Gracien. Loras and Tinko looked at each other excitedly. They couldn't believe what they were hearing. "But they won't do any good," continued Gracien. Loras and Tinko were confused by his solemn tone.

"Won't do any good?" repeated Tinko. "Why not? How could they not help us?"

"Because they are imprisoned," said Gracien. His voice was a mixture of sadness and anger.

"Imprisoned!" shouted Loras, "Where?!"

Gracien paused for a moment. "In Reysa."

"What?!" Loras and Tinko shouted together.

"They are imprisoned in Reysa," repeated Gracien. "They've been locked up there for their entire lives." Loras and Tinko couldn't believe what they were hearing. They looked back and forth between each other and the captain, unable to think of anything to say. There were too many questions. Finally, Loras gathered himself enough to ask one.

"I've lived in Reysa my entire life. If there were a hundred and fifty Reytana jailed in the city, I would have seen them. *Somebody* would have seen them."

Gracien simply shook his head. "Their prison is underground in the heart of the cliff. That's why nobody has ever seen them."

A vision appeared in Loras' mind; a cold, dark cave full of children chained to the walls. A shiver went down his spine. *Their whole lives,* he thought. He couldn't imagine a torture worse than that.

"We have to free them!" shouted Loras.

"After we take back the city," replied Gracien.

"But couldn't they help us to take back the city?" asked Tinko.

Again, Gracien simply shook his head. "The Fallen ones have lived their entire lives in a jail cell. They are not trained for battle. We don't even know if they can speak. Rey-willing they were still able to receive their light even though they have been cut off from the sun, but even so, they are still barely more than children. I would not free them just to have them killed in battle."

"But—" Loras continued but Gracien raised his hand to cut him off.

"They will be freed *after* we take the city." The look Gracien gave the teens let them know that the discussion was over, but he could tell by their faces that Loras and Tinko were still distressed.

"I think that's enough questions for now," said Gracien, releasing the sternness in his eyes. "If you're worried that our plan has some holes in it, remember this—we are about to go to war, and in war nothing goes according to plan." He bent over and pointed a finger at Tinko's forehead. "Ultimately, it won't matter what we planned here," he turned and poked his other finger in Loras' chest, "but what we found in here."

Gracien gave the boys a smile and then left them to go inspect the energy orb at the back of the ship.

"Just one time, I'd like somebody to point to my heart instead of my head," grumbled Tinko.

"Maybe after tomorrow, they will," said Loras. He put his hand over his friend's shoulder and the two looked out over the bow of the ship toward an uncertain future that was rapidly approaching.

Regan watched as the line of hovercraft in front of her gently rose and fell over the bow of her own ship. The calming movements of the flying vessels ran in direct opposition to the rapid and disjointed thoughts that were racing inside of her head. It was too much. She started to become dizzy and had to sit down.

"I thought floaters loved being up in these things," snorted Belkore from his cell in the back of the ship. He was noticeably queasy. "Why don't you ask if we can walk the rest of the way? I'll let you ride on my back." Regan ignored the prisoner. She took a deep breath and tried to clear her head, but it didn't work.

"Try closing your eyes," suggested Xander from the cage next to Belkore. He was also struggling with the flight, but not as much as the other two.

"It's not the ship," said Regan. "The ship is fine. In fact, I rather like being up here." She shot a sharp glance at Belkore. "I'm just..."

"Scared?" interjected Belkore.

"Anxious," said Regan.

"Well, of course you are," said Xander. "I'm sure you're not the only one. No shame in being a little excited." Belkore gave Xander a disgusted look and turned away from him, muttering under his breath.

"Want to talk about it?" asked Xander.

"Not particularly," said Regan.

"Ok," said Xander amicably. He waited a few moments before continuing. "Because if you wanted to talk, I've been told that I'm a great listener. A better talker; but also a great listener." Still Regan remained quiet. The only sound was the gentle whooshing of the hovercraft wings as they lifted the ship slowly up... and down... up... and down.

"You're worried about what will happen when we get to Reysa," continued Xander.

"I'm worried about what will happen when we get to Reysa..." whispered Regan, half to herself.

"You should be," growled Belkore. Regan caught a glimpse of the knowing smile that spread across his face. She immediately turned to him.

"What's that supposed to mean?"

"Oh nothing," sighed Belkore, his smile growing. Regan got up and approached his cage. Belkore put his hands behind his head and leaned against the bars in the back of his cell.

"Do you know something?" she demanded. Belkore only smiled. Regan looked over to Xander. "Do you know what he's talking about?" Xander shot Belkore a piercing look, but then he sighed and bowed his head. He thought for a moment before answering.

"Regan, do you know how a Tormada's parents are chosen?"

Regan looked confused. "What does that have to do with anything?" she said.

"Do you know how it's done?" Xander repeated.

"Something about collecting them out of the water when they arrive at their city," said Regan. "I don't know. They don't let tormen down at the collection pools and, as of three weeks ago, I was a torman, so it didn't really have anything to do with me."

"Right," said Xander, struggling with where to begin. "So, you know that Tormada don't actually give birth."

"Except for the Omegas," corrected Regan.

"Yes, except for the Omegas," replied Xander. "For the rest of us regular old Tormada, our parents are *assigned*."

"What do you mean, assigned?" asked Regan.

"If a Tormada wants to adopt a child, then they have to be the ones to pluck the babe from the collection pool once it arrives in Reysa or Gartol. They have to be the first Tormada that the baby sees. It is this actual act of pulling the child from the water that forms the parental bond between child and parent. Once that bond is formed, the baby is forever linked to their parent. They love them. They obey them. They will do anything for them. And that bond can never be broken. It is a part of their being."

"Ok, so what does that have to do with anything?" Regan asked, still confused.

"What do you think happened to your 'Fallen' Reytana? The ones who died during the war?" asked Xander.

"We're not supposed to talk about it."

"But what do you *think* happened?" Xander continued.

"Well," said Regan, "I guess I always just assumed they were captured or something. Like I said, we weren't supposed to talk about it, so I never really gave it much thought. You should ask my brother and Tinko. They have all sorts of theories."

"The Fallen Reytana were captured," said Xander, "but that's not the important part. The important part is *who* captured them."

Understanding began to creep over Regan's face. "My gods," she whispered, "Gartune adopted the Lost Reytana."

"Not just any Gartune!" interjected Belkore gleefully.

"There was only one Gartune who pulled the Reytana infants from your collection pool," said Xander. "My father."

Regan's eyes widened with horror. "Hadrian?! The Fallen Reytana were *assigned,*" she could barely get the words out of her mouth, "to your *father?*" She looked back and forth frantically, trying to process the new information as fast as she could. "So that means..."

"Yes..." said Xander. "They are tied to my father. They will obey whatever he tells them."

Regan's knees became weak and she sat down on the deck. "I think I'm going to be sick," she said.

Xander stood and walked to the front of his cage. "I don't know what his plans are for them. Maybe he doesn't plan on using them. After all, they aren't warriors. Last I saw of them, they could barely speak. But those Reytana aren't coming back to help you in this fight. That you can be sure of."

"Wait," said Regan, slowly lifting her head. "*The last you saw them?*"

"Ha!" jeered Belkore. "This is the best part!"

"You've *seen* them?"

"I was in charge of their welfare while I was in Reysa," said Xander carefully.

"But how can that be—" Regan answered her own question before she could finish it. "They're in *Reysa?*"

Xander nodded his head.

"Where?" cried Regan. "There is no jail large enough to hold one hundred and fifty Reytana anywhere in the city!"

"That's because it's under the city."

A shiver ran down Regan's spine. She remembered how cold and empty she had felt living in the Hole for only a short period of time. A mixture of fury and despair filled her heart. Her eyes began to water. She turned away from the prisoners in order to hide her face.

"Regan..." Xander said softly but she raised her hand at him and walked away.

The shadows grew long in the valley as the sun began to set over the Crescent Mountains. Twenty bird-like vessels floated up and down as they approached the city of Reysa.

It was almost time.

CHAPTER THIRTY
Basecamp

Twilight painted the tips of the tallest buildings in Reysa with a golden brush. The rest of the city was a dark silhouette against the auburn sky. Even though daylight had faded, the sun shield remained above the city. It had not retracted since Loras, Regan and Tinko escaped. Rankin had ordered it so. It was the first ordinance that he had instituted as the new governor. He said that it served as a reminder that the Gartolians were always there, always watching, even while the Reysene slept.

At this hour, the Gartolian base camp lay in the shadow of the city. Torch lights began to glow at evenly-spaced intervals throughout the rows of tents. A soft light emanated from the door of the large command center in the middle of the camp. Two Gartune soldiers stood at either side of the door, staring straight ahead. A group of eight Gartune, marching two abreast, patrolled the perimeter of the circular building while the muffled sounds of a one-sided argument leaked out of the command center door.

"Where are my tanks?" shouted Hadrian. "They should have been here two days ago!"

"They should be here by the morning," said Morlo. The tone of his voice did not convey the certainty that Hadrian was looking for.

"You told me the same thing yesterday, and the day before that!" seethed Hadrian. "Are you lying to me again, Morlo?"

"No, your highness, it's just that they had some trouble getting through—"

"I don't want to hear excuses!" interrupted Hadrian. "The Reytana could arrive at any time." The king stood over the shorter Gartune and pressed an angry finger into his chest. "And if they get here before my tanks, it's *you* who I will hold responsible. And trust me, you will not enjoy the consequences of that failure."

"I understand, your highness," whispered Morlo, looking at his feet. Just then the doors swung open and two Gartune sentries entered, holding a much smaller man in between them. They shoved the man forward and he awkwardly fell to his knees on the hard dirt floor. He took turns coughing and muttering curses while water dripped from his matted hair and dirty clothes. He spit, wiped his mouth, then spit again before rising up onto one knee and lifting his head.

"We found this waif trying to climb up the old cliff path to Reysa," said one of the sentries. "He claims he was looking for you."

"I was beginning to wonder if you had forgotten about us," said Hadrian to the man on the floor. "That would have been a costly mistake on your part."

"I never forgot, your 'ighness," said Declin in between another round of coughs. "I got 'ere as fast as I could. 'Ad to take da river and it's been awhile since I 'ad da occasion to travel dat way." He rung out one of the sleeves of his shirt and formed a muddy puddle on the floor. "Normally, I would 'ave walked, but I knew you needed me 'ere quickly. So, 'ere I am."

"And what do you have for me, waif?"

"Dey are comin'" said Declin, still trying to catch his breath. "I left before dem but dey weren't far behind."

"Which *way* are they coming from?" asked Morlo.

"'Tavian's Pass is what dey told me and dey had no reason to lie. Dey may even be at da end of it right now."

"So Rankin was right," replied Hadrian.

"Should I move the army to the mouth of the pass, your highness?" asked Morlo eagerly.

Hadrian studied the waif silently for a good deal of time before answering his commander. "No..." said Hadrian thoughtfully. Declin and Morlo both gave the king a confused look. "You wouldn't be playing both sides again, would you, old friend?"

Declin's face changed from confusion to anger. "I didn't nearly drown myself to come down 'ere and lie to ya!" said the waif at a volume that he instantly regretted. Hadrian raised one eyebrow at the torman. Declin adjusted his tone.

"I mean... I wouldn't dare to lie to ya, your 'highness. The floaters are comin' through da Pass, you can be assured of dat. And if dey aren't 'ere already, dey will be soon. Dat you can also be certain of."

Hadrian stroked his jet-black goatee while continuing to study the waif. The flames from the torches inside the room reflected off of the meticulously polished bands of metal that adorned his wrists, shins and forehead.

"You say you came all this way to tell me this, and yet my guards say when they found you, you were scaling the cliff to Reysa. So tell me... are you really here of your own volition or were you simply caught?"

"I swear, I was comin to find ya!" exclaimed Declin.

Hadrian raised his arms to the side and looked around the room. "I've been right here. Seems to me that the big command center at the middle of camp would be the first place I would come looking. Yet you were trying to get into the city. Why?"

"Thought ya might 'ave been in da capitol, is all," replied Declin with a slight quiver to his voice.

"Then why not take the lift?" asked Hadrian as he started to slowly approach the kneeling waif.

Declin snorted. "Ya 'tink those guards o' yours is just gonna let some wanderin woodsman take a ride on up to da city? Especially *now*?"

Hadrian stood over the kneeling waif and continued to stroke his goatee while he thought. The longer he stood, the more agitated Declin became. "Look, your 'ighness, I ain't lyin to ya. But if ya don't believe me 'den can you at least 'ave 'dese two lock me up somewhere? All this kneelin ain't doin my leg any favors."

Hadrian grunted then nodded to the guards who brusquely lifted Declin to his feet.

"Morlo, take a regiment to the mouth of the pass and have them sink the forest turrets," ordered Hadrian.

"But if the Reytana are here, we won't have the time to—"

"You'll have time," said Hadrian before Morlo could finish. "Even if the Reytana are already here, they won't come out of the pass until morning. Take the soldiers and sink the turrets and then wait in the forest. Do not approach the mouth of the pass. At first light, the Reytana will emerge. Let them come all the way out of the valley before you engage them. Cut off their retreat and force them toward the rest of us. Do *not* let them back into the pass, do you understand?"

"Yes, your highness," said Morlo with newfound determination. "I will drive them to you like nimbers to a hungry mendkin!"

"Just remember who the mendkin is..." replied Hadrian. "Now go. You have your orders." Morlo pounded his chest twice with a closed fist and then spun excitedly and stomped out the door. After Morlo left, Hadrian nodded to the two guards to let them know they could retake their posts outside the building. Once they, too, had exited the room, Declin nervously shifted his weight back and forth between his good leg and his bad while grinding his hands on his walking stick.

"So, if 'der is notin' else dat you be needing me for, your 'ighness, I will be on my way."

"I'm afraid you won't be going anywhere, old friend," replied Hadrian. "You're going to have a front row seat for this one. And I hope, for your sake, that your information is accurate. If I so much as see one hovercraft come from the sea or from behind us on the plains, I will personally see to it that you are loaded into a tank and fired into the heart of the Reytana."

"Tank?" replied Declin a bit confused. "Granted, it were dark when I got 'ere, but I didn't see no tanks out der in da camp..."

Hadrian turned to the waif with a small smile on his face.

"No... you didn't, did you?"

CHAPTER THIRTY-ONE
Ambush

Dawn was minutes from breaking in Octavian's Pass when Loras awoke from his half-slumber. The Reytana armada had landed several hours ago and Gracien had recommended that everyone use the time to rest up before morning. *Easier said than done*, Loras thought as he stretched his arms.

Loras had drifted in and out of consciousness for the past two hours, and he found himself more tired than if he had not slept at all. Every time he drifted into sleep, he immediately started to dream of the upcoming battle. The dreams didn't last long though, as inevitably he always wound up dying in some new and spectacular fashion. Often, he found himself at the wrong end of a Gartune eüroc. Twice he was shot by a tank and once he was run over by one. He even somehow managed to fly a hovercraft straight into the cliffs of Reysa. Each time he died in a dream, he jerked awake, wide-eyed and sweating. Now that morning had almost arrived, Loras found that he was thankful to be relieved of his dreams and ready to face reality.

The valley floor was bustling with commotion. A few stragglers that had sought their sleep on the ground rather than on the hovercraft deck were climbing aboard their ships. The hum of solar energy igniting the hovercraft began to reverberate through the valley. Ship after ship gently lifted off of the ground. Gracien had parked the fleet right before the last bend that led to the mouth of the Pass. From there, it was a straight shot of about a thousand yards to the base of Reysa.

Loras climbed aboard the lead ship and found Gracien giving final orders to his lieutenants. The majority of the Reytana fleet were to advance on the Gartolian base. While the enemy was engaged, Gracien would fly his hovercraft and the energy orb, up to the city.

From there, Gracien and a small contingent of Reytana would sneak into the capital and fill the lotus' orb in the courtyard. With a full supply of solar energy, they could then activate the city's defenses and provide support for the Reytana fighting below.

The lieutenants each took turns clasping forearms with their captain before heading off to join their own ships. Gracien turned to Loras. The leader of the Reytana had a glow to him that Loras had never seen before. Determination radiated from his entire being. Just looking at him filled Loras with courage. He knew at that instant that he would follow Gracien anywhere, even if it meant to his death, and was certain that everyone else in the army felt the same way. With that knowledge, Loras felt for the first time that, maybe, there was a chance of winning the battle to come.

"Are you ready, young warrior?" asked Gracien as he took his post at the helm of the hovercraft.

"I've been dreaming of this day my entire life," said Loras as he stood beside the Reytana captain, "but I don't think I've been ready until just now."

"Good," said Gracien. "Because it's time." Gracien beckoned to the helmsman and the hovercraft lifted off of the ground to join the other ships in the air. At the same moment, the sun began to peak over the Crescent Mountains and flooded the valley with light. The hovercraft drifted into their "V" formation and sped toward the mouth of Octavian's Pass. Sunlight glistened off of the metallic wings as they curved around the last bend in the valley. Gracien's ship led the charge.

Gradually, the valley widened and the slope on the southern side leveled, giving way to forest. Straight ahead, the cliffs of Reysa rose out of the horizon. At its base, the Gartolian camp sprawled from the mountain wall to the sea.

As the ships emerged from the mouth of the valley, Gracien raised his hand and the lead ship slowed its pace. The trailing ships decelerated to match. They cruised forward slowly. Up ahead, the Aeil River escaped the forest and cut across the plain toward Reysa. Here, the river was only about twenty feet across and smooth as glass—a far cry from the wide, gushing torrent of water that could be found near its source in Woodhaven. Giant bird-like shadows crossed the sparkling river as the hovercraft soared overhead. Gracien frowned as he scanned the area in front of him. He ordered his ship to slow even further.

"What's wrong?" asked Loras. "Why are we slowing?"

"Something isn't right..." said Gracien. Just then, something in the forest caught his eye. Loras thought he saw light flash off of a metal structure in the ground. Then it was gone. Gracien ordered his ship to stop. He studied the forest floor. Suddenly, there was another shiny reflection on the ground, then another, and another. Large circles of dirt began to rotate and rise out of the forest floor. Gracien had just enough time to yell "They're in the forest!!" before the first shot exploded from the trees.

Loras flew backward as the front of his hovercraft burst into a shower of wood and metal. His back hit something hard and it knocked the wind out of him. For several seconds a ringing filled his ears as he gasped for air. Blotches of white light obscured his vision. He squeezed his eyes shut to try to make them disappear. Darkness enveloped him as he sat clutching his ears.

After a few seconds the ringing dissipated and was replaced by the sounds of people shouting. The ship lurched backward as the helmsman attempted to regain control even though the vessel was now missing its front half. Loras opened his eyes and saw a bright clear sky above him. The white splotches were gone. He attempted to stand but was immediately thrown to the deck again as the hovercraft banked hard. It was then that Loras got his first glimpse of the destruction.

The armada was in disarray. Some ships were pointed toward the forest and firing relays of solar flares into the trees. Others were heading back for Octavian's Pass. Loras could see that several ships had sustained damage; more damage than he thought was possible in such a short amount of time. He looked into the forest to find where the first shot had come from. A steady *thud, thud, thud* of ammunition fire rang out from several cylindrical turrets that had emerged from the ground. Loras did not see any Gartune, but he occasionally spotted a violet cloak flapping from behind one of the turrets, so he knew that they were there.

"Back to the Pass!" someone shouted from a hovercraft close by. The ships that remained disengaged and turned back toward the valley. They flew as fast as they could, but a trail of turret fire peppered their retreat. Each ship sustained heavy damage to its stern by the time it was out of range of the Gartolian weapons.

Loras' ship was the last to join the fleet. It sputtered and landed at an awkward angle, throwing Loras and two other Reytana over the side. Once again, the air was knocked from Loras' lungs. He wheezed and clutched his chest. Two strong arms then grabbed Loras and lifted him off of his feet. He turned to the Reytana, expecting it to be Gracien, but it was not. It was the helmsman.

No sooner had the helmsman assisted Loras than he was rushing off to help someone else. Loras watched him run into the chaos of burning ships and injured Reytana. He squinted his eyes, trying to take in the scene, but it was just too hard to believe. The sense of optimism that had filled his heart just minutes ago was replaced with cold despair. *Had they lost the fight already? It can't be over so soon. It can't!* Loras looked around. He had to find Gracien. The captain would know what to do.

When Regan regained consciousness, she immediately noticed two things; the first was the overpowering smell of charred wood and metal. The second was an excruciating pain in her forehead. The pain was so bad that Regan was afraid to open her eyes, for fear that the daylight might make her head hurt even more. Instead, she lay on her back with her eyes squinted closed and listened.

The crackling of burning wood was all around her. Every now and then she heard the moan of collapsing metal. Acrid smoke filled her lungs, making it difficult to breathe. She coughed and rolled onto her side. She realized that she couldn't shut her eyes forever so she decided to open them, despite the pain that it might cause.

Regan slowly opened her right eye. Much to her relief, the pain in her head did not increase. At first, everything was brown and blurry. Then it started to come into focus. A heap of broken wood and metal, all that remained of her hovercraft, lay smoldering only a few feet away. Behind that, all Regan could see were trees.

She spun around to try to get her bearings and almost slammed into two large, black boots topped with metallic shin plates. Regan froze. Just beyond the legs in front of her, she spied the cages that had held the Gartune prisoners. Their doors were torn open. Regan was too scared to look up at the Gartune in front of her. But when a hand reached down to help her up, her fear subsided. She took the hand in hers and allowed herself to be pulled up to her feet. The smirking face that she met was not the one that she expected to see.

"Well look what we have here," sneered Belkore. "My, my, my... that's one nasty scratch you've got on your head there. Why don't you let me take a look at it?" His grin widened as he lifted his hands toward Regan's head. Instinctively, she leapt backward out of his reach. The strength of her jump surprised her, and she flew several feet off of the ground and landed only steps away from the fiery rubble behind her. Belkore's grin transformed into a snarl as he began to stalk his prey. "That's fine with me," he said. "More fun this way."

Regan looked from side to side, searching for any of the other Reytana that had been aboard her ship, but no one was to be found. Belkore laughed. "Look all you want. There ain't no one here but you and me." Then a voice came from behind Belkore.

"You never were one for a fair fight, were you, Belk?"

Belkore looked to the side, but he did not turn around. "I was wondering if you had survived the crash," he shouted over his shoulder. "I was going to go looking for you, but I found something more interesting instead." He turned his eyes back to Regan.

"You hurt my feelings, old friend. But no matter. I'm here now. Why don't you and I take this fine opportunity and see if we can't rejoin the rest of our brethren? I'm sure my father will just be overjoyed to see us. Well, you anyway. He probably hopes I was killed. In fact—new plan! You go, and I'll stay here. What do you say?"

"Oh, I'm going," replied Belkore, closing the distance between himself and Regan, "but I'm taking a prize with me."

"I'm afraid I can't let you do that, old friend."

"Oh, and you think you can stop me, coward?" sneered Belkore.

"He's braver than two of you!" replied Regan as she slowly circled away from Belkore and her way toward Xander.

"Is that so?" said Belkore. "Let me ask you something. Did he ever tell you how his brother *really* died? Or is he still going with that 'hit by a hovercraft cannon' story?"

Regan looked at Xander. He stared hard at Belkore but said nothing.

"He hasn't? Oh, well allow me to tell you what really happened. It's much more *enlightening.*"

"Choose your next words carefully, old friend..." said Xander.

"So, there's little Xan," continued Belkore, ignoring Xander's warning. "And he's been assigned as big brother Lex's steward during the battle. A steward has several jobs: he carries the Gartune's gear, sends messages, and most importantly, he *cleans up* the Gartune's victims."

"Cleans up?" asked Regan. She had stopped advancing toward Xander and instead remained frozen to her spot, unsure of what to do next.

"Murders," said Xander. "He means murders. The steward is in charge of finishing off the wounded enemy soldiers." Regan's jaw dropped.

"Exactly!" cried Belkore. "Except that, apparently, little Xan here didn't have the stomach for it."

"I was five!"

"You were a coward!" continued Belkore. "And because you were a coward that couldn't do his job, a wounded Reytana was able to sneak up on your brother and kill him! There was no hovercraft, no massive explosion. Just a scared little boy. *That's* who you've put your faith in, little girl."

Belkore began to advance again on Regan. She looked quickly over toward where Xander was standing. The prince lowered his head slightly. Regan could see a brief flash of guilt on his face, but it quickly vanished and was replaced by his normal, mischievous smile. Suddenly, he reached down to the ground, picked up a pebble and threw it at the back of Belkore's head. Belkore reached his hand up and blood came trickling through his fingers. Enraged, he finally turned around to face Xander.

"*Did you just throw a rock at me?!*" yelled Belkore.

"Oh relax," replied Xander, picking up another, larger stone off the ground, "it was only a pebble. Now this one," he tossed the stone up in the air. "This one might leave a mark. So why don't you leave that girl alone?"

"A coward *and* a traitor!" shouted Belkore. "First you attack your own sister, and now you protect *a floater!* All of those little chats while we were cooped up. I heard everything! You have fallen for this... *girl!* You choose her over your own blood!"

"Well she's much prettier than you."

"You know, you may be right about your father not wanting to see you again. I'll bet if he knew who you *really* were, he'd want you dead! Your sister was right about you all along. She always knew what you were hiding."

"Careful, Belk. You've been talking about my family an awful lot lately and that's a dangerous path," said Xander. "You think you know them? You have no idea. Why don't you just stick to me."

"The Gartune I knew is gone!" shouted Belkore. "It has been replaced by this weakling that I see in front of me! I guess all of those years living with the floaters has turned you into one!"

"You call me weak, and yet you're the one about to attack a defenseless girl."

"She's not defenseless!" shouted Belkore. "Look at her! She's a Reytana! You can't even see it because you're blinded like a love-sick pipken. She is the enemy!"

"She is not my enemy," said Xander softly. He started tossing the stone in his hand up in the air to himself. "If you want her, you're going to have to go through me. And as I recall, that hasn't worked out very well for you in the past, old friend."

"You're no friend of mine, traitor!" shouted Belkore. He ran at the Gartune prince, each foot cracking the ground where it landed.

"Here we go," said Xander. Rather than chucking the stone at the charging Belkore, he tossed it lightly in the air and yelled "Catch!" Belkore took his eyes off of Xander for an instant to watch the stone arcing up into the air. That was all Xander needed. In a flash, he reached behind his back and grabbed the piece of jagged metal that he had been concealing and threw it at Belkore. The makeshift dagger plunged into Belkore's chest. The Gartune looked down at the length of metal sticking out of his ribs, then up at his assailant with a mixture of shock and anger. He coughed once, fell to his knees and then disappeared into a cloud of purple dust. Xander and Regan watched as Belkore's aura slowly lifted up and floated west toward The Scales.

Regan stared at the spot where Belkore had disintegrated. She opened her mouth, but words would not come out. Xander saw her shock and put his arms around the girl.

"It's ok," he said, holding her close to his chest. "Nobody is going to hurt you."

"He just.... just... disappeared."

"That's the first time you've seen one of us die. Sometimes I forget how innocent you are." He pressed her head into his chest and stroked her hair gently. "It can be rather... unsettling to see for the first time. But that's just how it happens. It would not have mattered if I killed him or if he died in his sleep. We all go back to The Scales one day. You will. And one day, hopefully a long, long time from now, I will. It is how the gods made us."

Xander and Regan stood together for what seemed like a long time, just holding each other. Eventually, Regan's heart slowed and she stepped back from Xander's grasp. "You saved my life," she said, her voice quiet but full of emotion. "Again. Why?"

"Do I really need to tell you?" Regan didn't answer. Seconds that seemed like an eternity passed. Neither of them spoke. The silence was broken by a loud crash. They turned to see the remains of the hovercraft deck fall into the burning rubble. A large cloud of smoke rose from the pile, causing Regan to cough as she stepped away from the wreckage.

"We have to go," said Xander.

"Where?" asked Regan. She didn't know if he intended to take her back to her own people or to his.

"Somewhere safe. The ship that held Damnar and Damina's cages was shot in half. They may have escaped. Knowing them, they probably ran for camp, but I can't be certain. They may have suddenly gotten brave like Belkore. They could still be out here."

Xander looked around in the forest for a few minutes, searching for his eüroc. He found it amid a pile of burning rubble. Luckily, Gartolian metal doesn't burn. Xander withdrew his staff from the wreckage. There wasn't a speck of ash on it, as if the weapon were impervious to the fire. After a quick, inspection of his eüroc, Xander grabbed Regan's hand and led her through the forest. The two walked in silence for several minutes. Regan kept looking around to try to gauge the direction that they were traveling, but everything appeared the same. She could not determine their path. Then, finally, the forest opened up and Regan was staring at five hundred yards of empty sand. Past that, she saw a giant steel cage connected to several large pulleys that went all the way up the rocky cliff to Reysa. The lift. Xander had brought them to Reysa's front door.

Xander pointed at the expanse of sand in front of them. "War is coming. Reysa is the only safe place for you, and if we're going to cross, we need to do it now."

Regan examined the length of sand in between them and the lift. The sand was not what bothered her. What waited at the end of that run is what had her worried. Several Gartune soldiers were guarding the lift. There was no way they could reach the elevator undetected.

"How do you plan on getting us on that thing?" she asked.

Xander smiled. "Do you trust me?"

Regan thought for a moment and was surprised at how quickly and unequivocally she arrived at her answer.

"Let's go," she said, and the two of them started toward the lift.

As she crossed the empty space between the forest and the lift, Regan felt an eerie sense of the battle to come. She looked down at the clean, white sand and could almost imagine it painted with blood. To her left, she could just make out the mouth of Octavian's Pass. It was littered with debris from the damaged Reytana hovercraft. Smoke wafted out of the valley. For the first time, she thought of Loras. She wondered if he was all right. She sensed that he was, but it was just a feeling.

Xander caught her staring in the direction of the pass. "If they're smart, they're on their way back to their cave right now."

"They won't go back," said Regan. "They can't."

Xander nodded. "No, I don't suppose they can. But they won't have much time to regroup. Look." He pointed in the opposite direction. Emerging from around the far side of the cliff was the Gartolian army. They had been hiding there, waiting for the Reytana to come to them. Now that the Reytana had retreated, Hadrian's army advanced toward Octavian's Pass.

"We have to hurry," said Xander. He and Regan increased their pace to a trot.

When they had gotten within earshot of the lift, Xander stopped and grabbed Regan's hands and pinned them behind her back. "Ouch," she yelled. "What are you doing?!"

"Trust me," whispered Xander. "Follow my lead."

By this time the soldiers guarding the lift had taken notice of the approaching Tormada. Two Gartune approached Xander and Regan, their eürocs at the ready. One of them held up a hand, but Xander ignored it, proceeding forward with Regan held tightly in front of him.

"Halt!" yelled the Gartune with his arm raised. "Stop right there!"

"Put your hand down before I cut it off!" shouted Xander indignantly. Instantly, a look of terrified recognition flashed across the Gartunes' faces.

"Prince Xander, we didn't recognize you," said the soldier as he dropped his hand to his side, sheepishly.

"I don't know why not," answered Xander. "Most people can recognize my good looks from a mile away." He winked disarmingly at the soldiers as he and Regan continued toward the lift, undaunted. The Gartune who had ordered Xander to stop looked relieved that the prince didn't appear angry with him. The other soldier was confused.

"Excuse me, sir—" said the other soldier. "Who is that with you?"

Xander turned over his shoulder while still continuing forward. The amicable expression was gone from his face. "Who does it look like? She's a prisoner, you idiot! Now tell your lackeys to open that gate and take us topside. I want the best possible view to watch the battle!"

Two Gartolians immediately opened the lift gate for Xander and Regan. The two Tormada didn't even break stride as they strode into the elevator. The Gartolians shared wary glances as if deciding who was to go up with them, then, the shorter of the two slipped into the steel cage. He threw the lever upward, keeping his eyes on the ground the entire time. Two giant pulleys on either side of the cage spun into action and the compartment jumped off the ground with surprising speed. Up they sped along the face of the cliff. The ride was surprisingly smooth for as fast as they were going.

The higher they rose, the further Regan's heart fell into her stomach. As the plains sank beneath her, she could now see the mass of Reytana hovercraft jumbled together just behind the bend in Octavian's path. All the ships looked damaged. She could see Reytana moving frantically all over the wreckage. She wondered if Loras was one of those specs.

What she saw when she looked to her left was even more disheartening. Rows and rows of Gartolian soldiers, led by an entire regiment of Gartune, were marching neatly across the desert plain. Soon, they would be on top of the Reytana. Xander was right. They didn't have much time.

CHAPTER THIRTY-TWO
Regroup

Loras jumped from the deck of one damaged hovercraft to the next, desperately searching for Gracien. All around him, Reytana shouted orders to each other as they attempted to fix as many of the ships as possible before the Gartolian army reached them. A cursory inspection of the fleet indicated that maybe five or six of the ships were capable of flight. The rest were either totally destroyed or would take several hours to repair—hours that they did not have.

As he boarded each ship, Loras asked the remaining crew if they had seen the Reytana captain. Some shook their heads, and many ignored him altogether. Fixing the ships was a higher priority than the whereabouts of their leader. *He has trained them well,* thought Loras. *Too well for his own good, it would seem.*

Loras hopped on to a hovercraft that was missing its stern. Reytana were running back and forth along the deck, salvaging whatever they could. Fire crackled and wood creaked as the ship moaned from its wounds. Amidst the chaos, Loras spotted a familiar face. Tao stood motionless, staring at an empty spot on the deck.

"Tao!" yelled Loras as he ran up to the Reytana. Tao slowly lifted his head from the spot that he had been staring at. There were tears in his eyes. Loras noticed that he was holding something in his hand—a golden bracelet, identical to the one he wore on his left wrist. Loras looked down at the deck in front of Tao's feet and saw the last bits of golden dust float away into the air.

"Oh no..." said Loras.

Tao simply shook his head. "Go," he said. "Find Gracien."

Loras didn't know what to say, so he obeyed Tao's wishes and continued his search for the Reytana captain. Finally, he saw a ship with a group of Reytana huddled together in a circle, tending to something on the ground. Loras could tell by their demeanor that whatever lay between them was not good. Effortlessly, Loras cleared the twenty-foot jump between his ship and theirs, landing on the center of the deck with a heavy thud.

"That must be Loras..." said a wheezing voice from the center of the Reytana. As Loras ran toward the group, two Reytana stepped aside, revealing the voice's source. It was Gracien. His face was pale and his look severe. Two gaping wounds—one under his left shoulder and another in the center of his chest—oozed blood, and a large stain on his tunic indicated a larger wound was in his abdomen.

Loras slid down to the captain's side. He looked helplessly at the other Reytana. "Can't you do something?" he pleaded. "You have to help him!" But the Reytana just shook their heads.

"There is nothing to be done, young warrior..." coughed Gracien. "At least not for me. For you, however, there is still plenty left to do."

The corners of Loras' eyes started to shimmer. As he looked back down at Gracien, tears fell onto the dying Tormada's chest. Loras immediately wiped them off of Gracien's bloodied tunic, embarrassed that they had touched the captain. More tears fell. He couldn't help it. Gracien reached up and grabbed Loras arm. His grip was strong, even in his last moments. The two Tormada looked at each other, unblinking, for several silent moments. It was as if Gracien was trying to transfer the last bit of strength that he had into the young Reytana.

Loras wiped his eyes. His chest was tight. He didn't realize until that instant how much Gracien had meant to him. In less than two weeks, he had been more of a father to Loras than anyone he had ever known. He wanted to thank his mentor but couldn't find the words. The look in Gracien's eyes told him he didn't need to.

"You need to go on, Loras. You need to fight."

"How?" asked Loras. "Most of our ships are damaged. Several soldiers are dead and more are wounded. And we've lost the element of surprise. They know we're coming now!"

Gracien smiled wearily. "They always knew we were coming, Loras. They've been waiting for us for eighteen years... just as we've been waiting for them. If it wasn't today, then it would be tomorrow or the day after. But there was no escaping this day. We are here now. *You* are here now. It is time to face your destiny. It is time for you to be who you were born to be."

"*My destiny?* What destiny?" said Loras.

Gracien pulled the young Reytana close. Loras could tell he was fighting for every breath now.

"Listen... to me," coughed Gracien. "There isn't much... time. You have to get the orb... into... the city. The rest of them... will fight for you... they'll hold them off... until you get... there." Gracien released his grasp on Loras and leaned his head back onto the ground.

"I can't tell them to go out there and fight while I fly away to the city. They'll get slaughtered! They won't listen to me!"

"They... will... follow... you," panted Gracien.

"Why?" asked Loras.

"Because... you... wear... the... ri—" before he could finish, Gracien's eyes rolled into the back of his head and his wheezing ceased. Slowly, his body began to dissolve into a fine, golden dust. The dust rose upward, surrounding Loras for a few seconds. Then, it was lifted into the sky by a gentle breeze that caught the golden cloud and carried it west.

A myriad of emotions surfaced within Loras. Sadness, shock, and anger each took turns trying to consume him. But underneath these emotions, something else began to grow. A fire swelled inside Loras until it eventually pushed all of his other feelings to the side.

When Loras looked up, he found that all of the Reytana were looking down at him. Each one of them had the same steadfast look on their face. They had never looked at him that way before.

"Your orders, sir?" said a Reytana behind him. Loras recognized the voice. It was Tao. He wore his wife's bracelet on his wrist. Judging by his face, you would have never known he had lost her only minutes before.

Sir? Why am I now a sir? Loras rose to his feet and turned in a slow circle, regarding each of the Reytana that surrounded him. Without fail, each one of them looked right back at him with the same resolute stare. *They are waiting for me to tell them what to do.*

"What's all this then?" came a voice from the far side of the deck. Climbing over the rail, came a sweaty and dirt-covered Tinko. His right ear was bloodied and he had a large scratch on his chin, but otherwise he appeared to be okay. Loras smiled as his friend came panting up to the group. He had never been so happy to see him.

"I've been looking all over for you," said Tinko, giving Loras a sweaty embrace.

"You ok, Tink?" asked Loras. "You look like you may have taken a tumble."

"Oh, you know me," said Tinko, wiping his dirty face off on Loras' stomach, "I'm bouncy. Besides, I don't have as far to fall as you behemoths."

"Have you seen Regan?" asked Loras.

"Not yet. I *did* see what was left of the ship that was carrying Xander and the other Gartune. The cages were ripped open and there was no sign of anyone."

"That doesn't necessarily mean that they're alive," said Loras, looking down at the spot where Gracien had just disappeared. "Regan was on Xander's ship. How badly was it damaged? Could anyone have survived?

"I'm sure she's alive," said Tinko, attempting to sound confident. "Knowing her she's probably playing nurse somewhere. There are a lot of hurt Reytana out there. They really got us good, Loras."

Loras looked back at the other Reytana. For the first time he noticed that each one of them had been wounded. Looking at their resolute faces, though, you wouldn't know it. They continued to watch Loras, waiting for instructions. Loras looked back at Tinko. Then he had an idea.

"I can't tell any of you what to do," said Loras addressing the Reytana. "But if you want to fight, then I'm going to fight with you. Tinko here knows the city as well as I do. He can get the orb into the capitol building while we hold off the Gartolians."

Tinko's eyes widened. "I'm going to *what?*"

Loras grinned down at his friend. It was the same grin he used to have when the two of them would sword fight with sticks after school. "You're going to take that orb," Loras pointed at the giant energy orb that had been moved off of Gracien's ship, "and you're going to fly it up there." He pointed up to Reysa. "And you're going to do it before the rest of us are killed. Sound like a plan?"

Tinko looked incredulously at Loras. Then he looked back and forth at the other Reytana for some sign of assistance, but their faces were stone. Finally, he sighed. "Only you would come up with a plan like that."

Loras shrugged his shoulders, "It's the best I could do." Suddenly, and in unison, the surrounding Reytana pounded their left fists to their chests. They each gave a quick nod before dispersing into the crowd of surrounding ships, shouting orders as they went. Loras and Tinko were left alone on the deck.

"Well, you've really done it now," said Tinko. "Only one question though, if I may." Tinko pointed over toward the hovercraft that held the energy orb. "How do you fly one of those things?"

CHAPTER THIRTY-THREE
Jailbreak

"That damn fool, Morlo," muttered Hadrian to nobody in particular. His violet cape flapped in the wind as he led his army toward Octavian's Pass. Behind each shoulder marched a long row of Gartune soldiers in perfect time. They made sure to maintain exactly three feet of distance behind their king. Hadrian was always the first into battle. *The tip of the spear,* as he called it. The rest of the army knew to keep their distance.

The Gartune were dressed as they always were; dark violet tunics and black kilts with metal cuffs and shin guards. The officers, and of course Hadrian, wore violet capes. The only new additions to the uniform were rectangular metal plates that covered the left forearm of each Gartune. In battle, these plates could transform into shields of different sizes—torso-length for hand-to-hand combat or body-length to deflect a solar cannon blast.

Behind the row of Gartune marched the several hundred tormen soldiers that completed the Gartolian army. They wore steel breastplates and helmets. Their pants and sleeves were the same violet color as the Gartune tunics. The first row of tormen carried long spears, and the subsequent rows were armed with swords or daggers. The trailing rows carried backpacks full of medical supplies and other equipment necessary to support the battle. These were the stewards; young Gartolians, some of which were not much more than five or six years old. They, too, stepped in perfect time, the result of a lifetime of training for war. Left, right, left, right. There was no room for deviation in Hadrian's army. And yet, that was exactly what Morlo had done—deviated from the plan.

"I knew he wouldn't be able to wait before he opened fire," grumbled Hadrian to himself. "Had to take the glory for himself... I gave him one job... *one job*! Cut off the retreat. Push them forward. But instead, he lets them flee back to the pass." Hadrian increased the pace of his march and the soldiers at his back immediately matched it. A cloud of dust rose from their ranks as they passed the great Reysene elevator and advanced toward the rubble at the mouth of Octavian's Pass. Nobody took notice that the lift's cage, which almost always sat at the bottom of the cliff, was currently at the top of the city.

A tiny *click* echoed off of the cavern walls inside the jail below Reysa. Then another *click*, follow by another.

"I *thought* I saw something chip off that cretin's staff when it rolled toward our cell," said Lucan. "Nice to see you still have a few tricks up your sleeve, governor." Dario wiggled a small piece of metal inside the lock. It clicked once more before giving way. The cell door slowly creaked open.

"Quickly now, we don't have much time," said Dario as he stepped out into the hall. "That was Gartolian turret fire we heard; I'd bet my life on it. That means Gracien has come through the pass. I never had a chance to send word about those damned guns they just planted in the forest. They've probably got him pinned down as we speak."

Lucan gingerly stepped out of the cell and joined Dario. A hundred golden eyes followed their every move, but none of the prisoners made a sound. A few stood up in their cells and walked to their doors, expectantly. Dario turned and started walking toward the exit.

"Wait," said Lucan. "You're not going to take them with us?"

"There's no time," said Dario. "We have to get to the capitol building as fast as possible without being seen. They would make that impossible."

"But what about him, at least?" said Lucan, pointing to the cell across from theirs. Two unblinking eyes stared up at them through the bars. Dario considered the young Tormada for a moment. Then, as if attempting to make up Dario's mind for him, the Reytana slowly rose to his feet and walked to his cell door.

"You owe it to him," said Lucan. "We wouldn't be standing here if not for him. He won't slow us down."

Dario nodded and quickly unlocked the Reytana's cell. The remaining prisoners all stood up in excitement and pressed their faces through the bars of their cells. Lucan raised his hand to quiet them. "We'll be back for you. I promise," he whispered.

The young Reytana cautiously stepped out of his cell and walked toward Dario. "If you're coming with us, you're going to need a name," said Dario. "I've been thinking about it. What do you say to Adem?"

The Reytana nodded and repeated the name slowly: "A-dem".

"He speaks," said Lucan. "I guess that solves that mystery. Why Adem?"

"It means 'brave.'"

Dario then turned and quietly trotted toward the door at the end of the cavern, with Lucan and Adem close behind.

None of the prisoners made a sound as they passed their cells. Somehow, they knew to keep quiet.

Dario slowed as he approached the last cell in the row. Around the corner was the door that led to freedom, but Dario knew from his previous visit that two armed Gartune stood guard on the other side of it. Dario approached the door cautiously, then hesitated.

"There are other ways out of here now," whispered Lucan. "What if we go out the way that Hadrian came in? Or we could go out through the new prison expansion?"

"I don't know where those doors lead, but I do know where this one goes," replied Dario. He reached instinctively for the golden wristband that he had always worn concealed in his sleeve, but then remembered that Xander had taken it off of him when he was captured. "I guess we're just going to have to do this the old-fashioned way. Come on."

Lucan and Adem stood, bewildered, and watched Dario walk casually up to the door and give two loud knocks. "Oh, boys," he shouted through the door, "cell number twenty-three could use some new sheets!" Then he jumped to the side of the door and crouched down. Lucan and Adem exchanged looks, then dashed to the other side of the door and crouched down as well. They waited, but nobody came through the door. Dario crawled in front of the door and pressed his ear to the small crack between the bottom of the door and the floor. He could barely make out muffled voices. They sounded agitated. And strangely, the voices seemed to be coming from further down the hall. Suddenly, the ground vibrated and Dario heard two thuds, one right after the other. Dust spilled under the door, causing Dario to cough. He lunged back to the side of the door and waited in his crouched position, ready to spring. The sound of footsteps approached, then two large, metal latches on the outside of the door screeched open. Dario clenched his fists in anticipation while Lucan reached his arm behind him to hold back Adem. Suddenly, the door swung open.

"Tell cell twenty-three to shove it!" roared a voice from the hall.

It was Xander.

Dario rushed through the door and pinned the Gartune prince up against the wall. He tightened his grip around Xander's throat. Xander did not resist. Instead, he looked almost amused as he was being choked out.

"Dario, stop!" yelled Regan as she came running down the hall. Dario turned in disbelief. He loosened his grip on Xander.

"I see that they've been feeding you well, governor," said Xander, rubbing his throat.

"Regan!" shouted Lucan as he came rushing through the door. "It really is you!" He ran to his former student and hugged her, his head only reaching her belly button. "Look at you! You're all grown up!"

"What are you doing here?" asked Dario, trying to piece together what he was seeing. "And why are you with *him?*"

"You're welcome, by the way," said Xander. He nodded his head toward where Regan had just come from. Behind her on the ground lay the two Gartune guards, unconscious. Two large cracks zig-zagged on the ground away from their bodies, meeting at a single point about twenty feet down the hall.

"*You* did that?" asked Lucan incredulously.

"Don't give him too much credit," said Dario. "He's done it before."

Xander shrugged. "You'd think they would have learned from the last time."

"Dario, he's with me," said Regan. "It's a long story but he saved my life. Twice, actually. You can trust him."

Dario and Lucan eyed the Gartune prince suspiciously. Xander raised his eyebrows and waved. Regan rolled her eyes. "It would be a lot easier to believe you if you weren't always fooling around," she said.

"Regan, I just knocked out two of my own men. If they don't believe me after that, they never will. By the way, how did you get out of your cell? I had a whole speech prepared for when I let you out."

"Save it," said Dario as he brushed past Xander and started running down the hall. "We have work to do. Come on!" At Dario's order, Adem ran out of his hiding place and followed Dario down the hall.

"Wait, who's this guy?" asked Xander.

"Adem!" yelled Adem as he chased after Dario.

"It's a long story," said Lucan, ushering Regan to join Dario and Adem. "I'll introduce you later. Now if you're with us, then come along!"

Xander paused for a few seconds, then shook his head and trotted down the dimly-lit hall after the rest of the group.

CHAPTER THIRTY-FOUR
Reflections

The remainder of the Reytana army gathered near the mouth of Octavian's Pass. Slowly, they began to form ranks. Out in the distance, they could see the Gartolian army steadily approaching. It would not be long before they reached the river. Their measured pace taunted the cornered Reytana, as if to say *we don't need to hurry, you aren't going anywhere.*

The Reytana had managed to fix seven of their original twenty hovercraft. Six of them were manned to capacity with soldiers, leaving half of the Reytana army without a ship. Loras was among those that remained on the ground to fight.

"So, is this what you imagined all of those days when you drifted off in class?" asked Tinko as Loras boosted him up onto the seventh hovercraft—the one bound for Reysa. Four other Reytana were aboard to help sneak the energy orb into city.

"Not exactly," said Loras, looking up at his friend. "But then again, none of this has been what I imagined it would be."

"You mean you didn't imagine the future of Reysa depending on me?" replied Tinko.

"Oh, that part is just as I imagined," said Loras, hoping that his smile was hiding his fear. Tinko returned the smile and Loras felt a bit braver. "Take care of yourself, Loras. Don't do anything I wouldn't do."

"That has never been a problem," said Loras. He waved to his friend and the hovercraft lifted off and flew away from the group. Loras turned away from his departing friend and was startled to see the entire Reytana army staring at him. The soldiers on the ground had formed into ranks, while the six remaining hovercraft waited in a semi-circle above them. He didn't know why, but Loras was compelled to move to the front line. As he slowly strode through the soldiers, each one turned and followed him until the entire army was again facing Loras, their golden eyes fierce and waiting. Loras looked over his army; a hundred Reytana ground forces, their golden cloaks flapping in the breeze, and a hundred more warriors in the hovercraft above them. *This part is how I imagined it,* thought Loras. Still, it was two hundred Reytana against an army of over a thousand. The odds were not in his favor. At that moment, Loras remembered his daydreams in professor Lucan's class.

I was always outnumbered then too.

A trickle of courage flowed inside of him. He lifted his face to the sun and let its warmth fuel him. The trickle of courage became a rushing river. Loras closed his eyes, clenched his fists and felt the energy flowing through his wristbands and into the two small pads in the palms of his hands. He squeezed them, and a fiery sword and shield sprung forth with an electric hum. A second later, Loras heard the same hum magnified two hundred times over. He opened his eyes and turned toward his Reytana, *his Reytana.* They were armed and ready for battle.

Words would not come to Loras, though he thought he should say something to his army. *Think! What would Gracien say?* Loras could hear the Gartolian army behind him. They were only a few hundred yards away now, but not a single Reytana eye veered from Loras. They were strong. They were ready. *They're waiting for me,* thought Loras. Then, Loras realized something. *They've been waiting for this for years. They already know what to do. I don't need to say a thing.*

Loras bent his head slightly, furrowed his brow and nodded to his army. Every Reytana bent their head to match his. As they did, confident grins spread across their faces. They were injured. They were out-numbered. They were cornered. Yet, they all smiled as they gazed upon their young leader. Loras couldn't help but return their smiles before he turned to face his enemy.

"Down! Here comes another squad."

Six pairs of Gartune boots ran down the street toward the city's outer wall. Dario and the rest of his cohorts huddled in the shadows of a small alley, watching the soldiers pass their location. Once they had passed beyond earshot, Dario peeked his head around the corner. He looked up and down the street for as far as he could see, but there was no one there. Everyone—Gartolian and Reysene alike—had flocked to the city's outer wall to view the imminent battle below.

When he saw that the coast was clear, Dario waved his hand and his group snuck out of their hiding spot. They raced up the sidewalk in the direction from which the Gartune had come. First came Lucan, then Regan with Adem at her back hip. The newly-freed Reytana had to cover his eyes to adjust to the light, even though they were in the shade of the sun shield. Trailing them was Xander, who, unsure if he should be walking normally or stealthily, was awkwardly vacillating back and forth between a bent-over trot and a casual saunter.

At Xander's suggestion, the group had decided to surface a couple of blocks outside of the capitol building, rather than taking the underground passageway straight up into the governor's quarters, for fear that there might be a regiment of Gartune stationed within the building. Lucan and Regan stopped right before the capitol building. In front of it, lined by a half circle of stone columns and neatly-trimmed bushes, was the Lotus courtyard. The giant orb lay dark and empty. Behind it, the towering glass wall of the capitol building stretched several stories high, curving gracefully into the sky.

Dario and Xander caught up to Lucan, Regan and Adem. The group crouched together behind a chest-high row of bushes. All five of them looked up into the windows of the capitol building, attempting to peer inside. They studied the rooms for several minutes. The room they were most interested in, the governor's quarters, was on the fourth floor. It, like all of the other rooms in the building, appeared empty.

"Everyone is at the wall, waiting for the show to begin," whispered Xander.

"Maybe," said Dario. "But just in case, you're going in first."

"Why me?" asked Xander.

"Because if they see any of the rest of us, they'll kill us immediately. You, they may have to think about first."

"Fair enough," said Xander. He got up from his hiding spot and casually began to walk toward the capitol building. On his way, he prepared two different rebukes for anyone that chanced to come upon him. One of them involved a threat, the other was more physical in nature. Thankfully, he crossed the vast courtyard without having to use either one.

Once he arrived at the side door, he slowly peeked his head inside, then motioned for his companions to come join him. Lucan, Regan, Adem and Dario snuck around the courtyard's perimeter, staying behind the bushes until they had to make a run for it. Xander held the door open and quickly ushered them inside.

The hallway was empty. They waited, listening for the sound of approaching footsteps. When they heard none, everyone followed Xander down the hall and up the stairs toward the governor's quarters. Each time they entered a new corridor, they let Xander go first, waited a few seconds, and then tip-toed behind him. They didn't travel as quickly as they would have liked due to Adem stopping to curiously peek inside every door that they passed.

"Will somebody please do something about the kid?" whispered Xander impatiently as Lucan pulled Adem out of a doorway.

"Cut him some slack," said Regan. "He's never been outside of his cell. This is a whole new world for him. He's trying to take it all in."

"Well can he take it in faster?"

Adem, sensing that they were talking about him, looked at Xander and nodded, then jogged up to join the rest of the group.

"Huh," said Xander. "He's smarter than he looks."

"At least somebody is," quipped Dario.

Xander sneered. "That's not fair. I look *extremely* smart. He's wearing a diaper. The bars are different."

"Are you two done?" asked Regan as she shoved past them, taking the lead. The group followed her to the end of the hall then stopped when they reached the governor's quarters. Xander strode up to the entrance, looked over his shoulder to make sure that the rest of the group was ready, then he lightly rapped his knuckles against the door.

"Really? You're knocking?" whispered Lucan.

"Yeah, I suppose you're right," said Xander. He took one step backward, lifted his leg and kicked as hard as he could. The door flew off of its frame and crashed into the room.

"Well, if anyone is in the building, they know we're here now," said Dario as he brushed past Xander and into the room. It was empty. Adem, Lucan and Regan followed Dario into his old quarters. Regan bent over what was left of the door and twisted the handle. It turned easily. She looked at Xander.

"My way was more fun," said Xander.

"I'm sure it was," said Regan.

"Ok, so I've gotten you here, Dario. Now what?" asked Xander. "Don't tell me we brought you back to your room just so you could take a nap."

Dario ignored him. He was shuffling through a row of dusty binders on a bookshelf in the back of the room. He settled on one titled "Sewer Schematics for Western Quadrant" and brought it to his desk.

"Ah, right. I always suspected that the key to winning this war was proper waste management," said Xander.

"You should have paid more attention to your city's sanitation system when you were in command here, Xander," said Dario with a wry smile. He flipped open the binder and rapidly thumbed through the pages. Lucan joined Dario and leaned over the desk curiously. The binder was full of numbers and coordinates, but none of them seemed to have to do with the sewer system.

"Quick—what time is it?" asked Dario.

"Almost ten in the morning, why?" asked Lucan. Dario nodded, but did not answer the question. He flipped three more pages until he found the section he was looking for. He reached under the side of his desk and pressed something. They heard a small *click*, then suddenly, the entire top of Dario's desk slid back to reveal a large panel of buttons and dials.

"Why, you sneaky nimber," said Xander as he watched the governor go to work.

Dario drew his finger down the page and stopped when he found the numbers that he was looking for. He then turned to the panel in his desk. The panel consisted of three rows of dials. The top one was labeled "morning," the middle one "afternoon," and the bottom row read "evening." Dario went to the "morning" row and found the dial marked "10" and turned it until it pointed towards a small label that read "3rd St. warehouse windows – outer rim." Dario then looked up toward the windows. A minute passed, then, far off in the distance, toward the western wall of the city, there was a flash of light as the sun reflected off of one of the few buildings that was not currently under the shadow of the sun shield. Dario smiled and went back to his binder. He slid his finger down to the next line on the page, then turned back to the panel and rotated the same dial to a mark that read "church façade – outer rim." He looked up again. This time, so did everyone else. They waited for two minutes. Then, once again, far off in the distance, sunlight reflected off of a building that had been in shadow just a few seconds before.

Xander's jaw dropped. He slowly walked toward the floor-to-ceiling windows of the governor's room. Regan joined him. Lucan remained at the governor's desk, transfixed by Dario's calculated process. Again and again, Dario found a number on the page, then turned the dial to a corresponding city structure. Each time he did, a minute or two passed before sunlight was reflected off a new building. As Dario progressed, he selected buildings located closer and closer to the center of the city. Eventually, surfaces underneath the sun shield were reflecting light.

"How is he..." whispered Xander as he watched out the window. Then he saw it. A semi-transparent ray of light bounced from each reflective surface to the one before it. The ray's brightness intensified as it moved along the chain of buildings toward the center of the city. "He's banking the sunlight off of the buildings," said Xander in awe. "But how is the light getting stronger?"

"Each reflective surface contains a hidden lens that I had manufactured," answered Dario without looking up from his panel. "The lenses amplify the light."

Dario turned the dial until it read "Zone 2 Apartment Roof." Regan followed the pattern of reflected surfaces to guess the location of the next structure. She stared at a five-story apartment building a few hundred yards away. Just as she began to think she had guessed wrong, a Reysene emerged onto the roof of the building and quickly trotted over to a small, glass shed. He entered the little building and began to crank something. As he did so, a large solar panel that encompassed the majority of the roof rotated slightly until it was ablaze with reflected sunlight.

Xander was in disbelief. He turned away from the window toward Dario. "All this time you had this?"

"Of course not. It took me almost ten years to build this," said Dario without looking up from his page. He rotated the dial again and the column of sunlight bounced off a building just a hundred yards away. "You didn't think I just sat up here twiddling my thumbs all day while you idiots ran things, did you?"

"So you've taught the Reysene to angle their windows, solar panels—"

"Pretty much anything shiny," interrupted Dario without looking up.

"All so that they reflect the sun toward..." Xander stopped himself. He looked admiringly at the governor. "*You sneaky nimber.*"

Dario arrived at the last number on the page. He found the corresponding label and then looked up at Xander. "You're going to like this," he said as turned the dial toward "Lotus courtyard." The entire western side of the building next to the capitol building slid down, revealing a giant mirror. The mirror rotated slightly to the left and then—

"Aaaahhh!" yelled Adem. He shielded his eyes from the rush of sunlight that flooded into the governor's quarters. Even Regan, whose eyes were used to the sun, had to squint against the reflected light.

"Quick!" yelled Dario as he ran toward the windows. "Help me with this!" He jumped several feet into the air and pulled a handle out from the ceiling. Hanging from the handle with one arm, with his free hand, Dario pointed across the room at another notch in the ceiling.

"Don't look at me," said Xander. "There's only one other person in this room that can reach a fifteen-foot ceiling."

"Regan!" yelled Dario, still hanging from the ceiling, "Grab the handle and pull with me!" Regan ran beneath the notch in the ceiling that Dario had pointed to and jumped. She came up a foot short. "Come on! You're a Reytana! Jump!" cried Dario.

Regan looked up at the ceiling and clenched her fists. She let the sunlight streaming in through the windows energize her. Then she bent her knees and jumped. She almost hit her head on the ceiling.

Frantically, she grabbed at the handle before she fell back to the floor. At the last moment, her fingers found the notch in the ceiling. She pulled hard, and a thin, thirty-foot-long sheet of metal came rolling out of a slit in the ceiling. Dario and Regan pulled the sheet of metal all the way to the ground. Dario motioned for Regan to move and the pair walked back slowly, changing the angle of the metal sheet so the light it reflected bounced into the courtyard.

The open petals of the Lotus gleamed as thousands of circular receptors began to illuminate. Each petal began to pulse, pumping golden light through twisting veins and into the giant globe at the center. A thin trickle of glimmering liquid dripped into the bottom of the globe. Then the trickle increased to a steady stream and finally, into a strong current of solar energy. The glowing liquid swished back and forth at the bottom of the orb, throwing beautiful golden reflections across the courtyard.

Dario kicked a tile in the floor, and a notch—the same size as the one in the ceiling—appeared under his foot. He pulled the metal sheet's handle down and inserted it into the notch then motioned for Regan to do the same.

"That... is... amazing..." said Lucan. "But how did all of the Reysene know what angle to turn their surfaces? The calculations had to be exact and always changing."

"Each one of those buildings has a binder like this one," said Dario pointing to his Sewer Schematics binder. "Granted, they aren't all named the same thing. Some of them are reference manuals for light tube repair or water purification— all subjects that would have been of no interest to prying Gartune eyes."

"Who did all of the calculations?" asked Regan.

"I did," replied Dario.

"That must have taken you ages," exclaimed Lucan.

"Fortunately, I had a lot of free time," said Dario as he joined the rest of the group in staring out the window at the filling energy orb. The liquid was now about a foot deep and steadily rising. But none of the liquid was entering the pipes which sent the energy throughout the city.

"But you forgot to open the pipes," said Lucan.

Dario walked back over to his desk and shook his head. "Only one pipe," he said. "And not until it's ready."

"Which pipe?" asked Regan.

"The one that leads to the cannons," said Xander. Dario nodded.

"Our only job right now is to help the army on the ground. The solar cannons can reach Octavian's Pass. If we can force the Gartolians back to their camp, the Reytana should have time to get up here... if they have any ships left."

"Can we control the cannons from here?" asked Lucan.

Dario shook his head. "They have to be manned, and they haven't been used for many years. I can't even guarantee they all work."

"Well, that's comforting," said Lucan. "And I'm betting they can only be fired by someone of your size?"

"Yes," said Dario. "I would do it, but I need to stay here to open the pipe when the orb has been sufficiently filled."

"I don't suppose Adem over there is much of a shot," said Xander. Adem looked back at the Gartune blankly. Everyone stared at the prince.

"You expect me to fire on my own people?" said Xander.

"*Are they* still your people?" replied Lucan. Xander stood thinking in silence, a frown on his face.

"Lucan's right," said Dario. "If you're with us, then you're against them. This is part of the deal."

Xander looked around the room as he struggled with his decision. He stopped when he met Regan's gaze.

"I don't even know what you're debating," said Regan. "You made this decision a week ago when you saved us from Septa in the forest. Then you made it again when you killed Belkore, and *again* when you freed Dario and Lucan from the prison. Face it, you're with us now."

"Well, when you put it that way..." said Xander. "Oh, all right." He began to head for the door. "Truthfully, I've always kind of wanted to fire one of those things. I just never thought I'd be shooting at the guys in purple."

"Do you know how to get to them?" asked Dario.

"Of course, I know how to get to them," said Xander indignantly. "I didn't spend all of my time twiddling my thumbs either, Governor. I know more about this city's defenses than you do, and unfortunately, so does my father. I told him everything. He knows the exact range of those cannons. As soon as we fire the first shot, he'll know how far he needs to move out of the way."

"That's fine," said Dario. "We just need to give the Reytana time to get up here. With any luck, we can hold off the Gartolian tanks from firing on our ships while they fly up to the city."

"There aren't any tanks," said Regan. "We could see the Gartolian basecamp on our way over here. Other than the tanks holding up the sun shield, there weren't any."

"Yeah, about the tanks..." said Xander.

"There's no time!" interjected Dario. "If there are tanks, then you fire on them after Hadrian retreats. Understood?"

Xander gave a mock salute. "I'm on my way!"

"I'm coming with you," said Regan, chasing after Xander.

"No!" said Lucan. "It's not safe for you out there. What if something happens?"

"That's exactly why I have to go," said Regan. "What if something happens to Xander? There's only one other person here that can fire that cannon."

"But you've never fired a weapon in your life!" said Lucan.

"I'll teach her on the way," said Xander, giving Lucan a wink. "It's easier than you think."

"Let them go," said Dario. "You're wasting time." Lucan frowned but did not offer further protest. And so, Regan joined Xander as they ran down the hall, no longer taking care to remain silent. A few seconds later, Lucan looked out the window and watched as the two Tormada crossed the courtyard and

disappeared into the city.

CHAPTER THIRTY-FIVE
Standoff

Regan and Xander quickly trotted down the sidewalk, making sure to stay in the shadows as much as possible. But as it turned out, stealth was not needed. As Xander had predicted, everyone was at the wall. In fact, they were almost to the outer rim of the city before they spotted a single person; an old Reysene woman who quickly darted back into her house when she saw the pair approaching.

"There's something that's been bothering me," said Regan as they turned down a side alley.

"Only one thing?" asked Xander.

"It's about that parental bond you spoke of on the hovercraft, the one between a Tormada and his parent."

"What about it?"

"Well, you said it's like an unseen power that pulls on the child and makes him do whatever the parent wants?"

"More or less," said Xander.

"And yet here you are, about to attack your own father? Don't you feel his pull on you?"

"Oh, I feel it. I'm just choosing to ignore it," replied Xander.

"You can do that?"

"Well, it helps that we don't like each other very much."

Regan thought about that for a moment. "So if you can ignore him, maybe the Fallen Reytana can ignore him as well?"

Xander shook his head. "Perhaps in time they could. But right now, he has complete control over them. Unless..."

"Unless, what?"

"Unless they had someone else to follow; someone whose pull was stronger."

Regan considered this, then increased her walking pace to a brisk jog. "Come on!" she said, "We need to get those Reytana on the ground up here!"

Xander and Regan jogged through the empty streets of Reysa's outer industrial zone. They stopped when they reached the warehouse that Dario had first selected when he began reflecting the sunlight toward the energy orb. Regan looked up and noticed that a mirror had slid down behind the glass of each window, amplifying the reflection of the sunlight. Unless you were looking for it, you wouldn't have noticed anything strange about the warehouse windows other than the fact that the sun was shining rather brightly off of them.

Xander inspected the windows too. "I've got to hand it to old Dario. He's a clever one."

"How long before you think he will have enough energy in the orb to fuel the solar cannons?" asked Regan.

"At the rate that thing was filling, I'd say not long. We need to be ready when he opens the pipe."

"How far to the cannons?" asked Regan. Xander pointed to where the street dead-ended into Reysa's outer wall. The massive stone structure rose thirty feet in the air. Several thin slits were interspersed throughout the base of the wall at torman eye-level. A large crowd of Reysene gathered around the Holes. At the top of the wall, several Gartune soldiers stood leaning on their eürocs. They were all looking down at the ground below. Some were smiling and pointing. One Gartune was actually laughing. Regan's heart dropped.

"We're too late," she said.

"Listen," whispered Xander.

"To what?" answered Regan. "I don't hear anything."

"Exactly," said Xander. "Battles are loud. The fun hasn't started yet, although from the looks of it, it's about to. Come on." Xander led Regan across the street toward a small, square building. They had to stop and hide several times when a Gartune started to turn their head in their direction. When they finally reached their destination without anyone raising an alarm, they both exhaled.

The squat building stood innocuously in the shadow of several larger structures. It had a flat roof and no windows, only a single door large enough for one Tormada to enter. Regan stood in front of the building, confused. "This can't be it," she said. "There is hardly enough room for the both of us to fit in there, let alone a solar cannon."

Xander ignored her. He inspected the door.

"Why don't you try the handle first this time?" said Regan.

"Good thinking," said Xander. He tried the handle. It did not budge. He tried turning it again, but it still would not move. He looked at Regan as if asking for permission. She stared back at him, waiting. Xander smiled, then stepped back and kicked the door, but it still wouldn't budge.

"Oh for Gods' sake," said Regan as she walked over and stood next to Xander, facing the door. "On three... one... two... three!" This time, both Tormada kicked the door at the same time. It did not fall backward, but it was jarred slightly from its frame. Two more kicks, and the door gave way. Regan pushed through the doorway and almost fell forward. The room had no floor. Instead, the entryway immediately gave way to stairs that descended beneath the city. She looked warily down into the darkness below.

"Follow me," said Xander. He took Regan's hand and put it on his shoulder, then led her down the stairs. Thankfully, the stairs did not descend very far, and soon Regan found herself walking along a flat corridor. The air in the corridor was cold and musty, the result of not having been vented in several years. Darkness surrounded them. Regan reached out her free hand and touched a wall. She slid her fingers across it as they continued on.

"How can you see where you are going?" she asked.

"I can't," said Xander. "But I've been down here a couple of times before. It's just a straight shot. Keep ahold of me. We're almost there."

"You'd think they would have put some lights down here," said Regan.

"Oh, it will be plenty bright here shortly. Ah, we're here," said Xander. He stopped abruptly and Regan walked right into his back.

"Sorry," Xander said. Regan grunted.

She heard a handle turn and a latch click. A vertical crack of dim light appeared, then widened as Xander pushed open the door. The two Tormada walked into a long corridor that curved to both their left and right for as far as they could see. Sunlight spilled through small slits all along the corridor's outside wall. In front of each slit was a large chair meant to fit a Tormada. Attached to the front of each chair was a long cylinder roughly ten feet long and four feet wide.

"The cannons," whispered Regan. "We're *inside* the wall."

"Pick a seat!" said Xander as he climbed into the nearest chair. Regan walked to the cannon on her left and almost tripped on a small pipe that connected the bottom of the chair to the wall. She noticed that each chair had a similar pipe connected to it.

"When those pipes light up, it's show time," said Xander. He wiped the dust off of a couple of dials on the face of the cannon in front of him.

"Wait! How do these things work?!" shouted Regan. She kept staring at the pipe on the ground, just waiting for it to light up.

"The wheels on your right and left are how you aim." Xander pointed to two large wheels on either side of Regan's chair. "The one on your left moves the cannon up and down. The one on your right moves it sideways. Try it out."

Regan pulled on the wheel to her left. It did not move at first, but then with a rusty creak it gave way and spun freely. The cannon in front of Regan tilted upward and nearly tipped her out of the back of her seat. Xander laughed as he tested the wheels on his own cannon. "You're a natural!"

Regan turned the wheel in the opposite direction and leveled herself out. Then she gently turned the other wheel, making sure to not force it too hard, and she gradually swiveled to her right.

"Ok, now how do you fire this thing?"

"Point yourself the other way and I'll tell you," said Xander. Regan didn't even notice that she was aiming directly at him. She quickly turned the wheel on her right in the opposite direction.

"The two levers in front of you. The shorter one primes the cannon. Hold it down for a few seconds and then pull the longer lever to fire. Simple as that."

"How do you know all of this stuff?" asked Regan incredulously.

"You forget I was only eighteen when I took over this place," said Xander with a shrug. "There wasn't much to do and, if you'd ever seen a Gartune get their metal, you'd know how teenage boys felt about weapons. Especially really big ones." Xander patted the cannon in front of him admiringly then nodded toward the wall in front of Regan's seat. Someone had drawn a crude bullseye with a person at the center of the target. The person wore a purple cape and had short, black hair. He wore a thin, silver crown around his forehead. Regan glanced over at Xander, but he was busy inspecting the controls of his cannon.

Dust covered her weapon so Regan reached down and began wiping off the levers that fired the cannon. She wondered how many times over the years they had been pulled. She imagined the Reytana who had sat in her seat before her, and glanced down the corridor, imagining it full of Reytana soldiers manning the defenses. Protecting the city. And now it was up to her; her and the prince of Gartol.

Suddenly, from down the hall, they heard an electric hum. Regan looked at Xander, her eyes wide. The hum got louder as it approached. Xander nodded his head. "Show time," he said excitedly.

All of a sudden, the corridor was awash with light. The pipes running along the floor to each cannon lit up with solar energy. Regan felt a jolt in her chair as her cannon was activated. The entire corridor hummed loudly as weapon after weapon sprung to life.

"Oh, I forgot one thing," shouted Xander. He pressed a button between his legs and a panel in the ceiling above him slid open. Regan did the same and both of their chairs rose through the ceiling into the open air. It took her eyes a moment to adjust to the change in light. When she was able to focus her vision, she saw five open-mouthed Gartune staring directly at her. From behind her she heard a hum and a *whoosh*. She turned over her shoulder and saw a large cloud of purple dust slowly rising into the air.

"Regan, fire!" shouted Xander. She turned back to face the Gartune. They had snapped out of their shock and were charging toward her. Frantically, she pressed the small lever on her cannon down. The cylinder in front of her began to hum and spin rapidly. She counted in her head, *one... two...* the Gartune were almost on top of her... *three!* She pulled the other lever and a white-hot flare shot out of her cannon with a loud *whoosh*. The five Gartune in front of her disintegrated.

Regan felt like she was going to throw up. The purple cloud of Gartune aura floated into her eyes. She squeezed them shut and her stomach heaved. A strange smell filled her nose—one that she had never known before. It was acrid and smoky, and as it made its way through her nostrils and down to her tongue, she tasted death.

Her head began to swim, and she became dizzy. Suddenly, a voice cut through the fog. "Regan—look!" shouted Xander. She opened her eyes and spun her chair around. Xander was pointing toward the ground. Immediately, Regan's head cleared, and she remembered why she was there. She turned the wheel on her left and tilted her chair downward toward Octavian's Pass. As the scene below came into view over the top of her cannon, her heart skipped a beat.

The two armies stood on opposite sides of the Aeil River, only twenty feet apart. The swollen ranks of the Gartolian army more than tripled the Reytana troops. Neither side moved. Regan squinted and made out two figures, each standing in front of their respective armies.

Regan assumed that the Tormada in front of the Gartolian army had to be Hadrian. Even from far away he appeared larger than the other Gartune. The Reytana standing in front of the golden army was at first a mystery, but the longer Regan stared, the more she knew in her heart who it must be.

The two armies stared across the river at each other in silence. The trickle of slow-moving water between them was the only sound. Sunlight glittered off of the river's surface in a kaleidoscope of colors. It was by all accounts a beautiful day.

I would have liked to have learned how to fish, thought Loras. *The right way, not...whatever I was doing back in the forest. I think I would have liked fishing. I wonder if Declin would teach me.*

Across the river, Hadrian frowned as he sized up the young Reytana. He seemed particularly interested in the band around Loras' forehead. "You're a bit young to be standing in front!" shouted the king of Gartol.

"I couldn't see from the back," shouted Loras. The corner of the king's mouth curved upward for an instant, then returned to his normal grimace.

"Nice headband you've got there," said Hadrian. "What's your name, boy?"

"Loras. What's yours?"

The king's brow furrowed deeper. *That may have been unwise,* thought Loras. *I wish Declin was here. He always seemed to handle dicey conversations with ease.* Loras suddenly realized that he hadn't seen Declin since they left the Hole. He started to miss the little waif. If he had been there, Loras would have asked him what to do next.

"You're one of the twins—the ones who escaped, aren't you?" said Hadrian. Loras said nothing. "Well, now I know why they hid you from me for all these years. Tell me, why return? You could have hidden in the forest with the rest of your kind. You could have survived…for a little while longer anyway. Why come back?"

Loras shrugged. "I live here."

"Not anymore," snarled Hadrian. "I'll make you a deal. You don't have to die this day. Neither do the rest of you. Come over here and kneel to me, and I give you my word that you will live. I'll even let you stay in Reysa."

Loras could detect a glimmer in Hadrian's eye as he made his offer. *I'll bet you'll let me stay in Reysa… you'll let me stay* under it *with the rest of the Fallen Reytana.*

"This is your only chance, boy. Cross the river and surrender to me or die where you stand."

Loras looked down at the water between them and shook his head. "Sorry. I don't swim."

Hadrian stomped his eüroc in front of him. The ground peeled away and shot out over the river, forming a small land bridge. "There, now you don't have to," he said smugly.

Loras pretended to study the bridge. "I don't know, it doesn't seem too sturdy. Why don't you go first?"

"You remind me of my son," replied Hadrian. "His mouth always got him into trouble too." Loras bristled at the comparison.

"I won't ask again," continued the king. "Surrender, or I send you and all those behind you to The Scales!"

Loras looked over his shoulder at the army of Reytana. Six hovercraft gently dipped up and down above them. A seventh ship was barely visible behind the others, with Tinko peering over the bow. Loras lifted his fist to his chest and pounded it once, then gave his friend a small nod and the ship peeled off toward Reysa. As the ship departed, the entire Reytana army lifted their fists to their chests in unison and pounded once. They looked at their leader, waiting for orders. Loras lifted the fiery sword streaming from his palm and yelled with all of the courage in his heart, "For Gracien! For Reysa!" and leapt over the river. Before he landed, the rest of the Reytana were already in the air behind him.

"Good for you, boy," said Hadrian. He lifted his arm and the metal sleeve on his forearm expanded into a shield that easily deflected Loras' attack. Loras tumbled backward, but quickly stood and composed himself. Sparks flew around him as Reytana fire met Gartune metal, but Loras paid no attention. He only had eyes for one person: Hadrian.

The king did not advance on Loras, but stood and taunted the young Reytana, twirling his eüroc. He retracted his shield and left himself wide open to attack. *Let him come to you,* said a voice in Loras' head. Loras crouched in a defensive position with his shield arm up. Hadrian smirked and took a quick step forward. Loras jumped back, almost falling in the river. Hadrian laughed.

"Do you even know how to use those things in your hands?" taunted Hadrian.

"Why don't you come and find out!" shouted Loras, embarrassed for having flinched.

Hadrian sighed. "Very well."

The king advanced slowly on the crouched Reytana. Once he was within striking distance, he began to circle. Loras turned his body, staying square with the king, but did not move his feet. Quick as lightning, Hadrian jabbed his eüroc at Loras' ribs. Loras barely raised his shield in time to deflect the attack. *Gods, he's quick. Quicker than Gracien, even.*

Hadrian swung his eüroc over his shoulder and grasped it in his shield hand then swung again. This time, Loras saw the strike coming. He jumped, allowing the staff to pass under his feet. His timing was right, but his jump was too high. Hadrian had enough time to perform the *bodong*. The king quickly stamped his eüroc into the ground, causing the dirt in front of him to form a small hill. He then used his eüroc to catapult himself onto the hill just as Loras was descending from his leap. Hadrian met Loras in mid-air and hammered the unsuspecting Reytana in the chest, throwing him down into the river below.

The force of Hadrian's blow forced Loras down to the river floor. For an instant, his whole body went numb. He looked and saw the sun shining brightly through the ripples on the surface. As he continued to watch, the sun got closer and closer, rapidly growing in size until it exploded into a burst of light right in front of him. He could hear yelling from the Gartolians. Then, two more suns appeared in the sky and came hurtling toward them.

Loras leapt out of the river. As he wiped water from his eyes, two explosions erupted from the middle of the Gartolian army. Rocks and bodies went flying into the air in the midst of two plumes of light.

"Back to the camp!" yelled Hadrian. Immediately, the army fell back. Their retreat was not panicked, but organized and efficient. They were almost out of range before the next two volleys of solar flares hit the ground. Hadrian looked one last time at Loras, still standing in the middle of the river, before he joined his army in retreat. Two bright explosions landed right where he had been, sending rock and dirt shooting into the sky. When the air had cleared, he was gone.

A cheer erupted from the Reytana army. They thrust their swords in the air yelling, "Rey-sa! Rey-sa!" Everyone looked up toward the city. Two more solar flares flew down from the western wall but fell well short of the retreating Gartolian army. Nearly fifty dead Gartolian bodies littered their wake. Several clouds of purple dust intermixed with the bodies.

It only took Loras a moment to collect his thoughts. Miraculously, the six hovercraft were still intact and hovering above him. The soldiers aboard joined the Reytana on the ground in chanting, "Rey-sa! Rey-sa!" Loras did not join in. He knew that their victory was but a small one, and if they did not act quickly, it would be inconsequential.

"Quickly!" he yelled. "To the ships! To the city!" Immediately, the chanting stopped, and the hovercraft landed, allowing the Reytana on the ground to board. Though they were forced to stand shoulder to shoulder, somehow, all of the soldiers fit onto the vessels. *That's not a good sign,* thought Loras. *It means we lost a lot even in that short battle.*

Loras climbed aboard last and the ship struggled to lift off the ground with its overloaded crew, but the craft eventually gained altitude and banked upward toward the city. Loras scanned the sky for any sign of Tinko's ship but found none. *It's on you now, Tink,* thought Loras. *Or all of this was just a waste of time.*

CHAPTER THIRTY-SIX
Help

Tinko was frustrated. The wooden sled that he had haphazardly constructed in order to transport the energy orb was barely holding together and making way too much noise as it slid over the cobblestone streets in the outskirts of Reysa. It was obvious from the sweat dripping down their foreheads that the four Reytana in charge of pushing the sled were not thrilled with Tinko's plan. *I should have just had them carry the damn thing on their shoulders,* thought Tinko. *At least then it wouldn't have made as much noise.*

Tinko raised his hand and the Reytana behind him came to a stop. He listened as several Gartune footsteps came running down the street. Immediately, Tinko jumped behind the sled to join the four Reytana huddling behind their precious cargo. It was fortunate that Tinko had ordered the orb's sled be constructed to look like a merchant's cart—tall, rectangular and covered with a tarp—in order to disguise the shape of the object inside. *At least I did that much right,* thought Tinko. This was now the third time that they were forced to hide behind the cart as a group of Gartune ran by.

The soldiers passed their location without even a glance at the large cart parked in the alley. The Gartune ran in the same direction as the previous two groups—toward the center of the city. *Not a good sign,* thought Tinko. *They're going toward the capitol. So much for sneaking the orb in undetected.* He began to regret his decision to land the hovercraft on the northern outskirts of the city, rather than just flying it directly to the capitol building. Even though it would have been the most efficient path, he felt it was just too risky. A vessel as large as the hovercraft would have been easily spotted and stealth was paramount during this part of the plan. So, he circumvented the perimeter of the city below the wall until he found an old abandoned warehouse with a roof large enough to land the ship. He had then ordered the Reytana to construct a sled out of scrap wood they found within the building. Not once did the Reytana question any of Tinko's decisions. Until now.

"What's your plan for when we get there?" asked one of the Reytana as he struggled to lift the back of the cart and push it forward. The wooden planks that served as the sled's rails screeched as they scooted over the uneven road. The Reytana's tone was not angry or judgmental, merely curious.

"I don't know yet. I guess I'll think of something," said Tinko, scanning left and right before stepping out into the street. He honestly hadn't thought that far ahead. Currently, his entire focus was on getting to the capitol building. That task in itself was daunting enough.

The roads narrowed as they approached the center of the city. Each one was lined with sidewalks on both sides, big enough for two tormen to walk side-by-side, or one Tormada to walk alone. Apartments, shops and offices butted up against each other, occasionally making space for a narrow alleyway in between. Many years ago, it would have been a warm and bustling thoroughfare, alive with Reysene working and shopping. Today, it was dark and empty; depressing, but preferable for clandestine activities such as sneaking an energy orb through the city.

Just as the Reytana succeeded in pushing the orb's cart into the center of the road, four Gartune ran out into the street ahead. There was no hiding this time. The Gartune instantly saw the large cart, and more importantly, the four Reytana behind it. The Reytana immediately dropped the cart and sprung into a defensive position around the orb. One of them grabbed Tinko and shoved him inside of their little perimeter. Just then, more footsteps came from the opposite direction. It was another troupe of Gartune. Tinko and the Reytana were surrounded.

"Ok, I know that I've been making all the decisions so far," said Tinko as the Gartune approached them from both sides, "but I want you all to know that I am currently open to suggestions." The Reytana did not answer him. Instead, they all pressed the small pads in their palms and sword and shield sprung from their hands. They began to move clockwise in a slow circle, their eyes fixed on the approaching enemy.

Tinko's mind began to race. *Think, you idiot! That's what you're good at. There has to be some way out of this.* Tinko searched the buildings surrounding the street, not sure what he was looking for. They all appeared deserted. All except one. Tinko spied the face of a young Reysene peeking out of a second story window directly across from their location. Once the boy saw that Tinko had spotted him, he raised his arm to show something clutched in his hand. Tinko couldn't make out what it was; maybe a rock of some sort, or a book? Whatever it was, it was heavy-looking, and the Reysene appeared as if he meant to throw it. The young boy stared at Tinko as if asking permission. Tinko gave a quick shake of his head, hoping that the Gartune didn't notice the gesture. The boy in the window raised his hand a little higher, thinking, perhaps that Tinko hadn't seen what he was holding. Again, Tinko quickly shook his head, a little more forcefully this time.

The Gartune were almost on top of them now. One of the approaching soldiers noticed that Tinko was staring at something in the building across from them. He followed his gaze to the young boy's window. Without a word, the Gartune pointed his eüroc at the window, pressed something in the staff's handle and a sliver of metal shot out of the end and sliced through the glass.

"Get down!" yelled Tinko, but the projectile had already shattered the window. Tinko couldn't see the boy anymore. It all happened so fast that he couldn't tell if he was hit or not. *Rey, please let him be ok.* Slowly, a hand rose out of the window. It was still holding the strange object. Then suddenly, the boy flung it out the window. The projectile landed at the feet of one of the Gartune. Tinko could see it clearly now, but he still did not recognize the object. It was a small, dark cube with white powder on the outside. The Gartune poked the cube with his eüroc. Nothing happened. The soldier bent over to inspect it closer. Tinko noticed little wisps of white smoke slowly emanating from the edges of the cube. The Gartune's nostrils flared as he sniffed the smoke. He jerked back, but it was too late.

The cube exploded in his face, immediately turning the top half of his body into purple dust. The bottom half fell to the ground and dissolved into another violet cloud. The other Gartune started yelling and turned their attention to the building where the cube had come from. Suddenly, several other cubes came flying out of the surrounding buildings. The soldiers scattered. These cubes exploded faster than the first one and by the time the last loud *bang* rung out, three more Gartune were down.

The Reytana didn't waste any time. They left their defensive formation and pounced on the scattered Gartune. A shower of blunt objects came raining down on the backs of the Gartune soldiers as they fought. Plates, bowls, vases, books, and all other sorts of household items were thrown out the windows of the surrounding buildings. Some inadvertently hit the Reytana, but the majority of the projectiles struck the Gartune. Though they did not appear to be doing much physical damage, they distracted the Gartune enough for the Reytana to gain the advantage in the fight. It was not long before all of the remaining Gartune were either dead or unconscious.

Tinko had not moved from the cart since the fighting began. Now, he ventured out into the cluttered street. He gingerly sidestepped a fork as he surveyed the surreal scene. It looked as if several kitchens' worth of dishes had been thrown out into the road. He almost laughed when he saw an unconscious Gartune lying face-down with on oven mitt on the back of his head.

Tinko looked up and the boy from the window was standing in front of him, and he was not alone. Slowly, several Reysene men and women began emerging from the buildings. A few of them stooped down to collect their belongings as they walked toward Tinko.

The boy from the window stood with a wide-mouthed grin as his neighbors joined him in the street. Tinko recognized him. His name was Asher and he had been a couple of years below Tinko at school.

"What were those... *bombs*... that you all were throwing?" asked Tinko.

"We made them," said Asher proudly. "We've been making them ever since you and the others escaped."

"You *made* them?" said Tinko incredulously. "How? Did they start teaching underclassmen bomb-making after I left?"

Asher smiled. "Ha, I wish. No, but they're not so difficult to make once you know what you're doing. A couple of the adults from the southern quadrant had been stockpiling these for years, apparently. Once things started to get really bad a couple of weeks ago—the shield staying up all day and the twenty-four-hour curfew—they started teaching other people how to make them. They said we had to be ready for when the Reytana returned. Somehow, they knew you were coming back soon, and we believed them."

By this time, the crowd of Reysene in the street had grown to over a hundred. They surrounded Tinko and his large, tarp-covered cart. "So, what's in there?" asked Asher, pointing to the cart.

Tinko lifted a corner of the tarp off of the orb, revealing the glowing liquid inside. Gasps rang out from the crowd. "You weren't the only ones preparing for the Reytana's return."

An older man stepped forward from the crowd and inspected the orb. "This is nearly the size of the energy orb at the capitol. With this much energy, we could re-activate the entire city's defenses," said the man.

"That's the plan," said Tinko. "Unfortunately, I have a feeling that a whole lot of their friends are going to be waiting for us." He nodded toward the Gartune on the ground. "Any ideas on how we can get this thing to the capitol building without it being destroyed first?" The older man thought for a few moments and then looked around at the Reysene surrounding him.

"I think I might have an idea," he said.

CHAPTER THIRTY-SEVEN
Surrounded

"Well, the nimber's out of the bag now," said Lucan, peering out the window of the governor's quarters. Dozens of Gartune had entered the courtyard below and were squinting up in his direction. The light bouncing off of the large metal sheet in Dario's room was almost blinding to those on the ground. "I'm surprised they're just sitting there. Why haven't they run up here to kill us yet?"

"Because they don't know how many of us there are," said Dario, walking to the window. "They can't see in here. It's too bright. For all they know, the entire Reytana army could be inside this building, waiting for them."

"Rey damn the army," said Lucan. "I'd take just a handful of them at this point."

"Why, Professor Lucan," said Dario with a tinge of amusement, "I never knew you had such a tongue. I think prison life has made you salty."

"I'll tell you one thing," said Lucan grimly as he watched another dozen Gartune enter the courtyard, "when they do finally decide to come up here, I'm not going back to that cell."

"Nor am I," said Dario. They both looked over at Adem, who was nervously pacing back and forth in front of the window. He hadn't blinked in over a minute, unable to take his eyes off of the scene below. One Gartune in particular had his full attention.

"It won't be long now," said Dario. "Rankin is down there. He'll send a party to scout the building and then once he finds out that it's just the three of us up here, he'll come for us. More importantly, he'll take down my reflector."

"Why don't they just destroy the orb?" asked Lucan.

Dario laughed. "Because they can't. Nobody can."

"What do you mean, *they can't?*" asked Lucan. "It's just glass, isn't it?"

"Calling that orb glass is like saying a Gartolian tank is made of wood. The thing is unbreakable. You can't dent it. You can't even scratch it. The same goes for the petals and the tubes of the Lotus."

"Well then if it isn't made of glass, what is it made of?"

"Nobody knows," said Dario. "Some say that Rey herself created the orb when she created the Reytana."

"You don't actually believe that," scoffed Lucan.

"I've inspected that thing hundreds of times. It's flawless," said Dario. "But to answer your question, I have no reason to believe that it was created by a god. But I also have no reason *not* to believe it."

Dario and Lucan watched the golden liquid swish in the bottom of the giant globe. The few shots from the solar cannons had drained a significant portion of the energy. It was refilling now, but there wouldn't be nearly enough energy available to activate any kind of defenses within the capitol building by the time the Gartune decided it was time to breach. And so they waited, helplessly.

Minutes passed and a small group of Gartune in the center of the crowd began to circle Rankin. After much pointing and arguing, they eventually nodded in agreement and turned toward the capitol building.

"Here they come," said Dario.

To Dario's surprise, it was Rankin, himself, leading the charge into the building. *Scouting party be damned; this is a full-on invasion! Patience never was his strong suit,* thought Dario. *He's probably worried that someone else will come and steal his glory.*

Adem looked frantically from the courtyard to Dario and then back again as the soldiers rushed into the building. "You," said Dario pointing at Adem. "Hide." Then he pointed behind his desk. Adem hesitated for a moment with his hands clenched to his sides. It looked like he wanted to fight.

Lucan walked up to the young Tormada and laid a hand on his shoulder. "It's okay," said Lucan. "Let us handle this one."

Dario nodded once more towards the desk and Adem eventually relented and jogged over and bent behind the desk. It wasn't long before they heard footsteps running up the hallway. They stopped right outside the door. There were a few indistinguishable whispers and then two Gartune rushed in with their eürocs raised. They scanned the room, but it appeared empty. Suddenly, the metal reflector fell to the ground and sunlight blinded the Gartune. Before they knew what had happened, two back-lit silhouettes ran out from behind the reflector and kicked the soldiers to the floor. One of the Gartune dropped his eüroc in the scuffle. Dario quickly pounced on it just as four more soldiers came running in through the door. Dario managed to take down two of them but was eventually overwhelmed when more reinforcements came running inside to help. Lucan, on the other hand, was incapacitated from the moment he kicked the first Gartune to the floor. He had landed awkwardly, and his knee buckled, making him essentially useless in the fight. His hands were already bound behind his back by the time the other Gartune eventually wrestled Dario to the floor.

Dario's bloodied face looked up at Lucan as his captors tied him up.

"Nice kick," said Dario as he spat blood on the floor.

"I should have stretched first", said Lucan uncomfortably as he sat cross-legged on the floor. "It's too bad," he said as he inspected Dario's bleeding head, "your face had just begun to heal."

At that moment, Rankin sauntered through the door. He grinned when he saw Dario pinned to the floor.

"I'm not surprised you would send somebody else first to do your dirty work," said Dario. "Aren't you Gartune officers supposed to *lead* the charges? 'Tip of the spear' and all that?"

Rankin laughed. "Being governor has taught me that the key to effective leadership is delegation. I guess that's something you never learned during your tenure."

"How many times do you really think you can cover up your cowardice before the others start to notice?" asked Dario. His comment was quickly met with a sharp kick to the ribs from Rankin.

"Oh, *now* he fights," said Lucan.

"Careful, Professor," said Rankin, turning to face the smaller man. "This is not your classroom."

"Dario's right. You're no leader," continued Lucan, undeterred. "These Gartune only follow you because they're afraid of what Hadrian would do to them if they disobeyed a superior. You couldn't inspire a pipken, let alone a Tormada."

"Ah, but there's where you're wrong, Professor," said Rankin as he pulled Lucan to his feet. "In fact, I have a little demonstration planned that I think you will find very... *inspirational.* Let's go for a walk, shall we?"

Rankin ushered Lucan and Dario out of the capitol building and into the courtyard. He pushed them right up against one of the Lotus petals and then forced them to their knees. The crowd of Gartune surrounded them, waiting to see what Rankin was about to do.

The newly-appointed governor of Reysa climbed atop the energy orb to address the crowd. He drew a breath, but before he could speak, something off in the distance caught his eye. Several of the Gartune in the crowd turned their heads in the direction of Rankin's gaze to see what he was looking at.

"What are they looking at?" said Lucan as he tried to see through the mass of Gartune legs.

"I can't see anything," said Dario. "But I hear something…a lot of something."

The streets surrounding the courtyard began to fill with Reysene. Ordinary common folk carrying sticks, pipes and other makeshift weapons began to stream out of buildings and alleyways until they surrounded the courtyard.

"There must be hundreds of them out there," said Lucan. He still couldn't see the crowd, but their presence was now undeniable.

"Fools! They need to get back inside their homes," said Dario. "Tormen are no match for Gartune, no matter how many of them there are. They will be slaughtered."

From the back of the crowd, four Reytana pushed a large cart towards the courtyard. The Reysene parted as the cart moved through them. On top of the cart sat a short, stocky teenager. The cart came to a stop and the teen stood up.

"Attention, purple idiots!" yelled Tinko from the top of his cart. "We have you surrounded. Throw down your sticks and surrender and I promise that nobody gets hurt!"

Lucan groaned. "You've got to be kidding me…" he whispered to himself.

"One of your students?" asked Dario. Lucan just shook his head.

A metal projectile went zinging past Tinko's ear. He lost his balance and almost fell off of the cart. The Gartune erupted with laughter. The soldiers closest to the crowd of Reysene stamped their eürocs in front of them, causing the ground to shake underneath the Reysenes' feet. A few fell, but none ran. Tinko dusted himself off and stood back up on top of the cart.

"Maybe you didn't hear me the first time!" he yelled. Another projectile flew past his head, but this time he ducked and continued speaking. "I don't want to have to hurt you, but you are leaving me no choice! Throw down your weapons now or face the consequences!"

From the top of the lotus' energy orb, Rankin yelled at Tinko.

"What is your name, boy?" barked Rankin.

"I'm just a humble citizen of Reysa. My name is of no consequence. Why do you ask?"

"Because I like to know the name of the person that I'm about to kill," replied Rankin.

Dario rolled his eyes then yelled up to Rankin. "Are you sure that you could take him by yourself?! Perhaps you should *delegate* someone else to kill him for you!"

"Oh, that's right," said Rankin, smiling down at his prisoners. "I almost forgot you two were down there." He then turned to address the crowd. "Citizens of Reysa, you are just in time! It appears that you have forgotten who your masters are. And so, in accordance with the laws of Gartol and King Hadrian himself, I have prepared a demonstration to remind you of your place. Bring the prisoners before me!"

Three Gartune lifted Dario to his feet and stood him in front of the orb, facing Rankin. Another two Gartune easily lifted Lucan and set him beside his fellow prisoner. The crowd of Gartune parted to create a clear view for the Reysene to witness what was about to take place.

"Before you, I present two collaborators who have decided, unwisely, to test the might of the Gartolian empire. The penalty for insubordination is the same here as it is in Gartol: death."

A murmur spread through the Reysene crowd. They looked up at Tinko to see what they should do, but the boy stayed silent. Rankin continued his speech. "And, to prove that we do not show favoritism when it comes to tormen or Tormada, we will begin with your former governor. We do not discriminate in Gartol." Rankin winked at Dario as he said his last line.

Once again, Dario was forced to his knees. "Oh, for Rey's sake, make up your mind! Up and down, up and down!" He grunted as he once again stumbled to his knees. He looked up at Rankin who pressed a button on his eüroc and two gaudy and unnecessarily serrated blades sprung from the end of his staff. *Of course,* thought Dario.

"You sure those will do the trick?" yelled Dario. "You don't want to drive a tank over me, just to be sure?" Rankin smiled and lifted the eüroc over his head. Just as he was about to swing the blades at Dario, a crash of breaking glass erupted from the governor's quarters above him. Rankin turned toward the sound and saw a large figure surrounded by broken shards of glass falling from the sky. He barely had time to raise his eüroc before Adem landed on top of him, flattening him against the top of the energy orb. Wide-eyed and breathless, Rankin stared up at the young Reytana as Adem's hands instinctively wrapped around the Gartune's throat. Desperately, Rankin swung his eüroc at his assailant, but before his blow could hit home, Adem released one hand from his stranglehold and caught the staff in mid-strike. He then twisted it in his hand so that the serrated blades pointed at Rankin's chest.

"Adem, no!" yelled Lucan from the ground. The crowd of Gartune stood motionless, watching the spectacle on top of the orb.

"Help me, you fools!" shouted Rankin. None of the Gartune moved.

As Rankin stared into the eyes of his assailant, a large shadow moved over the courtyard. A loud hum echoed off of the walls of the surrounding buildings as six large shapes emerged around the side of the capitol building. Everyone looked up, including Adem. Rankin saw his chance and quickly pushed the blades away from his chest and toward the Tormada on top of him. Adem moved back just in time to avoid the main thrust of the blades, but he didn't move fast enough to avoid them altogether. One of the blades sliced through his right thigh and he screamed out in pain. Just as Adem lifted his head to yell out, a solar flare shot past him and hit Rankin directly in the chest, creating a smoldering hole right through the center of the Gartune. Rankin looked down at the crater in his chest, then back up at his assailant. In seconds, purple dust covered the top of the energy orb and Rankin was gone.

Giant wings flapped slowly over the orb as one of the hovercrafts lowered from the sky. Purple dust scattered throughout the courtyard.

"Drop your staffs! Get on your knees and put your hands over your heads!" yelled a voice from the hovercraft. The Gartune did as they were told. The hovercraft lowered and several Reytana jumped to the ground and began binding the hands of the captives. One Reytana walked up to Tinko's cart with a huge grin on his face.

"We'll take it from here, Tink," said Loras to his friend who was still standing on top of the cart.

"I really think I had things under control," said Tinko. "A couple more seconds and they would have surrendered. I'm fairly certain."

"Well if you like, we can leave and you can find out."

Tinko pretended to consider the offer for a moment and then shook his head. "Nah, you came all this way. You might as well stay. Besides, these guys are tired of pushing this thing." He patted the orb underneath his feet.

Loras called to some nearby Reytana and they all got behind the sled and pushed the cart toward the center of the courtyard. When they got there, Lucan and Dario were helping Adem down off of the orb. The young Reytana looked like he was more in shock than in pain as Lucan carefully inspected his wound.

"He'll be fine," said Lucan. "The blade didn't go too deep. You Reytana heal so quickly anyway—this will probably be gone by tomorrow." Dario smiled at Adem and patted him on the shoulder. Suddenly, Adem wrapped his arms around Dario and embraced him. Tears began to stream out of the young Reytana's eyes. Dario returned the embrace, smiling. Lucan grinned up at him. "I guess it was a good thing we brought him after all, huh?" Dario closed his eyes and nodded, still embracing the boy. When he finally looked up, he saw Loras, standing proudly in front of him.

"You did well, Loras. But where is Gracien?" he asked. Loras simply shook his head. Dario nodded again and released Adem from his embrace. "Well, I guess we'll have to think of something on our own then."

"We've been doing that a lot lately," replied Loras. "So far, we've gotten lucky."

Dario sighed. "Let's hope that luck continues. We're going to need it."

By this time, most of the Reytana had disembarked the hovercraft and were organizing the Gartune prisoners into small groups in the courtyard. In between the mass of Tormada, Regan came running through the crowd and jumped into her brother's arms. Loras was equally as surprised at seeing his sister as he was with the sudden show of affection. He recoiled for a second before returning his sister's hug.

"I could see you!" shouted Regan excitedly. "I could see you down at the river! Was that Hadrian you were talking to? Were you scared? I was scared! They let me shoot a cannon—a *cannon*! I think I missed my first two shots, but then Xander told me where to aim. Oh, I hope I didn't hit any of you! Are you okay? You look okay. I shot a cannon!"

"Slow down," said Loras as he smiled at his sister. "Wait, that was you who fired on the Gartolians?"

"Yeah! Me and Xander," as she said his name, Xander came walking through the crowd.

Immediately, Loras lit up his ray blade and pushed his sister behind him. "Stand back!" he yelled.

"Nice to see you too, Loras," said Xander.

Regan pushed her way between the two Tormada. "Loras, stop! He's with us. He saved my life. And he saved yours at the river. You have to believe me."

"It's true," added Dario, joining the group. He laid his hand on Loras' sword arm and lowered it slowly. "He helped Lucan and I escape the prison. I'm not sure why... but he's with us."

Loras looked suspiciously at Xander and then at his sister before deactivating his sword. "I have an idea why," said Loras.

Once his friends had had their moment, Tinko whipped the tarp off of the cart with a dramatic flourish. The golden liquid inside the orb shimmered with light. Suddenly, the crowd of Reysene began to cheer. Tinko looked down and saw his old professor frowning at him.

"That was quite a speech, Mr. Tinko. You're lucky it didn't get you killed."

Tinko hopped down off of the cart. "Loras told me that I needed to draw their attention for a few moments. I think I succeeded pretty well in my task."

"Oh, so you were in on the plan too, were you? Why am I not surprised?" Lucan turned to Loras, but his frown was waning.

Loras wrapped his arm around his professor's shoulders. "I never thought I'd say this, but I'm relieved to see you, Professor. After our escape, I wasn't sure I'd ever see you again. You move pretty good for an—" Lucan raised an eyebrow "— for a *scholarly* man, such as yourself." Then he turned toward Dario. "And thanks for the assist out there. How did you do all of this?" Loras pointed up toward Dario's room and the adjacent building with its wall of reflected sunlight.

"Maybe someday I'll show you," said Dario. "But first, we need to fill this thing up before Hadrian has time to regroup." He beckoned for several Reytana to help lift the Hole's energy orb above the Lotus. They carefully tilted the orb, spilling its contents into the empty globe below. The cheers from the Reysene grew louder as the orb filled.

"Now what?" said Loras.

"Now," said Dario as the last bit of solar energy was transferred, "we take the fight to them!"

CHAPTER THIRTY-EIGHT
Seige

Hadrian grunted under his breath as the cheers of "Rey-sa!
Rey-sa!" echoed down from the city on the cliff. *They won't be
cheering for long,* he thought.

The king stomped through the camp looking for his
second in command. Everywhere, the Gartolian war machine
was in full effect. It had been eighteen years since the army
last fought, but it might as well have been yesterday. A cluster
of triage tents had been rapidly constructed at the south side
of the camp to tend to those who sustained wounds at
Octavian's Pass. Each regiment of soldiers—both Tormada
and torman—had already re-grouped, re-stocked and started
preparing for the next round of battle. All they needed were
their orders.

Hadrian arrived outside of the command center and
shouted through the open doors.

"Morlo!" shouted the king. "Get out here, now!"

The Gartune commander humbly emerged from the command center.

"Your highness—" he started to speak but Hadrian cut him off.

"You had *one* job! Just one!"

"I know, my king," said Morlo with his head bowed low. "One of the Reytana spotted us before we had planned on attacking. We had no choice. We had to open fire."

"You were impatient as always," seethed Hadrian. "I should have known you could not be trusted. I must have been out of my mind for allowing you to begin this battle. The task was so simple; the instructions so clear. Even *you* should have been able to follow them!"

"My king," said Morlo. "They have won nothing. Our troops took only minor losses and we are ready for the counter-attack."

"And what of the tanks?" said Hadrian slowly.

Morlo raised his head slightly to look at the king. "They are in place and ready for your command."

"Finally," said Hadrian. "Then let us not waste any time. The Reysene have enjoyed their little victory long enough. It's time to shut them up once and for all. Bring up the tanks!"

Morlo nodded, "Yes, my king!" then rushed out of the command center and disappeared into the camp.

Once Hadrian's conversation with his commander had ended, a Gartune sentry approached the king.

"Your highness, Damnar and Damina have returned. They are waiting inside and wish to talk to you."

"I don't have any time to waste on those two fools. Tell them they can speak to me when the battle is over," replied the king.

"But, sir," said the sentry, "they say they have some information. Information about Xander... and Septa." Hadrian was already heading back into the camp, but Septa's name stopped him in his tracks.

"They know what happened to my daughter?"

"They wouldn't tell us," said the guard. "They said they would only tell you."

"Out of my way!" shouted the king as he stormed past the sentry and into the command center.

Reysa's command center, spanning the entire top floor of the capitol building, was full of activity. Panels and monitors that had been dark for years were alive and humming. Methodic beeps, pulses and flashing lights emanated from all corners of the room. Several Reytana took posts behind the panels and began adjusting knobs, pressing buttons and reading monitors. In the middle of the room stood Dario, giving orders like a seasoned general. Xander and Regan silently watched the Reytana work from the corner of the room.

"You know, I always thought that Reysene were kind of... disinterested... when it came to this kind of thing," whispered Xander to Regan. "But this is impressive. Reminds me of how they do it on the ground."

"Well, the Gartolians haven't been the only ones fighting a war for hundreds of years. We've had just as much practice as you," said Dario.

"Maybe," said Xander. "But you're still not as good as us." A concerned look flashed on Xander's face as he remembered something. "There's something I need to tell you," he said.

Just then, the room began to shake. "More hovercraft?" asked Regan, peering up out of the window.

"Those aren't hovercraft..." said Xander as he ran toward the windows. "Dario! You need to activate the city's forcefield—*now*!"

"Why?" said Dario, annoyed with being interrupted. "They've only got light artillery down there; nothing that can do any damage from that range. I'm charging up the cannons. *All* of the cannons. It's time we wiped that camp off of the ground!"

"Look!" shouted Xander, pointing to the ground. From their vantage point at the top of Reysa's tallest building they could just see down to the Gartolian basecamp. It looked like hundreds of tiny squares arranged in a perfect grid with thousands of little specs marching in between them. Right next to the camp, something was happening. The ground was opening up. Giant square holes in the desert were sliding open and large, menacing vehicles were rising up through the widening gaps.

"Tanks," said Regan. "How did they—"

"Forcefield up!" yelled Dario. "Full power to the southern perimeter shields!" The Reytana manning the circuit board nearest Regan rapidly turned dials. An electric hum began to swell outside the room. Down below in the Lotus' courtyard, six large tubes flooded with light. Regan watched as the light shot through the tubes toward the southern wall of the city. It was only seconds before the light reached the perimeter and illuminated the large pipe that ran atop the great wall. Several other pipes ran parallel along the outside of the wall at ten-foot vertical intervals. With the Lotus feeding it energy, the southern face of the city wall was striped in gold.

A shimmering light began to emanate from the wall. Then, a translucent liquid began to form a dome over the city. The liquid swirled slowly creating irregular floating shapes that reflected a myriad of colors when the light hit it.

"Southern shield deployed," said the Reytana at the panel next to Regan.

"Will it be able to stop those things?" asked Regan, pointing down to the tanks.

"We're about to find out." said Dario.

The last tank platform completed its ascent from its underground chamber and the four hydraulic columns that supported it locked into place as the Gartolian war machines slowly rotated their turrets up toward the city.

Morlo didn't waste any time giving his command. The instant the turrets stopped turning he yelled "fire!" and the tanks launched their projectiles up at the city. The iron cannonballs, ten feet in diameter and made out of a combustible Gartolian alloy, flew toward their target. Twenty feet from the city's wall, they collided with the golden forcefield and shattered with a magnificent explosion of splintered iron and refracted light. The forcefield flickered briefly, but then the golden liquid resumed its steady, molten flow, unbroken.

"Ten degrees down... fire!" yelled Morlo.

Another relay of cannonballs sped toward the city. This time they struck the cliff just below the wall that held the forcefield's light tubes. Other than some very loud explosions and nominal dents in the rock, the projectiles did not have much of an effect. Morlo grimaced.

"Twenty degrees west... fir—"

"Belay that order!" shouted Hadrian, marching up to the platform at the center of the tank regiment. "Repeat the trajectory of your initial volley. Target the forcefield!"

The turrets on the tanks rose slightly and then fired in unison. Again, the cannonballs collided with the forcefield and exploded in a dazzling display of sound and color. The shield flickered twice before regaining stability. Hadrian smiled. "Again!" he yelled. "Maintain current trajectory. Keep hitting the forcefield!"

"But, your highness," said Morlo, "our fire is not penetrating the forcefield. It's having no effect."

"Isn't it?" said Hadrian, raising an eyebrow. Another round of tank fire rang out. The projectiles struck the shield and exploded as before. This time, it flickered a few seconds longer before settling.

"You have your orders!" said Hadrian. He then turned and walked briskly back toward the camp, a look of satisfaction on his face.

The Gartolian tanks pounded Reysa's forcefield relentlessly. Once a tank had exhausted its payload of ammunition, the metal platform on which it sat lowered back into the ground and another tank immediately rose to take its place. Underground, the massive cavern was built like a freeway, twelve lanes wide. Each lane held three tanks. While one was firing above, another waited to replace it, while the third tank was being reloaded with ammunition. Hundreds of giant cannonballs lined both sides of the lanes. Gartolian-operated cranes quickly moved back and forth between the rows of cannonballs and the tanks, lifting the ammunition and loading it into the back of the tanks. It was a spectacle of Gartolian engineering and efficiency. Morlo's secret project may have taken longer than expected to complete, but now that it was operational, it was a devastating weapon.

Reysa's command center shook again as another volley of Gartolian tank fire hit the forcefield. Dust fell from the ceiling and the lights flickered. However, none of the Reytana manning their controls seemed to notice. They were too involved in their work. But Dario's face was wrought with concern.

"The forcefield is holding," said the Reytana at the shield controls. "But it's using a lot of energy."

Dario looked down at the energy orb in the courtyard. Already, about an eighth of it had been drained. "My little sun-bouncing trick won't be able to refill the orb at the rate that it's draining," said Dario. "And once night comes..."

"The tanks are firing at will right now. Maybe we can slow them down a bit," said Xander. "Divert some energy to the solar cannons. I'll take some of the Reytana with me and we'll see if we can't slow down their assault."

Dario shook his head. "I need the Reytana to guard the prisoners." Down in the courtyard, the Reytana had the Gartune collected into small groups. The guards paced slowly between the prisoners, their heads pointed toward the southern wall. With each explosion, the look of concern on their faces deepened, while the Gartune began to quietly snicker.

"Your soldiers are wasted down there." said Xander. "They would be more effective at the wall." A wry grin spread on his face. "As for the prisoners, I know just the place we could lock them up."

Dario thought for a moment, then nodded. "I suppose Hadrian did us a favor when he expanded our prison. Ok, take them underground and put them in the empty cells. But leave plenty of Reytana to guard them. The last time Hadrian visited the prison, he came in through a different door. There is more than one way into that dungeon, and I don't want anyone from below sneaking up there to free *any* of them."

"Understood," replied Xander.

Loras rushed into the command center just as Xander was leaving with his new orders. Xander clapped a hand on Loras' shoulder as he passed him. "Oh, by the way, nice work out there, Loras. Couldn't have done it better myself."

"Your dad says hi," said Loras, brushing Xander's hand off his shoulder. Xander laughed and left the room.

Loras walked over to Dario and stood next to him at the windows. They watched as the forcefield sustained another barrage of tank fire.

"Will it hold?" asked Loras.

"Not forever," said Dario.

"How long do we have?"

"Once the sun goes down," said Dario grimly, "so does our shield."

Dario and Loras watched out the window in silence. Twelve brightly-colored explosions flashed before their eyes. The floor shook and more dust fell from the ceiling. Dario brushed it off but Loras did not. He was lost in thought.

"There's only one thing we can do," said Loras. "For our shield to stay up, *theirs* must come down."

"Loras," said Dario. "Gracien knew that taking down the Gartolian shield was going to be a suicide mission. That's why he insisted that it was him that did it." He sighed. Another barrage of cannon fire shook the room.

"He was the strongest among all of us, and even then, his odds of succeeding were slim. Nobody knows how to get on the floating tank. We've been watching for years and have never seen anyone get on or off. And even if you did get inside, there's no way of knowing what is waiting for you."

"It's the only way," said Loras. "Somebody has to do it."

Dario turned and looked Loras up and down. "Do you even know how to swim?"

"No, but I've had a few lessons in not-drowning lately. So that's something."

Dario sighed again and shook his head. This time when the cannonballs hit, it took the forcefield several seconds to stop flickering. He looked down at the Lotus rapidly pulsing solar energy into the six veins that fueled the shield. He would have to open up six more to fuel the cannons. Once he did so, the orb would drain twice as quickly. They might not even make it to the night.

"How are you going to get down there?" asked Dario. "I'm sure Hadrian has the lift covered by now. They'll shoot you down the minute you step aboard. And the mountain pass is too dangerous now with all of the explosions above it. You'd have shards of cannonball raining down on your head."

"You leave that to me," said Loras. "Just keep all of the Gartolian attention up here."

"Very well," said Dario.

Loras clapped the governor on the back and walked toward the door. Just as he was about to leave, Regan ran up to him and hugged him.

"Two hugs in one day?" said Loras. "Who are you and what have you done with my sister?"

"Just be careful," said Regan. "This isn't playing with sticks after school. This is real." Loras looked at his sister. Concern was plastered all over her face. He was so used to seeing disapproval or embarrassment when she looked at him that he wasn't quite sure how to react to this new sentiment. He started to revert to one of his old, sarcastic comments but Regan put

her hand to his mouth just as he was about to open it. "Don't,"
she said. "Just try not to kill yourself."

This time Loras smiled at his sister's familiar tone. "I'll do
my best," he said, and he walked out the door.

Loras ran through the courtyard to the sound of exploding
cannonballs. The last of the Gartune prisoners was being
ushered away by Xander and a handful of Reytana. Loras still
had a hard time seeing Xander as one of the good guys. He was
fairly certain that this was all some sort of long con. But what
was the end game for the Gartune prince? After what he had
done the past few days, he could not return to Gartol. That
much was certain. Son or no son, Hadrian would have the
prince locked up… or worse. So why then? Could all of this
really be for Regan? A new current of emotion entered into the
maelstrom that was already churning within Loras' head. He
forced his mind to settle. There were more important things to
focus on at the moment. The new, uncomfortable relationship
between his sister and his old arch-enemy could wait for
another day. As if he could sense that he was thinking about
him, Xander spotted Loras and gave him a small nod before
continuing on his way with the Gartune prisoners.

Loras could feel the heat from his headband and wristbands
warming his skin. He did not need to look at them to know
that they were glowing. Inside his chest, his heart pounded
fiercely, yet he felt oddly calm. He knew what he had to do.
Though he did not know what obstacles lay ahead, somehow,
he knew that he had the strength to overcome them. *After all,
look what I've already achieved today.* Never in his wildest dreams
had he imagined that he would ride in a Reytana hovercraft or
meet King Hadrian on the field of battle *and live to tell about it.*
And after all of that, somehow, he had managed to liberate the
city of Reysa from the Gartune, just like he had dreamt for so
many years. It was crazy to think about, and yet, he had done
it. He, Loras, on this day, had done all of that. Now, his greatest
task lay before him. It might be naive to think he was capable

of accomplishing it, but he didn't care, for now he knew that the outcome of his next mission was solely up to him. And that, in itself, was a comforting thought.

Before long, Loras reached the eastern edge of the city. Once there, he quickly scaled a four-story building that butted up against the perimeter wall. When he emerged on the roof, he was fifteen feet above the wall. He looked down and was almost blinded by the dazzling sunlight reflecting off of the rippling sea. Before he had time to debate his decision any further, he walked to the opposite end of the roof and took a deep breath. *Here we go,* thought Loras. He closed his eyes, bent his knees and ran. Three large strides easily crossed the width of the roof. Loras opened his eyes just as his right foot was planting for his jump. He panicked. His right leg straightened, and his momentum sent the top half of his body flailing over the planted leg. Arms wind-milling at his side, he balanced precariously on the edge of the roof. Below him, the enormous distance to the sea smacked him in the forehead and pushed him back up straight. He fell backward on to the roof.

Embarrassment washed over Loras. He looked over his shoulder to see if anyone was watching, even though he knew no one was there. The blue sea stretched out before him, calm and beautiful. It mocked him. Loras felt shame in his heart.

Then he decided something. *I'd rather be afraid than ashamed.* With fists clenched, he rose to his feet. He looked out into the ocean and scowled. His heart began to pound in his chest once more.

"I'd rather be afraid than ashamed," he repeated out loud. Then he closed his eyes, lifted his arms from his sides, and jumped.

Water has played an important role in the history of the conflict between Reysa and Gartol. Not only is the Aeil River responsible for delivering each city it's precious Tormada, but the Delucean Sea has occasionally served as a battlefield. Both the Reysene and Gartolians regard the sea with trepidation. Given the choice, both races would much rather do battle on solid ground. However, from time to time, one of the armies would take advantage of the other's apprehension and launch a surprise attack from the sea, even though it meant risking the wrath of it's custodian.

- Chapter Nine of *The Crescent Wars*, by Nicholas Baston

CHAPTER THIRTY-NINE
The Tank

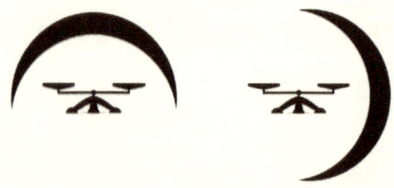

Gartolian tanks and Reysene solar cannons exchanged fire into the afternoon. Xander strode along the top of Reysa's perimeter wall, weaving between solar cannons as he shouted orders to the Reytana manning the weapons. A relentless chorus of hums and whooshes rang out as the cannons unleashed shot after shot at the Gartolian tanks. However, their attack didn't seem to be having much of an effect. The solar flares hit the steel sides of the tanks and simply washed over them in an impressive explosion of light.

Meanwhile, Reysa's forcefield was waning. Each time a Gartolian volley hit it, the shield wavered for several seconds before reforming itself. Xander knew that it was only a matter of time before they would have to make a decision to either cease their attack or take down their forcefield. They did not have enough solar energy to maintain both.

Then he had an idea.

"You there!" he pointed toward the Reytana manning the cannons closest to the Gartolian basecamp. "Target the command center!"

The Reytana nodded and turned their cannons toward the large, circular building at the center of camp. They unleashed a round of shots. The command center was made of steel, but it was not of the same impenetrable thickness as the tanks. The solar flares dented the roof. Several shouts rang out from the ground. All of a sudden, a group of Gartune went running toward the command center. Once there, they created defensive perimeter around the building.

Xander watched from his perch on the wall and smiled. *That should even things out a bit.* "You three, keep firing on the command center," he ordered. "The rest of you, power down for a moment."

While the three Reytana continued their fire, Xander gathered the remaining soldiers into a group and relayed new instructions. Several of the Reytana nodded approval at their new orders. A few of them even had smirks on their faces when they returned to their weapons. They climbed back into the seats of the solar cannons and awaited Xander's command. Meanwhile, more Gartune had joined the perimeter defending the command center. Each time a solar cannon fired on their location, several Gartune would stamp their eürocs into the ground, causing a large mound of rocks to form in the area where the solar flare was heading. The projectile then smashed into the rock pile before it could reach the building behind it. It was a laborious procedure for the Gartune as they constantly had to race to the location of the next shot before it could strike the camp. The Reytana were skillfully varying the trajectories of their shots to keep the Gartune scrambling. Thanks to the Gartune's efforts, no more flares were getting through to the command center. They were effectively at a stalemate again. But there was one difference. The tanks were not nearly as protected as before.

"Now!" yelled Xander. The rest of the Reytana opened fire toward the tanks. However, instead of targeting the tanks themselves, the Reytana targeted the platforms underneath them. Even though there was hardly any area where the platforms were not covered by the tank above them, the Reytana still managed to sneak in a few shots before the Gartolians realized what they were doing. Three tank platforms were disabled before Morlo redeployed a regiment of Gartune to the front of the platforms. Within seconds, the Gartune had built up mounds of rock in front of the tanks. Solar flares smashed into them, causing dirt and rock to fly everywhere. After each hit, a couple of swift eüroc stomps built the mounds back up.

And so, the battle continued on. The Gartolian tanks now had to maneuver around the rock piles in front of them in order to get off a clear shot. This slowed their assault considerably. Even though the tanks had sustained no damage, Xander's strategy was having an effect.

While the Reytana waged war with the Gartolian basecamp, Loras was attempting an equally arduous task—learning how to swim. It had taken him what seemed like forever to resurface after his dive off the cliff. Once the initial shock of hitting the ocean had subsided, he frantically flailed his arms and kicked his legs back and forth. He could barely keep his head above water, let alone propel himself through it. It was all he could do to keep from drowning. He swallowed an unhealthy amount of water and struggled to breathe between coughs. After about a minute of flailing without any success, Loras gave up his attempt at moving forward. Instead, he decided to concentrate on just breathing, so he flipped over onto his back and floated for a minute, staring up at the sky.

The sun did its job. Loras could feel the strength returning to his tired muscles. Once his breathing had returned to normal, he decided to make another attempt at forward motion. This time, he remained on his back and swept his arms in large circles at his sides. He didn't know what to do with his legs, so he just let them drag under the water. *Better to just concentrate on one thing at a time,* he thought. It was not elegant, but it moved him toward his destination, and it kept his head from sinking under the water.

The floating shield tank rose out of the water a hundred yards away. As he paddled forward, Loras lifted his head out of the water and looked back toward Reysa. The Gartolian basecamp was taking heavy fire from the solar cannons, but they were still able to return fire at a consistent, though slower, rate. Reysa's forcefield flickered and wavered each time a barrage of tank fire hit it, but it was still holding. *They're doing their part, now I have to do mine,* thought Loras as he twisted his head to look toward the tank that controlled the Gartolian sun shield. Much to his dismay, it didn't seem to be any closer. *Could that thing be moving away from me?*

Loras held his breath and ducked his head under the water. He could make out the hull of the tank way off in the distance. Bubbles were emitting from the end of a spinning propeller that was attached to the back of the tank. *It is moving away from me. How could they possibly have seen me coming?* Then Loras saw the chain attached to the bottom of the tank. It stretched down to the ocean floor where it was tethered to an enormous anchor. Relief and recognition dawned on Loras. *Of course it's moving, just like the shield tanks on the ground move. It's moving with the sun. It's still possible that they haven't spotted me.*

With newfound determination, Loras began to paddle harder toward the tank. He was halfway there when he felt something brush against his leg. He froze, hoping that it was just a bit of seaweed or maybe a fish. Then it happened again and this time it was undeniable. The thing that brushed against his leg was a hand. This time it didn't brush—it tugged. Loras shoved his head under the water and was face to face with one of the most beautiful creatures he had ever seen. A water nymph; her long, wavy hair flowing all around her perfectly oval face, stared at Loras with inquisitive blue eyes.

Loras froze, waiting to see what the nymph would do next, but she simply floated and continued to stare.

Surprisingly, Loras felt no fear toward this strange creature. Perhaps it was her beauty that disarmed him, or the unthreatening way that she regarded him. Either way, Loras was as equally enthralled with her as she appeared to be with him.

She wants to know what I'm doing, thought Loras. He nodded toward the floating tank. The nymph frowned. Her blue eyes became darker, which in turn, made them even more stunning. They mesmerized Loras.

The nymph nodded toward the anchor on the ocean floor. Loras peered through the water and eventually saw what she was motioning to. It wasn't the anchor; it was the condition of the ocean floor surrounding it. Just as the three shield tanks on land had carved enormous gouges in the ground, the floating tank had dragged the anchor along the seabed, causing a huge rift that ran straight through a large coral reef. The anchor had done enormous damage to the ocean floor. In addition to the dark, muddy trench that it had carved through the center of the reef, Loras could see that the surrounding coral had begun to die as well.

That tank is killing the sea bed. No wonder the nymph is mad. He looked back at the woman floating beside him. She now wore a frown. *How do I convince her that I only want on the tank so that I can destroy it?* Loras waved his hands in front of his head making large semi-circles while blowing bubbles out of his mouth to represent an explosion. After doing so, he immediately realized that he was out of breath, so he re-surfaced for air.

Gods, how long was I down there? Two, maybe three minutes? I can't hold my breath that long. What is going on here? He ducked his head back under the water and was alarmed to see not only one face, but now three. They slowly bobbed up and down in the water and watched him with their large, sapphire eyes. Loras pointed to the anchor and then to the tank and re-enacted his explosion pantomime, this time being even more dramatic when he waved his arms and blew bubbles. The nymphs were confused. Then, one of them whispered something into the ear of the first nymph and a look of recognition came over her. She thought for a moment and then rapidly swam away. The other two nymphs followed her. Loras watched them until they were out of site. Suddenly, his lungs contracted and he became dizzy. He was beyond breathless. He was drowning. Loras fought his body's natural instinct to open his mouth for air. With all of his might he pushed his head out of the water and gasped for breath. Blotches of white light dotted his vision as he sucked in oxygen as fast as he could. Eventually, his lungs re-inflated and he started breathing normally.

What just happened?! Loras thought to himself as he began to calm down. *How did I go from being perfectly fine to completely out of breath?* Then he realized that it had happened exactly when the nymphs left him. Had they been the ones allowing him to hold his breath for so long? Loras thought that must have been it. He promised himself to remember the effect they had on his breathing if he ever ran into them again. He had a feeling that he had not seen the last of them.

Loras took two deep breaths and then resumed his slow, labored swim toward the tank. After fifteen minutes of strenuous paddling, he finally reached his destination. Up close, the tank was enormous. It was even larger than the three on land. The giant iron leg stretched out of its turret and extended all the way up to the shield. Loras looked up and could barely see where the leg connected to the massive disc in the sky.

Loras recalled the one time he had stood on top of a shield tank. It was dark and raining that day, but if memory served him correctly, there was a hatch right behind the turret. However, reaching the top of this tank was going to be a challenge. Before, he was able to use his Reytana ability and simply jump to the top of the tank. Without a solid surface to push off of, jumping was out of the question this time. He had no other option but to climb. It was a particularly difficult task because there was nothing to grab onto. The hull of the ship was a smooth, solid surface. Loras had to press his arms and legs hard against the metal in order to form enough friction to pull himself up, but not before slipping back into the water several times.

After many unsuccessful attempts, he finally pulled himself up to the top of the ship. He shook himself off and tip-toed softly to the back of the tank. Slowly, Loras peered behind the turret. There was nothing but smooth, solid metal. Loras frowned and walked to the other side of the turret. Nothing. He then retraced his steps and walked back to the front of the tank, thinking that he must have missed something. But the tank was completely solid. Not only was there no hatch, but there weren't seams of any kind. It was as if the entire vessel had been shaped from one solid piece of iron.

Loras sat down to think. There had to be some way inside this thing. He wondered if the Gartolians inside knew he was there. Then Dario's voice spoke to him from inside his head. *Gracien knew this was a suicide mission...* Suddenly, Loras knew where the tank's hatch was. His heart sank. He stood up, hoping that his intuition was wrong, then walked to the edge of the tank and peered over the side. *Well, only one way to find out.* Loras dove back into the water then propelled himself under the tank with a few awkward strokes. Somehow, he had more success swimming underneath the water than above it. He took several more strokes toward the center of the vessel. The rhythmic *whoosh, whoosh, whoosh* of the propeller at the rear of the ship filled his ears. Once he had reached the center of the tank's hull, he looked up and saw it—a large, rectangular door with an iron wheel for a latch.

Loras began to feel his lungs burn. He looked back the way he had come. It would take him some time to swim out from under the tank; time that he did not have. The nearest source of oxygen was inside the tank. He made the snap decision to go for the hatch rather than try to swim for the surface. Loras reached up and tugged on the wheel connected to the hatch. It did not budge. He pulled harder, exerting energy that he did not have. His lungs were on fire. Each tug of the wheel seemed to burn the last bits of air in his chest. The sound of the propeller churning the water became louder. Loras' extremities began to tingle. He could feel his eyes bulging in his head. There was only time for one more tug on the wheel. He summoned all of the strength he had left in his body and pulled. The wheel started to turn just a tiny bit before everything went black.

Loras' hands fell limply off of the wheel. His body went numb as he slowly drifted away from the hatch. The water's current pushed his lifeless body toward the back of the tank and the propeller's churning blades drew him closer and closer. Loras' eyes rolled into the back of his head as his body was sucked toward the propeller.

His head was inches from the blades when a rush of water came roaring from the opposite direction and pushed him away from danger. Two strong arms wrapped around his chest. Suddenly, Loras' vacant body was filled with life. His lungs filled with air and his eyes shot open. Instinctively, he opened his mouth to breathe, but a large hand immediately covered it up. Behind those fingers, a shadowy figure began to come into focus. She had some similarities to the other nymphs that Loras had encountered earlier; she had the same flowing hair, the same blue tint to her skin, but she was darker... much darker. In particular, her eyes were solid black. There were no pupils and no irises. Just solid black like an eel. They were also too large for her face, almost double the size of normal eyes. Looking into those black orbs, Loras did not detect good or evil, only power.

Behind this woman, Loras could see several other beings swimming around in the darkness. They looked like the nymphs that he had seen earlier. They swam in slow circles behind their queen—for she was undoubtedly their leader— as if they were protecting her. Loras didn't see how she could have needed any protection. Nothing in the water, other than maybe Lyse herself, could have been any threat to the creature before him.

Once Loras had closed his mouth, the nymph queen removed her hand and nodded toward the hatch. Loras looked up and saw that the wheel had indeed turned slightly on his last attempt. The queen placed her hand on Loras' chest and a surge of strength filled him. He knew that it would only take one more turn and the hatch would open. With newfound strength, Loras swam to the hatch and turned the wheel. This time it gave way without a fight. The hatch slid sideways, and light poured from the opening.

Loras swam up through the entrance and was surprised when his head quickly surfaced above the water. He swam away from the opening and his feet found a solid floor. Slowly, he stood up in a waist-deep pool that was inside of a large, brightly lit room. The room appeared to span the entire width and at least half the length of the vessel. On one side of the pool was a dock of some sort, and a ladder. Attached to the dock was a small submarine. *So that's why Dario never saw anyone come in or out of the tank.*

Loras waded over to the ladder and pulled himself onto the dock. Then he saw the windows.

One side of the room was made up entirely of windows, with a large glass door at its center. Behind the windows, Loras could see a dim room that must have been the control center for the tank and the sun shield. The back wall contained several glowing monitors with graphs, numbers and squiggly moving lines. There were rows and rows of brightly lit buttons. Some of them flashed. More important than all of that, though, were the five Gartune standing behind the windows, looking out at Loras.

Two of the Gartune had confused looks on their faces. Two others looked angry and ready to rush through the door. The fifth Gartune, the one standing nearest to the door, had a knowing grin on his face. He said something to his companions, and they began to laugh. Then, he pressed a button near the door and Loras heard the hatch at the bottom of the pool slide shut. At the same time, the water began to rise.

The Gartune gave Loras an evil smile from behind the glass. One of them waved at him. Standing on the dock, the water was now at Loras' knees and rising rapidly. He looked down into the pool and saw something move. A large, dark shape circled gracefully in the water. Then something touched his leg. Loras looked down and saw two blue eyes staring up at him. The smaller nymph from earlier. She waved her hands to the side of her head and made two semi-circles while blowing bubbles out of her mouth. It was the same motion Loras had made to her when he communicated his intentions to blow up the ship. Loras nodded to the nymph and the two of them waded toward the back wall.

The large, dark shape that had been circling began to rise out of the center of the pool. Water cascaded off of her dark, wavy hair as the nymph queen emerged from the rising water and turned toward the control room. Before the water level covered his head, Loras looked back at the terrified Gartune staring out from behind the windows. He couldn't help himself. He waved.

The water level continued to rise until the entire room was full of water. With his nymph companion once again touching his arm, Loras was able to hold his breath with ease. He watched as the nymph queen raised her hands and an incredible current blew open the control room door. The Gartune began to panic as water swirled around them. Soon, she was in there with them, swirling around as they feebly attempted to strike her with their eurocs. Loras held onto a handle on the back of the wall while the water churned around him. The blue-eyed nymph grasped him around the waist and the two of them watched the chaos unfold within the control center. The queen was a blur as she wrapped herself around the submerged Gartune and threw their bodies against the control board, shattering monitors and windows alike. It was not long before the five Gartune came floating, unconscious, through the door and out into the pool room.

With the nymph still grasping on to his shoulder keeping his lungs full of air, Loras swam into the control center and found the button that the Gartune had pushed to flood the pool room. He pressed it and the water quickly began to drain from both rooms.

As the water receded, Loras was able to assess the damage that the control room had taken during the nymph queen's assault. It was bad. Very bad. Sparks shot from behind several buttons and two of the monitors were making a hissing sound while smoke curled from their sides. Suddenly, an alarm sounded and a large, red button began to flash in the middle of the console.

Loras looked around, frantically. Back in the main pool room, the nymph queen stood in the water with her arms crossed. The five Gartune floated face down in the water around her. The smaller nymph, the one who had been assisting Loras, stood next to her with a concerned look on her face. The queen's face was harder to read, but Loras thought he saw a hint of satisfaction.

Great, thought Loras. *Now what.*

Smoke continued to fill the small control room while the alarm echoed off of the walls. The entire left side of the console was now sparking and sizzling. It wouldn't be long before the entire thing caught fire. But Loras hadn't accomplished his mission. The shield was still up and he was running out of time.

The flashing red button at the center of the console drew Loras' attention. There was no label saying what it did. In fact, none of the buttons had any labels or indications of their functions. Not that it mattered—most of them were probably fried at this point anyway.

Above him, Loras heard a loud creaking sound come from the top of the tank. It was the unmistakable groan of bending metal. *Oh no,* thought Loras.

The tank began to tilt.

CHAPTER FORTY
The Shield

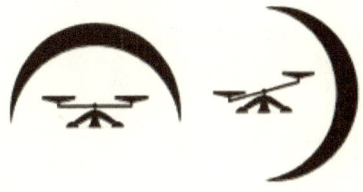

"That's not good."

Xander watched as the sun shield above Reysa began to falter. Several sections of the mechanical arm attached to the floating tank had collapsed in on themselves, causing the shield to dip in that direction. Sparks flew from the compromised joints each time a section collapsed and a terrible creaking sound of metal on metal filled the sky. Xander noticed that the other three tanks on the ground had come out of their ruts and adjusted their normal courses in an attempt to compensate for the damaged arm but now the three healthy arms were noticeably straining to support the ailing shield. Alarms sounded from the tanks below as their wheels spun rapidly, kicking up clouds of sand.

"That thing is coming down," said Xander.

Several of the Reytana who were manning the solar cannons followed Xander's gaze toward the sun shield. The eastern edge of the massive disc was dipping closer and closer to the city.

"Rey help us," whispered one of the Reytana. He looked at Xander. "What do we do?"

The rest of the Reytana had all stopped firing on the Gartolian basecamp and stared at Xander, waiting for orders. How quickly they had accepted him as their commanding officer. For years, he had struggled to get his own Gartune to respect his leadership. *Not that I ever did anything to deserve it*, thought Xander. But after only a few hours, these Reytana who had been his enemies his entire life, now looked to him for guidance. Right as their city was about to be destroyed. The irony almost made him laugh.

"Do you hear that?" asked Regan. She and Dario looked up at the ceiling of the command center. Above them, they heard the unmistakable sound of metal bending.

"Retract the roof plates," said Dario.

A Reytana sitting at one of the control stations turned a lever and the metal plates that covered the domed roof of the capitol building slid backwards. Everyone stopped what they were doing and looked upwards through the glass ceiling. Sparks showered on to the roof above them. Little puffs of smoke rose from the panels after each spec of fire hit the glass. Through the haze of smoke and sparks they saw the shield. It was almost on top of them.

"Oh my gods," said one of the Reytana.

There was a loud crack and the shield jerked downward even further. A new shower of sparks rained down on to the roof.

Dario and Regan exchanged a look. They were both thinking the same thing. Loras.

Immediately, Dario jumped to action. He ran towards the largest of the control stations and shoved one of the seated Reytana out of the way.

"Do you think—" said Regan.

"Yep," replied Dario as he began pressing buttons on the console in front of him.

"But how—" continued Regan.

"I don't know what he did but he did something." He nodded towards the eastern wall of windows. Down below in the ocean, the floating tank was listing badly to one side. Regan looked worriedly down at the ailing vessel.

"I'm sure he's fine. I'd be more worried if the shield *wasn't* about to collapse. The fact that it's failing means that he was at least partly successful."

"Partly successful?" exclaimed Regan. "The shield is about to fall on the city!"

Loras pounded on the flashing red button in the middle of the console but nothing happened. The alarm still blared in the control room and he had to hold on to a chair that was bolted to the floor in order to keep from falling over as the tank continued to list to the side. Water from the pool room entered through the broken windows behind him and sloshed up against the left side of the console as the ship tilted further in that direction. All of the lights and monitors on that side of the board flickered and then went out. Loras looked around frantically for any other button that he could push to get the shield to retract.

He smashed his fist into anything he could find. One button caused a mechanical revving sound to briefly start from above him and a spark of hope flickered in Loras' chest but that was immediately extinguished when the revving turned into a horrible crunching and grinding noise which caused the entire tank to shake.

Behind him, the nymph queen and her smaller consort watched Loras struggle. They stood directly out of the water which meant that their bodies were tilted at the same angle as the ship. It was an off-putting effect which caused Loras to do a double-take when he saw them standing like that. His mind became distracted by the distortion of physics which the nymphs displayed but then an extra loud crash from above jarred his attention back to the task at hand. However, it was becoming more and more evident that there was no way to retract the shield. The damage had been done.

Xander watched another section of the shield arm collapse on itself, sending a shower of sparks everywhere. The giant metal disc was now perilously close to the top of the capitol building. He knew that Reysa's command center was on the top floor which meant that Regan was on the top floor. He had to do something and it had to be fast.

The Reytana soldiers continued to look at him, expectantly. Their solar cannons hummed with light energy, just waiting to be fired.

For the first time, Xander noticed that the Gartolians had stopped firing on their position. *Why waste the ammunition when the shield is about to do more damage than they ever could?* He considered taking advantage of the momentary ceasefire and re-firing on the Gartolian basecamp. But what good would that do if they were about to be crushed by a giant, falling shield?

Xander closed his eyes and put his hands to his head. *Think!* But thinking had never been Xander's strong suit. Try as he might, he couldn't come up with any ideas. All he could do was stand there and listen to the humming of the solar cannons.

The solar cannons...

"I have an idea!" shouted Xander.

Everyone in the command center had stopped what they were doing. Everyone except Dario who frantically ran between control stations, shoving anyone who got in his way. The rest of the Reytana stared up at the sun shield, waiting for the inevitable. Even if they tried to descend the hundred flights of stairs down to the ground, what difference would it make? The shield would fall there as well. There was nowhere to escape to.

Suddenly, a golden beam shot past the windows and struck the sun shield with a blast of solar energy. Everyone, including Dario, rushed to the windows to see where the beam had come from. Dario had to squint because the beam of light was blindingly powerful, but it was undoubtedly coming from the perimeter wall. All of the solar cannons were simultaneously firing on the same exact spot on the shield, creating a singular beam of light.

"How are they doing that?" asked one of the Reytana. "The solar cannons can only fire individual shots. They can't fire a continuous beam.

"They can be adjusted to," replied Dario. "It would take someone who knew what they were doing. Someone who had a lot of free time on their hands and liked to play with things he shouldn't be playing with..."

"Xander," said Regan.

"He must have figured out how to alter the cannon fire. Look! The beam is holding up the shield," said Dario.

Sure enough, the shield's descent had stalled. The disc began to glow orange where the solar beam hit the metal.

"It's too hot! The beam is going to punch right through the shield!" exclaimed a soldier.

Dario shook his head as he considered the situation. "That shield is made to reflect solar light. I think it will hold."

"You *think*," said Regan.

Dario shrugged. "It's the only chance we've got."

"Governor!" yelled a Reytana at one of the control boards. "You need to see this."

Dario rushed over to see what the soldier had discovered. On the console in front of him, the Lotus capacity meter was blinking.

"Well, that's going to be a problem," said Dario. The Lotus was already down to forty percent capacity when it had just been at seventy-five a couple of minutes ago. The continuous stream of solar cannon fire was draining the energy at an unsustainable rate. The Lotus would be empty in a matter of minutes.

Dario looked back up at the shield. Not only had it stopped its descent but it was slowly tilting backwards towards the ocean. The beam was pushing it back.

As the shield moved, sun light—real sun light—reflected off more of the buildings on the western side of the city.

"Quick!" yelled Dario. "Somebody get me the sewer schematics manual. We need to bounce more light!"

Inside the tank, Loras felt the water around his knees start to shift in the opposite direction. He looked behind him and, sure enough, the angle that the two nymphs were standing in the water began to correct itself towards vertical. The ship was flattening out.

Huh, thought Loras. He looked back at the control console to see which button had fixed the issue. At that moment, the entire board burst into flame. *Well, whatever I did, it's done now.*

Loras felt a tug on his arm. The smaller nymph stood behind him and beckoned towards the pool room. She pantomimed the explosion motions with her arms. Loras nodded in agreement. "Yep, time to go."

He took a deep breath then jumped through the shattered control room windows and into the pool room. The nymph kept one hand on Loras and used her other arm to propel the two of them towards the hatch. Loras kicked his legs to help but he was pretty sure the nymph was doing all the work.

They reached the closed hatch at the bottom of the pool but on the inside of the ship, there was no wheel to open the door. *Oh no,* thought Loras. He remembered that one of the Gartune had pressed something inside of the control room which had caused the hatch to slide shut. Loras looked up towards the control room but all he could see through the water were flames. Whatever mechanism the Gartune had used to control the hatch was now on fire.

Suddenly, Loras felt an insanely powerful rush of water surge behind. He looked back and saw a black shadow streak towards the hatch. The door exploded when the shadow struck it. Loras and the nymph were immediately caught in the current behind the streaking shadow and sucked through the hatch. They tumbled and flailed for several seconds until the current dissipated and they found themselves a surprising distance away from the tank. Next to them, the swirling black shadow coalesced into the shape of the nymph queen.

Loras frowned at her. *If you could have done that the entire time then why did you...* She narrowed her eyes at him, as if reading his thoughts. *Oh, nevermind.*

"Zone three, building six. Tilt thirteen degrees west!"

Dario barked orders to a Reytana who turned a series of dials on the board in front of him.

"Tilt the roof reflectors on building four and twelve towards building nine, then adjust up by four degrees."

On the west side of the city, building reflectors turned and angled themselves to catch the sunlight that was creeping in due to the sun shield's partial descent. The light energy bounced off of the metal panel several floors below them in the governor's quarters. The Lotus petals pulsed as the light hit them, feeding liquid energy into the orb, but it was still draining faster than it was filling.

Above the capitol building, the solar cannon beam continued to hold up the sun shield. The metal glowed an angry red around the spot where the beam struck it, but it didn't appear to be melting.

Sweat dripped off of Dario's brow as he flipped a page in the sewer schematics manual. He needed to move faster.

"Zone eight, building nine. Shift southern reflectors up ten feet and then tilt three degrees east!"

Dario spared a glance out the window to watch the reflectors on the western buildings move. Just behind building nine, he noticed, for the first time, one of the shield legs from the ground tanks. It was bending badly. Even from far away, he could hear the metallic creaking that was coming from it. It got louder and louder until, finally, it cracked in half.

Dario looked up as the shield began to rapidly descend towards the capitol building.

"Deactivate the perimeter shield!" Dario barked. "Divert all power towards the solar cannons!"

"But sir," responded one of the Reytana. "We'll be—"

"Just do it!"

Hadrian stood outside of the command center in the Gartolian basecamp and watched as the sun shield descended upon Reysa. Morlo stood next to him. The grin on Morlo's face widened the closer the shield got to Reysa's capitol building.

"It won't be long now, sir," whispered Morlo into the king's ear. Hadrian ignored him.

Suddenly, the glowing globe of the perimeter shield dissipated around the city. The solar beam shooting from the solar cannons doubled in size as the Reysene diverted all of their power towards pushing back the sun shield.

"Look, your highness. The city is defenseless. Now is our chance."

Hadrian thought for a moment before answering.

"That's it," said the king. "Bring up the tanks. All of them."

The solar cannons shook as they continued to fire on the falling shield. The hum from the barrels became almost deafening and the Reytana struggled to hold the overloaded weapons in place. Light pulsed violently through the energy tubes feeding each cannon.

"We can't keep firing like this!" a Reytana shouted towards Xander. "The cannons weren't meant to hold this much energy!"

"And look!" yelled another soldier. "The shield is starting to melt at the center. We're going to punch right through!"

They were both right. The cannons were starting to overheat. The adjustments that Xander had made to the weapons weren't meant to last this long. The cannons were not built for sustained continuous fire and they would soon fail.

At the same time, Xander could see the glowing red area at the center of the shield was starting to liquify. If the beam punched through the shield, it would be catastrophic. The rest of the shield would fall and the city would be crushed.

"We need to split the beam!" shouted Xander. "You half—" he pointed to the soldiers at his left. "Divert your aim towards the left side of the shield. You half—" he pointed to the soldiers to his right. "Divert your aim towards the right side. Push it back!"

The Reytana followed their orders and split their beam into two separate beams, each one as powerful as the original beam that had successfully held the shield before one of the arms broke.

It worked. The sun shield's descent halted just before it reached the top of the capitol building.

That's when the tank in the water exploded.

The arm extending from the floating tank quickly shattered once the vessel exploded. After that, the remaining two shield arms bent and then snapped like twigs, unable to hold up the weight by themselves. The only thing keeping the shield from falling from the sky was the two solar beams shooting from the solar cannons. But they were not up to the task. The shield, once again, began to descend on the city.

On the ground, thirty-six Gartolian tanks lined up with their turrets pointed towards the city.

Hadrian did not hesitate.

"Fire!"

All around him, the solar cannons shuddered and then one by one, began to burn out. Xander looked to the sky for the last time. The sun shield fell. The glowing center was directly above the capitol building and falling fast. He thought once more about Regan. He just hoped whatever happened next, happened fast.

A resounding boom sounded from the Gartolian basecamp. Xander turned and saw dozens of giant cannonballs flying in their direction. *Not leaving any doubt, eh dad?* He closed his eyes and waited for the inevitable.

A woosh of air almost knocked Xander off of his feet as the cannonballs shot overhead. He opened his eyes just in time to see the ordnance slam into the face of the sun shield. An ear-splitting clang reverberated through the air. Once gain, Xander nearly fell forward as a second volley of Gartolian cannonballs flew overhead and then struck the shield with a thunderous boom.

The shield tilted backwards.

Xander stood up and tried to orient himself. His ears were ringing. Several of the Reytana around him were holding their ears with bewildered looks on their faces.

"Keep firing!" Xander shouted.

The soldiers manning the few functional solar cannons collected themselves. They aimed their beams at the center of the shield as another wave of Gartolian artillery struck the disc, shoving it back.

"Sir, I don't understa—"

"Fire again!" barked Hadrian, ignoring his second in command. Thirty-six tanks fired in unison, shooting off another volley of cannonballs directly at the shield.

"But the shield... the city..." sputtered Morlo, "they were about to be crushed. We would have won!"

Hadrian whipped around to face his bewildered commander.

"What would we have won? There would have been nothing left to conquer! I will not have some malfunctioning machine steal my victory from me!"

Morlo looked like he was about to say something but then stopped. Instead, he just shook his head, unable to comprehend what was happening. Up above, a final wave of Gartolian artillery, combined with the Reysene solar cannon beam, succeeded in pushing the shield away from Reysa. The Reysene immediately cut off their beam and the glowing perimeter shield began to reform around the city while the crippled sun shield fell in to the sea.

"Oh crap!" sputtered Loras. Once the shield fell in to the sea, a tidal wave erupted from its edges and shot towards Loras' location. He turned away from the wave and began to frantically swim in the opposite direction but he hardly moved at all. The wave gathered strength as it barreled down on him.

"We need to get out of here!" shouted Loras to his nymph companion. But instead of speeding them away, the nymph calmly placed her hand on Loras' shoulder and pushed him under the water. Down, down they went until they reached the sea bed. Above them, the giant wave tore along the surface, leaving a trail of somersaulting current in its wake.

Loras turned in the water and watched as the sun shield slowly sunk to the bottom of the sea. A cloud of mud erupted from the ocean floor where the disc hit. Floating in the middle of the cloud was the black form of the nymph queen. Right before the dirt particles enveloped her, she looked back at Loras. Her face was full of rage.

The damage to the coral reef that the tank's anchor had created was nothing compared to the devastation that the giant shield caused when it crashed into the sea bed. Loras knew there would be repercussions for his actions. The nymph queen had only helped him because she wanted to stop the tank from damaging her domain. Now, he had gone and made things worse. The final look that the queen had given him left no doubt that there would be a reckoning for this betrayal.

The nymph yanked on Loras' arm. It was time to go. They looked into each others' eyes as they circled upward toward the surface. Her watery gaze was full of emotion. There was fear—fear over what they had done and for what might happen to them as a result. There was also excitement to have escaped with their lives. And there was something else; something that Loras didn't have much experience with so he didn't recognize it at first.

Just before they reached the open air, the nymph swam in front of him, looked him in the eyes and kissed him. More warmth than he had ever known filled his body, but only for an instant. As soon as her lips left his, she pushed his head above the water and released her grip on his arm. Loras gasped for air as if he had been holding his breath for hours. By the time his breathing had returned to normal, the nymph was long gone and, though the sun shone brightly overhead, Loras felt a little bit cold inside.

CHAPTER FORTY-ONE
Revelations

"I still can't believe we're alive," whispered Regan as she looked through the windows of Reysa's command center. It had been thirty minutes since the Gartolian sun shield was blasted into the sea and the late afternoon sun flooded the courtyard of the capitol building. The Lotus' petals were pulsating with energy as golden liquid poured into the orb at its center. Out in the sea, half of the sun shield stuck out of the water. In its shadow, the last remains of the shield tank slowly bubbled beneath the waves.

"He really did it," Regan said to herself. She looked around at the other Reytana in the command center. They had only taken a few moments to watch the shield fall into the sea and then went directly back to manning their posts. There was still much work to be done, but, for the first time, there was an air of confidence in the room.

"You should have more faith in your brother," said Lucan as he joined Regan at the window.

Regan turned to her old professor with an eyebrow raised. "This, coming from *you?* The same teacher who reprimanded Loras on a daily basis for the better part of three years?"

"It was for his own good. Look at him now—he's the savior of Reysa!" said Lucan proudly.

"Just don't let him hear you say that," said Regan. "This day is going to give him a big enough head as it is."

Lucan looked over his shoulder to where Dario was standing. He could tell that the governor had been listening to the conversation and was deep in thought. Finally, Dario raised his head and looked at Lucan. He gave a small nod.

Lucan turned back to Regan. "Regan, there's something that I need to tell you."

Suddenly, three loud booms rang out from the courtyard. Regan and Lucan both looked down. Their jaws dropped. There, standing in the courtyard, was Hadrian. With him were the hundred Gartune that had just been captured. But the worst sight of all was standing in front of them. A hundred and fifty filthy, scantily clothed Reytana teenagers cowered with their hands covering their eyes, shielding them from the sun.

"Rey help us. He's freed them," said Lucan. All of the Reytana in the command center looked up from their stations.

Hadrian struck his eüroc into the ground three more times. The ground splintered away from him and the sound echoed off the walls of the courtyard. Dario joined Regan and Lucan in peering down through the windows.

"This was always his end game," said Lucan. "To make them fight for him. He knows we won't kill our own."

"No, I don't think so," said Dario. "He'd rather they had stayed in prison forever. That's why he built the damn thing—so he could control us and keep The Scales from balancing the equation. He didn't want to risk the Fallen Reytana being killed and re-born. Right now, he controls the balance. As far as The Scales are concerned, the Tormada are even because there are an equal number of Reytana and Gartune alive. The Scales do not know that Hadrian has incapacitated such a large number of our ranks. If these Reytana were to die, he might lose control of that situation. No, this... this is a last resort."

Hadrian stamped his eüroc three more times and then, sensing that he had the occupants' full attention, shouted up at the capitol building.

"Dario! I know you're up there. Deactivate the city's defenses and surrender yourselves and I will let you live. Refuse, and I will order your brethren here to attack everyone inside. There is no escape. Give yourself up now or I will make sure that I'm personally waiting at your pool of life in two weeks to scoop up the aftermath of today's battle, just like I did with these ones!" He nodded toward the young Reytana shuffling nervously in front of him.

Inside the control room, nobody moved. Silence dragged on as everyone waited for somebody to say something... to *do* something. How quickly the tide had turned once again. And just when they thought they had finally gained the upper hand.

Dario turned to Lucan. "Tell her," he said. "It's time."

"I know about the Fallen Reytana," said Regan, "I know how Hadrian *collected them* when they were babies." There was disgust in her voice. "Xander told me all about it. I know that they now have a connection to him and will do what he says."

"That is true," said Dario. "They are bonded to Hadrian. They will follow him even against their own will if it comes to that. But there is a stronger bond; one that supersedes the paternal connection that Hadrian stole."

"What bond is that?" asked Regan.

"The bond to their king," interjected Lucan. "Or in this case, since their king is somewhere splashing around in the sea... to their *queen*."

Regan's eyes widened. She looked back and forth between her professor and Dario. Both of them regarded her with dead seriousness. She started to speak but then stopped. Then she started again.

"No... no... it can't be me..." stuttered Regan. She shook her head back and forth, refusing to accept what she had just heard.

"Ah, but you *are* the queen," said Lucan as he tried to comfort his former student. "That is why we hid you all of these years. That is why we sent you to Gracien and the Lost Reytana. And that is why, eighteen years ago, I plucked you and Loras from the river before Hadrian could collect you in the pool of life."

"The aura of King Atholos lives within you," added Dario. "And the aura of King Calan, all the way back to Octavia. We Reytana have a royal blood line. It is one of the ways in which we differ from the Gartune. Our kings and queens are born kings and queens, and we follow them whole-heartedly and without question until the day we die. And you, Regan, are our queen."

"But, it doesn't make any sense. How did you know I was the queen when I was just a baby? I'm no different than any of those poor Reytana down in the courtyard. How did you know to collect me from the river before I got to Hadrian?"

"Because you wear the rings," said Lucan. He gently angled Regan toward the window so she could see her own reflection. Then he brushed back the hair behind her ears.

"What? What am I looking at?" asked Regan.

"Clench your fists," said Dario.

"What?"

"Just do it."

Regan clenched both of her firsts together as tightly as she could. Suddenly, she saw in the window a golden ring appear behind her left ear. It was like a large earring except emblazoned into the side of her head. She quickly swung her head to the other side and there was another ring in the same exact spot behind her right ear.

"The twins wear the rings..." she whispered to herself.

"I stood upstream of the river for days looking for that mark," said Lucan. "It disappears from an infant shortly after they are collected and doesn't resurface until they receive their light." At this point he bowed his head regretfully. "It was one of the hardest things I've ever done in my life, letting all of those other children flow past me when I knew the fate that awaited them. But finding you and your brother was too important. The leader, or in this case, *leaders,* of the Reytana could not be imprisoned."

Regan thought for a moment. "So that means Loras..."

"Wait," said Dario with a confused look on his face. "You didn't know Loras was king? Didn't he tell you?"

"He doesn't know!" exclaimed Regan.

"But he wears the crown!" shouted Lucan. Regan gave him a confused look. "The headband that Loras wears, it is the symbol of the king. Didn't Gracien tell him what it meant?

Regan shook her head and laughed. "He said it shot fireballs."

"Unbelievable," said Dario, turning away from the window to think. "How could he not have told him?"

"He must not have thought he was ready," said Lucan, thoughtfully.

"Wait a minute," said Regan. "You can't just blame Gracien. He wasn't the only one who hid the truth from us. You didn't tell us either!"

"That was to protect you," said Dario. "If you were captured, I didn't want anyone to know who you really were. But I figured once you were safe with Gracien and the others..."

"Regardless," interrupted Lucan. "The Lost Reytana know what Loras' circlet means. They know the truth even if he doesn't. All you have to do is look at the way they regard Loras. They follow their king. Now you need to do the same for those young Reytana out there."

Regan shook her head again. "This is all wrong. It should be Loras to lead them, not me. Can't we wait for him to come back?"

Three more booms rang out from the courtyard.

"This is your last chance!" yelled Hadrian. Some of the Gartune began to prod the young Reytana forward toward the door of the capitol building. They looked around, confused, but did not resist.

"Look at them, Regan," said Dario. "They are lost. Right now there is a terrible struggle going on inside of each of them. They don't want to listen to Hadrian, but their bond compels them. You can free them from that. You need to lead them! It is time for them to know who their queen is."

Regan looked down into the courtyard at the hundred and fifty Reytana shuffling back and forth. Many of them were still covering their eyes from the sun. The source that was supposed to strengthen and comfort them was causing them pain because it had been kept from them for their entire lives. She looked down and realized that her fists were still clenched. She gazed at her reflection in the window to check and see if the rings were still glowing behind her ears, but what caught her attention instead was the golden fire that was shining in her own eyes.

She turned to Dario. "Tell me what to do."

Dario smiled and nodded. "First things first, there's something that I need you to wear."

The courtyard was eerily quiet considering the number of people that occupied it. The young Reytana had finally started to acclimate to the sun and only a few still shielded their eyes. But they all were listless and confused as they looked around and tried to process their new surroundings. Outside, the tank fire had slowed now that Reysa's defenses were operating at full capacity. Occasionally a cannonball would explode off the city's shield, but it was more of a probing for weaknesses tactic than a full-on assault.

Hadrian stared up at the top floor of the capitol building but did not see any movement. *He's really going to make me do this,* thought Hadrian to himself. He eyed the Reytana shuffling around in front of him. *Very well. Time to drive the herd.*

"Fine, have it your way, governor!" yelled Hadrian. He motioned for the Gartune to push the Reytana forward. Then, a voice called out from the street behind him.

"Hello, Father."

Hadrian slowly turned. Xander stood alone. He leaned slightly on his eüroc while his violet cape fluttered gently in the breeze. There was a small, mirthless grin on his face.

"Now that's a voice I wasn't sure if I'd ever hear again," said Hadrian.

"Would that have been your preference?" asked Xander.

"To be determined," responded Hadrian.

Xander grunted. "So how do you like what I've done with the place?" he asked as he opened his arms out wide. Hadrian scowled.

"All of this, right under your nose," snarled Hadrian. "If I didn't know any better, I would have thought Rankin was in charge the whole time."

"Nah, Rankin was too busy whoring in Spirea to pay any attention to what was going on here."

Hadrian's eyes narrowed further. "I'll be sure to discuss that with him the next time I see him."

"Hmm," said Xander. "That's going to be tricky."

"Enough!" shouted Hadrian. "I've heard what you've done and I'm willing to chalk it up to living with the Reysene for far too long. Now, come stand by me and try to learn something. We will address your deficiencies when we return home."

"I'm afraid that isn't going to happen," said Xander.

"What did you say to me?" said Hadrian in a voice barely above a whisper.

"I'm afraid that isn't going to happen," repeated Xander. "You see, I *am* home."

"I don't think I heard you correctly," said Hadrian, his violet eyes deepening. "Repeat that one more time."

Xander nodded his head upward. "I'm with them."

Just then the rooftops of all of the buildings surrounding the courtyard were full of Reysene. The citizens of Reysa, mixed with their Reytana protectors, filled every rooftop, balcony and window. From around every corner, hundreds of armed Reysene flooded into the streets. A large band of citizens led by Tinko appeared in the street behind Xander. Several of the Reysene were carrying their makeshift bombs. Others carried whatever weapons they could find in their homes—hammers, shovels, even a few brooms.

"I see..." said Hadrian, surveying the crowd. "Interesting choice. But, a torman with a hammer is still just a torman." He struck his eüroc into the ground and a fault line shot directly at a nearby group of Reysene, causing them to topple backward.

"And what is a king without an army?" shouted a voice from above the courtyard. Everyone turned and looked up at the capitol building. There, standing in the window that Adem had burst through hours before, stood Regan. A golden cape whipped vigorously in the wind behind her. Both of her shins and forearms were covered by twisting, golden strings and around her forehead was a glowing headband.

"A king is a king with or without an army, young lady," shouted Hadrian. "But as you can see, I happen to have one. Or is the sun in your eyes?"

"You *stole* that army. It is not yours to command," shouted Regan from the window.

"You're half right," answered Hadrian. "I did steal it. But they are most definitely mine to command. Would you like me to show you?"

Regan said nothing and simply glared down at the Gartune king instead.

"Very well, then." said Hadrian. He lifted his hands in the air and addressed the Fallen Reytana. "Come, my children! No longer are you prisoners. Today, you are proud Tormada! Come and fight with your father against those that would do us harm!"

As if in a trance, the Fallen Reytana turned toward the Reysene that surrounded them. The Gartune fell back toward the center of the courtyard, letting the Reytana move ahead of them. Hadrian urged the Reytana forward. "Go! Go, my children! Fight for your father!"

The Reysene in the streets exchanged glances, questioning whether or not to engage the approaching Reytana. A few begged the young Tormada to stop, but their pleas fell on deaf ears. The Fallen ones' eyes began to glow as they approached their enemy.

"Stop!" yelled Regan. "Children of Rey, hear me!"

Immediately, the Fallen Reytana stopped and turned back toward the capitol building to face Regan. Hadrian's outstretched arms slowly fell to his sides. *It's not possible,* he thought. He looked up at Regan, still standing in the window. "Who are you?" he shouted. Somehow, she looked familiar.

"Who am I? I am the one you have been seeking! I am the one you missed; the one that escaped! And now I am back to free my people. Children of Rey, look on me! My name is Regan and I am your queen!"

Immediately, as if pulled by some invisible force, the Fallen Reytana fell to one knee and bowed their heads. The Reysene in the surrounding streets and buildings did the same. The few Gartune standing in the middle of them looked around, not sure how to proceed. Hadrian stood tall as always.

"A fine speech for a girl in a window," shouted Hadrian. "But I cannot see your rings from here. Why don't you come down and show them to me, so you can prove who you really are?"

Regan did not move. For an instant, uncertainty flashed across her face. The Fallen Reytana slowly rose their heads to Regan, awaiting their orders, but she did not speak. Just then, Xander yelled out to the crowd, breaking the silence.

"Citizens of Reysa, protect your queen!" he shouted.

"Protect the queen!" repeated a few voices from the crowd. "Protect the queen!" they shouted again, louder. The Fallen Reytana rose to their feet. "Protect the queen!" they repeated together as they began to advance on the Gartune in the courtyard.

Fueled by the sudden burst of fealty, Regan jumped out of the window to join her brethren. She closed her eyes, lifted her face to the sun and clenched her fists. Solar energy pulsed through her body. The bands encircling her forehead and arms glowed fiercely. And she floated.

Down below, Gartolian steel clashed with fiery swords and torman weapons. Small explosions rang out amongst a chorus of yells and screams. Through the center of it all, Hadrian's voice boomed through the ruckus shouting orders. There was no panic in his voice, though his position was dire. Finally, Regan opened her eyes and looked down.

The Lotus sat directly below her and there was a soft yellow glow emanating from underneath her feet. To the left of the Lotus, Regan spotted three Gartune surrounding a small group of the Fallen Reytana. The young Tormada huddled together as the violet-eyed soldiers moved in for the kill. Before they could reach their prey, a golden blast erupted in front of them. The surprised Gartune looked up and saw Regan hovering above them with her fists pointed in their direction. Liquid fire flowed through her wristbands down to her hands and two more flares shot at the Gartune's feet, sending them stumbling backward. Realizing that they were no match for the Reytana queen, the Gartune quickly turned and ran in the opposite direction.

Regan looked for more targets. It did not take her long to find them. Most of the Gartune had chosen to engage the defenseless Reytana. However, they were not defenseless for long. Hovering above the courtyard, Regan unleashed a storm of fire. She shot flare after flare into the crowd.

She continued to spin and fire, her face a hardened mix of anger and determination, as she circled over the battle below. Gradually, as some of the energy began to drain from her body, Regan lowered herself toward the ground. Once she had landed, a voice shouted her name. Regan turned toward the voice and saw Xander struggling to force his way through the crowd. She began to call out to him when a hand grabbed her shoulder and spun her around. There, in front of her, stood the king of Gartol.

"So, the queen has returned," said Hadrian. He tilted his head to the side so that he could see behind her right ear. A golden circle was emblazoned into her skin. When he saw the ring he nodded, approvingly.

"Still, you don't have any idea what to do, do you?" said Hadrian, sizing up Regan. "That's ok. You'll learn. I'll see to that."

"Regan!" shouted Xander. He was right behind her now, along with three of the Fallen Reytana. "Go! Protect your queen!"

"No!" shouted Regan as the Reytana jumped and landed in front of her. She tried to pull them back, but it was too late. One of the Reytana let out a sickening grunt and, suddenly, Regan was covered in a cloud of golden dust. She coughed, choking on the aura of the slain Reytana. Before she could regain her breath, Xander strode through the death mist and squared off against his father.

"This has been a long time coming," said Xander as he positioned himself in front of Regan. The king tapped his eüroc and a gleaming blade, identical to the one that adorned Septa's staff, sprung from the end.

"I see that there is no saving you now, boy" said Hadrian.

"It looks that way," agreed Xander.

"Very well. Perhaps The Scales will send me something more worthy after I dispatch you."

As the king circled his son, several nearby Gartune saw what was happening and formed up around the combatants. They created a small circle to keep Xander from escaping. Xander noticed Damnar and Damina in the group. The twins looked nervously between the king and the prince, unsure who to root for.

Xander saw their indecision and shook his head with mock disapproval. "And after all we've been through," he *ts*ked. The twins looked down, too embarrassed to make eye contact.

"Enough!" shouted Hadrian. "Fight or get out of my way!"

Xander shrugged and threw a half-hearted jab at his father who effortlessly swatted it away. Hadrian scowled as Xander pranced, bouncing on his tip-toes in a circle around the king and then threw another lazy jab. This time the king swatted Xander's eüroc down into the ground with so much force that it cracked the stone.

"Stop embarrassing yourself and fight, you imbecile!"

Xander smirked. He reversed the direction of his circle, prancing backward this time. He twirled his eüroc in front of him, mockingly. *Come on, Dad, let's see that famous temper of yours.*

The flamboyant twirl did it. Hadrian charged at his son.

Immediately, the smirk left Xander's face. He pressed the button on his eüroc and released his *tre'ance*. Three short prongs emerged from the bottom of his staff, forming a miniature tripod. Just as his father was about to reach him, he slammed his eüroc into the ground. The prongs stuck to the stone, holding the end of the staff a single inch above the ground; just enough to allow it to swivel from its base. Xander moved both of his hands to the top of his eüroc and then jumped to the side, angling the top of the staff toward him. His plan worked. The enraged Hadrian charged angrily past the spot where Xander had been standing, unable to stop himself in time. As he passed by, Xander swung his body in a horizontal arc, using the staff as leverage, and kicked the king in his back, knocking him to the ground. Hadrian landed at the feet of two Gartune. They quickly bent down to help their king to his feet. Infuriated by having fallen for Xander's trick, Hadrian jumped up and shoved off the aid of his soldiers. He turned to face his son. A small trickle of blood crept from the side of his lip. With eyes locked on Xander, Hadrian wiped the blood off his mouth and then studied his hand.

"Perhaps you learned something after all," said Hadrian.

"Lex and Septa weren't the only ones in the family who knew how to fight," replied Xander coolly. His eüroc was still planted upright next to him, the *tre'ance* holding it in place. Off to the side, Xander noticed Damnar slowly emerging from the circle of spectators, his eyes transfixed on the *tre'ance* at the bottom of Xander's eüroc. Damnar took another step forward to take a closer look and as he did so Xander quickly pulled the top of his staff toward him and then let it go. The tip of the eüroc struck Damnar squarely in the forehead before springing back to its upright location. The stunned Gartune stumbled backward, holding his bleeding forehead in his hands. Xander winked at him. "Now you know why I picked it."

Suddenly, a large explosion erupted in the circle between Xander and Hadrian. A cloud of dirt and solar fire surrounded Xander making it impossible to see. A strong gust of air blew down from above. Xander looked up and saw the giant wing of a Reytana hovercraft flapping over him. The vessel lowered itself, revealing a row of solar cannons all pointed at the circle of Gartune on the ground.

"Where is he? Where did he go?" shouted a voice from the bow of the hovercraft. It was Dario. As the dirt from the explosion cleared, Xander could see several Gartune bent over and coughing, but one was missing. Hadrian was gone.

Elsewhere, the fighting had all but finished. The few Gartune that remained dropped their eürocs once the hovercraft made its appearance. The air was a mixture of gold and purple dust. Xander waded through the murk in search of his father but to no avail. Then, he found someone he was happier to see.

At first, the only thing he saw through the dusty air was the golden glow of the bands encircling her wrists and forehead. As he got closer, the light emanating from them began to illuminate the rest of her form, giving it an almost celestial appearance. Her back was to him, but she turned her head over her shoulder once he was within a few feet. She smiled before she saw him.

426

"I'm starting to lose count of the number of times you've saved my life," she said.

"Oh, I'm keeping track," said Xander as he walked slowly toward the Reysene queen. "Three. I've saved you three times. Twice just today, actually." He looked warmly into her eyes. "And I expect you to make it up to me."

Regan smiled as she wiped some dirt off of his tunic. "We'll see," she said.

"I can live with that," replied Xander. The two of them looked over the scene unfolding around them. Once again, the Gartune were separated into small groups. Whereas before, the captives had retained a look of defiance while they were being restrained, now they simply sat on the ground with their heads bowed. They knew the battle was lost.

Throughout the courtyard and the adjoining streets, the citizens of Reysa welcomed back their Reytana. Men and women mingled with their long lost Tormada, shaking their hands and giving them hugs. The Fallen ones were showered with tears and affection. Though they were unable to effectively communicate with the Reysene, they happily knelt down to receive their embraces. For most of them, it was the first time they had ever smiled.

Regan turned back to Xander. "Where did he go? Is he dead?"

"My father?" replied Xander. "No, he's not dead. He'd never allow himself to do something as stupid as getting killed."

Regan let out a small laugh. Xander wiped some dirt off of her cheek and smiled at her. Then without a word, she folded into his arms and laid her head against his chest. The two just stood there holding each other, oblivious to the commotion around them. Xander began to say something but Regan stopped him.

"Don't", she said. "You'll just ruin it."

Xander laughed. "So, do I finally get to call you queen?"

Regan looked up at him, surprised. "Finally? You knew?"

"Of course I knew. Ever since that day outside my cell when you three were talking about the contents of your letter. *The twins wear the rings.* I knew it could only mean one thing. And it explained a lot, actually."

"Wait, how could you hear us? We were whispering."

"Regan, I don't think your brother knows how to whisper. Speaking of Loras... I don't see him anywhere. Has anyone told him yet? If not, maybe we should consider keeping it a secret. I mean, a city really only needs one ruler and it seems like you've got that job locked up."

Regan looked around. Everywhere the Reysene were beaming at her. Even the Fallen Reytana were smiling ear to ear. Some of the Lost Reytana pounded their chest with their fists and nodded when she caught their gaze. Dario and Lucan stood together with Adem and beamed proudly.

"What do I do now?" asked Regan.

Xander took her back into his arms. "I'll help you think of something," he said.

CHAPTER FORTY-TWO
Rematch

Loras lay on his back and stared up at the sun. The waves broke on the beach and ran up around his toes. He did not know how long it had taken him to swim ashore, but he knew that he was exhausted. Every muscle in his body was spent. So, he just lay there and let the sun do its job.

As he was re-energizing, Loras thought about the blue-eyed nymph. In fact, he had been thinking about her the entire time he was swimming to shore. He couldn't get her out of his head. It wasn't just the kiss. *Although, that wasn't exactly your typical first kiss,* he mused. And it wasn't the way she had kept him alive just by touching him. No, it was the way that he, himself, had felt while she was with him. Somehow, she had made him feel warmer. Not the way that the sun warmed him—that felt more like being fueled. But rather, something inside of him had felt more alive when she was there.

Loras laughed to himself. *Look at me, acting like a love-sick pipken. If I'm not careful, I'll turn into Regan.* He turned over and looked up at the city on the cliff. *Regan. I hope she's all right.* He felt confident that she was ok. After all, she had Dario and Lucan up there with her. And Xander. He wasn't sure how he currently felt about Xander. Maybe that was something that he could put off for a while longer. There was enough going on in his head right now to worry about the Gartolian prince's relationship with his sister.

When he felt that he had sufficiently recovered from his swim, Loras lifted himself off of the beach and started toward Reysa. He would have to be careful sneaking past the Gartolian basecamp. Although it appeared that all of their attention had turned to building rock mounds in front of their installments in order to protect them from Reysa's artillery, which was now at full strength thanks to Loras. The tanks had all but ceased firing at the city's forcefield. There was no point anymore. The cannonballs didn't even cause the shield to flicker when they hit it now. Every once in a while they would fire a single round at a different area of the shield, probing for a weakness, but each time the result was the same.

Loras skirted around the base of the cliff as he made his way to the narrow path that he had previously used to escape the city. It was a risky choice, but not as risky as attempting to take the lift all the way up to the city. It might still be manned by Gartolians. At a minimum, someone would see the cage going up the face of the cliff. No, the trail was the best choice. Plus, the mounds that the Gartolians had erected in front of their base shielded the bottom of the cliff from their view. He would be well up the slope before anyone would have a chance to see him.

The entrance to the path had just come into view when Loras stopped in his tracks. He did not see or hear anyone, but he could *feel* someone watching him from above. Then a trickle of rocks fell off the cliff and onto his shoulder. Loras froze, letting the pebbles cascade over him. There was a small ledge not far overhead that covered his position. It was possible that whoever was up there could not see him where he was standing. Then another, larger rock came rolling down the cliff. Loras made a quick mental calculation and decided to let the rock hit him, rather than jump out of the way and risk losing whatever concealment he might have. The rock struck him squarely on the top of his head and bounced to the ground. Loras let out a grunt but did not move.

Then he heard it. A laugh. A woman's laugh, and a familiar one at that. He looked up. For an instant, he had to squint because sunlight was shining brightly off the side of the figure standing on the ledge. Eventually, the dark form started to come into focus. Half of her body, from her hip to her face, was covered in metal. The sun blazed off of it. Tattered, jet-black hair blew in front of the living part of her face. A strong gust of wind revealed a mirthless half-smile and one, furious purple eye. *Septa.*

Septa struck her eüroc into the ledge that she was standing on, causing it to crumble under her feet. She deftly rode the rockslide to the ground, landing in front of Loras without so much as a stumble.

"I was wondering if I would ever see you again," said Septa as she strode toward Loras. Her left arm was missing. In its place, a solid piece of metal was molded around her torso. It stretched from her waist all the way up to her neck where it attached to a half mask of similar material. The missing arm did not seem to have affected Septa's confidence as she sauntered toward her prey.

Septa looked Loras over and noted the golden bands around his wrists and forehead. She nodded. Loras could not tell if it was approval or mockery. "I see that you've made a few improvements since we last met. Tell me. Have you learned how to use those?" She pointed toward the wristbands on Loras' forearms.

For a second, Loras' instincts told him to retreat from the approaching Gartune. But it was only for a second. Instead, something else directed Loras. It wasn't courage. At least not the kind of courage that an experienced warrior felt before he entered a fight. But it was something almost as powerful. A mixture of confidence, earned from the day's events, mixed with a tinge of anger that compelled Loras to stand his ground.

"I thought you were dead," said Loras, staring Septa directly in her eye.

"Nearly," said Septa. "But as you can see, I *also* have made some improvements." She tapped her metal side with her eüroc. It made a metallic *ting* when it hit. Septa smiled admiringly at her new body.

Nothing is getting through that, thought Loras. *Even another solar cannon shot would probably just bounce off.* "I'll bet that thing itches something terrible though," said Loras.

The smile instantly vanished from Septa's face. She gave her eüroc a quick strike into the ground. Loras lazily lifted his leg and the fault line went zooming under him.

"You guys need to learn some new moves," said Loras.

"I think I would like your tongue," replied Septa matter-of-factly as her blade sprung from the end of her eüroc. She began to spin the weapon in her hand. It was amazing. She controlled the staff just as well with one hand as she had with two.

Loras pressed the pads in both of his hands. Fiery sword and shield sprung to life. "Come and get it," he said as he tilted his forehead slightly toward his adversary.

The two Tormada made a circle in the sand as they sized each other up. Half of their circle lay in the shadow of the cliff. When Septa stepped out of the shadow, her metal half reflected the sun and made it difficult for Loras to look at her. She saw Loras squint and she stopped circling, thinking that she had the advantage in the sun.

Loras raised a hand to his face in order to shield the glare off of Septa's metal body. She grinned and smashed her eüroc into the ground in front of her. This time, instead of a fault line, a shower of rocks and sand came shooting out of the ground toward Loras. He barely had time to raise his shield in order to deflect the attack. Septa laughed.

"What's the matter? Haven't seen that one before?"

Loras lowered his shield but continued to squint and cover his eyes with his sword hand. Septa sent another shower of rocks at him. He ducked at the last instant and they went flying over his head.

"Come to me, boy. Come and meet your fate," said Septa, beckoning to Loras. She walked backward, further separating herself from the shadow of the cliff. This time it was Loras who smiled.

He lowered his hand from his eyes and came charging out of the shadow. The glare from Septa's metal half still shone brightly, but it did not appear to affect Loras as he ran toward her. When he was ten feet from her, he jumped up into the air and raised his sword above his head. An expression of surprise flashed for a moment on Septa's face as she looked up. Loras placed his body directly in between the sun and Septa so that he was a black silhouette highlighted in golden sunlight as he descended upon her. At the last second, Septa raised her eüroc to meet Loras' sword. Sparks flew everywhere as the two weapons met. Loras leaned in toward Septa so that he was only inches away from her face. Their clashing weapons screeched and sparked between them.

"You must not know Reytana very well..." said Loras, his eyes narrow and glowing. "We don't like to fight in the shade!" He quickly spun and swung his ray blade at Septa's knees. She jumped, barely clearing the sword. As she did so, Loras raised his shield and caught her under the chin. Golden sparks flew off of Septa's mask as the shield struck her jaw. Her head whipped back, but she still managed to land on her feet.

Sensing that she was vulnerable, Loras advanced on the Gartune princess. Once he was within arm's length, he was instantly hit with a violent kick to the stomach. He stumbled backward but quickly regained his stance. Septa spun her eüroc again, undaunted.

"Very clever, boy," she said, advancing on Loras. "I thought it odd that you were shielding your eyes from the sun, but then again, you are weak. However, you must not know Gartune very well either. We don't care if it's in the shade or the sunlight—we just like to *fight.*" With that she unleashed a murderous flurry of strikes at Loras. Her eüroc was a blur as it spun in all directions from her single arm. It was as if she had three weapons, not just one. It was all Loras could do to stop himself from losing a limb as her blade sliced through the air. While defending himself, he suffered several painful strikes to his ribs and one to the side of his head that almost knocked him unconscious. Though the blow didn't knock him out, it did knock him off his feet. He looked up from his back, panting. This time, it was Septa that positioned herself in between the sun and Loras as she stood over her victim.

"You fought better this time. It's a pity. In time, you may have actually given me a challenge. I guess we will never know."

Septa wiped her eüroc's blade on her cape; cleaning it for the kill. She then lifted it slowly above her head until she saw the light of the sun reflecting off of it and onto Loras' face. Though he couldn't see, Loras knew that her half-smile was back. He lifted his hand to his eyes once more, this time earnestly trying to see his attacker, rather than tricking her.

"It's ok," she said. "You can close your eyes if you want."

Loras' golden eyes stared unblinking at the black silhouette above him.

"Good for you," said Septa. She swung.

Everything happened very quickly. When Septa's strike was about halfway home, it was stopped by a long staff, but it wasn't a eüroc. It sounded like wood. Septa turned quickly in the direction that the staff had come from, but no sooner had she turned her head than the tip of the staff struck her on her good side, knocking the wind out of her. Then the staff swung around and struck her on the back of the head. Her unconscious body fell on top of Loras with a heavy thud.

"Sorry 'bout dat. Didn't mean for her to land on top of ya. I imagine she's a bit heavier now 'dan before."

Loras pushed Septa off of him and a familiar hand reached down to help him up.

"Declin!" shouted Loras and he lifted the waif off the ground with an enormous hug.

"Ay, you can put me down now," said Declin. Loras ignored him and instead threw him up into the air like a child. Before Loras could catch him, Declin whacked him on the side of the head with his staff, causing Loras to raise his hand to his ear and Declin to fall to the ground. Loras smiled and picked the waif off of the ground, dusting him off as he did so.

"I should'a just let her kill ya," grumbled Declin as he shook sand out of his hair.

"Did you see? Were you watching?" asked Loras, excitedly.

"Aye, I saw," said Declin.

"Did you see me trick her out into the sun? How smart was that?!"

"Yeah, yeah, you're very clever. I 'spose that's why I 'ad to save ya."

Loras went in to give the waif another hug, but quickly thought better of it and threw his arm around his shoulder instead. "Where have you been?" asked Loras. "So much has happened today. You're not going to *believe* what I've done."

"What *have* you done?" The voice was not Declin's.

Loras looked down and saw fear in the waif's eyes. He turned around and standing right behind him was Hadrian. Loras froze. Hadrian locked eyes with the young Reytana and then looked at the ground where his daughter lay unconscious. His gaze shifted to Declin. Then back at Loras.

"So we meet again. Loras, right? You seem pretty proud of yourself, boy. Tell me, was it you that sunk my tank?"

Loras said nothing, but his wet hair made the answer obvious.

"You must be a pretty good swimmer. A rare talent for a Reytana. You must be very proud."

435

Again, Loras said nothing. He rubbed the pad in his sword hand with his thumb and considered pressing it. Hadrian raised an eyebrow, as if sensing Loras' thoughts. But then reason prevailed and Loras gave up any thought of attacking the king.

Hadrian studied him in silence for a few moments, frowning slightly. Recognition flashed in his eyes.

"Do you have a sister, Loras?" the king said slowly.

Loras started to open his mouth. "Don't—" whispered Declin from behind. Hadrian bent over to look at the waif and addressed him for the first time.

"Declin. Old friend. Why am I not surprised?"

"I'm sorry, your 'ighness. Dis boy is no match fer yer daughter. I couldn't stand to watch her kill 'im is all. Weren't a fair fight. I didn't save 'er life just to have 'er kill a stupid boy."

"Just a stupid boy..." said Hadrian, once again regarding Loras. He bent his head toward Loras' right ear as if looking for something. "You know, you look just like her."

Loras clenched his fists. He could not bite his tongue any longer. "If you hurt her, I swear to the gods I will kill you!" he shouted. Hadrian struck Loras in the stomach with his eüroc, causing him to double over and gasp for air.

"Never swear to something that you can't back up, Loras," said the king matter-of-factly. He snatched the wristbands off of Loras' arms. Loras did not resist.

"F—father..." came a shaky voice from the ground. Septa rubbed her head and groggily looked up at the men standing above her.

"And *you*—I gave strict orders for you to stay in Gartol while you were recovering. You're lucky you're not a cloud of purple dust right now."

"You think this one ever had a chance against me?" she asked, nodding at Loras.

"You were just knocked out by a waif!" shouted Hadrian.

Septa bowed her head in embarrassment. "So just kill them both and be done with it," she said under her breath.

"I don't think so," said Hadrian rubbing his goatee. "No, I will take something from this day. Perhaps, it was not a complete loss after all."

"What are you going to do with us?" said Loras, finally regaining his breath.

The king smiled. "I'm going to take you back to Gartol with me, Loras. And you—" this time he turned his gaze to Declin. "I just got an interesting report about you, old friend. We have some unfinished business to attend to once we get back."

"Gartol?" said Septa. "But the battle isn't over! We can still—"

Hadrian raised his hand to cut her off. He turned his gaze towards the ocean and the half-sunk shield that shimmered in the afternoon sun. Then he glanced up at the city on the cliff. A cannonball burst off of its golden shield into a million pieces. He sighed. "Come," said Hadrian. "It's time to go home."

There have been eight great wars between Reysa and Gartol. In between, there have been countless battles, feuds, and skirmishes. So then what classifies as a war?

Is it the length of time that the conflict encompasses? No. Some wars lasted only a few days. There have been blood feuds that have lasted years and we don't refer to them as wars.

Is it the impact that the result has on The Crescent? Partly. Although, prior to the Gartolian occupation of Reysa, not much changed in either society following the conclusion of the previous seven wars.

One could say that Gartol and Reysa were continuously at war. So why separate out eight individual confrontations? And how do we determine the start and end of individual wars when the fighting is virtually ever-present?

It's fairly simple, actually.

A war ends when one side runs out of Tormada.

The next one starts when they return.

- Chapter Twelve of *The Crescent Wars*, by Nicholas Baston

EPILOGUE

Regan stood on the top of the capitol building and greeted the sun as it rose over the Crescent Mountains. It was a ritual that she had adopted over the past several weeks. The sun cleared her head and gave her the energy she needed to get through the day, which was a much more daunting task now that she was the ruler of Reysa.

Like he so often did, her old professor decided to join Regan on the roof. Lucan was not a huge fan of heights, but, as he told Regan on several occasions, eighteen years of limited sun takes a toll on everyone—torman and Tormada alike. Now that the shield had come down, he was going to take advantage of every moment he could to soak up those precious rays. There wasn't any better place to do that than on the top of the capitol building.

Regan welcomed the company. Lucan had become an invaluable advisor since her reign began. She had sought his opinion on a variety of topics; from how to handle their Gartune prisoners, to how to structure the new government.

There were several new positions to fill. Some of them had been easy. Dario was the obvious choice to take over as commander of the army. Tinko had become her chief strategist, a job that he had been born to do. Other appointments had been trickier. The biggest challenge was deciding what to do with Xander. Everyone knew that the Gartolian prince was now with the queen. They didn't hide their relationship and after his showing during the battle, most people accepted his presence. But some were still concerned that the prince had ulterior motives. He was, after all, a Gartune.

Regan sighed as she turned her head from the rising sun and looked down at what was left of the Gartolian camp. The rows of tents and military pavilions were all gone. Hadrian's retreat had taken less than an hour; an impressive feat for such a large undertaking. But that was the Gartolian way. There was precision and efficiency in everything they did, even losing battles. They packed up everything and descended into the underground tunnel that the tanks had emerged from. The last thing they did was to slide the tunnel doors shut. Regan had tasked Xander with figuring out how to open those doors. She wanted to see what the Gartolians had built right on her doorstep, for no other reason than she wanted some warning before the next time they decided to emerge. But for as much as he had tried, Xander was unable to open the tunnel doors. For all they knew, the entire Gartolian army could be sitting right underneath them, waiting. It was one of many thoughts that kept Regan up at night.

After a minute of watching her stare at the remains of the Gartolian camp, Lucan had a pretty good idea of what she was thinking.

"If he could open the doors, he would," said Lucan. "He's even asked for help, which, for him, is saying something."

Regan smiled. "Maybe he's finally maturing."

"Maybe he's finally found someone to make him grow up," said Lucan.

Regan blushed.

At just that moment, a heavy-breathing Tinko climbed over the ladder that led to the roof.

"If you're going to keep insisting on coming up here every day, we really need to consider installing a lift. Because this is getting out of hand."

"Good morning, Tink," said Regan, giving her much-shorter friend a warm hug.

"Good morning, your highness," muffled Tinko into Regan's abdomen.

Regan released the boy and gave him a friendly frown. "I told you that you didn't have to call me that."

"Regan, I am a citizen of Reysa, and you are the queen. I really kinda do."

"Well, you don't need to when it's just us. It makes me feel awkward."

"Awkwardness is part of the job, I'm afraid," said Lucan. "At some point, you're going to have to get used to the fact that the eyes of this city follow you wherever you go. From now on, you will always be the center of attention."

Regan sighed. "This job was made for Loras. He always loved being the center of attention." She turned to Tinko. "Have we heard any news from our lookouts at Gartol?"

Tinko shook his head. "No, nothing yet. But I'm sure he's there. They've probably just got him underground somewhere. Hadrian must know who he is, and he wouldn't harm something so valuable. It wouldn't make strategic sense."

"Wouldn't make strategic sense," Regan repeated. "He's my brother, Tink. And he's your best friend. He's not some piece on a game board."

"With all due respect," interjected Lucan, "right now, that's exactly what he is. And if we want to get him back, we need to start thinking strategically as well."

Tinko joined Regan in looking out over the remnants of the Gartolian camp. Eventually, his gaze shifted from the camp to the mouth of Octavian's Pass. The residue of battle was still visible. Several craters of scorched earth marked the spots where Regan and Xander had fired upon the Gartolian army. Unfortunately, many soldiers on both sides had been vanquished before their attack had forced Hadrian to retreat.

Tinko frowned. "Professor, something about the battle has been bothering me for a while," said Tinko. "What was the final count of Reytana infants that returned to us after this last battle?"

"Forty-seven babes were pulled from the pool of life. Why do you ask?"

"The math doesn't add up. Between the ambush at the pass, the fight at the river, and then the fighting up here in the courtyard, we lost way more than forty-seven Reytana. Do you think that the Gartolians stole more of our infants? Maybe they went further up the river—closer to Woodhaven—and captured them there?"

Lucan shook his head. "No, I don't think so. Lyse would never allow it. She protects the infants on both sides of the river until they are very close to their destinations. When I plucked Regan and Loras, it was just before the river emerged from the forest. If I had gone any further upstream, I'm sure that Lyse would have stopped me. She probably would have also killed me."

"So then why weren't all of our dead Reytana replaced?"

Lucan shuffled a bit. "Dario is the one you should really be talking to about this."

"Oh, come on, Professor," prodded Tinko. "You know more about the Tormada than anyone else in this city. Besides, you've never been one to withhold knowledge from eager, young minds." Tinko looked at Regan for assistance but she seemed distracted.

"Very well. I will tell you what I know, but you should still talk to Dario or one of the other Reytana if you want to know more."

Tinko instinctively sat down on a ledge and looked up eagerly at his professor. It was like he was back in school again.

"From what I have surmised, The Scales exist first and foremost to maintain the balance of power. And that means that sometimes, not everyone returns."

Tinko appeared confused, so Lucan continued. "The Scales are just that—a scale. They only tip when one side is heavier than the other. During battles, like the one at Octavian's Pass and the brief one we had up here in the courtyard, Reytana and Gartune were both killed at roughly the same time. It makes sense then, that their auras would reach The Scales at the same time."

The strained look on Tinko's face made it apparent that he was trying to work out the solution but was still having trouble. "Think of it like this, Tinko. If the aura of two Gartune and two Reytana reach The Scales at the same time, would The Scales tip?"

Understanding dawned on Tinko's face. "They wouldn't, because the weight on each side would still be even," said Tinko.

"Correct," replied Lucan. "The Scales only tip when their balance is off; when one side sustains more casualties than the other. I suspect, during the initial ambush, that most of the Reytana who died were replaced because the Gartune did not sustain many fatalities. During the confrontation at the river between Loras and Hadrian, the Gartune sustained more losses thanks to Regan and Xander's assistance. During this time, more Gartune were replaced than Reytana."

"Then during our fight up here in the courtyard?" asked Tinko.

"That one would be more difficult to predict. Both sides sustained roughly the same amount of losses, but again, it all depends on exactly *when* the deaths occurred. I imagine it only takes a few seconds for the aura of a fallen Reytana or Gartune to tip The Scales into the lake on Za'Dyn Mountain, thus releasing the aura back into the water. It's only when equal amounts of aura reach both sides of the scale at *exactly* the same time, that The Scales don't tip."

"So, what happens to the aura that doesn't get spilled back into the water for reincarnation?" asked Tinko.

"I suspect it is just... collected," explained Lucan.

"Fascinating..." mused Tinko.

Just then Regan let out a little moan. She rubbed her forehead and grimaced.

"Are you ok?" said Tinko. "You don't look so well. And I noticed that you haven't been eating much lately."

"It's nothing," said Regan, continuing to rub her temples. "I've just felt a little... off... lately." She gave Tinko a weak smile. "Must be the stress of the job."

Lucan examined the queen. She seemed a bit peaked to him. He took one of her hands in his. It felt clammy.

"Seriously, it's nothing," said Regan as she took back her hand.

"Maybe, but I think the doctor should take a look at you anyway. Mr. Tinko, can you please go fetch him?"

"Anything for my queen," said Tinko. He turned and walked back to the ladder. As he descended, they heard him muttering about an elevator.

"You're lucky to have him," said Lucan.

"I'm lucky to have all of you," replied Regan as she turned her attention to the courtyard below. It was nearly seven in the morning, which meant training was about to begin. The Fallen Reytana had taken to their lessons like a mendkin to moonlight. It wasn't only the sword and the shield that they had picked up quickly, but also the basic fundamentals of being a person. For beings that had spent their entire lives in silence, language came surprisingly easy to them. It had only been a few months, but almost all of them could not only speak coherently but read and write a little as well.

It helped that they had excellent teachers. All of the Lost Reytana had volunteered to teach their younger brethren in some way or another. Be it language, swordplay, or even the basics of being part of a civilized society, there was always an older Reytana there to help one of the young ones. During their mentorship, several of the older Reytana had grown very close to their pupils and had decided to adopt them. Only a few of the Fallen remained without a mother or a father. Regan was confident that, when the time was right, they would all be adopted. In the meantime, a group of tormen Reysene had taken it upon themselves to foster the remaining Reytana until proper parents could be found. Of course, Lucan was the head of this group.

A few Reytana had begun to fill into the courtyard and began stretching for their morning exercises. The first one to arrive was always Dario. And right behind him, without fail, was Adem. Adem was the first of the Fallen to be adopted. The Gartolians hadn't been gone two hours before Dario informed the young Reytana that he would be his new father. Somehow, Adem had known exactly what that meant and the two had been inseparable ever since.

Lucan smiled when he spotted Dario and Adem walking together in the center of the courtyard. Adem was excitedly trying to show Dario some new maneuver he had just learned. He swung his sword wildly in front of him and ended up singeing the cape of a nearby instructor. Dario apologized to the instructor, then patiently took Adem's arm and corrected his form. He watched approvingly as Adem practiced the maneuver again, except slower this time.

"Fatherhood suits him nicely," said Lucan.

"And you as well," said Regan. "What you're doing with the orphans is invaluable, professor. I can't thank you enough."

"Ah," said Lucan, waving his hand dismissively. "It's nothing. Besides, it won't be long before they're all adopted. Then I'll have to go back to enhancing the hearts and minds of the regular old tormen children."

"Hey, I was once a regular old torman child!" said Regan. "They need enhancing just as much as everyone else."

"True, but *you* were never a torman."

"I suppose not," said Regan. "How were you able to keep that secret for so long? I know if it was me, I wouldn't have been able to do it."

"I almost slipped a few times," recalled Lucan with a chuckle. "There were several instances when I wanted to tell your brother to start acting like a king!"

"I'm not sure that would have gone over like you wanted," said Regan.

"No, probably not. I would have hated to see how Loras acted if he thought he was royalty."

They both laughed.

"I miss him," said Regan.

"I miss him too," said Lucan. "We'll get him back. I promise you we will."

Regan smiled at her professor, but her eyes said that she didn't entirely believe him.

"What's all this about you not feeling well and why am I just now hearing about it?" Xander leapt lightly over the ladder and onto the roof. He nodded at Lucan as he strode over to Regan and put a concerned hand on her head.

"Is this why you haven't been eating?" he asked, moving his hand from her forehead to her cheek.

"It's nothing, really. Just stress." said Regan.

"I told you that you've been doing too much. You should let me take some of it off your plate. After all, I did basically run this city for five years. I think I know what I'm doing."

"Like I said the last ten times you offered, thank you but I need to do this myself. The Reysene need to see that a Reytana is in charge. For real this time. I don't want anyone thinking that you're pulling my strings like you did with Dario."

A mischievous grin crept on Xander's face. "Pulling your strings, eh? You mean like *this* string?" He playfully plucked an imaginary string on Regan's side and she jumped backwards.

"You two get a room!" shouted Tinko from the opposite side of the roof. He had the doctor with him.

"Oh good, you're just in time!" said Xander. "The patient was starting to get unruly." Regan playfully shoved Xander with her elbow. "See what I mean!" he said.

The doctor examined Regan in silence for several minutes. It was not the first time that he had attended to her, but it was the first time as the queen. Normally, the doctor liked to joke and make conversation while he was checking out a patient. There was a time when Regan was ten and she thought she had broken her arm. The doctor had unloaded what seemed like an endless supply of jokes on her. She couldn't believe how many jokes he knew. She guessed it was just part of being a doctor. But as the doctor's silence continued and his examination got longer and longer, concern began to grow among the group.

"So, what's the story, Doc?" asked Xander. He was starting to get agitated. The doctor said nothing. Instead, he rummaged through his bag and eventually emerged with an instrument that he had already used twice.

"I said, what's going on?" asked Xander again, his voice raised. The doctor raised his hand to quiet him. He continued to examine Regan.

As he progressed, his expression varied between confusion and concern. Several times he rummaged through his bag, looking for a tool that apparently did not exist. Each time he returned to Regan with the same mixture of worry and confusion. The tension among the group was palpable. Finally, the doctor zipped up his bag and shook his head.

"What does that mean?!" shouted Xander. "There must be something you can do! You're a doctor for gods' sakes!"

"There's nothing I can do," said the doctor, staring down at his bag. Xander lost it.

"This is all your fault!" he pointed at Lucan. "I told you not to push her so hard! She wasn't ready for all of this!"

Lucan started to respond but the doctor interjected.

"Actually, I suspect it's *your* fault," said the doctor. He looked up at the Gartune with an odd expression on his face. Xander was so worked up that he couldn't speak. Regan placed her hand gently on Xander's shoulder and a calm came over him. He looked at her and then took a deep breath and placed his own hand on top of hers.

"Doctor, please," said Regan calmly. "It's ok. Just tell us what is wrong with me."

The doctor looked from Xander to Regan as if he was looking at one person. Then he smiled. "There's nothing wrong, my queen. You're pregnant."

End of Book One.

THE OMEGA PROPHECIES
CHAPTER ONE

Loras sat on the ground of his subterranean cell and imagined the sun. With closed eyes, he let the warmth in his mind radiate down his neck and through his entire body. Not until each finger and each toe had touched a delicious trickle of warmth did Loras release the image in his mind. Slowly, the warmth left him and the chill of his cell pressed hard against his skin. He clenched his fists and some lingering heat deep within him rose to the surface and fought with the cold until, eventually, a lukewarm equilibrium was reached. There was no cold. There was no warmth. There was just air. Loras let out a sigh and opened his eyes.

It took a few seconds for his surroundings to come into focus. The cell didn't offer much by way of scenery. Three roughly hewn walls of thick rock and a row of iron bars in front encompassed Loras' small, square cell. A thin blanket on the floor made up his bed and a hole in the corner his latrine. The rest of the cell was empty. Over the past three months, Loras had memorized every inch of it. He could close his eyes and trace every contour in the rock walls, each crack in the floor and each stalactite in the ceiling. Before he had taught himself the sun visualization trick, memorizing his cell had been the only thing he could think of to keep his mind occupied; to keep him from going insane.

For a Reytana like Loras, being trapped underground was more than imprisonment; it was torture. As one of Rey's Tormada, Loras needed the sun like tormen needed food and water. It was how he drew his power. It was what fueled him. Cut off from the sun, Loras was quite literally suffocating, so much so that he almost didn't make it through the first couple of weeks after his capture.

The first few days were the worst. Stuck in the cold, dark cell, alone and confused, Loras nearly lost his mind. Madness began to visit him in his dreams. Suddenly, he wasn't alone in his cell. His twin sister, Regan was there too. But she wasn't alone. Xander, the prince of Gartol—Reysa's sworn enemy—stood next to her and the two of them laughed at Loras as he cowered in the dark. Xander kissed his sister and then winked at Loras. The couple laughed harder. Loras tried to stand and fight Xander but some unseen power held him down. He could not move. Xander and Regan laughed even harder. He tried to scream but no sound came out of his mouth. Then they were gone, and everything was black again.

As the days went on, Loras was visited by similar dreams. Sometimes it was his sister and Xander laughing at him. Other times, his old school teacher, Professor Lucan, was standing over him with an admonishing scowl. Even friendly faces like his best friend Tinko would turn on him, saying that his imprisonment was payback for all the times that Loras had teased him.

One day, Loras dreamt that his old waif companion, Declin, was standing outside his cell whispering through the bars. Loras had not seen Declin since the two of them arrived at Gartol. But he had heard him. They had been put in separate cells, and Loras could sometimes hear Declin's screams from down the hall as he was mercilessly interrogated for the first couple of weeks. However, he had not heard a sound for quite some time. Loras assumed that his old companion was dead. He was ashamed to admit that the thought relieved him. He didn't think he could stand to hear much more screaming.

But now, the old waif stood battered and beaten, but very much alive outside of Loras' cell. He whispered something through the bars, but Loras couldn't make it out. Declin nervously looked around and then beckoned for Loras to come closer. Groggily, Loras waved an arm at Declin.

"Go away... you're not real," said Loras. Declin kicked the bar in front of him and the sound echoed through Loras' cell. "Leave me alone," whined Loras.

"Get your floater arse off of da ground and get over 'ere!" yelled Declin. This time, Loras could hear him quite clearly.

"You're dead!" yelled Loras. "This is all just a dream!"

"Come over 'ere and I'll show ya how dead I am!"

"Fine," said Loras as he grudgingly got up from the ground. "If that's what it will take for you to leave me alone." Just as Loras stepped within a few feet of his cell bars, Declin reached through one of the gaps and poked Loras with something sharp.

"Ouch!" yelled Loras and he jumped backward, holding the spot where Declin had stabbed him. He looked down and there was blood on his fingers.

"Der! Still tink dat I'm not real?"

"Ok, now I'm undecided," said Loras as he licked the blood off his fingers to see if it was real.

Declin rolled his eyes. "Dey don't make 'em much thicker dan you, do they? So how is ya holdin' up?"

"I'm still alive," said Loras, "which is more than I may or may not be able to say about you."

"Ay, they gave it der best shot, they did. But ol' Declin ain't no pipken."

"Ok, well then assuming that you're not dead, how did you get out of your cell? What are you doing here?"

"I came to check on you, dummy! Ain't the first cell I've 'ad to break out of in my time, and likely won't be da last. Unless you plan on makin' this yer new home, I recommend you do da same."

"Great! Then let me out of here!"

Declin shook his head. "Ain't as easy as dat. I don't have no key."

Loras looked confused. "Then how did you get out?"

Declin smirked. "Yous gotta work for it." As he said this, he tossed the sharp object that he had used to poke Loras into his cell. It clattered on the ground behind him. Just then, the sound of footsteps came from down the hall.

"Dis be where I leave ya," said Declin, turning away from Loras' cell.

"Wait!" shouted Loras, reaching through the bars. "You've got to get me out of here! I don't know if I can make it much longer. It's so cold. I can't breathe down here!"

Declin turned back and whispered to Loras, "Just because your body is trapped down 'ere doesn't mean your mind has to be." And with that he turned and disappeared down the hall.

Loras grabbed the sharp object off of the floor and tried to jam it into the lock of his prison door, but the keyhole was much too small. The footsteps grew closer. Loras jumped back into his bed and covered himself with his blanket just as the footsteps reached his cell. Two Gartune sentries stared down at him through the bars. Loras pretended to be asleep. One of the sentries tapped his eüroc against the bars, but Loras remained still. The other Gartune grunted, and then the two of them walked away.

As he lay there, he tried to imagine that he was back in Reysa. It was difficult. The underground cell made it hard to remember anything bright or warm, but he tried anyway. He imagined fighting with Tinko with tree sticks in the street after school. He remembered the wind flowing through his hair as he flew on a giant hovercraft through Octavian's Pass. Each memory only lasted a couple of seconds before the cold washed it away. Loras became frustrated. He decided to concentrate on something simpler. He thought of the sun.

At first, it was nothing more than a yellow dot in the back of his mind. But the more he concentrated, the larger the dot became. As it grew, warmth began to fill Loras' body. He concentrated harder. Beads of sweat began to form on his forehead. Still, he concentrated more until the sun became so large that it filled his mind completely. Heat radiated all over Loras' body. Suddenly, he realized that he had been holding his breath the entire time. As he opened his eyes and gasped for air, darkness slapped him in the face. The sheen of sweat covering his skin immediately chilled, sending a tingling sensation all over his body. It was a shock to the system, but a welcome one. For the first time in a long time, Loras felt alive.

Over the following weeks, Loras taught himself how to ease the transition from hot to cold when he did his visualizations. He found that he only needed to warm himself a few times a day in order to fight off the cold. It helped that he also had a new way to pass his time. Digging.

The object that Declin had given to Loras was a rudimentary pickaxe made out of stone. At first, Loras had thought that Declin used it to pick the lock of his cell, but as he examined the worn edges of the tool, the truth became clear. Declin had dug himself to freedom. And Loras would have to do the same. Fortunately, Declin had left one of the edges of the axe sharp for him.

There were several benefits to digging. It was hard work, but the labor was cathartic. It also helped Loras to focus and kept his mind from wandering back to dark thoughts. He also slept better, mainly because he was so exhausted. He was grateful to find that the deeper his sleep, the less likely he was to be visited by dreams. Most importantly though, digging gave him a goal. And with the goal, came hope.

It was not easy sleeping over the top of a hole, but Loras had gotten used to it. Now, as he lay on his back and inspected what was left of his dirt-caked fingernails, he had a decision to make. After weeks of digging, his tunnel was nearly complete.

Two days ago, he had begun to hear noise on the other side of the tunnel wall. There were no voices, only mechanical sounds; clicks and hums and something that sounded like steam escaping. There were other sounds too. The intermittent clanging of a hammer hitting an anvil. There was the screech of a circular saw. All sounds that might have come from a blacksmith's shop. But no voices. There were never any voices.

Loras knew that the only way out of his cell was through whatever room his tunnel had led him to. For two whole days he had patiently listened with his ear to the rock and had not heard the sound of anyone speaking. Even so, he had a feeling that someone was there, working. The question was, could he overpower them? And if he could, then what? Loras had been blindfolded when he was brought down to his cell. He couldn't remember how far he had walked or in which direction. But Declin had found a way out, so it must be possible. He had to at least try. Staying locked up in his cell was no longer an option.

Loras descended into his tunnel and crawled the twenty feet until he reached the end. It was not easy going for a nine-foot-tall Tormada to squeeze his way through such a small space, but Loras had gotten over his claustrophobia long ago. After weeks of digging, the walls of his little tunnel were like a second home—one that he hoped to soon be rid of.

When he reached the end of the tunnel, he carefully scraped the last bits of rock off of the wall in front of him until he estimated that only a couple of inches separated him from the room on the other side. He tucked the makeshift pickaxe into the back of his pants where he could quickly retrieve it if necessary. It was worn down to a thin sliver. *It did the job,* thought Loras thankfully.

Loras took four steps back into the tunnel and lowered his head. He listened and could quite clearly hear the rhythmic clanking of metal on metal in the adjoining room. He timed up the strikes and then right as a clank was about to sound, he ran forward, dipped his shoulder and burst through the wall of his tunnel.

He may have underestimated exactly how little rock was left in the wall, or he may have been just a bit too excited to escape his cell, but either way, Loras' momentum met little resistance. He ended up sliding several feet into the adjacent room. The clanging stopped.

Loras looked up from the floor. All he could see was a cloud of dust in a large, dimly lit room. As the dust cleared, shapes began to form all around him. Every inch of the wall and ceiling contained some sort of tool or machine. There wasn't a single empty space. A track ran around the circumference of the room. On it, a small mechanical creature zoomed back and forth, gathering and replacing objects on the wall. The creature paid no mind to Loras as it grabbed a large wrench-like device and sped on down the track. Loras wondered if that was what was making all of the noise he was hearing.

"I wondered when I would be seeing you..." said a low, rumbling voice from behind Loras.

I guess that answers that question, thought Loras as he leapt onto his feet and spun around to meet the voice. A Gartune stood bent over a table in the back of the room, his back to Loras. *Gods, it sounded like he was right behind me.* Loras kept his guard up and walked slowly toward the Gartune. As he approached, he began to realize how large the Tormada was. Even bent over, the Gartune was taller than Loras.

The Gartune continued to pay no mind to his intruder. Instead, he gave his full attention to the object on the table in front of him. As Loras approached, he was able to see what the Tormada was working on. It looked like a metal net. The Gartune's fingers were a blur as they weaved delicate metal strings in and out of the net. Loras had never seen such craftsmanship, and the speed at which the Gartune was working was incredible. Loras stopped his approach and just stood, mesmerized, watching the Gartune go about his craft.

A few more seconds passed before the Gartune tied the last knot in his net. Then, without leaning up from the table, he threw the net at Loras, yelling "catch!" Awoken from his trance, Loras reached out at the last second and caught the net in his hand. As he did so, the net burst through his fingers and impossibly thin wisps of metal expanded rapidly from Loras' hand and wrapped around his entire body. Before he knew what had happened, Loras was immobilized by a hundred unbreakable metal threads.

The Gartune, still bent over his table, turned his head slightly toward Loras. His skin was a darker tone than most Gartune, although it was hard to tell because it was almost entirely covered in dirt and grime. He was also clean-shaven, which was also odd as Gartune men held their goatees in high esteem. His thin mouth was spread into an enigmatic smile and the one eye that Loras could see seemed to have specs of white within the purple iris.

"What's your name, boy?"

Loras struggled briefly with his restraints to show that he would not be a willing captive. "My name is of no concern," said Loras, trying his best to sound brave.

The Gartune chuckled and turned to completely face Loras. His other eye was golden. "Well hello, Ofno Concern. My name is

Hyperion. Welcome to your new home."

GLOSSARY

Adem
One of the Fallen Reytana.

Aefort
Master Gartune tracker. Lives in the forest with his children, Damnar and Damina.

Aeil River
The main river of The Crescent. Forms from a waterfall at Za'dyn mountain then splits into two tributaries. One branch of the Aeil leads to Reysa, the other leads to Gartol.

Arsdale
Forest city.

Asher
Reysene teenager.

Atholos, King
Reysene king. Died at the end of the Eighth Great War.

Aura
The essence of a slain Tormada. A powdery dust that floats to The Scales after a Tormada is killed. Some qualities of the deceased Tormada are retained within the aura.

Battle Plains
Mostly desert area that expands from the base of Reysa all the way to Hadrian's Canyon. The site for most of the great wars.

Belkore
Gartune. Childhood friend of Xander.

Bodong
Tactical maneuver performed by the Gartune in which they
strike their eüroc into the ground, causing a small hill to form
in front of them. They then catapult themselves onto the top
of the hill where they can meet a Reytana who has jumped
into the air.

Calan
The second Omega. Born to Reysa. Sought to bring peace to
The Crescent through unifying the two races. Created the
hyper-rail. Assassinated at a Summit meeting by the
Gartolians.

The Crescent
The civilized portion of the planet Torma. Called "The
Crescent" because of the shape that The Crescent Mountains
form along the western border. Tormen are the main
inhabitants.

Crescent Mountains
Large, curved mountain range that forms the western border
of The Crescent. The peaks of the mountains are said to be
uncrossable.

Damina
Gartune tracker. Twin brother is Damnar. Father is Aefort.

Damnar
Gartune tracker. Twin sister is Damina. Father is Aefort.

Dario
Reytana. Governor of Reysa.

Declin
Waif. Lives in Woodhaven.

Dellwood Forest
Large, wooded area that extends from The Crescent
Mountains to the Battle Plains.

Delucean Sea
Enormous ocean to the east of The Crescent

Drohnus
The third Omega. Born to Gartol. A fierce and maniacal
warrior, responsible for two centuries of war known as "The
Plague of Drohnus." Thought to have died attempting to
climb Za'dyn Mountain.

Eüroc
Gartune weapon. A bow staff made from a composite of
stone and metal alloy. Can transform through its *tre'ance*.

The Fallen Reytana
Those Reytana that were killed during the Eighth Great War
but were not returned to Reysa as newborns.

Gar'on
The god of stone and metal.

Gartol
The home of the Gartolians. The city is halfway built into a
cavern and sits mostly in shadow.

Gartolians
The citizens of Gartol, pledged to the god Gar'on. A hard
and violent race.

Gartune
Tormada created by Gar'on to rule over the Gartolians. Can

manipulate the ground forming small hills and creating minor tremors. Excellent engineers. Their eyes turn violet when they receive their metal at age eighteen. Sometimes referred to as "diggers."

Gracien
Reytana captain.

Hadrian, King
King of Gartol. Fierce Gartune warrior. Father to Lex, Septa and Xander.

Hadrian's Canyon
The canyon that leads to Gartol. Changes names to reflect the current king or queen of Gartol.

The Hole
A large cave within one of the Crescent Mountains that serves as a hideout for the Lost Reytana. Had previously been used by Declin's family to smuggle goods.

Hyperion
The fourth Omega. Born to Gartol. A master engineer responsible for the creation of many Gartolian advancements, including the eüroc's *tre'ance* and possibly the sun shield.

Hyper-Rail
Hyper-fast railway that connects Reysa to Gartol. Built through a joint effort between the Reysene and Gartolians during the rule of Calan. Uses both solar energy and magnetism for propulsion.

Lem
Waif.

Lex
Gartune. Eldest child of Hadrian. Died during the Eighth Great War.

The Lift
Giant elevator that connects Reysa to the ground level.

Loras
Reytana. Eighteen years old. Regan's twin brother. "Wears the rings."

The Lost Reytana
Those Reytana that disappeared before the end of the Eighth Great War, leaving Reysa undefended. Have not been seen for eighteen years.

The Lotus
Solar energy collection device in the courtyard of Reysa's capitol building. Contains a large orb at its center and is surrounded by several leaf-like structures and tubes for distributing the energy throughout the city.

Lucan
Reysene professor.

Lyse
Water elemental created by Rey and Gar'on to rule over the waterways. Custodian of the Tormada newborns as they travel from The Scales to their city.

Mendkin
Giant, furry woodland creature. Harmless unless it is hungry.

Miles
Waif bartender in Woodhaven.

Morlo
Gartune. Commander in the Gartolian army. Responsible for creating the underground tunnel from Gartol to Reysa.

Nimber
Raccoon-like forest animal.

Octavia
The first Omega. Born to Reysa.

Octavian's Pass
Valley that skirts the base of the northern half of The Crescent Mountains.

The Omegas
The children of the Tormada. Since their creation, the Tormada have only given birth four times. These children possess both the powers of the Gartune and the Reytana. Omegas do not have to wait until their eighteenth birthday to receive their powers – they are born with them.

Pipken
Forest animal. Slightly larger than a rat.

Rankin
Gartune. Formerly the chief ranking Gartune in Reysa before Xander's arrival.

Ray Blade
A Reytana weapon. A sword made out of light energy.

Regan
Reytana. Eighteen years old. Loras' twin sister. "Wears the rings."

Rey
The goddess of the sun.

Reysa

The "city on the cliff." Home of the Reysene. Sits atop the northern terminus of The Crescent Mountains where the mountain range meets the Delucean Sea.

Reysene

The citizens of Reysa, pledged to the god Rey. An ethereal and cooperative race.

Reytana

Tormada created by Rey to rule over the Reysene. Can harness the power of the sun which allows them to jump to extreme heights as well as form weapons out of solar energy. Reytana's eyes turn gold when they receive their light on their eighteenth birthday. Sometimes referred to as "floaters."

The Scales of Torma

Tormada regulatory device atop of Za'dyn Mountain. Responsible for keeping the number of Gartune and Reytana even. Can reincarnate deceased Tormada by dipping the slain Tormada's aura into the Aeil River, thus starting the incubation period that creates new Gartune and Reytana. Protected by "The Guardian.

Septa

Gartune. Princess of Gartol. Fierce warrior. Middle child of Hadrian. Siblings are Lex and Xander.

Spirea

Forest city.

The Summit

Meeting location for the Reysene and Gartolians built at the exact midpoint of the Hyper-Rail line.

Sun Shield (aka Hyperion's Shield)

Mechanical marvel created by the Gartolians in order to block the sun's rays from hitting Reysa. Held up by four arms that are connected to four tanks at the base of the city. Hyperion is rumored to be its inventor.

Tao

Reytana guard.

Tinko

Reysene. Best friend to Loras.

Torma

Planet created by the gods Rey and Gar'on. Indigenous race is the tormen. Civilized portion of the planet is referred to as "The Crescent."

Tormada

Super-human race created by Rey and Gar'on in order to rule over the tormen. Rey created the Reytana in order to rule over the Reysene. Gar'on created the Gartune to rule over the Gartolians. Both the Reytana and Gartune can grow up to nine feet tall and have a lifespan double or triple that of a torman. Each race has unique powers that are derived from the god that created them.

Tormada cannot reproduce. When they die, their aura returns to The Scales and they are reborn through a two week incubation process as they travel from Za'dyn mountain, along the Aeil river to their assigned city. Tormada grow like normal tormen until their eighteenth birthday when Reytana receive their "light" and Gartune receive their "metal." At this point, they receive their powers and begin to rapidly transform into full-grown Tormada.

Tormen
Human-like race created by the gods Rey and Gar'on. At first, all tormen lived together peacefully. Later, their allegiance toward either Rey or Gar'on forced them to split off and form two separate cities – Reysa and Gartol.

Tre'ance
An enhanced modification to the eüroc such as a projectile or blade. Each Gartune may select their own *tre'ance* once they receive their metal

Waif
A torman who did not choose to be a Reysene or Gartolian and so must live in the woods.

Wapas
Mosquito butterflies that can suck the light out of Reytana.

Woodhaven
Forest city located at the point where the Aeil River splits.

Xander
Gartune. Prince of Gartol. Youngest child of Hadrian. Siblings are Lex and Septa. Chief ranking Gartune within Reysa.

Za'dyn Mountain
The tallest peak in The Crescent. Home of The Scales of Torma. Unclimbable.

ABOUT THE AUTHOR

Nathan was born on July 31st, 1981 in Dayton, Ohio. He currently resides in Columbus, Ohio with his wife, Stephanie, and three children: Ellie, Neil and Leah. When he isn't writing, he owns and operates Blue Avenue Media, a multimedia production agency in Columbus.

He is a fan of all things fantasy – from books to movies to fantasy sports. The first fantasy book he ever read was an old copy of *The Hobbit*, given to him by his grandmother. He has been hooked ever since. Some of his favorite fantasy book series include *Mistborn*, *The Kingkiller Chronicles*, *The Lord of the Rings* and *Harry Potter*.

Hyperion's Shield was a passion project written in two month increments over the span of five years. The idea of the Tormada first came to Nathan on a long train ride in Europe, and the rest of the story evolved from there. Nathan claims that writing this novel was his greatest literary achievement since winning the coveted Power of the Pen competition in eighth grade.

Lastly, Nathan would like to thank everyone who has supported him along his writing journey and hopes that there are many more novels to come.